MEMOIRS

OF

ANDREW WINPENNY,

COUNT DE DEUX SOUS;

COMPRISING

NUMEROUS ADVENTURES IN DIFFERENT COUNTRIES.

By FRANCIS GLASSE, Esq.

AUTHOR OF " NED CLINTON," " JOE OXFORD," &c. &c. &c.

" How, when competitors like these contend,
Can surly virtue hope to fix a friend?"

LONDON:

PUBLISHED BY J. CLEMENTS, LITTLE PULTENEY STREET,

FOR THE PROPRIETORS OF

THE ROMANCIST AND NOVELIST'S LIBRARY.
1841.

MEMOIRS OF ANDREW WINPENNY,

COUNT DE DEUX SOUS.

CHAPTER I.

" By education most have been misled,
    So they believe because they so were bred;
    The priest continues what the nurse began,
    And thus the child imposes on the man!"

" Ill fares the land, to hastening ills a prey
    Where wealth accumulates and men decay."

THE sceptic says, " man does everything by custom; " he affirms, too, that honesty, dishonesty, justice and injustice, are but names, attached by us to certain actions, according to the education we have received.

Education and custom, most assuredly, hold dominion over man ; if they did not, how could it happen that a deed which in one country is denounced as being criminal, in another state brings commendation and pecuniary reward to the individual who has perpetrated it ? For example, in the Spartan and some others of the states of olden times, theft, when ably achieved, was considered so highly meritorious and honourable, that he who (like the brave Spartan youth, whose bowels were torn out by the stolen fox he held under his frock) died perseveringly denying a robbery by him committed, was considered as having been a hero, not only meriting the admiration of his own time, but also worthy of having his fame transmitted down to posterity by the ablest historians among his applauding countrymen.

In modern times, throughout all countries, the successful robber is applauded for his masterly conduct. Yea ! he is rewarded with the proudest distinctions. In fine, robbery leads to great wealth, and, under monarchical governments, overgrown wealth ensures aristo-cratic rank to its possessor, which, with management, is made to yield him and his posterity a perpetuity of power and place, at the suffering people's expense.

To illustrate this fact, scrutinize into the long list of aristocratic titles. There it will be found, that, with few exceptions, these honours have been granted to the spurious issue of royalty, and to unsparing plunderers, some of them ruthlessly terrible slayers of their fellow-men—others, practitioners of the law's infamy, or else robbers of the state they were paid to serve ;—a few, perhaps, owe their advancement to the more hazardous, yet less dishonest, practices of gaming, sycophancy, and usury.

Those noblest spirits of mankind, the aboriginal tribes of North American Indians, openly reward the bravely-daring thief; but civilized governments, actuated by baser principles, covertly render tenfold greater services to the very vilest of thieves, even to such as risk nothing themselves, but cold-heartedly administer to the law's impositions and delays—to men who preside over courts, where, so terrific is the iniquity practised, millions of money are annually pillaged and partitioned out among harpies, who well know that the proper owners of much of that wealth are incarcerated in prison, or else lingering life away in hopeless pauperism.

The more dispassionately we examine into the subject, the better shall we satisfy ourselves that theft is not thought to be dishonourable in the most civilized of countries. The crime, when publicly detected, may be punished ; but that is only in ordinary cases, where persons of no influence are the criminals, or the crime itself accords not with the views of men in power.

To exemplify the assertion just made—a state minister, whose administration is marked by unnecessary warfare, the grossest public rapine, a greedy seizure of places for his progeny, and of wasteful pensions for the partisans of corruption, usually retires from office, rewarded with an advanced title and a large grant from the public purse, instead of being brought to a public trial, and ignominiously punished for his infamous misdeeds.

Then again; that man who joins not in parliamentary debate, yet is (as if ironically) termed " the speaker," as likewise lords—chancellors, herds of ambassadors (twenty of whom would not have been paid equal to one physician by the Athenians, who valued public men according to their deserts) and other enormously overpaid servants of the state, after they have realized immense fortunes from the golden showers poured on them at the nation's expense, are allowed to further burden it by getting pensions granted for themselves, and not unfrequently for their wives, children, and affinity. Yet as these abuses are imposed on the state by men in authority over it, common sense is so outraged to meet their pleasure, that they are not denominated and considered what they really ought to be—so many infamous thefts.

The sceptic must be correct in his assertion ! Honesty, dishonesty, justice and injustice, are words only, which the great bandy about at pleasure, and attach to individuals according to their success in life ; were they otherwise, the incongruous laws of civilized states would be pronounced barbarous and infamous.

Justice, as she is administered, sentences to death the poor man convicted of crime, which the great employ armies to perpetrate ; and she unhesitatingly transports him for a petty theft to a distant colony; thus putting the community to great expense, and punishing it to improve the condition of the guilty.

Honesty should be sought after at the fountain head of justice ; and here is a specimen of the disinterestedness of the fair dame. A certain court of chancery took charge of a million of money bequeathed to its care by a superannuated merchant, to accumulate at compound interest for half a century, and this honest court charged only the interest upon the million during the half century for abusing the trust.

If the scales of justice were fairly poised, dishonesty and injustice would not triumph over humanity and right, as they do in the regulations for private lunatic asylums, which are a cruel mockery of human liberty. Any sane person may be seized and incarcerated for life, to serve the interests or gratify the malice of another, for when once got within the walls of a private mad house, he is beyond the reach of juries and the law.

Unquestionably, the directors of certain public companies must be sceptics to the heart's core. They cringe to get themselves employed in the direction, but when snugly seated there, bribe the most compliant of the law tribe to assist them in concocting a deed of settlement, of a nature to ensnare the other proprietors in the meshes of their deadly net. They put the company to an expense for costly feasts, at which, to blind the uninitiated, they trumpet forth in set speeches the praises of each other. And does not every one know that they grant extravagant salaries to the partisans whom they employ, without regard to their qualifications, while that in jobs understood only by themselves, they (like a prodigal monarch, throwing his grievously taxed subjects' money among a mob of foreigners) lavish away the company's funds right and left, until the company is brought to a state of insolvency by the very men employed to uphold it ?

Yes ! these deeds, and many more such, are the every-day deeds enacted by certain directors; yet, like the assassins of the arch-butcher Cæsar, these directors are all of them " honourable men !"

Assuredly, the words honesty, dishonesty, justice and injustice, can be no more than cant terms. If what they seemingly represent really existed, is it not impossible that there could be any exorbitantly over-paid bishops ? For who in the shape of man, having the two best of these monitors to guide him, could be so wickedly degraded as to preach humility and poverty, while himself living, bloated with pride, and distressing an entire county for money to uphold his princely extravagance, and to fund or purchase more than a princely revenue in land for his posterity !

Should unsophisticated honesty and justice rise from their present prostration in certain persecuted kingdoms, what, in their hallowed names, would become of their bishops ? Poor wretched saints ; would not their consciences smite them ! Honesty and justice would advocate the clothing of soldiers in all the cloth a munificent nation gives for their use ; not curtail their garments to enrich honourable general officers with the tailor-like spoil, and gloss over the transaction by terming the price paid for the overplus cloth—their off-reckonings! Nor would honesty and justice consent to burthen a people, by making them pay three general officers for each of their regiments, and an admiral for every one of their ships.

Honesty and justice would condense the laws of a country, and thereby do away with the great cause of lawsuits. Honesty and justice would abolish iniquitous corn-laws, which cause the toiling multitude to eat their bread at twofold its proper price, that a tax of thirty millions of pounds may be levied to uphold landholders, who, as honest men, should themselves repudiate the infamous monopoly; and it is the imperious duty of legislators, however heavily they may tax the unprotected, to facilitate their obtaining that essential to life and great boon of the Almighty—their daily bread. Honesty and justice would make the judge blush at sitting in the seat of judgment until his salary had been reduced to less than one-third part of what this luminary of inconsistency now receives.

The whole of Europe, the republics of Switzerland alone exempted, affords incontrovertible testimony, that, as far as two of these qualities are concerned, the sceptic is not mistaken in the opinion he has advanced; therefore, should honesty and justice be sought after, it is either in Switzerland, or in some happy republic across the Atlantic, where they are to be found.

We, however, have numerous casuists, who, contrary to the sceptic's opinion of the reality of these qualities, boldly assert, that dishonesty and injustice have taken up their permanent abode with us, and that they shine forth in all trades and professions; in evidence of which, they insist on it, that he who cheats with most effect is the best craftsman; while that religion itself is made a trade of, wherein the grossest impostors are the most successful professors. In a word, these learned casuists and the sceptic are at variance on every point; but philosophy whispers, that there may be much sound truth in both their opinions; and that to bring about a wholesome reformation of errors and abuses, it is necessary to expose and attack bad institutions, establishments, and manners; for is it not a law of the moral world that what is at once seen, despised, and laughed at, never long endures? Therefore, leaving the generous reader to form his own judgment on my character by the following memoirs, wherein every particular, however detrimental to my fame, shall be related with candour, I proceed to their relation, first briefly observing, in extenuation of my faults and of those of my associates, that the enlightened Jesuit maintains, that "education moulds the conscience, and crime cannot be greater than the conscience makes it."

CHAPTER II.

The addled egg to market sent
Will pass its muster well,
Provided that, by accident,
We do not break the shell."

" The worldly priest, to sport an equipage,
Luxurious feed, and fill his silken purse,
In legal strife too often will engage
For tithes or dues, which gains him many a curse."

PRIDE is more costly to many persons than hunger, cold, and clothing.

Sensible as I feel of this truth, I shall strenuously endeavour to get rid of so worthless an attendant; for that the stately dame accompanies me everywhere I have good reasons for believing, inasmuch as I perceive her to be a shadow-like companion to nearly the whole of my acquaintances.

To prove myself sincere in my professions, I shall, in penning these my Memoirs, pay the strictest possible regard to truth; and, however incredible the circumstance may appear to high-minded aristocratic personages, so far gain the victory over pride as to waive those pretensions to exalted parentage which many persons in my situation would build largely upon.

To be brief, then, I have strong grounds for being satisfied as to the identity of my parents on the maternal side; and, however mortifying this moiety of information may be to the pride attendant on many possessors of ancient titles, assuredly it is all man can rest assured of on this side of the grave.

The good woman, Diana Winpenny, who fed and clothed me until I had entered into my nineteenth year, invariably called me her child; and as she was not in easy circumstances in life, I can see no reason for believing she would have performed those parental duties by me without an adequate reward, had I not really been her offspring, while that she never received any pecuniary remuneration on my account is quite certain. However, as it is in the line of possibility that I may leave legitimate issue behind me, who, to fabricate another pedigree for our family, may be desirous of tracing out my descent, I shall now publicly avow that I have repeatedly heard the well known accoucheur who ushered me into the world, as also two aged dames who were present in Diana's chamber at the time of her delivery, solemnly declare me to be truly and indisputably her own offspring.

My parentage is far from being flattering to pride; yet it may be worthy of observation here, to show the great uncertainty attached to heraldic honours, that had Diana Winpenny been the eldest sister of a king of Madagascar, instead of a poor countryman's wife, which she was at the period of my birth, I should, though illegitimately begotten, as her first-born son, in due course of inheritance have been entitled to wear the crown of Madagascar. Unfortunately, however, poor Diana, my mother, although she was less depraved than are many exalted ladies, well known to fame, in every clime and country of our world, yet was not so chaste a character as the sylvan goddess, her namesake, is represented to have been. Indeed, to confess the unwelcome truth, she had been seduced into numerous *liaisons* previous to the epoch when she committed the most egregious act of folly she was guilty of in the whole course of her existence—namely, that of marrying a poor distressed man.

The Diana from whom I claim descent passed away most of her juvenile years as one of that dependent class of people said to be the peculiar favourites of heaven. She was numbered among those whom holy writ assures us "to give to is to lend to the Lord;" that light-hearted tribe who are studiously shunned by the great, but, happily for themselves, set all the learned counsellors of the law at defiance, and triumphantly laugh at their wily tricks and quibbles; in short, Diana was a vagrant—a common beggar, who possessed neither goods nor money to serve as lures to those insatiate sharks. Her parents, too, and their ancestors, for a century or more, had likewise been mendicants.

A beggar girl, however, when she happens to be pretty, may become an object of admiration to exalted personages of the opposite sex; and provided her cunning equals her beauty, there is no calculating to what pinnacle of grandeur the little upstart may climb her way.

To pass over the days of her early youth, about the period of her attaining her fourteenth year, my mother's charms found favour with a certain celebrated tragic actor on the London boards, who, after having given her some necessary instructions in the mysteries of his profession, kindly procured her an engagement at the theatre to which he belonged; and but from this kind of interest, it is too well known that no songstress nor actress can ever justly hope for success.

The flowery path of pleasure, laying as it now did before her, the young gipsy, for such she had recently been, frisked and wantoned so extremely to her heart's delight, that the goddess her namesake could scarce have tripped along the sylvan greensward more lightly than my parent daily tripped to and from the greenroom of the theatre at which she exhibited her fair person in performance as one of the daughters of Thalia. Unfortunately, however, although dangers are to be encountered in every state of life, none other perhaps is so replete with them to the virtue of fair woman as the life of an actress; for actresses are looked upon as fair game for every debauchee, while to the theatre it is that the most unprincipled, debauched, and heartless of them resort.

To tell the many ordeals her virtue was exposed to, and where Diana triumphed or when she fell, I shall not attempt, as the narrative would prove too voluminous for my memoirs; besides, there are certain book-making personages in the community, who pretend to be minutely conversant with the private history and adventures of every recently-deceased person, any way remarkable for relaxity of morals, or other notoriety; and charity forbids that I should deprive one of these enterprising scribblers of the fruitful opportunity which Diana Winpenny's conduct as an actress may afford him for earning additional literary fame, as well as for gaining him more bread.

If, however, the reader of these pages should deem me remiss for not bringing to his notice more of the *faux pas* committed by my maternal parent than what I consider it necessary to touch upon, I must appeal to his philanthropy, and request of him to make allowance for the feelings of a child desirous of sparing the memory of his mother, as likewise that he will bear in mind that there may be many sons living who have substantial reasons for being actuated by the same sort of delicacy.

My mother, according to general report, when first engaged as an actress, was one of the liveliest girls ever met with; but though surrounded by flatterers (and what female that is young and beautiful can be without them?) she possessed no true friend. Her situation, in regard to danger, is comparable to that of a moth, fluttering about a brilliant chandelier, lit up by a multiplicity of bright lights. She could not escape—it was impossible. A pigmy would have a better chance of success, when facing a giant in open combat, than could a lovely girl with a versatile heart and warm passions, such as my mother possessed, of escaping the innumerable snares set to entrap her; and artful depravity, backed by wealth, was perpetually at work for that purpose.

When virtue stoops to frailty, it signifies little who is the despoiler. Therefore I pretend not to say who it was that triumphed over the innocence of my maternal parent. The journalists of her day, who busied themselves in every amour and adventure in which this famed actress was engaged, less scrupulous than I am, attribute the victory over her to different persons. One gives the tragic actor who elevated her from mendicity credit for the exploit; another, and probably with greater reason, fathers the act upon a certain Protestant bishop, celebrated for his professions of sanctity; a third attributes the honour of this conquest to a tailor, who, from having bartered his own wife away to a state minister in exchange for an army contract, and afterwards his daughter for a similar remuneration, became one of the wealthiest commoners of his day; a fourth newspaper authority pronounces a Quaker, who was a great advocate for promoting marriage among the blacks, to have been the happy achiever of this triumph; a fifth unhesitatingly declares the lady's citadel of virtue was stormed by a learned judge of the Ecclesiastical Court; yet, notwithstanding these authorities, a celebrated court journalist boldly asserts, that an Israelite from the Stock Exchange bartered away a portion of some weighty differences received by him on a settling day in exchange for Diana's virtue.

The knowledge I have gained of the world has made me somewhat of a philosopher; and I care not which of the aforesaid reports may be the true one, or whether they are all calumniously false: yet, though I possess sufficient wisdom to know that neither the good nor the evil deeds of its parents ought to bring either honour or dishonour on their offspring, and consequently that hereditary titles are distinctions opposed to the spirit of justice and common sense, still (such is the selfishness of human nature, that) I cannot avoid deploring the misfortune I shall have to relate as having befallen my mother, because thereby I was doomed to make my appearance in the world—a poor unfriended boy, instead of being born to great honours and abundant wealth.

Having touched lightly on my mother's frailties, by referring only to newspaper accounts of them, when I might have adduced stronger matter, I shall, with the same filial tenderness towards her, avoid saying more of her amours than what is absolutely requisite, preparatory to explaining the particulars of the misfortune I have alluded to as having, most untowardly for my interest, befallen her.

Multifarious as may have been Diana's gallants, it is an assured fact, that, to gratify a bishop who supported her in great splendour, she—poor ill-advised woman!—about ten months previous to my birth, discarded the whole of them except the right reverend father himself; and the circumstance is equally well authenticated, that several months subsequent to the period of her confining her affections to this proud churchman, a prince of the blood royal of a foreign kingdom made tender overtures to her, which, by the sage bishop's advice, she accepted, and consequently became the envied mistress of this royal, and, and as the fulsome journalists of the day styled him, august personage!

To a person unacquainted with the artifices resorted to by courtiers, it might appear almost incredible that a Protestant bishop, endowed with a revenue exceeding that of two, or perhaps three, royal princes, should voluntarily resign his favourite *chere amie* to one of that class; but he who knows anything of a court must avow that this concession is quite natural, and one which may always be expected on an advantageous occasion, such as the transfer of an expensive mistress afforded promise of being to the proud prelate.

The bishop was a thorough trained courtier—one who, by blowing hot and cold to fall in with the tide of favouring events, had, from being, when a stripling, a waiter at his father's tavern, risen to be a great church pluralist, when, by means of plagiarism, proved by his compilations from the writings of abler men, he got up a few political pamphlets, of a standard suitable to the talents of state ministers, who had the giving away of bishoprics and sinecures which weigh down the nation, and notwithstanding our divine's propensity to litigation about tithes and dues, by their aid contrived to step into an episcopal see; for the ladder of ambition is the less liable to slip when it has been firmly fixed in the mud. Ambition, however, is not to be contented as long as there is a higher post to be gained; consequently, my mother's *ci-devant* supporter, the bishop, by bribes and promises, now brought her over to exert all her influence with the royal prince, her paramour, to procure the promise of his influence to get him elevated to an archiepiscopal see as soon as one fell vacant.

Here again a novice in worldly affairs might fall into a mistake. He might imagine that the bishop, in his eagerness after promotion, imposed too weighty a task on his fair friend; but this novice ought to be told that our bishop did not calculate without his host; for that female influence it is which puts mitres on the majority of the bishops, while not one perhaps owes his lofty situation to his Christian humility, though many of them, from being sycophantic schoolmasters, get possession of their pastoral crooks.

Not to digress more respecting a class of men who, the sceptic says, cannot be reformed, unless by doing away with the golden temptations strewed in the state clerical gentlemen's way (and which are many and manifold in a nation whose established church is said to cost more than the churches of all dispersed christians throughout the world), it must be mentioned that all things were going on swimmingly between his royal highness the prince, the right reverend father the bishop, and little Diana, the *ci-devant* gipsy mendicant; when, alas! as mine and her ill stars ordained, she caught the small-pox, and although her life was fated to be spared, the boon was accompanied by the total loss of beauty, in place of which, to her inexpressible horror, the young actress's once lovely features were left deeply seamed by the ravages of that unsparing disease, which also rendered the pupil of one of her lately bright eyes frightfully white and sightless.

CHAPTER III.

" Why for her children should the wife express
More fond affection, and the husband less?
The reason, if I rightly judge, is this,
She knows them her's, and he scarce thinks them his!"

" A woman's tongue is her sword, and she never suffers it to grow rusty."

A PRINCE may be readily pardoned for entertaining a penchant for a pretty actress; but he would be deemed insane, were he to live with, and continue enamoured of, a one-eyed, poor, pock-marked girl. The royal personage in question was so extremely disgusted with the altered condition of his Diana, that almost immediately after her recovery from the small-pox he broke up her establishment, without making her a pecuniary present, or settling on her a stipendiary allowance. This conduct from a person of royal birth may be thought extremely brutal; yet, have we not examples of such in many a continental prince? Besides, some allowance may be made for his highness, inasmuch as his affairs were embarrassed; but in vindication of the bishop's barbarity nothing can be adduced. He, most unfeeling man! soon as my parent's misfortune had happened, posted away from the capital to make a visitation to his diocese; and, finding his late mistress had lost all pretension to beauty, and that he had no church preferment to hope for from her good offices, left unanswered her letters, and refused to hear the applications she strove to get made to him in her behalf.

Young and pretty actresses seldom are provident. Indeed, how is it to be supposed they can see brooding storms when gold in profusion falls into their laps? My poor mother, in her short career of pleasure, had not only been one of the gayest of the gay, but also one of the most thoughtless of the thoughtless; the consequence of which last failing was, that within a short month from the time of her being ejected from her sumptuous dwelling, she found herself penniless, and destitute of everything requisite for her support.

Want now overtook the unfortunate young woman, and absolute starvation stared her in the face. She not only was without a friend, but could follow no profession; for at the theatre where she had been employed her services were refused, and her person was regarded with scorn. She could find no alternative, and, therefore, although *enceinte,* prepared herself to resume her pristine trade of a beggar.

To be born a mendicant, and continue óne through life, may not, perhaps, be a hard lot, especially when the mind accords with the lowly situation; as those persons are happy who enjoy good health, are satisfied with such things as are merély necessary, and who desire not superfluities, luxuries, riches, or distinctions; but to rise to greatness from the condition of a beggar, and then suddenly fall back into mendicity, must be truly galling, and make the vagrant's crutch one of the weightiest that can be carried.

My poor mother, whom in these memoirs I have somewhat prematurely called Diana Winpenny, was spared the mortification of resuming her old avocation, but it was to stoop to a lot scarcely a whit better than mendicity—in short, it was to marry a poor man, one who had recently been a footman; yet from her alliance with him it was that she became entitled to bear the sirname of Winpenny.

Everything is judged of by comparison. I think I hear the reader commiserate the piteous lot of my hapless parent. We, however, often form a false estimate of the happiness of others; and who can pronounce that Diana Winpenny's present situation, although deprived of that treasure—her beauty, blind of an eye, and united by wedlock to a man at once ignorant and poor, was not preferable to that of a person afflicted with total blindness, loathsome scrofula, outrageous insanity, an ungovernable temper, or some other of the equally severe afflictions with which Providence not unfrequently visits the wealthy and the great.

The venal journalists of her day, who had hitherto shown themselves most ready to trump forth the actions of my mother, took no notice of her marriage; but when the hymeneal ceremony was over, the newly wedded pair were permitted to retire to a cottage in Surrey, which they did, as guests, to the bridegroom's mother, a hard working washerwoman, without having the place of their retreat, or any other circumstance regarding them, blazoned abroad in the public prints.

To abbreviate this part of my story, I shall merely state, that in the aforesaid cottage I was ushered into the world in less than two months after the newly-wedded couple had taken up their abode in that lowly dwelling; and shortly afterwards, to save my maternal parent's character from the opprobrium which would otherwise have been attached to it by our ignorant and rustic neighbours, taken to the parish church, and christened there by the names of my mother's husband.

Here again is an incontrovertible proof that all is mere chance which relates to hereditary succession. Provided my legitimate father, Andrew Winpenny, the legitimate son of Moses and Rebecca, should by right of succession, traced from an ancient genealogical tree, become entitled to a principality, a dukedom, or to any other title or estate, I, Andrew Winpenny, the second, because so christened and born of the body of the wife of the aforesaid Andrew, should, although known to be no more his child than that of the Grand Mogul, indisputably succeed to all the titles and estates to which he, the first Andrew Winpenny, could by law make good his claim. Unfortunately, however, the good villagers, Moses and Rebecca, whom both the common and ecclesiastical law pronounces to have been my grandparents, were of very low origin; and therefore, unless it were by an able *ruse de guerre,* there could be no hope for me of obtaining either title or estate in virtue of my descent from them.

We are all the sport of circumstances. My mother, Diana Winpenny, whose charms, perhaps, equalled those of the fairest of King Charles's favourites, and whose virtue, unquestionably, was of as exalted a character as was that of the celebrated Moll Flanders, nevertheless, unlike Barbara Villiers, Mrs Pegg, Lucy Walters, Nell Gwynn, and the aforesaid Moll Flanders, who, all of them, saving the last adventuress, were enriched out of the national purse, and had sufficient influence to get their sons and daughters honoured by that prelude to aristocratic titles, the word Fitz placed before their names—she, poor, ill-starred woman, neither could get me so enriched, or so honoured; but, alas! was herself doomed to spend the bitter dregs of her life in miserable poverty.

Amatory swains assert that love may exist in a cottage; yet, without denying the assertion, I can take on me to say, that where poverty is its companion, the urchin god will soon spread his wings and depart, leaving the lovers to themselves to deplore his absence, and contemplate their own folly. He did this with Andrew and Diana Winpenny, long before I had arrived at a suitable age to know he had ever been an inmate of their humble cot.

Life glides away like a shadow. Though our years are few, numerous are the wrongs heaped upon us, and the changes we are destined to undergo.

At the expiration of a few years, spent in the cottage of my nativity, I had grown to be a strong, hale youth; but in that time my grandmother's phantom of life had passed away, and she now laid deposited in her last earthly resting-place—a neighbouring churchyard. The good woman's death, however, so far from benefiting her son's affairs, proved seriously injurious to them; for she had enjoyed a small life-annuity, granted by a gentleman with whom, report said, she had lived on very familiar terms, and which materially aided in supporting the joint-household expenses; but that source of revenue being stopped by her death, my father was put to great straits to support himself and family.

All creatures are strongly prompted by generous nature to love and provide for their offspring; yet it so happened that my father, who, by the time I had completed my fourteenth year, had three other children by his wife Diana, not only did not show that parental love and regard for me which he displayed towards my brothers and my sister, but he would often evince downright hatred, by beating and otherwise ill-treating me, without justifiable cause. Moreover, on my mother's interfering on my behalf, he would quarrel with and reproach her with the circumstance of my birth. My mother, on the other hand, who, woman-like, never could cease deploring the loss of her beauty, and that of the magnificent establishment her charms had procured for her, would frequently shed involuntary tears on contemplating the person and miserable prospect of her first-born son, clothed as I was in mere rags; and sometimes she would exclaim, " Oh, my poor Andrew, were it not for the misfortune which deprived thy mother of her charms, thou, even thou, wouldst have been a great man—perhaps a bishop, a lord, or a prince."

Apostrophes of the kind now mentioned had better not have been made; for when the husband overheard them, they served to aggravate his anger to a pitch of fury, and not only made him more reproachful and violent to his wife, but also more tyrannical and cruel to me. Diana, however, who had never, since her marriage at least, been remarkable for the gentleness of her disposition, could ill brook these sallies of an ungovernable temper, and therefore she would retaliate in terms as reproachful as those made use of by her husband, and also valorously defend her first-born child, both by her tongue and her talons, which last were often made to leave vestiges of their sharpness on his face.

Lovers' quarrels may lead to a renewal of tender bliss; but matrimonial strife, when it has been of long duration, and between an ill-sorted pair, is of so diabolical a nature, that it should be defined as a curse, which makes a hell upon this earth for the suffering pair; and of this violent character were the quarrels which took place between Andrew Winpenny and his spouse—the once lovely Diana.

Providence is said to be just in all its ways; and providentially, the fire which burns violently seldom endures long. Shortly after I had entered into my nineteenth year, an epidemic which much prevailed in our neighbourhood released Andrew Winpenny, the senior, from a great portion of his troubles, and his wife Diana from the possibility of enduring more earthly sufferings, by depriving her of mortal life—or, as the goodly say, " taking her to a better world," when, aided by a little assistance from the parish, the disconsolate husband contrived to give his departed wife a tolerable decent burial, in the same grave with his own mother.

With the flight hence of my maternal parent's spirit all things unfavourable to her memory should be forgotten, as it behoves man, when he contemplates the errors of woman, to remember his own.

CHAPTER IV.

" Wherever God erects a house of prayer,
The Devil always builds a chapel there."

" Entreat the elder women as mothers, the younger as sisters, with all purity."
WESLEY'S SERMON ON WHITFIELD.

" Beloved of his God, but abhorred of men; the omniscient judge at the grand assize shall ratify and confirm this, for England and its metropolis shall know there hath been a prophet among them."
FROM A DISSENTING PREACHER'S TOMBSTONE.

WIDOWERS find favour in the eyes of the fair sex; for women know that men who have been rivetted in the chains of Hymen have stooped to slavery; and consequently, custom being everything to man, that they are prepared for, and in most cases anxiously ready to return to, a state of vassalage.

My lawful father, Andrew Winpenny, had scarcely seen deposited his wife's body in our parent earth, ere he turned the eyes of affection upon the daughter of a neighbouring miller; and she, having passed the zenith of her charms, and being still a spinster, with no great share of beauty to recommend her in the hymenean market, was pleased to smile approbation of his love-suit. The pair now came to a proper understanding, and were shortly afterwards joined together in holy wedlock; indeed, so ready were they on the occasion, that the auspicious ceremony was performed within four months from the date of my mother's departure from this land of trouble.

My father, who had treated me with redoubled severity after my poor mother's death, behaved with a still more wanton cruelty from the day of his bringing home a second wife; in short, such was his conduct, that apparently he was determined to send my soul on the great voyage of futurity, as a companion to that of my mother, or else to drive me an outcast from his roof; while his spouse, faithful in this instance to her matrimonial vow of obedience, aided his vile efforts, not only by treating me with vixen-like fury, but also by invariably giving me a scanty allowance of food, always chosen from the very refuse of her miserable larder.

The treatment I received was not to be borne by a lad of spirit; and I, becoming thoroughly disgusted, formed the determination of flying from my father's roof. Fortune, too, the gentle dame so often abused by the ungrateful, but who not unfrequently assists man in his worst exigencies, and heaven knows, has done me many a good turn, smiled on this occasion, by most opportunely throwing a treasure of money in my path. The way she took of bestowing this boon upon me was as follows:—I had been sent to a village some miles from home by my unkind mother-in-law, ostensibly to deliver a message to a cousin of hers, but in reality that she might get rid of me until a little feasting party was over, to which she had invited her parents at our cottage that day. After delivering my message, I was trudging on my road home in the dusk of the evening, tormented by a very keen appetite, with nothing in the shape of food to gratify it, when my foot chanced to strike against something which jingled at its touch in the middle of the turnpike road, which having picked up and examined, excessively to my delight I discovered to be a small money bag, containing one sovereign, two half-sovereigns, and twenty-six shillings in silver.

In my rapture of joy at this lucky event I was more than once on the eve of proclaiming my good fortune. Prudence, however, saved me from that danger, by whispering in my ear that my secret must be kept inviolate in my bosom, or my treasure would be ravished from my person. Time, however, was not to be lost, for I was apprehensive of losing my money, and most eager to enjoy ease and freedom; therefore, on the following Sunday morning, at a time when my father and all the family save myself were away from home, on a visit to my mother-in-law's parents, I most unceremoniously departed from the lowly habitation of my nativity, with my pecuniary treasure in my pocket, and a bundle containing a change of raiment in my hand; nor did I feel any boyish regret at the bold step I was taking. Worldly people usually consider that education to be the best for youth which conduces the most effectually to the attainment of those objects the most desired in life, and which they are destined to keep in view; and experience gleaned by me from my intercourse with mankind, since the time of my clandestinely quitting the humble cottage of my nativity, has satisfied me that no erudition, however great, can make amends for a false education; yet, as to what may be a false education I shall give no opinion, but leave that nice point to be settled by the sceptics and the learned, and content myself by observing, from my own experience, that most assuredly diffidence and modesty are great drawbacks to a young adventurer. For my part, I was free from those incumbrances; but ignorance furnished assurance to my character, and that too when shame would better have become me.

I was master of no learning to boast of. To write and read were the whole of my scholastic attainments. Mine, however, according to my then erroneous ideas, was not a false education; and that inasmuch as my father, by his own example, had taught me numerous of the little pilfering ways by means of which numerous agricultural labourers, and other people in humble life, contrive to keep their cottages supplied with good food, from the fields, farm-yards, and fish-ponds of their more wealthy neighbours; still, however, when all has been said that can be urged against him, it must in candour be avowed that my father's were only thefts suitable to his morality and to his name; for Win-a-penny, be it known, was his maxim, fixed as that Winpenny was his name; and he would say to me, when in a jocular vein, but which was very rare, " Win your penny, my boy, honestly if you can ; yet win it at any rate, and when you can."

My mother, who had witnessed the tricks of life, as they are practised, in all their intricacy, by place and pension-hunters in the higher circles, laughed at and despised the aforesaid pitiful maxim of her husband.   She knew that no man could well hope to arrive at a pinnacle of grandeur, either in the church, the law, the service of arms, or as a state minister, governor-general, or ambassador, by the practice of honesty, truth, and modesty.   " Andrew, my dear boy," the good woman has often said to me, " always bear in mind that he or she who would thrive in this world should be acquainted with modesty only by name, and, when necessary, must flatter, promise, and deceive, but always with due discretion.   As to robbery," she would add, "the person who has gained a character for sanctity may talk largely of his honesty and conscientious scruples, while he robs, betrays confidence, and commits other impositions, wholesale and with impunity."

Poor, unfortunate Diana! grievously would she sigh and lament while counselling me in this motherly manner: doubtless the recollection of those once favoured lovers of hers, the royal prince, the holy bishop, the contract tailor, the actor, the wealthy Jew, the Quaker, and the learned judge, together with that of their worldly maxims and conduct, rushed thronging upon her much embittered imagination, whenever she so lectured me for my future advantage in this transitory life.

Thus ably tutored, apparently I had only to follow the maxims laid down for my guidance, that, if favoured with common luck, I might in due time become a great and a wealthy personage.   How far my subsequent conduct has proved me worthy of my education the impartial reader must be left to decide, and I trust his decision will be the result of his own sound judgment, and not shaped after the opinions of renowned and learned judges or doctors of ecclesiastical courts, who open not their mouths but to give vent to musty precedents, and who, though they thoroughly satisfy us of the character of their own education, whenever opportunity offers, by legally stripping us of all the goods and money we possess, and heartlessly leaving us to perish in misery and want, yet pretend to know more than others do of the exact period at which the infant mind is capable of receiving impressions, as also of the only regular habits which (as exemplified in themselves) they assert are benefits to be felt to the close of life.

Heaven be praised, I am no proctor, and never shall sit as a judge in an ecclesiastical court. Hitherto my lot in life has been to act, not to preach, and pretend to more knowledge and probity than my fellow-men.   Contenting myself, therefore, with what I have stated as to my education, I shall proceed with my story.

After quitting my father's cottage, I trudged briskly along the road for nigh two hours before I slackened my pace, when, seeing the door was temptingly open of a Methodist meeting-house, erected almost adjoining the village church, I entered the sacred building for the purpose of resting myself while divine service was being performed.   Here I may observe, that I had frequently been made to attend our parish church,; not, however, that my parents were religious characters, or, indeed, at all with the approbation of my mother; for she, poor woman, having no fine clothes to appear in, had never, from the day of her marriage, gone to a place of worship.   Moreover, since her intercourse with the bishop, she had imbibed the notorious Priestley's opinion, insomuch that she hesitated not to declare she hated all religious establishments, and thought them sinful and idolatrous.   It was in accordance with the commands of my father that I had gone to church, as he, to procure occasional employment from our rector, to gather in or thrash his tithe corn, used to say that he must hold a candle to the devil, and verily I am inclined to think that he held the clergy to be of affinity to his Satanic majesty.   In the meeting-house I had entered I was doomed to have my senses of hearing and seeing most completely astounded.   Never before had I heard so impressive a discourse, or witnessed such theatrical action, as the minister treated his audience to on that occasion.   At his pleasure, hell was made to yawn widely for the wicked, and the gates of paradise were thrown off their hinges to admit the righteous ; while, to increase their force on the imagination, his terrific threats and most blissful promises were accompanied by blows of the evangelical man's clenched fist, dealt with thundering force on the cushion before him. " It is a wonderful pathetic discourse, and touches the heart to the quick," I overheard several staid dames say to each other, and I make no question that they thought as they spoke ; for sobs and sighs, groans and tears, with their eyes turned up towards heaven, were given by them as accompaniments to certain of the threats and promises which it seemed had occasioned the most disturbance to their tender consciences.

After the service, a subscription was entered into at the chapel-door for the family of a dissenting clergyman, who had emigrated rather than undergo the ordeal of a public trial for a nameless offence, sworn against him by the waiter at a coffee-shop, when, so strong was their disbelief of his backsliding, and so great the sympathy of the worthy congregation, stirred by the representations and entreaties of their Wesleyan minister, that they showered down their silver offerings, until the plates held out for receiving them were literaly piled up with money.

About an hour after my quitting the meeting-house, as I was passing through the town of Guildford, a gentleman addressed me, saying, " My lad, hold this horse for me ; I shall be back with you in less than a quarter of an hour," when, having put his steed under my care, he hurried away after a dashing young damsel, who was walking at some little distance down an adjoining street.

I loved horse exercise, and, for a boy in my lowly situation, was rather an adept in that noble sport, having very frequently been employed by the miller, our neighbour, whose daughter my father married, to take his nags to and from a distant pasture ; and now, without hesitation, or more delay than was requisite for its owner to remove himself out of sight of me, I mounted the horse, and expeditiously quitted the town, when I pushed forward, with more than the speed of a post-boy, to Farnham, a distance of ten miles. " I have had a rare pleasant ride," said I laughingly to myself, while walking the charger through the main street, to let him get cool after the journey ; "riding, however, too far, I find is severe exercise, the fatigue of which would soon counterbalance the pleasure ; therefore my next stage of the journey shall be performed in some easier manner."

With me, unless the ability fails, to will a thing is to do it ; and before many minutes had elapsed since my making the little soliloquy just related, I was comfortably housed, with a glass of negus and a plate of ham sandwiches before me, in the parlour of the Crown ; meanwhile my horse stood unsaddled in the stable of that establishment.

" Landlord," said I, after having gained the unsuspecting man's confidence by a plausible tale, " I shall leave the horse I came here upon in your custody, until such time as the kind gentleman who lent it to me sends for it home to Guildford." The landlord, glad to have what he considered a profitable inmate for his stables, readily promised to take good care of the steed, when, having discharged his little bill, I walked away from the town, on the Winchester road, and was soon overtaken by a stage-coach, on the roof of which I procured a seat, and thus proceeded on my travels, laughing most heartily in my sleeve to think how and when the gay Lothario, its owner, would find his horse.

No hero, however proudly seated in his triumphal car, ever enjoyed more ecstatic delight than my juvenile heart rebounded with during that my first journey, travelling upon a stage-coach ; but then, unlike the hero whose deeds leave him rivers of human blood to account for to his Creator, not one gout of the precious stream had I ever shed, or caused to be shed.

Pleasure such as I felt is indescribable ; therefore, all I shall add on the subject is, that my situation appeared to me to be like that of a captive who had just burst his prison bars, and happily effected his escape from loathed incarceration and the power of his persecutors. Indeed, such was my exultation, and so lively was my imagination, that I repeatedly whispered to myself, " Drudge away, Andrew Winpenny, the senior, and gain your penny how and when you can : still wilt thou be a poor man ; but he, the Andrew who is called thy son, without drudging at all, will do his endeavours to live more nobly by his wits, and to make his fellow-men his footballs."

The corporeal exertions which I had made during that, to me, most eventful and pleasant day, had fatigued my body ; and I not being one of those restless persons who lie awake in their beds, musing upon trifles, at those hours which ought to be devoted to sleep, after terminating my journey and enjoying a comfortable supper, retired to bed at the hotel the coach put up at in Winchester, to pass away, in one uninterrupted sleep, the entire night.

CHAPTER V.

"Hang sorrow, and drive away care;
The parish is bound to find us."

"Gay's doggerel lines tend to show that mirth and pauperism could be companions in olden times; the 'heaven-born minister,' too, must have been of this opinion, as, when he bribed the militia conscripts to serve in foreign fields of glory, he sent their spouses to the parish, as an honourable place of sojourn; but now that numerous poor-law commissioners, salaried with their thousands, lord it over the pauper race, nothing better is allowed for their food than oatmeal gruel, that banisher of corpulency and merriment, from the monstrous bastiles erected to uphold place and punish poverty."

My landlord was a thrifty character, who well knew how to manage with his customers; consequently, as I had no luggage for him to detain as security for the bill I owed, he took the prudent step of calling on me to discharge the little account, previous to my returning to the comforts of my pillow.

Boniface's cautious conduct had left me no account to settle with him previous to my departure on the following morning; therefore, as soon as I had quitted my bed, which was at an early hour, I hastened away from the inn, to proceed on my journey.

The morning was beautiful, and an excellent night's repose had thoroughly refreshed my limbs; therefore I proceeded on foot upon the road I purposed to travel, and felt that gaiety and joy revelling at my heart which healthy youth alone can be alive to, but all the potentates of the earth, with all their much-vaunted powers, can neither insure for themselves nor bestow upon others.

A light heart is an excellent companion; and provided he enjoys good health and the blessing of liberty, the man who journeys through life without one is but a simpleton for his pains. Thus I have constantly thought, for I am satisfied that the proudest honours and the greatest wealth are but incumbrances to the miserable mortal who carries about with him the leaden load imposed by care. The continuance of human happiness, however, like that of all terrestrial things, is dependent on many contingencies, and not the least pressing of those is the necessity that exists of frequently satisfying man's animal appetite. On the occasion in question my sense of hunger appealed to me so very forcibly, that after reaching the sixth mile I gladly entered an ale-house to procure a substantial breakfast, to satisfy the ravenous wolf within me.

The facetious woman, my hostess, when putting the meat on my table, was curiously inquisitive to know what could have brought a young fellow like me on his travels, with an hungry stomach at that time of the morning: but I recollected the old saying, that "a still tongue makes a wise head," and suffered her not to elicit any true information from my lips; but soon as I had contented my appetite, I resumed my journey, when, after walking the distance of two or three miles, I bargained with the driver of a Portsmouth chaise-cart, and for a trifle of money got accommodated with a seat in his vehicle to that famed maritime town.

He who would be acquainted with life in an humble walk should occasionally travel in mean habiliments, and frequent those taverns, of which there is one at least in every large English town, known as the "beggars' house." Chance, on the present occasion, conducted me to a favourite place of resort of the god Momus. It was a mean-looking dwelling, but its sign "The Crowing Cock," which stood conspicuously placed over the entrance-door, served as a faithful augur of the unsophisticated merriment which took place withinside the dwelling. The cock, however, with all his triumphant crowing, would have been wofully misplaced had he been stationed where he was to announce the approaching dawn, for that was a time when the visitors there were always revelling their time away in the sweet embrace of the pacific god Morpheus, and when they might defy the vigilance of Apollo, assisted by the crowing of all his cocks, to awaken them: in fine, this cock, though the emblem of triumphant crowing, served as the sign to an inn wherein mirth and jollity reigned only when crowing cocks and the rest of the feathered tribe were at roost. To an inn which, in the day-time, was surpassed by none for the peaceful and regular conduct of its inmates, but at night was invariably made the theatre of ribaldry, feasting, and debauch; in mockery of which real scenes, probably it was, that the cock over the doorway had been shaped and moulded with his beak open.

After I had taken a glass of ale and a biscuit in the aforesaid then quiet inn, I left my bundle with the landlord, and amused myself by walking about the town and viewing its fortifications, together with the shipping lying in the harbour there. In the evening, highly delighted with what I had seen, I returned back to the Crowing Cock, where everything was going on regular and peaceful, the same as when I had left that house. Presently, however, the shades of night began to obscure the earth, when, proportionately as the darkness became greater, distressed-looking objects flocked into the house, some of whom, to all appearance, were blind, and others lame or deformed, but all of them martyrs to sickness, or aggravated misery of one description or other.

For my part, I avow that I never possessed a redundant share of the amiable quality denominated tender-heartedness; nevertheless, on the present occasion, kindly feelings were harrowed up within my breast at the sight afforded by so many miserable objects of my own species; for the men and the women, the boys and the girls, were all of them, in some shape or another, most grievously afflicted.

He who judges of another by outward appearance usually is mistaken in his conclusion. The summons to a good supper, about an hour after night-fall, brought every one of the mendicants together in the common sitting-room—the apartment allotted for them to mess in. They were merry as so many grigs, and most of them freed, as if by magic, from their several sicknesses and infirmities.

It was a pleasant sight now to behold the happy set, amongst whom envy and pride—those fiend-like curses, too frequently attendant on the great—apparently were unknown. The landlord, mistaking me for one of the happy fraternity, which was most excusable, inasmuch as beggars appear in all garbs and disguises, placed a chair for me, and invited me to sit down, which I unhesitatingly did: as to a boy like me, who had never—no, not once in his life—fared sumptuously, the roasted goose, the apple-pie, the plum-pudding, the sausages, and the boiled mutton and vegetables, displayed on the board, were temptations too many and too great to be resisted: in short, at that moment of temptation, such were my feelings of friendship towards the good things I saw, that I would have risked losing all my money, and my wardrobe to boot, rather than have quitted the apartment without having first gratified my appetite with a share of them.

Professed mendicants, who travel the country for their subsistence, were it not for their intemperance, would be a very long-lived class of people; for the lightness of their hearts, and the great exercise they take in pure air, are undeniable promoters of longevity. Excesses, however, of any kind, may kill a giant, and mendicants are notorious for those they commit. They seldom entertain scruples of conscience regarding their amours or their feasts, but thoughtlessly enjoy both to their hearts' full content: and he who imagines that the doctrine of a temperance society could convert a set of mendicants, need only to preach it to the merry-hearted crew to discover that his doctrine and his labour might as well have been given to the winds.

On the occasion I am now relating, vain would be my efforts were I to attempt recounting one-half of the gormandizing which took place. No set of friars, revelling unseen by the eyes of laymen, could gluttonize much more voraciously than did these jovial beggars. They demolished to the last ounce of each dish on the table, and they drank of small and of strong beer in proportion to what they ate. In fine, theirs was like a Norwegian feast, at which one article serves only as a prelude to another, until nature, wearied by repletion, is made to exclaim, over and over again, " Hold, for heaven's sake, enough!"

With hirelings, under a monarchical government, the monarch's name is trumped forth as that of the god of their idolatry; and however weak in intellect or detested by the nation the monarch may be, his or her health, as the case may be, is invariably the standard toast at their public messes, on the removal of the cloth. Here, however, more sincerity was used; for no sooner had the cloth disappeared from the board, and the pipes and their accompaniments been placed there in its stead, than a snowy-headed mendicant, standing up, as also did the companions around him, raised his brimming glass of punch to his lips, when he gave aloud, with peculiar emphasis, the well-known old standing toast among genuine mendicants, and quaffed off a large portion of its contents.

Smoking, drinking, story-telling, and ribaldry, were now resorted to by the party, to make time pass merrily away. The more juvenile portion of the company, however, quitted the bacchanals, to adjourn to the far end of the room, where we all of us, boys and girls alike—and I was one among the number—played many a strange prank with each other; nor is this surprising, considering that we, no, not one of us, had been tutored by fastidious masters, who, no matter how learned and precise they may be, teach that which they themselves rarely or never practise. After a rather protracted term of enjoyment that way, the fair mendicants of the adult party grew tired of drinking spirits and water, when they brought away with them from the convivial board a one-eyed fiddler, who, by-the-by, passed as totally blind in the day time, and to the tunes extracted from his violin the youngsters soon commenced cutting capers. Let those persons who know of none more natural or better, loudly and vehemently, if they please, extol court and aristocratic balls, where pride, vanity, and affectation reign triumphant in almost every fair female's bosom; or, should they prefer such, their acclamations may be bestowed on opera dances and other public assemblies, got up expressly for the gratification of persons in high life : but, for my part, to make me truly happy, give me the mendicants' dance, when the mendicants themselves, who merrily foot it with me, have thrown aside for the night their crutches, their assumed infirmities, and all the tricking arts of their venerable trade; that, with unsophisticated mirth, and hearts buoyant as if grief had never reached them, they may be prepared to give and to receive all the delight which the happy can reciprocally share and bestow.

Yes, grant me, kind fortune, whenever I wish for it, to enjoy the sprightly dance, with all the delight I felt at the Crowing Cock ; and I shall rest satisfied that enhanced bliss, derived from dancing in more refined society or to sweeter music, will never fall to my lot.

CHAPTER VI.

" *Simon.*—Obadiah, think'st thou that the common beggar is the meanest of his tribe ?
" *Obadiah.*—Verily, friend Simon, I believe the proverb, 'the richer the man the greater the rogue,' applies to all the begging community."   THE HONEST QUAKERS.

THE cares of the world weigh but lightly on those favoured mendicants who have become thorough proficients in the calling. Unlike agricultural or manufacturing labourers, they rise not from their pillows at early hours of the morn, when the god of sleep most invokes them to his embrace, but revelling in his arms at some cheerful inn, they dream delightful dreams, or slumber away the time until the fumes arising from the preceding night's debauch have all been dispersed, and a comfortable hot breakfast awaits them.

The hours for business now approach, and the mendicants array themselves in their robes of office; when some of them, like fair coquettes, put on their paints and patches; others, unknowingly, copying after Hercules and Vulcan, take in hand their clubs or their crutches, and duly prepared for the grand business of life—the great work of imposition—they sally forth, refreshed and invigorated, from their several places of abode. They are all of them rogues and impostors; but arrant impostors as these vagrants are, who shall dare to say that their impositions equal those of certain empirics, who unhesitatingly poison their patients without even having ascertained their complaints? Or who could be so besotted as to compare these impositions with the grosser frauds of some men in this world who call themselves divines, and preach up as gospel what no man gifted with common sense can comprehend or believe? In short, the crutch of a beggar, when the real merits and demerits of their possessors have been examined into, ought not to be thought one-half so dishonourable as the supporters of many lordly coronets; and who is there living that, provided he knew the scales of divine justice were ready poised to weigh those things against each other, would not a hundred-fold rather travel the unexplored road to eternity, answerable only for having carried a mendicant's stick in preference to a heathen bishop's crook, or some of the precious emblems of office of certain favoured courtiers high in dignity?

To conclude this subject. Avowedly the trained beggar is a lying impostor. Let us, however, ask, whether the professor of any other one of the trades or professions by which man acquires his subsistence is a whit better than this beggar? And, if honestly replied to, we shall be told that the craft and mystery by which all live is of a similar nature to each other; and, moreover, that the key-stone of most of the trades and professions is based on the rock of imposition.

I passed away most happily a great portion of another day with the light-hearted mendicants and little Celia Selina Carolina (for beggars in low life, just the same as titled ones, love to christen their children with a variety of names), the pretty lass who had footed it away so merrily with me, having strained her ancle in the dance, or, what answered the same purpose, said that she had done so, stayed at home with me the whole time, when she communicated many of the secrets of her profession, and resorted to a variety of coaxing arts to induce me to become one of their joyous fraternity.

With regard to fair woman, it is said, "when she deliberates she is lost;" but for a youngster, such as I then was, who had previously met with nought save wickedness from the world, it proved so tempting a thing to be tempted by all the persuasive arts of a most tempting little maiden of about my own age, that I never deliberated, but most readily agreed to everything her winning tongue proposed to me; and, consequently, I was in almost as fair a way of becoming a professed mendicant as any newly-appointed prime minister can be of becoming a state pauper.

In pretty Celia Selina's society the hours were made to glide most pleasantly away with me, till at length came the time for that feasting and revelry with which my associates always recompensed and consoled themselves for those rebuffs which their professional employment had exposed them to during the earlier part of the day. The mendicants were now in as good humour as on the preceding day, and the dinner was of the same substantial and excellent quality, but several of the fraternity present at yesterday's meal had taken their departure from the town to campaign elsewhere, and in their place two or three newly-arrived beggars took their seats at our social board.

It was now, just after the standing toast had been drunk, that an opportunity was afforded me for hearing the old white-headed beggar, the father of the crew, declare his sentiments regarding the poor laws of England, he having been drawn into the declaration of his opinion by one of the newly-arrived members of the community, who, it seems, had so greatly mismanaged his affairs as to have recently been the inmate of a poor-house, wherein, according to his statement, he was restored to lost health, occasioned by excess of good living, by means of the spare diet allowed them, but which, he said, had brought him to the very verge of starvation.

"And well may it have done so," observed the hoary-headed patriarch of the gang, "for the poor laws threaten ruin to all that comes within their vortex. They are the curse of the country, and I fear will bring to pauperism even the most experienced members of our profession. The poor laws destroy the resources of the country, and while they increase the numbers to be supported on a common fund, paralyze the industry by which the fund is reproduced and maintained. The most direct and irresistible evidence is likewise afforded of their tendency to discourage prudence or foresight—to confer a premium on profligacy and improvidence—to render economy a useless incumbrance on poverty—to annihilate all the relations of kindness and sympathy between the rich and the poor—to dissolve domestic ties among the poor themselves, and to convert our rural parishes into Indian plantations, peopled with harsh masters and with refractory slaves. In fine," concluded the hoary mendicant, "if the poor laws are much longer administered in the way they now are, the farmers must most of them become mendicants, and our trade consequently be so overstocked with members, that there will be no possibility of living by it."

"I see how it is," said a swarthy, ill-looking gipsy man, who, it appeared, had recently been driven from the pursuit of his old avocation and that of his forefathers by the prosecution and punishment he had met with for pretending truly to tell people's fortunes, "none but your licensed thieves and rogues are now permitted to earn a living. A license qualifies any rogue as a field ranter, while a few shillings suffice to pay for the license of a hawker and pedlar, when they both of them may go at large about the world, ranting their humbug, or cheating every one they can manage to defraud with downright impunity."

"Ah, Cooper," rejoined the white-headed veteran, "so you would have your craft licensed, I see. Apparently you don't exactly approve of the law which punishes such of the enterprising part of the community, as common knaves and impostors, who pretend to fortune-telling, the use of spells, or similar mysterious feats of skill."

"Confound all such laws," exclaimed Cooper, "they have driven me to my wit's end to know what to do to obtain a good living. What think you of it, grey head, of my turning wizard?"

"It would not answer your purpose, my Norwood friend," answered the old vagrant, "for, since the laws against wizards, witches, and witchcraft have been abolished, nobody cares a doit about the crimes attributed to them; indeed, imaginary crimes require the fertile inventions of the lawyer tribe to set officious fools at work to hunt them out for punishment; otherwise, they being mere phantoms, would cease to be thought of, even among the most ignorant of the vulgar."

"The law is like a lop-sided vessel," now remarked a wooden-legged mendicant, dressed in the garb of a sailor. "It leans all on one side. Look now at the corn laws, don't they force the poor and the needy to eat their bread at double the price which it ought to be, that the rich landholder may pocket one-half of the money? And are we not forced to pay ten times its value, as the duty on our tobacco, because that the law-makers love to grind down the poor, to save their own purses?"

"Ah," rejoined the ancient beggar, "Jack tar has spoken the truth, the plain truth, and nothing but the truth: poverty is slavery in all countries; but here, in this land, everybody knows that to be poor is to be overtaxed, trod on, and cheated by everybody, and in every way. Howsoever, as to fortune-telling, which we were talking of, it was not until lately that our betters were allowed to gull the public without fear of punishment, by predicting for money this or that luck as likely to befal their customers; while we, who foretell fortunes by the stars or the palm, are still to be punished by fine and imprisonment for our predictions. It is all gross injustice," added he, after a pause, and taking a printed paper from his pocket. After observing it had been given to him on the morning of that day, he read aloud its contents, which were as follows:—

"Phrenological Predictions.—Persons meditating any important change in their pursuit, parents, before deciding on a business or profession for their children, should consult this science, as their fortunes depend on the choice harmonizing with its predictions. Terms, five shillings and upwards.

"PROFESSOR SMITHSON.

"No 90 Market street, opposite the Swan (inner private door).

. "The responses of the science, as far as will conduce to the future welfare of youth, are given for the same."

The mendicants passed many jokes upon the professor's advertisement, which they seemed to think a clever contrivance for imposing upon the ignorant and unwary; but the general opinion was, that the government would not long tolerate the telling of fortunes through the agency of bumps in the skull, as, if permitted, it must serve as a licence or loop-hole for admitting all the trickery of fortune-telling into general practice.

After having terminated these remarks, Cooper, the Norwood gipsy, who apparently had been absorbed in meditation on the communication just made, rousing himself from his reverie, spoke as follows:—"It don't signify what you say, bumps or no bumps, a pretty lass may venture to tell gentlemen's fortunes. Knowledge, I know, beyond what they themselves possess, is deemed a crime by the magistrates, who scruple not to send even the learned astronomer to prison, to labour for weeks among common felons for having cast a nativity; yet may a pretty lass venture to tell a gentleman's fortune, for where is the wretch to be found who is cold-hearted enough to inform against a pretty girl? or where is there a brute of a magistrate that would convict her?"

The mendicants were now busily at work feeling the bumps on each other's heads, and I, having first indulged myself in a sly laugh, addressed my fair young friend by saying, in a whisper, "Celia, my dear, let us feel each other's bumps, and you shall turn fortune-teller, for none other is so fit for it."

"I agree to your proposal, provided you will accompany me about the country," said the pretty lass, when she having smiled a sweet smile of her approbation, we spontaneously rose from our seats, to dance a merry jig to the music of the one-eyed fiddler.

—————

CHAPTER VII.

"For many a year in honest trade I early toil'd and late ;
Paid rent and tax—nor once refused to pay the poorhouse rate,
Till times grew bad, and trade decreased, and troubles gather'd fast,
And all my cares and ventures fail'd,—to this I came at last."

"In England, the much vaunted land of liberty, truly deplorable hath been the seaman's lot. Thousands of the brave but thoughtless fellows have been seized upon like felons, and punished without trial by close imprisonment in tyrannically governed ships ; yea, kept there in twofold slavery, to toil and to fight until killed, maimed, or worn out."

"We wonder not that such profusion's shown ;
Shameless they give, who give what's not their own."

HE who is habituated to early rising, finds it irksome to be slumbering in bed at late hours of the morning ; and I, notwithstanding that I had footed it away most merrily on the preceding night, was up betimes, when I sallied forth from the Crowing Cock, to enjoy a walk before our breakfast was in readiness for us.

I unpremeditatedly bent my steps towards the harbour, when having arrived there, and while I stood leaning over a rail, looking at the shipping, in the hilarity of my heart I broke forth into the following soliloquy :—"Here am I, free as the wind blowing around me ; for, happily, this is no land of slavery. I am young, and the world is to me as a luxuriant garden, abounding with delicious fruit, all ripe and ready for those who know how to gather it. My poor mother's advice shall not be thrown away upon her friendless child. He it is who will show honour to her memory by attending to her precepts, and carving his own way to fortune. No foolish scruples nor qualms of conscience shall check his advancement ; for, knowing the world to be peopled with knaves and fools, he will unscrupulously hold fast what he gets ; while, by believing in the promises of none, yet administering to the vanity of all persons, he gleans more and more, until those riches are his in abundance, which, properly spread, cause all other advantages to accompany them."

"Jack, my boy, how long is it that you have been ashore ?" now asked of me one of two very ill-looking fellows, habited in the garb of sailors, most abruptly interrupting my soliloquy. I stared at the questioner for a brief space, thinking he had mistaken me for some other youth, and then replied to him by saying, that I had lived ashore all my lifetime, and had never been aboard ship. "The youngster has run his vessel ; lay him aboard, Ned," now peremptorily said one of these ruffians, interlarding his short speech with several villanous oaths.

Not liking the appearance of things at this moment—though still I could form no conjecture of what the sailors wanted—I looked sharply about me, intending to make the best use of my legs in taking French leave of the unmannerly rascals. I might as well, however, have spared myself the trouble I was taking, as before I advanced half a dozen yards on my road, a severe blow from a bludgeon, inflicted on the back part of my head, brought me sprawling on the ground ; when in less than two minutes I had been seized hold of and thrown headlong to the bottom of a boat, into which my brutal assailants jumped after me, and then lost no time in pulling at the oars to a vessel anchored at the outermost part of the harbour.

The rascally crimp—for such he proved to be—had inflicted rather a severe blow on my head, which bled so freely during the time we were in the boat on our way to the tender ship—for such she was—that on my arrival on board I was nearly insensible. The surgeon, however, dressed my wound, and bandaged up my head ; when I was put to rest myself in a hammock, the motion of which, combined with that of the ship, which laid at single anchor, pitching violently—for it blew fresh—made me grievously sick, when in attempting to relieve my sufferings by getting out of the hammock, it flew from behind me, and I fell prostrate with great force on the ship's deck.

"Confound the lubber," coarsely vociferated the surgeon's mate, who had dressed my wound, and at the moment of my fall had been engaged within a few feet of me administering professional aid to an Irish patient by bleeding him, "confound the young lubber; he has knocked the basin over, and spoilt my waistcoat."—"The devil bother him!" exclaimed the Hibernian; "by Jasus, doctor, but I'd sarve it out to him, if so be my arm was done bleeding, and bound up dacently. I say, doctor, dear—sure it has bled enough—bandage my arm, will you?—that's a good jontleman."

This was a bad time for entreaty. The patient might as well have invoked a post as expected of a ship's surgeon to bandage up his arm until he had first attended to his soiled waistcoat, which he now did, aided by the boy in attendance on him, who brought soap and water for the purpose. The mischief, however, was not great, as, happily for the disciple of Galen, the apron he wore reached up to his breast, and therefore his waistcoat was very little the worse for the accident; but, as regarded the Irish patient, he, of the three sufferers of us, had the most cause for regret, for, although a robust man, he was brought to the very verge of fainting from exhaustion before the surgeon could spare time to bandage up the vein he had opened of his arm.

After passing twenty-four hours in a state of misery on board the tender, I, together with six or seven more impressed persons, were conveyed in a boat belonging to that vessel to the Zephyr frigate, anchored outside of the harbour. Here somewhat more liberty was allowed to us than had been in the tender, where, it should be observed, we had been treated worse than convicted felons pent up in a common gaol.

My head was still very sore; but I was no longer sea-sick, and having a set of blunt tars about me, who were willing to enter into conversation, I consulted with one or two of them regarding what steps I ought to take to procure my liberty. They, however, soon set me right on the subject, by communicating the melancholy truth that freedom at that time was tolerated in British sailors only when they were not wanted for his Majesty's service, and consequently that I could have little or no chance of regaining mine long as the war lasted, except, indeed, I should effect my escape from the ship, or happen to lose a limb or an eye in the service of my country; in which last case they said that, provided my recommendations were good, I might be granted a pension, perhaps sufficiently large to keep life and soul together for the rest of my days. "But," observed I, in the simplicity of my heart, "I can be of no use here, for I am no sailor; nor did I ever, until yesterday, behold even the outside of a ship."

The tars laughed at my innocence, till presently one of the most ruffianly of the crew turning the quid in his mouth, declared that "their boatswain would soon make a sailor of me; for d'ye see, Jack," added he, "you are young and able, but many of the lubbers the crimps send here are old chaps, who, most of them, are stiff-legged or stiff-fingered, just as though they had been tailoring on shop-boards all their lives."

To narrate more of my conversation with the sailors is unnecessary, but I now plainly discovered I had fallen into the most loathsome state of bondage that any landsman, disliking the sea service, can possibly fall into; repining, however, could be of no avail, and of this I was so sensible, that I resolved to put the best face I could on my misfortune, and to bear my captivity with fortitude. But he who has sipped from the cup of sweets, ere it was dashed from his lips, cannot forget the sweet draught he has been deprived of; though, perhaps, had he been permitted to drain the cup to its bottom, the bitter dregs engendered there might have cured him of all desire of ever tasting of such another cup.

For my part, I regretted my separation from little Celia Selina with infinite regret, and tears involuntarily started to my eyes whenever I contemplated the mendicant's highly preferable state of life to that of the impressed landsman, doomed to waste his best days in a hated ship; and yet I was sensible that I should have been reduced to a state of mendicity in a very few days, had I not fallen into the clutches of infernal crimps.

At the time this deplorable event befel me, it so happened that my money was safe in my pocket, but then it had been reduced by one half from what it was previous to my falling into the society of the happy mendicants. The two days' expenses at the Crowing Cock had eased me of fifteen shillings, in addition to which I had lightened my purse by several purchases made, and the loan of five shillings to accommodate pretty Celia Selina; but it may be observed, that she would not have needed this sum, only for the circumstance of her having sprained her ancle, and so missed the opportunity of accompanying her mother to a neighbouring fair. Still, poor as I was, I have my doubts whether there was a single sailor before the mast, belonging to the proud frigate I was on board, who could have produced even ten shillings, though that paltry sum might have been made available to procure him great advantages. Compared to my shipmates I was rich, for I had a sovereign and a shilling in my purse; but the loss of my clothes vexed me; and, as not one man out of our free-born crew was permitted liberty to go on shore, I got a Jew slopseller to carry a note to Portsmouth for little Celia, who promised me he would use his best endeavours to procure an answer from her, and to bring me off my clothes. However, all the satisfaction I got by this measure was that of recovering a single shirt, which, by the Jew's account, the landlord had sent me word was all he could find belonging to me; while, as to Celia, it appeared she was away on an excursion to some country, fair on the business of her profession, at the time when the Jew called at the Crowing Cock; therefore my note was left there for her, but from that day to the present I have not received an answer to my epistle.

The second day after that of my embarkation we hove anchor and made sail; but as the captain carried sealed orders, not to be opened until we were in the latitude of Madeira, nobody in the ship knew to what place we were bound; consequently, innumerable were the conjectures formed on the subject, and that the more as we were victualled for a long voyage.

I now had ample opportunity afforded me for contemplating the life of a sailor, which notwithstanding all that had been trumpeted forth in its favour, is one of unceasing drudgery. The sailor cannot call a single minute his own. Alike, day and night, he must obey the shrill notes of a boatswain's whistle; while for the most trivial neglect of duty, or negligence of any kind, he is liable to be punished more severely than most felons are for their crimes. In short, a British sailor, though, as far as manly qualities go, inferior to no man, was at the time in question so extremely degraded, from the arbitrary nature of the naval service, that scarcely any other class of men in any country are reduced to the same lowly state of degradation.

When misfortunes overtake us, we are apt to think them worse than those by which other persons are afflicted; for, most indubitably, almost everything in life is viewed in a wrong light —and, perhaps, no persons in life are either so happy or so unhappy as the world would make them out to be. My fate certainly appeared hard, to have been seized upon by crimps, and doomed to be made a sailor, and banished to foreign realms, like a condemned criminal; yet, when we were employed upon long and tedious night watches on our voyage, the landsmen on board the Zephyr, who had been victimized by crimps, related our tales to each other; and I found that my case was by no means comparable for hardships to those of many others among us—one of which, as a humane hint to administrations that encourage, or even tolerate, the infamous trade of crimping men, I will summarily record.

" Since, shipmates, you are pleased to signify a desire to be made acquainted with my story," said the relator, a man apparently verging on his fortieth year, "I have to inform you that my father was a small farmer in the neighbourhood of Brentford, and on his dying, which happened when I was in my twenty-fourth year, I succeeded to the tenantry of his farm; and about a year afterwards, wanting a helpmate, married an amiable young woman, who made me an excellent wife, by whom I have six children now living.

" My father left little wealth behind him, and my wife brought me none; but, for a time after our union, our joint frugality and industry made our affairs go on swimmingly, insomuch that we were getting before the world, for we had spare money in store.

" The sun of prosperity does not always shine. An increasing family—the galling pressure of tithes—and almost year after year a change of times for the worse, gradually altered our condition; till at length, though we fared harder than our labourers, we could no longer make both ends meet. When we were in this woful state, often have I been compelled to part with implements of husbandry and articles of household furniture, to enable me to pay exorbitant poor-rates, to support the idle and the worthless, who fared better than myself.

" But, shipmates," resumed the broken-down farmer, after having wiped away a tear or two from his care-worn face, "not to harrow my own feelings or tire your patience by an unnecessarily long tale, I shall pass over the minute relation of our misery, and leave you to judge how it must have been increased, year after year, from the time when I had a good, well-stocked farm, to that of my possessing no article worth a single shilling. When my family were reduced to a state of utter destitution, I was taken into custody by a writ from the Court of Requests, and carried to Whitecross street prison, in London, for a debt of one shilling and sixpence."—(Here several dreadful oaths from the lips of his warm-hearted hearers interrupted the *ci-devant* farmer in his story.) After which, and his having listened to some commiserating remarks, the honest man resumed as follows:—

"I thought my case was a very cruel one; but when I had been afforded time to look around me at my companions in the prison, my sentiments underwent an entire change, for I and my family, d'ye see, messmates, are all of us young and hearty, and strong enough to earn our bread by our labour, while, incredible though it may seem to you, there were now pointed out to me three wretched debtors, whose united ages amounted to two hundred and twenty years, and who were lingering their last days away in squalid misery, just removed from starvation for debts, which, summed up together, amount to only four shillings and tenpence!

"But this is not all. I could freeze your very hearts with horror at the relation of what passes in that loathsome gaol. One poor father of a large family I saw brought there for a debt of fivepence: he, however, was released from his troubles, for he died of apoplexy shortly after his being brought to the prison for incarceration; but what became of his starving family heaven only knows.

"In my behalf fortune again smiled, for an old friend came forward to liberate me from prison; but law and poverty had forced me to move from one place to another, and I had been apprehended in rather a distant part of the country: consequently the expenses of my arrest, though I had been taken for only one shilling and sixpence, were made by the law's chicanery to amount to a score of pounds—all which large sum my friend paid; yet, generous and kind-hearted as this most excellent man is, he protested against the hardship of his being made to pay so dearly for justice administered against a poor man; when against a rich one in England, he said, justice could never be made to act; as a proof of which bold assertion, my dear friend adduced the circumstance of his having recently lost upwards of a hundred pounds by a lawyer, who had himself pocketed fifty thousand pounds belonging to his clients, and then laughed at these dupes of his, and threatened one of them with a prosecution for daring to cast an imputation on his character. Thus, my friend said, the boasted laws of Britain had not only left this wholesale rogue unpunished, but had even tolerated his proceedings; while, moreover, that in genteel society he had become a great favourite, as a natural consequence of his increased wealth."

Several loud ejaculations, indicative of indignation at this part of his narrative, almost stopped the unfortunate man in his story; however, he perseveringly concluded by saying, that his friend sent him to Portsmouth, to negotiate for the passage of himself and family to Canada in a ship on the eve of sailing, which passage money his friend had intended to pay, as also to give him a sum to enable him to begin a new career in the world; but that, the morning after his arrival at Portsmouth, having left his family in bed at the inn where he put up, he himself went to the harbour to make some necessary inquiries; when there, his person had been seized upon by a gang of crimps, who conveyed him on board the tender, from whence he had been removed to the Zephyr frigate, to be made serve the King, while his poor wife and children were left penniless, to struggle in an unfeeling world against misery and starvation; or, in accordance with his own words, to become "parish paupers."

Unfortunate man! Miserable as may have been the predestined fate of his helpless wife and children, how much more threatening would have been their situation, had the humane poor law of a subsequent period been in operation! A poor law which is the appropriate companion of a Reform bill that diminishes the suffrage, and by means of placemen barristers, who sack their thirty-five thousand pounds annually from the taxes, impedes the rate-payer in establishing his right.

CHAPTER VIII.

" He was of that noble trade
That demi-gods and heroes made,
Slaughter and knocking on the head,
The trade to which they all were bred;
And is, like others, glorious when
'Tis great and large, but base if mean."

THE reading portion of the community have long had their patience put to a severe ordeal by the monotonous stories related by voyagers of their doings, seeings, and sayings on board a ship; and this, notwithstanding that a ship, after all has been urged that sophistry can invent in its behalf, is most indubitably the very worst prison that a man can be incarcerated in.

Presuming companions, abominable accommodation, the smallest possible comfort, and the greatest personal danger, may justly be enumerated in the long list of grievances of which the impressed landsman has to complain when he is compelled to serve on board a ship.   In fine, such not unfrequently is his miserable situation that he would inevitably destroy himself had he sufficient time left at his disposal to reflect upon it; his persecutors, however, apparently sensible of this, leave him no leisure time for thought, but almost unceasingly harass the poor wretch, driving him to and fro, aloft and below deck, and forward and aft, as though he were an animal of a meaner nature—a dog or a monkey to come and go at the bidding of any jack in office, shaped in the shape of a man.

Knowing, therefore, as I do by experience, what is the life of an impressed landsman when serving on board a king's ship, I shall weary no reader's patience by detailing any particulars relating to it, but pass on to other matters, after briefly observing, that all the inventive faculties of mankind for torturing the innocent of his own species must have been strained to their full stretch, when a worthless administration, paid and employed to do justice to everybody, yet devised and enforced the means of supporting their nation's grandeur by torturing their fellow-men in the frightful way that impressed landsmen are tortured; indeed, no class of priests, in the pomposity of their pride, have ventured to foretel any punishment comparable to it for barbarity, as the lot of the wicked who deviate from their creed in the state of futurity.

Our sealed orders, when they were opened off Madeira, were found to contain instructions for the commander of the Zephyr to proceed with her to the West India station, and we arrived in the Carribean Sea within five weeks from that time, and two days afterwards anchored in the harbour of Port Royal, in Martinique.

The season was sickly at that time, and the yellow fever raged to a frightful excess, while we, as new comers, soon were made dreadful sufferers from its violence. Forty of our crew died within a fortnight from the day of our arrival, and among them was the poor farmer, whose story is related in the last chapter, as also another of the pressed landsmen, who had been shipped from the tender about the time I was.   My youth and spare habit of body were circumstances in my favour, and I had the good fortune to escape a visitation from the then prevailing scourge of the western tropic; but a seven weeks' confinement to a ship, with salt provision, bad rum, and filthy water for my daily ration, had by no means reconciled me to the miseries attendant on a sea life; therefore, I was continually upon the watch for a favourable opportunity of effecting my escape from the Zephyr frigate.

The discipline carried on in the British navy was at that time extremely severe, and deserters from it, no matter whether they had been pressed into the service or that they entered into it voluntarily, could expect to be shown no mercy when they had the misfortune to be retaken.   Of this last mentioned fact I was very sensible, and I also well knew that it would be a futile task to attempt hiding myself anywhere in the island of Martinique.

This beautiful island at that time belonged to Great Britain, but the French settlers dared not to harbour or conceal deserters from the British service, either of the army or the navy, for great was the penalty attached to this offence. For the same cause no ship captain would take any person from the island, unless he had a permit from the government there.

We had been in harbour about a month, when a Spanish brig of war from Porto Rico, which had been caught at sea in a hurricane while cruising in our neighbourhood, entered the harbour of Port Royal, as we were taught to believe, to procure shelter.

There is a favouring time for all things, and I was now doomed to discover that resolution and perseverance may triumph over great difficulties. One of the lieutenants belonging to the Spanish vessel was an Englishman, and it so happened that I being on shore in attendance on our captain, who, on the death of his personal serving man, had taken me into his service, as he said, on account of my cheerfulness and activity, contrived, by means of little services rendered at a coffee-house to him, to scrape an acquaintance with this officer, who, it should be mentioned, lodged only a door or two from my captain's quarters.

The officer in question appeared to me a man after my own heart; his lofty spirit commanded respect from every one, while his easy manners gained the goodwill of many; but I subsequently found that he was a man whose education would have done honour to a Spartan of olden times. No scruples of conscience disturbed his breast. When it could be achieved with safety, this extraordinary personage would unscrupulously have robbed from the church or chapel of any religious class of the great community of the world. He would have taken away its plate, its valuable shrines, or its wine, but disregarded the sacred wafers ; and when the act had been achieved, he would have gloried in his robbery, and turned his booty to the best account.

After a growing intimacy of some days, I thought I had delved into the character of this remarkable lieutenant, and that I could bring him into the humour of furthering my views. Accordingly I ventured to open my heart to him, by confiding to him the tale of my grievances, and hinting at my eagerness to effect my escape from servitude in the British frigate.

I was correct in my conjecture, and my confidence was not misplaced ; while, to prove the force of opinion, I avow, that from that day forward I have thought the better of myself for the just estimate which I then formed of this intrepid man.

"My boy," said he, after having mused over certain parts of my tale, but assuming, as he spoke, the manner of a man not to be played with, "those who mean to deceive always have recourse to oaths, but your little pranks satisfy me that you are worthy of being served; therefore I shall at once tell you what to do that you may regain your freedom, and you, youngster, in return, must tell me as candidly whether you dare to perform what I propose."

The gallant officer now communicated, as a secret, that his ship was to depart at midnight, and told me he would furnish me with a sleeping draught, to be put into my captain's grog that evening, when all I should have to do, he said, would be, after dosing his allowance, to possess myself of what valuables the captain had on shore with him, and then hasten to an appointed spot at the water's edge, where he himself and a boat's crew would be in waiting to take me off in their boat to the Santa Maria, whose anchor would then be apeak, and the canvass of her courses lying loosened from her yards.

The prospect now held out to me of escape from the man-of-war filled my heart with joy, and I was warm in expressions of my thanks to the lieutenant for his generous offer, though inwardly resolved not to commit the robbery he had made a condition of our agreement; for, Jesuit like, I was willing to take all the good I could procure for myself, and to shirk all the evil. Consequently, for the sake of escaping, I readily agreed to the terms proposed by him; when the preliminaries having been arranged, everything else was speedily settled between us, for the lieutenant was not so much a man of words as of deeds.

My captain, who lived in perpetual dread of a visitation of the yellow fever, which had carried off so many of his crew, led a very recluse regular life on shore, and kept early hours; and I, having duly received the promised sleeping draught, administered it to him in his last cup of the night, which, by-the-bye, happened to be one containing medicine, and therefore in that nauseous mixture the new ingredient was not discernible. The effect, however, proved admirable, as the patient was thrown into a sound sleep almost before he could retire to his bed.

Having satisfied myself of the naval captain's condition, I locked the door of his chamber upon him, and, with the key in my possession, took a hasty departure from the lodging-house to attend with punctuality to my appointment.

I found the brave lieutenant waiting for me on the beach smoking a cigar, and pacing backwards and forwards opposite to his boat, which lay, ready manned, a short distance out at sea. Having gently hailed me in the dark, and ascertained who I was, he addressed me by saying, "Well, boy, all's right, I see, for here you are; but say, what booty have you brought from the king's officer?"

"Noble sir," replied I, "I gave the captain his dose, which set him asleep, but ere I could do more, I was disturbed by some one approaching the chamber, which made me glad to escape without ransacking his locker;—indeed, I fear I am now being pursued.".

"You are a swab and a lubber; I thought better of you," exclaimed the lieutenant, swearing several bitter oaths. "Howsoever, you may stay behind and be —— to you."

At this declaration I most earnestly entreated of the lieutenant to take me away with him, saying I should be flogged to death if he left me to the captain's mercy.

The lieutenant listened to me with more patience than I expected he would have shown, and then, after a pause of some duration, which filled my mind with painful apprehension, he said, "Well, youngster, though I suspect you are not of the value of a pinch of oakum, I shall overlook your neglect of duty in not having pillaged the naval captain, and I will take you off with me."

I warmly thanked the brave man for his kindness to me, and he, after smoking a few whiffs of his cigar, said, "The wind's fair, and with spread canvass we shall walk over the wide waters in a giffy;" and then, in the Spanish tongue, he hailed his boat, which instantly put to land, and we were seated in her, and she was bending her way to the brig almost immediately.

"Keep a still tongue in your head, as you value a whole skin," said the lieutenant to me while the boat was being rowed to the brig; "as, d'ye see, lad, we have queer hands aboard, who think no more of skinning a living Protestant than bleeding a pig."

"By the shade of my mother," thought I, "I have stepped out of the frying-pan into the fire. Here's a pretty business I have made of it; my life lying at the mercy of the merciless."

My sensations at this time were anything but pleasant, yet in ten minutes we were alongside the brig, when I saw additional and stronger grounds than heretofore for stirring my fears. Half-a-dozen ferocious, half-naked blacks, armed with a brace of pistols and a cutlass each, stood in the ship's gangway to receive us on board; meanwhile a number of Creole Spaniards were assembled on the after-deck, engaged in noisy conversation; while bustling blacks, intermixed with men of colour of all castes, thronged the waist and fore-part of the vessel.

I knew not one word of what was said, but the truly savage appearance of the ship's crew might have appalled the heart of a stout man in my situation, and I scruple not to avow that I involuntarily shuddered as I hastily contemplated the busy scene around me; and I would have thought myself happy to have been once more in safety on board the Zephyr, even though doomed to receive a severe punishment for the offences I had committed against naval discipline.

The lieutenant of my acquaintance, whom for the first time I now heard called by the name of Jones, having exchanged a few words in conversation with his captain, in which, I presume, he made his report of the duty he had transacted at Martinique, called me into the presence of that commander, who, however, took no particular notice of me, but employed himself in issuing orders; upon which all became bustle in the ship, till presently she was under weigh, gliding rapidly through the water with her stern to the shore.

My friend the lieutenant now told me that there was a hammock ready for me, and bid me descend from the deck under the guidance of a flat-nosed black fellow, whom he pointed out, saying he was a gunner's mate, who would be my messmate and look after me.

Accordingly, as this was no fit time for idle talk, and I was not altogether at my ease respecting Lieutenant Jones's conduct, I followed after the black in silence till he stopped between decks, and made signs to me to signify which hammock I was to turn into. This too I presently did, though I felt myself extremely disgusted with my berth, the bedding of which was still warm from the perspiration of some person who could not have risen many minutes from it; while, from the peculiar oily odour arising from the bedding, and which well-nigh poisoned my nostrils, I felt convinced that the individual in question could be no other than a glossy-skinned black.

The favoured child of fortune, who is daily pampered with delicacies, and has a heart quite at ease, may be as fastidiously nice as he pleases in the quality of his bedding, but the less favoured mortal, who happens to be situated in such a way as I was on this untoward occasion, even the most delicate lady might readily pardon for submitting in silence to occupy the sleeping quarters allotted to him. Besides, while I lay tumbling and tossing my body about in my loathsome bed, perspiring like a sunflower from the effects of intolerable heat, always inevitable in low situations within the tropics, but made almost suffocating where I was, from the confined air between decks of our crowded ship, and also feeling myself, as I did, within an ace of being poisoned by the horrid stench bequeathed to me by my prede-cessor, I could not fail reflecting upon the lieutenant's advice, whereby he had cautioned me to keep a still tongue in my head, that I might be spared from becoming the victim of a crew who thought no more of skinning a living Protestant than of bleeding a pig.

In the midst of astounding difficulties, when I get a little habituated to them, somehow I always find my courageous spirit rise with the occasion; and now, while I lay in the black man's hammock, perspiring almost to death, ironically I whispered to myself, "Truly I am in comfortable quarters, no one ever had a warmer berth;" when, soon as I had soliloquised in this way, I felt more mastery over myself, and shortly afterwards fell into a profound sleep.

CHAPTER IX.

"A sail! a sail! a promised prize to hope!
Her nation—flag—how speaks the telescope?
They own the signal, answer to the hail,
Hoist out the boat at once, and slacken sail."

A NEW day had scarcely dawned on the luxuriant islands of the West Indies, when an uncommon bustle on the ship's deck awoke me from sleep to a painful sense of my condition. The watch below were now turning out of their hammocks, for all hands had been piped upon deck, and my new messmate, the gunner's mate, not having observed that I was already awake, gave me a rude tweak by the nose, as a preliminary step to his signifying to me that my presence was required above. I obeyed the ungenteel summons with alacrity, and in a trice was among the bustling crowd upon deck; yet, before I could get there, a shotted cannon, fired from just over my head, startled me not a little, at the same time that it filled my mind with conjectures, intermixed with apprehensions, that the Zephyr was paying us an unwelcome visit.

Every man of the crew was now at his quarters; but having had no particular station allotted to me, I kept beside my messmate, the gunner's mate, whose post was at a long brass twelve-pounder, the sternmost gun on the larboard side of the brig. However, I had not been here many minutes before Lieutenant Jones ordered me aloft into the mizen-top, and from thence I had a fine view afforded me of the passing scene.

A strange sail, evidently a large vessel, was in sight, and her appearance had occasioned our captain to pipe all hands upon deck, and to send every man of the crew to his quarters. When we neared upon her, it was discovered that she was not a ship of war, yet, in defiance of our signals to her to bear down to leeward of us, she continued steering a course away from the Santa Maria, with all her canvass spread to the wind. Another and yet another gun was fired, but still she changed not her course, although we gained fast upon her. At length, having come within half-gun range of the stranger, we fired a shot at her rigging, which passed through her mizen-staysail, when her commander, no longer daring to resist our pleasure, backed his mainsail, and we passed close to windward of him. Through a speaking-trumpet he was now hailed by our captain in the Spanish tongue, to which his reply was in English. Lieutenant Jones next hailed him, asking what ship it was, where he was bound to, and in what consisted the cargo. "The Stately, from London bound to Jamaica, with plantation stores," was the reply, given in a hoarse, rough voice.

Men who best know their own species are always suspicious of, and rarely confide in, the word of others, when better security can be obtained. We now manned a boat, in which Lieutenant Jones proceeded on board the Stately; and after a lapse of twenty minutes our boat returned back to the Santa Maria, followed by one belonging to the Stately, rowed by two sailors, and bearing in her the ship's commander and one of his passengers.

On his mounting to our deck the merchant captain looked around him with fearful surprise, caused by beholding our warlike appearance and formidable crew, who were most of them drawn up two deep in the gangway, each individual armed with a brace of pistols stuck in a waist belt, and a sabre suspended from his thigh. The brass cannon, too, of which we had eighteen pieces mounted upon deck, were ready run out, and a gunner stood to each with a lit match.

The knowledge he had of mankind, which made our dreaded commander dubious of the veracity of Captain Edgar, now prompted him to order me down from the mizen top, that I might be present to hear what the merchant skipper and Lieutenant Jones said to each other, for though he knew I could not be catechised on the subject by any individual on board save Jones himself, yet he bore in mind, that when he next put into port he could employ some person to question me, and thus ascertain whether his lieutenant had in any way deceived him. Accordingly, Captain Edgar, in my presence, and before all the superior officers of the brig, was now interrogated by Lieutenant Jones on all points regarding his vessel, and also made to produce his bill of lading and ship's papers of every sort, which documents were attentively looked at by our captain, although he could not make out a word of their meaning.

At length, after much questioning, and a severe lecture given him for not having laid to immediately he had been signalled from our ship of war, the merchant captain was dismissed by our commander, and allowed to return to his vessel; not, however, without receiving a caution that, as he valued his future safety, he was on no account to let it transpire in Jamaica that he had been boarded in the Caribbean Sea by a foreign ship of war; but as to our brig's name, it was not permitted to any one on board us to make it known to him.

The mercy that our commander had thus shown to Captain Edgar, by not having captured his vessel, and made prisoners of every soul on board of her, I acknowledge, considering what I had seen of the crew of the Santa Maria, extremely astonished me. Our captain, however, had cogent reasons for showing this great lenity, inasmuch as a West Indiaman, though a large and good ship, was not worth his capturing, when freighted, as the Stately was, with nought save plantation stores. Had he captured her it might have brought a British cruiser in search of him, and consequently occasioned the loss of his war-brig in return for the worthless prize; or, under any circumstances, the ill-timed capture must have compelled him to quit his present cruising-ground. "You ought to consider yourselves highly favoured by fortune to have escaped uninjured from a set of barbarians, who think no more of skinning living Protestants than of slaughtering so many pigs," thought I, when looking at Edgar and his companions, while their boat was passing over the rough ocean under our stern, on her way back to the Stately. Presently, however, the frail little boat was alongside that ship, when soon I saw it hoisted astern of her, and the merchantman making all the sail she could to get at a safe distance from the Santa Maria.

From not understanding anything of the Spanish language, I could only guess at the sentiments of our crew with regard to the Stately having been allowed to depart from us without overhauling her, and in safety; yet, assuredly, if a true judgment could be formed from the gestures and manners of our people, I should take on me to pronounce that the desperate band felt disappointed and angry on the occasion.

The business of subordinate heroes is to blindly obey orders, and not to reflect upon their nature, or presume to question them; consequently stir and bustle are great promoters of discipline among organized bodies of men, and, to judge by his conduct, our commander was perfectly well acquainted with this truth. To use a vulgar adage, he was one of those persons who look before they leap; and I saw his keen eyes busily employed, reading, as it were, into the sentiments of his people, before he issued his orders to them, or in any manner disturbed their cogitations on the subject of the merchantman's departure. This brave commander's general policy, as I afterwards found, was to balance parties against each other, and employ spies in the councils of every faction.

Our brig was all this time lying to, with her mainsail aback, yet making some headwa
before the trade wind, which blew at the rate of five knots an hour. Till now, Captain Quirorga, for this was our commander's name, issued his orders through a speaking-trumpet, when
in five minutes our yards had been braced round, and the ship's sails were filled from the
larboard quarter, bearing us along at a steady rate upon a new course.

All the crew, except the watch, which constituted one-third, were now permitted to retire
below to their quarters; and my friend the black gunner unceremoniously introduced me to
the rest of our messmates, when, from the top of an arm-chest, we soon demolished our breakfast, which consisted of yams, biscuits, and coffee. To use a maritime term, I was now
most completely out in my reckoning; for I neither knew where we were bound to, nor could
understand the language of any individual on board the Santa Maria, save only Lieutenant
Jones, and he had not deigned to speak to me since our embarkation, except to give orders,
and that before every one.

Difficulties and dangers often serve to infuse energy into a youthful character, and have a
tendency to form a man, of all others, the fittest to brave the storms of life, and to rise superior
to the machinations of envious rivals and open foes. Seeing the difficulties of my situation
as I now viewed them, I resolved to make it a rule with me through life to study, as much as
I could, the language, customs, and leading peculiarities of character of those persons with
whom I associated; and, in accordance with this determination, I now set myself to work in
picking up what words I could of the Spanish language.

On the second morning after our falling in with the Stately, we made land, and towards
evening came to an anchor off an island which I have since learnt was Santa Cruz, at that
time the seat of government of the Danish governor in the West Indies. Next morning, before
the day dawned, we hove anchor and made sail from this picturesque island; when, after a
chase of some hours, thanks to our superior sailing, we came up with a strange-looking,
lugger-built vessel, painted black from stem to stern, which had passed in sight of our anchorage-
ground the preceding evening, and in search of which doubtless it was that we had hove anchor
and made sail at the early hour we did.

On nearing this vessel, we discovered she had a thronged crowd of people on board, and
that they were in a state of no small confusion. The intention of her crew seemed to be that
of running her ashore, anywhere they could, on the island of Porto Rico; for they kept steering
their lugger steadily on the same course, with all her canvass set, direct for the land there.
However, at length the fears of her crew apparently had been exchanged for the feelings of
satisfaction, as all at once, and before it had become necessary to resign the hope of successfully
running their vessel ashore, her crew, at having made out some signal of ours, suddenly put
her about, when, under easy sail, she came majestically over the waters towards us.

Presently the Santa Maria and the slaver, for such this last vessel proved to be, were nearly
alongside of each other, when a few words having been exchanged through their speaking-
trumpets between her commander and ours, a boat was lowered from our stern, and while the
vessels laid to, Lieutenant Jones and a boat's crew, of which, by the captain's order, I made
one, paid a visit to the Guinea-man. To a person unaccustomed as I was to such a sight,
the thronged deck of a slaver, with a full cargo of Africans on board, could not be otherwise
than distressing. The suffering wretches here were chained together by pairs, and so many
in number that they crowded every plank, save alone at the officers' quarters, the aftermost
part of the lugger's deck; yet half the negro slaves were at that time below, secured under
hatches.

I could know nothing of the conversation which took place between Lieutenant Jones and
the commander of the Guineaman, but that it must have been an amicable one admits of no
question, as, on parting, the two officers shook each other's hands with great cordiality; and,
moreover, the slaver's captain sent a basket of things of African produce in our boat as a
present to Captain Quirorga.

"Andrew," said Lieutenant Jones to me, as I sat beside him, on our way back to the
Santa Maria, "see what canting sectarians of our misgoverned country have done for the
sake of ruining the British colonists, because they themselves have no property in the colonies. By getting the oppressively-taxed, half-fed people at home to sign petitions in behalf
of a population infinitely better off than their own labourers, and who work not half the

hours of their squalled factory people; they have stirred the British negroes to a state of insubordination, and procured their own nation to be a party against the landholders; nor will they cease stirring discord, until the lucrative colonies in this quarter have become the property of the well-governed United States of America.

I neither knew nor cared anything concerning the mal-administration of West India affairs, and consequently attempted making no reply to the lieutenant's sarcastic observations; but, several hours after we had rejoined our brig, the slaver and the Santa Maria were snugly anchored in the harbour of Saint Juan, at Porto Rico, in berths convenient to each other.

CHAPTER X.

" A crowd of shivering slaves of every nation,
    And age and sex, were in the market ranged:
Each bevy with the merchant in his station:
    Poor creatures! their good looks were sadly changed."

" Methinks at meals some odd thoughts might intrude,
    And conscience ask a curious sort of question,
About the right divine, how far we should
    Sell flesh and blood."

CAPTAIN QUIRORGA and the captain of the slaver proceeded on shore together as soon as their vessels were safely anchored; and shortly after daylight next morning an order arrived from our captain for Lieutenant Jones to proceed on shore, and take me along with him. Accordingly we went on shore together to our commander's residence, but the cautious lieutenant, conjecturing from the order he had received that his captain was resolved to have me present, as a check upon him when the English language was used, wisely made a merit of necessity by communicating to me some little secrets regarding the commanders of the two vessels, and the nature of the service they were engaged in, so that I might fully understand how I was to act, to avoid in any way betraying or injuring him with his commander.

By the secrets alluded to, I was given to understand that the slaver, though she was known in the Spanish trade as the Santissima Trinidada, was in reality no other than the celebrated vessel the Saucy Jack; and that, although ostensibly the property of a Captain Robertson, of Porto Rico, she absolutely belonged to some wealthy members of the Society of Friends, who resided in a certain great metropolis, and who, from the gains realized from three successful voyages made by this lucky vessel from the coast of Guinea, had already more than tripled the capital embarked by them in this most lucrative speculation.

Captain Robertson, it appeared, was the managing man of all the concerns which these conscientious Quakers carried on betwen the West Indies and the coast of Guinea; consequently he was well known, and in great credit at Porto Rico as a general merchant. He always remained there, when the lugger was away under Spanish colours; but whenever she made a trip to any of the neighbouring islands, which, the better to disguise the nefarious business she was kept for, usually was once between each voyage of hers to the coast of Guinea, then Captain Robertson invariably went commander of her, with a different crew on board, and the Saucy Jack's papers.

By Lieutenant Jones's discourse, it further appeared that Captain Robertson was a zealous partisan of, and correspondent with, the Anti-Slavery Society, and that, assisted by a brother-in-law of his, who was a missionary, and a famous dissenting parson, employed in Jamaica, he had been a great instrument, according to the cant of the society itself, in converting whole gangs of negroes to the blessings of Christianity; or, in plain language, he had stirred them up to insubordination, which threatened to entail on themselves and their posterity misery and starvation.

The preceding information having been communicated to me by the lieutenant, together with some confidential cautions respecting how I was to conduct myself in the presence of our much-dreaded captain, he, to secure me in his interest, just as we were landing, presented me with a dollar, telling me it would more than suffice to defray what expenses I might incur on shore.

We proceeded to our captain's lodgings, where we found him closeted with the commander of the slaver, and a puritanical looking man, remarkable for an abundance of red hair, whom I soon discovered was the celebrated Captain Robertson.   This famous man, it seems, had not been able to master the Spanish language sufficiently to converse in it on business ; therefore Lieutenant Jones had to interpret between our commander and the alternate captains of the lugger.   The Spanish captain of the slaver commenced the conference, by the production of his ship's papers, whereby was shown the number of slaves he had brought with him into Porto Rico, how many he had lost by death, and what the cargo and expenses of the voyage stood them in hard dollars.

The accounts having been examined, and explained to the satisfaction of Captains Quirorga and Robertson—for, to my surprise, I found that my commander possessed an interest in the lucrative concern—directions were given by Robertson that the slaves, who were at that time undergoing the process of being cleansed for the express purpose, should be landed as soon as practicable, and taken to the slave-market.

The Spanish captain of the slaver departed to visit his lugger, and the remaining three gentlemen sat down to breakfast ; meanwhile the mistress of the lodging-house, Mademoiselle Delisle, as she was called, though a woman with half-a-dozen of her own children about her, took me under her maternal care, and gave me a most delicious breakfast, as a part of which were several sorts of tropical fruits—one of them the rich pear, named the aracado, which is highly esteemed, and eaten with salt meat.

Mademoiselle Delisle, both at and after our breakfast, seemed to regard me as an unfortunate youth, in whose welfare she felt interested ; but all attempts at conversation between us proved unavailing, therefore, what could be the kind-hearted female's motive for feeling concerned on my behalf I could not possibly conjecture.   When we had idled away an hour or more at breakfast, a sailor came to the lodging-house, to notify to the gentlemen above stairs that their presence was called for in the market, as the slaves had all been disembarked from the Santissima Trinidada.   The trio of enterprising heroes, on receiving this summons, sallied forth to visit the slave-market, and I, of course, followed at their heels, when, such was the sight I witnessed, that I feel assured I shall never forget it on this side of the grave.

The squalid, emaciated, half-famished negroes, just landed from the slaver, were bound together with cords, by pairs, in the market-place—men and women, boys and girls, having been carefully lotted, according to their size, age, and sex ; and, in most cases, in accordance with their shades of colour, which are greater than a European, who has not visited the slave colonies, or the slave-market anywhere, where Africans are bought and sold, can well have an idea of. For my part, although I had been aboard the Santissima Trinidada, and witnessed the crowded condition of her decks, yet I could not but feel astonished at counting five hundred and forty newly-imported slaves drawn up in the market, to think how it could have been possible for so great a number to have been stowed away, much less to have continued in a state of existence, on board so small a vessel as was this slave lugger.   My astonishment, however, was afterwards augmented, on finding she had sailed from the river Gambia with seven hundred on board, one hundred and sixty of whom had died during the month of most dreadful incarceration in their infernal prison, where the space allotted to each for sleeping room was materially less than what a dead human body is pent in when coffined.

Before the abolition of the slave-trade by the British Government, and until the time when it employed its ships of war cruising to make prizes of the freighted slave-vessels of other nations, and out of the pockets of its home tax-payers paid the seamen head-money for the slaves so captured by them, the traffic of slavery, as related to conveying the slaves from Africa, was carried on in a far more humane manner than it has been since that period ; for formerly respectable merchants were the traders ; and, inasmuch as security is the foundation of property, they took especial good care, for their own sakes, as well as from principles of humanity, not to crowd their vessels too full of slaves.   Since then, a set of unprincipled, desperate adventurers, have carried on this traffic ; and to make the gain more than commensurate with the risk, the hard-hearted race crowd their vessels almost to suffocation, in a way at which humanity is made to shudder.   However, when we take into consideration the great encouragement held out for illicitly carrying on this trade, as, for example, that the crews of war ships find it is their interest never to fall in with an empty slaver, and leave a certain latitude free for them ; and also that the governors of Spanish islands give every encouragement and protection in their power to those who embark capital in slaves and slave-ships, how is it to be wondered at that this branch of commerce should be a most thriving one? In truth, the temptations for embarking money in this way are so great, that they must be irresistible to unprincipled, avaricious men. The great glut of prisoners made in African warfare—the royal mode in practice there of selling subjects, in place of extracting wealth from them by taxation—and the almost innumerable malefactors which the African chiefs have to dispose of, are peculiarities which render slaves so very plentiful, that they may be procured almost for nothing along the whole line of slave coast. Slave importers certainly act a most brutal part in so exceedingly crowding their vessels; yet, in mitigation of their crime, it may be adduced, that they save the lives of hundreds of wretches every year by bringing them from their native land; for the African kings and princes, when they cannot sell them, not unfrequently make a promiscuous slaughter of their unfortunate prisoners, and sometimes from a sort of royal pride, invariably carried to an excess in despotic countries, have their court-yards paved with their skulls, as did that renowned warrior—the King of Dehomy.

But royalty, such as I speak of, and war, with its interminable train of horrors, are scourges imposed by craft and power on suffering mortality; still, however, after all has been urged pro and con that subtile argument can adduce, it is questionable whether the African method of transporting troublesome characters is not almost as humane as the Malthusian or British mode, which is very chargeable, in place of being profitable, like the African plan. Indeed, some scores of pounds are thrown away for making a British free-born subject become an indifferent slave, to a pelf-hunting emigrant countryman of his own; and this, in most instances, because a dozen men, often very ignorant ones, give it as their opinion that he has taken an illegal oath, robbed, or otherwise defrauded some person to the tune of a few shillings, or poached a head of game from the land of a rich man, who by no possibility could have missed it.

To resume my story:—It was truly amusing to a person like me, who at that time was not overstocked with the ductile feelings of philanthropic sensibility, to hear the bargaining and the cavilling which took place in the vending and the buying of this cargo of human beings. To particularize these transactions would be impossible, yet it may not be unworthy of observation, that the old saying relative to each sex being the best judge of the qualities of the opposite one, was, according to appearance, completely verified here, inasmuch as the planters' wives, and the fair Creole ladies, were the chief examiners and purchasers of the Negro men; while the planters themselves, and numerous other gentlemen of Porto Rico, as likewise those who had come from the neighbouring islands to be present at this sale, more particularly scrutinized into the faults and the perfections of the Negro slave girls, and consequently became the chief dealers in them.

CHAPTER XI.

"' Steer, to that shore!'—they sail. ' Do this!'—'tis done;
' Now form and follow me!'—the spoil is won.
Thus prompt his accents and his actions still,
And all obey, and few inquires his will;
To such, brief answer and contemptuous eye
Convey reproof, nor further deign reply."

" And glory long has made the sages smile;
'Tis something, nothing, words, illusions, wind—
Depending more upon the historian's style
Than on the name a person leaves behind."

THE slave cargo of the Santissima Trinidada having been sold to great advantage, the trio of captains, who were more or less concerned in the adventure, commemorated the event by a rare carousing match together at my commander's lodging, when they quaffed their burgundy and champagne, their hock and their claret; and, for the frolic's sake, were attended upon by the three prettiest jet black girls of all which the slaver had brought from Africa on her last voyage. The lasses, without having been landed, had, to serve their fantastic humour, been bought in at low prices by these bashaws, and at the dinner in question they attended, habited in new white muslin dresses.

At this luxurious feast arrangements were made by the three successful heroes for employing the two vessels on a new service, differing much from that in which they had recently been engaged ; consequently the day following the craftsmen were set to work on them both, and so zealously did they labour, that a few days afterwards no person who had not been made acquainted with the transformation could have known the old black-sided slaver, changed, as she now was, into a bright yellow painted brig—a wicked, rakish looking vessel, bearing the British flag, and for the twentieth time, re-christened the Saucy Jack. The Santa Maria was also much altered in appearance, inasmuch as she now was rigged differently from what she had been, with her masts considerably more stooped ; while in place of her being a black-sided vessel, she exhibited no less than three colours, her larboard side having been newly painted a bright yellow, her starboard a light green, and her stern a glaring white.

The three captains had their heads full of business on this important occasion. Soon, however, as the Saucy Jack was ready for sea, and had got a few tons of marketable goods shipped on board of her, her anchors were hove to her bows, and sail was made on her to quit the harbour, under the command of the *ci-devant* merchant—the notorious Captain Robertson, who, never losing sight of the character he had assumed, with puritanical gravity now asembled his crew upon deck, and offered up prayers for a prosperous voyage, leaving his worthy colleague, the Spanish captain, long as he himself might stay away from Porto Rico, to act the merchant's part there in his stead.

While these events were taking place, I should observe that I was mostly detained aboard ship, being permitted to go on shore only when my commander required my services there, to act as a check upon Lieutenant Jones when he was employed fulfilling the office of interpreter ; but at those times I was afforded ample opportunities for gleaning much information, and what I learnt gave me no little insight into the rascality of the characters I had to deal with, and was of a nature to fill the mind with fearful apprehensions for myself.

The Creole lady, my captain's hostess, on two occasions got an English sailor, who could converse with her in Spanish, to tell me I should do well to make my escape from the Santa Maria, and all persons belonging to her ; yet, as I knew not how to accomplish this exploit, nor what were the lady's motives for furnishing me with her advice, I attached no great importance to it, and this the less as Captain Quirorga had in some degree won my good-will, by his having presented me with a few dollars, and given me to understand that he would be the making of my fortune.

Three weeks had elapsed after the departure of the Saucy Jack, and still the Santa Maria lay at anchor in the harbour of Porto Rico ; but on the twenty-second day an express boat from Jamaica brought letters both for our captain and his colleague, who acted the merchant's part, but so recently had commanded the slaver, and with the dawn next morning we hove anchor, and made sail from Porto Rico, shaping our course into the wide Atlantic, but still keeping in sight of land. The trade wind bore our vessel onward at a rapid rate, and during the second and third day of our voyage we sailed at a pleasant distance along the coast of the majestic island of St Domingo, after which we stood further from the land, and continued doing so until we had weathered the easternmost end of Cuba, when we sailed some considerable distance along the coast of this very long isle, and afterwards stood more to the north, until eventually we reached the channel of the Gulf of Florida, at sixty or seventy miles distance from Cuba.

We had now been a whole week at sea from Porto Rico, and in that time seen a number of small trading vessels, though, contrary to the custom of a ship of war, we had either kept our course or stood away from them. One thing, however, should be mentioned here, which is, that the night after quitting the harbour of Porto Rico our commander caused his vessel to be disguised, by affixing a ready-prepared black stripe of canvass along her sides and round her stern, of a sufficient breadth to cover the painting ; and so well did this answer the intended purpose, that I am thoroughly satisfied no seaman, however familiar his sight might have been with her bright sides and stern, could, even through the best spy-glass, have made out the Santa Maria from on board a vessel passing near to her at sea.

At all times we kept a sharp look-out from the mast head ; yet now the orders given to the man stationed there were more pointed than customary, and he was specially enjoined to look out for vessels coming along with the gulf stream ; meanwhile we ourselves kept dodging about in such a manner as not very materially to lose head way.

We had been three entire days cruising about here, during which time we had seen several small vessels passing with the gulf stream, which, so far from molesting, we did not even approach near to, when at day dawn on the fourth morning we discovered a large deep-laden merchant-man coming in full sail towards us. The wind and the gulf stream both favouring, she neared us very fast, meanwhile our captain examined her most minutely. Indeed the spy-glass was scarcely a minute from his eye till she had approached so near to us, that his crew evidently surmised he intended letting her pass, as he had the small vessels, unmolestedly on her voyage.

The crew were mistaken. Suddenly a signal for the stranger to lay-to was hoisted by our commander's order, and presently a gun was fired athwart the stranger's bows.

Further contumacy would have been altogether unavailing, and of this the merchant captain must have been sensible, for his mainyard was almost instantaneously backed, when we went to windward of him, and then lying-to, spoke him through the speaking-trumpet. I was aloft in the foretop, and therefore knew not exactly what was said; but thus much I made out, that she was an English ship from Jamaica bound to London, and to the best of my hearing she was called the Columbine, or by a name nearly approximating to it.

A boat, in which, besides her crew, were Lieutenant Jones and several petty officers, with ten foremast men, was now despatched from us to board the merchantman; and almost immediately after they had mounted her deck the British colours were struck, and her sails braced to the wind, to bear her on a different course to that which she had previously been on. We also made sail, shaping our course the same as the merchantman; and to shorten the tale, it suffices to say, that two days from this time we arrived in company together at a small barren, uninhabited rocky island, near to which we both cast anchor, and which rock I have since learnt lies not far remote from Turk's Island, so justly celebrated for its salt.

The ship we had so unceremoniously taken proved a glorious prize, and our crew considered the taking of her as a glorious affair, for barren, empty-handed glory would have been no glory with them. But should we bring truth to the test, who shall say that this buccaneering exploit was not as glorious an affair as the taking of a proud Danish fleet by a nation at peace with the Danes? Successful power, however, will ever dictate its own conditions, and use even long-established laws as links of a chain to bind the weak.

We had scarcely dropped our anchors off the rocky isle before the boats of both ships were hoisted out, to be kept constantly employed landing the merchantman's cargo, which was a rich one, consisting of sugar, rum, coffee, and pimento. There was a circumstance on this occasion which created no little astonishment in my mind, which was, that there were no people of her own crew, no, nor her captain, the poor fellow whose voice I had heard speaking us through his trumpet, at the present time on board the Columbine. I own I felt strange suspicions regarding my unfortunate countrymen; but the lieutenant's advice to me respecting the necessity of my keeping a still tongue in my mouth was always fresh in my memory, therefore I took especial good care to evince no curiosity on the subject. However, shortly after this time the real truth came to my knowledge, told from the lips of Lieutenant Jones, and which happened in this way. I was employed one day helping to discharge her cargo, when he took me into the merchantman's state cabin to treat me to a glass of grog, and, being himself rather elevated by liquor, in the hilarity of his heart he made a sort of boast to me of his humanity, telling me how Captain Quirorga had ordered him to kill the merchant skipper and all his crew, and to throw their bodies overboard; instead of doing which, he added, he had served some grog out to them with a powerful sleeping-dose mixed therein, and when this had operated, and their senses were chained in sleep, taken them out of their hammocks, and, after lashing them by pairs back to back, cast their bodies into Davy's locker. The captain, he remarked, from not having imbibed his proper allowance of the grog, had been awake when taken from his bed, and consequently, being a powerful man, he had given the crew some trouble to make away with him, insomuch that they found it necessary to inflict a blow or two on his head before they succeeded in lashing him to the ship's steward, which however was done, and they perished overboard together.

Two days after our arrival at the rock, and while we were busily engaged landing the mer-chantman's cargo, a sail hove in sight, on which Captain Quirorga lost no time in shortening his cable, preparing his ship for action, and getting everything ready to give chase to the stranger. She, however, was soon discovered making direct for the island, and presently we hoisted a signal at our mast-head, which, by the assistance of his telescope, Captain Quirorg saw her promptly reply to. The wind was favourable, and the stranger vessel soon approached sufficiently near to be examined by the naked eye, when a man stationed at the mast-head proclaimed her to be the Saucy Jack, and so she proved. In less than two hours she lay anchored a few cables' length from the West Indiaman, our prize.

Captain Robertson, from the Saucy Jack, and Lieutenant Jones from the prize, now proceeded on board the Santa Maria, when the former, who never divested himself of the cant of Methodism, with puritanical precision desired his interpreter to make it known to Captain Quirorga that the Lord had heard his prayer, and thus far made his voyage prosperous. He now called for a bottle of old hock, and also one of Spa water, and having mixed their contents in a large bowl, the confederated captains drank the invigorating draught between them, and then, without further ceremony, proceeded to the transaction of business.

By the discourse which now took place, it appeared that Captain Robertson was the person who transmitted the information from Jamaica which occasioned our sailing from Porto Rico, and subsequently making a prize of the merchant ship. As to the death of the captain of that vessel, a gentleman with whom Robertson had been intimately acquainted, the news of that event apparently afforded him pleasure; inasmuch as on hearing it he observed to Captain Quirorga, that he had been a man hostile to the dissenting interest, which was the main cause why he selected his ship for their prize, when he might have named another of equal, if not greater, value; but, turning up the white of his eyes while he spoke, he terminated this discourse by emphatically remarking, that with the blessing of Providence he yet hoped to see all the enemies of the dissenters exterminated, after many a rich cargo belonging to them had been shared out among his worthy confederates.

The indefatigable Robertson was extremely desirous of hastening the Saucy Jack through the present business, so that she might be re-chartered for the coast of Africa, where, excessively to his annoyance, the French, the Portuguese, the Spaniards, and the Brazilians, whose ships of war never molested their slavers, were enjoying a monopoly of this most lucrative trade; consequently, as Robertson's pleasure was law with us, the most able hands of our three vessels were set to work to load the Saucy Jack from the part of the merchantman's cargo not landed; while such was the alacrity with which the men laboured, that at the expiration of five days the disguised slaver was full of cargo, the weight of which sunk her upper deck as near as safety permitted to the water's edge.

Captain Robertson was no novice in his business. He now filled up a forged bill of lading, which showed to a cask what cargo he had on board, as also the day on which he had sailed from Jamaica for New York. This task achieved, with her hatches properly battened down, as a requisite precaution against bad weather, away went the Saucy Jack on her voyage to New York.

Quirorga was a worthy colleague of his friend Robertson. They neither of them were men to lose time when an adventure could be advantageously achieved; therefore, in furtherance of the plan they had on hand, all hands of us were busily kept at work landing the residue of the merchantman's cargo, and stowing it away between some rocks with that which had previously been landed, where it might be conveniently covered over with tarpaulings.

When we had completed the business of landing and stowing away her rich cargo, the merchantman was got ready for a long voyage in ballast, and, thanks to the able management of Robertson, good ship's papers awaited her, by which she was represented to be an American ship, named the John Adams. Her place of destination was Chili, for which she sailed with eight hands on board, under Lieutenant Jones's command, just one week after the Saucy Jack's departure. Lieutenant Jones received instructions to sell her to the best advantage, and forward bills of exchange to St Thomas's in the West Indies for the money she fetched; but after disposing of the ship, he himself and his eight men were to return to Porto Rico in a small sloop, which he had orders to purchase at Chili for the express purpose.

After the John Adams had quitted us, our crew had little or nothing to do, but the ship was still kept at anchor off the rocky isle whereon lay deposited our valuable West India produce. The treasure was intrusted to the care of two petty officers, who bore the character of being sober men, none other of the crew being permitted to set foot on shore, from an apprehension that they might make free with the rum, and thereby create disorder amongst us,

The Saucy Jack had been away a full month, when towards evening one day a sail hove in sight, bending her course for the rocky isle, but she was too far off for signals to pass between us; while, from the wind not being fair, there was no prospect of her reaching the isle before night-fall; consequently Captain Quirorga, as a precautionary measure, slipped his ship's cable with a buoy attached to it, and set sail to reconnoitre the stranger.

We all conjectured it was the Saucy Jack, and so she proved to be; the beautiful little vessel floated light as a cork, having scarcely ballast enough on board to enable her to keep the sea. Next morning we lay anchored nigh each other in our former berths, when the large boats belonging to both the ships were employed carrying freights from the rock to the Saucy Jack, which vessel, after seven days' labour in freighting her, was again so full of colonial produce, that we had to batten down her hatches once more that she might be sea-worthy; she, however, had now on board of her all that remained of the captured ship's cargo.

The sagacious Robertson, in his anxiety to get the Saucy Jack ready for the slave trade, had brought with him a set of ship's papers ready to fill up. By them it appeared that the vessel had taken in a cargo of Jamaica for the neutral island of Saint Thomas; and he now carefully entered the colonial produce and other goods she had on board in his false bill of lading, which being done, the two ships hove their anchors.

Great, however, as may have been his anxiety to depart, still the ever methodical Robertson detained the ships lying-to, while he assembled a portion of their crews on the deck of his own vessel to perform the ceremony too common among greater powers, of putting up prayers for success in an unholy cause. This ceremonial having been gone through, the two ships made sail in company together from the rocky isle; but that there might be no evidence to adduce of their acting in collusion, they shortly afterwards separated, the Saucy Jack to make the best of her way to a good market for her colonial produce at Saint Thomas's, by passing along the coast of Saint Domingo and of Porto Rico, and the Santa Maria to sail between Saint Domingo and Jamaica, into the Caribbean Sea; from thence, with her black canvass stripped from off her bright sides and her showy stern, to cruise nearer to the continent of America, ostensibly in search of Columbian ships, but in reality to capture the vessels of any nation where she could do so with apparent safety; and also to deceive the maritime and commercial world, by making it appear she had been employed in a quarter far distant from that vessel, and consequently could have had no transactions with the notorious Saucy Jack.

CHAPTER XII.

" Let not his mode of raising cash seem strange,
Although he fleeced the flags of every nation;
For into a prime minister but change
His title, and 'tis nothing but taxation:
But he, more modest, took au humbler range
Of life, and in an honester vocation
Pursued o'er the high seas his watery journey,
And merely practised as a sea attorney!"

On our voyage between the islands of Cuba, Hispaniola, and Jamaica, we saw a number of small trading vessels passing in all directions; but made no signals to them, nor did we alter our course to approach near to any one of them. Our crew, however, examined the strangers with hawks' eyes, and seemed to think it a violation of their rights that any weaker vessel than ours should be allowed to pass us unplundered.

Hitherto we had acted the part of a treacherous wolf in lamb's clothing; but soon as we had got well away from the trio of large islands, the black canvass was stripped from the sides and stern of the Santa Maria, when she appeared on the wide waters in all her artificial beauty. Our course was also changed; for now we made sail with the wind astern of us, till in a few days we were embayed in the Gulf of Mexico. Here, in this long-celebrated quarter, we continued cruising for several weeks, during which time we visited the Bay of Honduras, and then shaped our course to the Musquito shore, the country of which always brings to mind the exploits of a notorious adventurer—a would-be cacique, who, for a puncheon or two of rum, is said to have purchased a principality, equal in size to a score or two of those of German sovereign princes. The possessions of the latter class, however, have a magical power; they qualify their master and every one of his blood for marriage with a reigning sovereign, and being provided for in a royal way by a nation who never before heard of the august race but his highness the cacique in question, on the strength of his possessions, could only procure large loans of money from among the greenhorns of Europe, numbers of whom, in return for the spoil reaped from them, he dubbed "Green Cross Knights," and "Grand Green Cross Knights;" an order of knighthood nearly as valuable as some of the orders of other princes, and, in the estimation of a true philosopher, intrinsically as good as that of the "fish-bone of Pellew," or the one instituted by a merry monarch in honour of a prostitute and her garter !

Hitherto nothing worthy of particular attention had occurred during this cruise ; but now, while we laid at anchor off the Musquito shore, at a time, too, when the mulatto king of the land and half-a-dozen of his ministers, with as many of his wives, were on a visit to our gallant captain on board his proud ship—and it should be observed that he seemed to be well known wherever he came to an anchor in this tropic—a small cutter, with three men on board, arrived in the bay where we lay, which brought despatches for Captain Quirorga from Carthagena, and, almost immediately after he had read them, the captain most cavalierly dismissed his royal guest, his ministers of state, and the rest of his suite, to hoist anchor, and shape our course towards the famous city of Carthagena, once the scene of exploits of the heroic Morgan, who, because a successful buccaneer, was twice entrusted with the government of Jamaica, and then, when his lawless power on the ocean had passed away from him, was not he doomed, by his weak, ungrateful monarch, to drag the dregs of life away in prison, merely because the king he served was desirous of gratifying the revengeful feelings of the Spanish king, and not as a punishment for crime or misdemeanour towards his own country, her monarch, or its interests ?

Though we bent our course towards Carthagena, we never approached near enough to that proud city for our vessel to be discerned from the shore in its vicinity ; but having, after some days' sail, made the land ourselves, we stood out further to sea, to cruise in the track of vessels voyaging between Carthagena and the West Indies. On the fourth day of our cruising here, " a sail in sight" was proclaimed by the top-man at the mainmast-head, when we crowded every stitch of canvass on the vessel; and though the stranger bore away from us with all her sails set, yet, after five or six hours of close chase, we got within gun-range of her. We now hoisted Danish colours, and signaled for her to lay-to ; but she neither brought to, nor otherwise noticed our signals. This *ruse de guerre* having failed, we hauled down the Danish flag, and hoisted the British in its stead, when immediately the unsuspecting stranger hoisted British colours, and lay-to to be hailed by us.

At this time necessity, backed by inclination and assiduity, had enabled me to master a little of the Spanish tongue ; and our wary commander, being desirous of deceiving the stranger as long as possible as to who and what we really were, now ordered all our blacks to keep themselves out of sight, and directed that none on board, save mulattoes and white people, should appear on the upper deck. These orders having been enforced, the captain directed me to speak the stranger, which accordingly I did, soon as we came within speaking distance, by hailing to ask what she was, whence she came, and to what place she was bound ; to all which her captain replied, that her name was the Snipe, and that she was the British packet from Barbadoes to Carthagena.

The preceding information having been given by him, her captain, in return, asked what we were ; to which I was ordered not to reply, but direct him to send a boat on board us, which I did, when the Snipe's commander, evidently disliking the appearance of things, directed that his main-yard should be braced to the wind, that he might make sail away from us.

Captain Quirorga, who could, when he pleased, be one of the gentlest-mannered men that ever held command over desperate adventurers, smiled on seeing the futile efforts the packet captain was making to shun all further scrutiny from him ; but his smile was almost instantly followed by an order to one of his lieutenants to fire two double-shotted guns, pointed at the stern quarter of the packet. The order was joyfully obeyed, and the effect caused by the harsh measure was almost magical. The guns had scarcely been discharged ere the men employed bracing round the packet's yard ceased their labours ; when all would have been still as death on board that vessel, had it not been that there was a little bustle and confusion on the after part of her deck, which, as we afterwards heard, was occasioned by one of the passengers who had got wounded. Captain Quirorga now directed me to speak to the stranger once more, to order her commander to come aboard us with his ship's papers, which order I fulfilled, when, without further hesitation, a boat was hoisted from on board the Snipe, in which her captain embarked, and it was soon seen being rowed towards us. Meanwhile, as if to make assurance doubly sure, a boat was lowered down from our stern, in which a very ferocious fellow, who was our first lieutenant, together with thirty men, all of them well armed, were dispatched away to board the packet. The commander of the Snipe looked extremely desponding when he mounted to our deck, and beheld our terrific crew, who almost to a man had come forward to show themselves; and verily, I think, men could not look more frightful than these ruffians now looked. The rascals were well acquainted with their commander's summary mode of doing business; consequently the grin of brutal satisfaction animated their ferocious countenances, for the packet's treasure, be it what it might, they knew was their destined booty.

What now passed on board the prize—for such, of course, she was to us—I knew not; but, on board us, Captain Quirorga contented himself with ascertaining from the mouth of her disconsolate commander, as well as from reference to her bill of lading, that the packet had actually got stowed away in her hold the large remittance of Spanish dollars, which, it seems, he had been previously informed the loan contractors in England had shipped on board of her, in payment of their instalment of the last loan taken by them for the Colombian government.

This information was amply sufficient for our captain, who had no idle questions to ask. He now ordered that his prisoner, the captain, together with the boat's crew, should be conveyed below into the gun room; and, in defiance of the remonstrances which the poor captain strove to make to our commander on this, to him, painful subject, the much-dreaded order was peremptorily complied with; but as the prisoners hung back, and would not go there of their own accord, they were forcibly conveyed below deck.

While the preceding conversation took place on board the Santa Maria, it seems that our first lieutenant had been employed in the task of unceremoniously lashing together by pairs the crew and passengers on board the packet, which he did with their backs to each other, and then placed them in confinement in the state cabin of their vessel, with several of his men as sentinels over them, who had orders given to them to blow out the brains of any captive who attempted to free his person from the cords with which he was bound.

After all proper precautionary measures had been taken to secure the prisoners, we dispatched another boat-load of our crew to the prize, to assist the lieutenant in ransacking her; when, to shorten the story, so expeditiously and effectually did we fulfil this business, that, within twenty-four hours from the time when the second boat's crew were sent, not only her valuable freight of dollars, but everything else that was deemed worthy of being taken out of the Snipe, had been conveyed on board of the Santa Maria.

The unfortunate commander of the packet, and the boat's crew which he had brought with him aboard us, were now re-conveyed to their own vessel; preparatory to which, on their quitting the Santa Maria, symptoms of joy became discernible on their countenances. Poor fellows! no doubt they thought it a happy event their getting away from us, and their hearts felt lightened of a portion of care at the prospect of rejoining their old companions in their own ship. "You are lucky fellows," whispered I to myself, as I looked at them passing over the fathomless blue ocean in their boat to rejoin the plundered packet; "yes, you will be the luckiest of the lucky, if you escape with your lives from a set of men who think no more of skinning living Protestants than of killing so many pigs!"

This my anticipation of evil was by no means erroneous. Alas! the genius of destruction was abroad, hovering over the poor sufferers' heads. They had scarcely rejoined their companions in misfortune, before our desperate lieutenant and his boat's crew of plunderers quitted the ill-starred vessel, most cold-heartedly leaving every one on board of her to perish by an untimely watery grave. To explain this lamentable circumstance, it is only necessary to add, that after our people had taken everything they thought fit from the cargo, as also all that was worth pillaging from the passengers and crew, they set themselves to work scuttling the packet —a job they so ably effected, by means of boring holes in her hull, that she had already sunk considerably in the water before they themselves quitted her, and most assuredly she would have gone to the bottom in less than an hour from the time our boat rejoined the Santa Maria had she been then left to her fate; nevertheless, so impatient was our provident commander to get rid of this floating evidence of his last piratical exploit, that he now fired a broadside into the fast-sinking vessel, and in consequence, amidst the cries of the poor wretches on board her, not one of whom had time afforded him, even had he got freed from the cords that bound him, to jump into the little boat alongside the vessel, she immediately gave a great lurch to leeward, and then disappeared in the bottomless ocean.

He who places the smallest value on the life of man, when the deaths of his fellow-creatures, even of thousands of them, can produce any personal advantage to himself, is, I must avow, unfit to be a hero. For my part, not having yet been sufficiently schooled in the school of heroic deeds, I shuddered as I looked at the ship's masts, while they gradually disappeared in the briny abyss, after the hull of the packet had gone down; yet that which had been performed here was literally nothing, when compared with the blasting of a mine, the storming of a town, or the driving of an unresisting enemy into a deep river to perish there.

Hundreds, yea, thousands of people may be mutilated or destroyed by either the one or the other of the last-named heroic exploits; but the sinking of the Snipe was a mere bagatelle—a trifling event, by which a paltry packet vessel was lost to her country, and seven passengers, and twelve men and boys who constituted the crew, were sent to a watery grave!

CHAPTER XIII.

"And thus their course they ran,
  Though right ahead the roaring breakers lay
A reef between them also now began
  To show its boiling surf and bounding spray."

"Immediately the masts were cut away,
  Both main and mizen; first the mizen went,
The mainmast followed."

"At last with swimming, wading, scrambling, he
  Roll'd on the beach, half-senseless, from the sea."

THE whelming ocean had scarcely resumed its ordinary appearance over the spot where the packet ship and all on board her had sunk, and must now have been sinking still deeper in her briny waters, before Captain Quirorga, who apparently, like most of the great men, his predecessors in the path of glory, meditated only on the future, and hardly bestowed a thought upon the past, had his ship's sails filled, to commence beating our way to Porto Rico, against the trade wind which blew almost right ahead of our proper course.

The captain, however, than whom no one knew better the nature of man, that same evening assembled his crew upon deck, when to furnish them with a sample of the pecuniary treasure we had taken out of the Snipe, and at the same time to put them in good humour, he broke open a few of the money chests, from which he served out twenty dollars each to every man aboard, telling them at the same time that the sum thus given would be sufficient for spending money at the first port where we went ashore; and that the prize-list should be made out against their arrival at Porto Rico, when every man and boy amongst us would be settled with according to the number of shares that his berth on board entitled him to receive. This promise, from the lips of a man of honour, who invariably kept his word, proved so pleasing to his crew, that we all, with one accord, answered our noble captain's speech by three tremendous cheers; and all circumstances duly considered, perhaps this mode of showing our approbation of his conduct was the only suitable acknowledgment we could have made to the brave man. An admiral or a general under a monarchy would be honoured by the men under them exactly in a similar way; yet prize-money with them is unjustly distributed, inasmuch as their commanders-in-chief scruple not at taking for themselves the portion of twenty or thirty thousand men; and their prize-laws bestow upon surgeons, purveyors, chaplains, and commissaries, each and every one of them, the allowance of one hundred fighting men—yea, and sometimes of more. With privateers, and among common pirates, honour and justice are more associated; they share as men ought to share spoils won by a participation of toil and danger; for, as the aristocratic practice of enriching the few at the expense of the great mass, reaches not where there is anything like republican rule, a few seamen's shares suffice for the commander of this description of heroes.

The ceremony of distributing the dollars having been gone through, and an allowance of rum from the packet's stores having been served out to every hand on board, such of the crew as were not on duty upon the watch proceeded below decks to turn into their hammocks, all extremely well contented with the events of the day, and the unambitious among us to contemplate the pleasing circumstance that two or three more such captures as the one we had just made would suffice to enrich us so that we should have nothing more to do in life than drink good liquor, smoke Havannah cigars, and revel our time away on shore amidst plenty of every sort, in the society of abundance of good-humoured lasses.

To make a windward passage against the trade wind which blows into the Gulf of Mexico is anything but a pleasant undertaking; it needs a good sea-boat, and a great share of patience in those who embark in her. For my own part, I prefer plain sailing to embarking in a voyage to windward, and at any time would much rather pass smoothly over the ocean, with the trade wind which blows almost from Madeira to Carthagena, than suffer the misery attendant on making a voyage, even of five hundred miles, against this almost unceasingly steady wind. There are men, however, whose study it is to act against nature and common sense; one of these, a West India captain, though he had a ship full of passengers, obstinately attempted making the voyage from Jamaica to England in the very teeth of the trade wind. The consequences were, that his passengers, who were most of them invalids, died, almost to the last person; and with a crew worn out by fatigue, a vessel strained in her timbers, so as to become dangerously leaky, and his provisions nearly expended, this obstinate skipper, after having beat against the trade wind for one hundred days, was compelled to change his course that he might reach the port of his destination, which, to the great injury of his owner, eventually he did with a much damaged cargo.

The Santa Maria continued beating about, continually tacking from side to side, and so violently shaken and tossed to and fro, that there was no comfort to be found for the human body in any position; till, at the expiration of a little more than a fortnight, we had made its head-land sufficiently to weather the island of Jamaica, so as to make what at Jamaica is termed " the windward passage," which is done by passing between Hispaniola and Jamaica. It is true that our captain might have saved time, and spared his crew no small fatigue, had he bore away sooner, to have sailed through the Gulf of Florida; but he had substantial reasons for acting otherwise, and being free from the incumbrance of passengers, apparently he was in no hurry to terminate the voyage. Moreover, this able commander, although he was as brave a man as any living, was a prudent officer, who in the main took good care of his crew; and, therefore, he must have felt a disinclination to be boarded, and perhaps overhauled, by a British man-of-war, which might readily have happened had he sailed by way of the Gulf of Florida. Policy required that he should get rid of the chests of dollars and the remainder of the booty, which he had made ours by capturing the packet, before any such a *rencontre* took place.

We had spoken many little vessels during the last fortnight's cruise; but evidently they were none of them worthy our attention in the way of prizes, for the captain permitted them all to pass after speaking them, and intimating to those on board that our ship was a Spanish man-of-war, cruising in search of Columbian vessels and of pirates. The last vessel spoken by us was in passing between Jamaica and Hispaniola. She was a small Bermudian trader, named the Rob Roy, bound from Jamaica to St Thomas's, and shortly after we had spoken her an ominous dark cloud in the horizon gave us warning that a tropical hurricane was brewing.

The omen told too true: we had barely time to strike our top-masts before the furious tempest overtook us, and the sea keeping pace with it, ran mountains high; while, as it kept invariably to the same point, blowing on the eastern end of Cuba, the captain and his officers became seriously concerned for our safety, fearing it would be impossible for us to weather the Cuba coast. We, however, kept the ship as close to the wind as the violence of the hurricane would permit; but the sea canted her head so to leeward, that she made more lee than headway; and the rigging got so strained with the working of the vessel, that even the faint hope we had entertained of being able to keep her off the shore was constantly diminishing; in short, unless the wind changed or subsided, we saw that to effect this object would be utterly impracticable.   Many of the sails blew into ribands—some of the rigging was carried away—yet, such were the exertions we made, that every stick which could possibly be struck we succeeded in lowering upon deck.

Shortly after it had become dark, captain Quirorga was alarmed by an unusual noise upon the deck, and, running up, discovered that every sail of the vessel, save only the foresail, was totally carried away.   The sight now was horrible, and the entire ship presented a spectacle as dreadful to the feelings as it was mortifying to human pride.   Fear had produced among many the helplessness of despondency, and among some the mischievous freaks of insanity.   Quirorga was firm amidst all the perils of his situation; but some of the crew were down upon their knees, clasping their hands, and praying with all the extravagance of horror depicted on their faces; while others, though not any great number, were flogging their images with all their might, calling upon them to allay the storm.   At this juncture one of the petty officers mounted to the deck with a case bottle of rum in his hand, and with an air of distraction and deep despair imprinted in his face, was strutting about in his shirt, when the captain, perceiving him to be on the point of giving liquor to the crew about him, with a blow of his clenched fist knocked the daring offender backwards, and then threw the rum bottle into the ocean.

The brave Quirorga endeavoured to bring the wavering part of his ship's company to a becoming sense of their duty as seamen, and their dignity as men.   He exhorted the sailors by his example, and strove to raise their spirits by assuring them the storm did not appear more terrible than some he had before experienced.   While the captain was employed encouraging his crew, we shipped a sea on the larboard side, which every one thought would have sent us to the bottom.   The vessel seemed to sink beneath her weight—she shivered and remained motionless; it was a moment of critical suspense, and by the tremendous sea thus shipped seventeen of our crew were washed overboard.

At this dreadful crisis the water rushed with incredible force through all parts of the vessel; yet the captain, finding she did not go down, exerted himself, in an extraordinary manner, to rouse his crew to a sense of their duty, and he succeeded in getting the splintered masts cut away, and what guns could be untackled thrown overboard—as also some spars and other things which encumbered the ship.   The pumps, which recently had been useless, were, by the exertions now made, once more set agoing: it was with difficulty, however, that some few hands could be procured to work them, and the captain seeing this to be the case, stood at them himself, at once to encourage the men by his example, and prevent them from quitting the arduous duty; for, although our present situation apparently was hopeless, this undaunted officer was determined that no effort practicable on his part should be wanting to the preservation of the ship and those on board her.   The water, however, gained upon us, notwithstanding all our exertions, and it was evident we could not long keep the vessel afloat.

About ten o'clock the hurricane was at its greatest height, when the sky was so completely obscured with black clouds, save only at intervals, when it was illuminated by vivid forked lightning, and the rain fell so thick, that objects were not discernible from the wheel to the ship's forecastle.   The pumps were again choked, and dismay was now painted on every countenance; but I shall not make a mockery of real sufferings by attempting, in the manner of a certain nautical novelist, to portray every shade of the countenances of our mariners on a dark tempestuous night; nor, like him, detail a twentieth time over how the wind sounds among the cordage, and the nether muscles of the hardy seamen's mouths, are brought into play.   Nothing was to be seen but unutterable despair, and silent anguish and horror wrought up to frenzy.   Scarcely a man of the crew was capable of making any effort that was useful, but all on board seemed more desirous to extinguish their calamities by embracing death, than willing, by painful exertions, to avoid, or at least procrastinate, their frightful doom.   About eleven o'clock we heard a dreadful roaring noise, resembling that of waves rolling against rocks; but the darkness of the night and the accompanying rains prevented us from discerning anything, insomuch, that if it were rocks, we might be actually dashed against them till we went to pieces without our perceiving them.   The wind, however, now lulled for a time, and the terrific sea seemed to have somewhat abated, which made the senses of the people return in some degree, and their stupefaction decrease.

We now discovered breakers, and large rocks without side of them, so that it appeared we must have passed quite close to them, and were now completely hemmed in between rocks and the land. At this frightful epoch our captain adopted the dangerous resolution of letting go an anchor, to bring the ship up with her head to the sea ; but scarcely had he let go the anchor before an enormous sea rolled over the vessel, which, in addition to its washing away many of the crew, overwhelmed and filled her with water, so that every one on board concluded she was unquestionably sinking. An African black at this juncture, with a presence of mind worthy of a thorough-bred British mariner took an axe, ran forward and cut the cable.

Thus liberated, the vessel again floated, and made an effort to right herself; but she was almost completely water-logged, and heeled to larboard so much, that the gunwale lay under water. We now endeavoured to steer as fast as we could for the land, which evidently was not at any considerable distance, though we were unable to discover it through the hazy weather. By great efforts in baling the ship righted a little, her gunwale was got above water, and she scudded before the wind, which still blew hard on shore.

The love of life countervails all other considerations in the mind of man, consequently the uncertainty we were under with regard to the shore before us, and all its dangers, was forgotten in the joyful hope of saving life, and we scudded towards the shore in all the exulting transports of a people just snatched from the jaws of death.

The gleam of happiness was of short duration—a tremendous sea rolling over the ship, broke over her stern, tore away everything before it, stove in the steerage, carried away the rudder, shivered the wheel to pieces, tore up the very ring-bolts of the deck, and conveyed the men stationed at the wheel, bruised and senseless, to the forepart of the ship, and then overboard.

When this terrific sea came rolling over us, I was standing near the wheel, and fortunately laid hold of the tafferel, which enabled me to resist in part the weight of the water. I was, however, swept off my feet, and dashed against the stump of the mainmast. The jerk from the tafferel, which I held very tenaciously, seemed as if it would have dislocated my arm ; but it broke the impetus of the motion, and in all probability saved me from being dashed to destruction against the mast.

I now floundered about in the water at the foot of the broken mast, till at length I got on my feet, and seized hold of a rope, which I held in a state of great embarrassment, dubious what I should do to extricate myself. At this instant I perceived my messmate, the gunner's mate, had got upon the capstan, and was waving his hand to me to follow his example. This I wished to do, though it was an enterprise of great risk and difficulty ; for if I lost the hold I had, a single motion of the vessel, or a full wave, would certainly have carried me overboard.

I made, however, a bold push, and fortunately accomplished my object. Having attained this station, I could the better survey the wreck, the deck of which was entirely under water, and I now perceived our surgeon standing where the water was most shallow, as if watching with patient expectation its rising, and awaiting the speedy death which must ensue. I called to him, but he shook his head in despair, and said in a lamentable tone, " It is all over with us," when, raising his hands, a whelming wave washed him far away into the ocean, where he was soon released from a state of suffering more deplorable than death.

The vessel was now completely water-logged, and while her larboard side was gradually sinking into the ocean, the deck, and of course the capstan, became too nearly perpendicular for me to remain on it, therefore I shifted my berth to the starboard side, holding fast by the gunwale, and allowing my body and legs to yield to the sea as its waves broke over me. Thus I continued for some time ; but the severity of the labour exhausted my strength and spirits, till the best hope I entertained seemed to be that of an early conclusion to my painful death, and I began to think seriously of letting go my hold, and of yielding myself at once to the fury of the waves.

The ship, which continually approximated the shore, at length struck the ground, which for an instant revived our almost departed hopes; but we soon found that it availed not, in the smallest degree, to better our condition. The crew now began to consult together about the best means of getting on shore, and I made an effort to reach the lee shrouds, to which many of our hands were clinging; but, ere I could accomplish the desperate task, I lost my hold and fell down the hatchway, the gratings of which had been washed overboard, together with the long-boat. Here I was for some minutes entangled among a heap of packages, which the violent fluctuation and dashing of the water had collected on the lee side, when, as the ship moved with the sea, and still more water flowed in, I and the packages were rolled about together, sometimes one and sometimes another uppermost, until ultimately I grasped something that lay in my way, made a vigorous spring, and gained the lee shrouds. I now called to my old shipmate, the black gunner's mate, to make his way to where I was, but he noticed my speech only by shaking his head in a truly desponding manner, staring wildly about him. Poor man! his spirit was subdued and his strength exhausted—despair had taken possession of his mind.

I had scarcely ceased talking to my honest messmate, when a tremendous sea rolled over me, shook everything from its place, and carried me, the brave Quirorga too, and I believe every other survivor on board us, along with it into the vast ocean. Death now seemed inevitable; yet, amidst all the confusion of intellect occasioned by my sudden immersion, it came to my recollection that if a man will throw himself flat on his back in the water, lie quite stiff and straight, and suffer himself to sink till the water gets into his ears, he will continue to float in this position.

The happy thought with which I was inspired was not thrown away upon me, for I threw myself on my back in the way just mentioned, and left myself to the disposal of Providence, when I floated with hardly an effort, and began to conceive faint hopes of pre-servation. After lying in this manner, committed to the mercy of the wind and the tide, without having once turned from my back, after a time my body struck upon a sandy beach, when, overjoyed at my providential deliverance, I made a convulsive spring to gain my legs, which I effected, and ran up a little distance on the shore; but I was so weak, and worn down by fatigue, and so unable to clear my stomach of the salt water with which it was loaded, that I suddenly grew deadly sick, when I felt apprehensive that I had only exchanged one miserable death for another—in a minute or two, however, I became senseless.

CHAPTER XIV.

"Night wanes—the vapours round the mountains curled
Melt into morn, and light awakes the world.
Man has another day to swell the past,
And lead him near to little but his last."

"The sun, which yearly melts the polar ice,
Has quite the contrary effect on vice."

THE morning of a new day had dawned upon the island of Cuba before I awoke to the slightest recollection of my situation. I was then lying in a bamboo and mud hut, stretched on the ground upon a wretched bed, made of the large leaves of the cabbage tree. A woolly-headed African negro and a mulatto woman, his wife, together with their four children and an infirm old negress, were my companions; but presently the six first-named went away from the hut to their place of labour in the field, leaving the aged woman to take care of me.

When my senses became sufficiently collected to contemplate my situation, I felt much grieved to think that my wealth and bright prospects had now passed away from me, for the Santa Maria, and everything living or dead on board of her, except a few straggling sailors, who had since been picked up from floating upon spars, or been driven on shore upon them, the negro man, previous to his going out, had, in Creole Spanish (which, thanks to my per-severance in acquiring the language during my late eventful career, I could pretty well make out), given me to understand had been ingulfed in the ocean, or shattered to pieces by the tremendous hurricane shortly after our beautiful ship struck upon the rock.

A good chest of clothes, which I had collected together by degrees, and upwards of sixty dollars, which I had kept deposited in my chest, were lost to me by the wreck of the Santa Maria, and, what was still worse, all the specie we had taken from out of the packet ship was gone for ever; therefore I could make no claim for the prize money on that head, should I live to reach Porto Rico once more, where I scarcely knew whether I ought to attempt going for although, from the destruction of most of our ship's crew, I should now have an equitable claim to a large sum as my share of prize money for the cargo of the Columbine, yet the uncertainty respecting how Captain Robertson might treat me and my claim, combined with the knowledge I had of the man himself, and of the dread character he bore, made me think he would not scruple a moment at depriving me of life should he deem it good policy, and this thought filled my mind with evil bodings on the occasion.

It may be imagined that I should feel no great regret for the lives of my companions who had so miserably perished; but he who reasons thus knows not the human heart. Man is a sociable animal, and let his intimate companions be who they may, he cannot see them snatched away by an untimely fate without deploring the sad event; besides, death, by visiting those immediately about us, forcibly reminds us of our own danger; therefore, in some measure, it is a selfish feeling which actuates us when compassionating the fate of such lost companions. But in addition to these general reasons for deploring the death of such a multitude of my own species, I was in many instances swayed by more personal motives, as amidst the most ferocious characters ever assembled together pleasing companions and warm-hearted friends are to be found; and it would be acting an ungrateful part towards the memory of the departed, if I did not honestly avow, that among the savage-looking, ignorant negroes and mulattoes, so recently my shipmates, many had acted kindly by me, and proved by their conduct in various instances that the face is not the counterpart of the heart.

When, in a most melancholy mood, I had mused for some time on the untimely end my shipmates had come to, the imminent peril which I had myself been in, and the present sad vicissitude of my affairs, suddenly I called to mind that two doubloons were in the fob of my trousers at the time we were wrecked; and scarcely did I recollect this circumstance ere, by signs and the little broken Spanish I was master of, I endeavoured to find out from the old negro woman what had become of my trousers.

The woman, who was a martyr to the worst kind of yaws, which had already eaten away some of her fingers, was also so extremely stupid that I could not bring her to understand what it was that I required; but at almost every fresh attempt I made to obtain the much-desired information, she would bring me yams or fruit, or some other article of produce of the country.

Kindness proffered at an improper time is scarcely considered such, and this negro woman's kindness, shown when I wanted to have my curiosity gratified and not my appetite for food, was even provoking to me; but there was no remedy save patience, therefore I ceased making signs or speaking, and stifled my feelings to chew the cud of reflection in silence.

The negroes in the West Indies, even in the island of Cuba, are infinitely better off than the peasantry of England. The industrious among them all have plenty of rum, sugar, coffee, tobacco, salt fish, tropical fruits, and vegetables of many kinds; and it is the negro race who supply the markets with pork, fruit, poultry, and fish.

These facts being made known, it cannot be wondered at that in my host's absence I was supplied with everything necessary in the eating and drinking way; for although the old negress either would not or could not make out my request respecting my trousers, she took care to put cooked yams, ripe bananas, plantains, and other fruits beside my bed. She likewise, by her prudent conduct, made it evident that she knew what was fit for a person in my condition, inasmuch as she kept from me the rum bottle—that solace to the mariner in his troubles, but which now might have thrown me into a burning fever.

About sunset my host and his family reappeared in their place of dwelling, when the worthy man expressed much satisfaction at finding me in so promising a state. The question uppermost in my mind now found vent, and, with the eagerness of youth, I asked my sable host to render an account of my trousers; when he, perhaps seeing my anxiety, smilingly said that I was in no fit condition to go abroad, and therefore need not be in a hurry to clothe myself. Presently, however, he opened an old chest which stood in a corner of the room, and had been covered over with branches of plantains, and taking from it the clothes I had worn at the time of the wreck, handed them to me on my bed, when, such was my anxiety to recover my treasure, that, without reflecting on my strange conduct, I most eagerly examined the fob of the trousers, and to my consternation found that it contained nothing. I felt again and again like one not crediting the evidence of his senses, or determined not to believe an astounding truth which he fears.

My good-humoured host, who was honest and sincere, for unprincipled missionaries had not been tolerated in Cuba to corrupt the negro population, seeing my distress, kindly relieved my mind by producing my two doubloons, when, giving them to me, he said he wished there were ten times more of them for my sake.

Not to dwell on this part of my history, I shall content myself by stating, that on the day following the recovery of my gold pieces, though still very sore from my bruises and suffering from fever, I contrived to leave my lowly bed, and sit up for a time under a shady mango tree near the hut; and two days after this my host brought a Spanish planter, his master, to see me. This gentleman had, from the time of my shipwreck, been away from his plantation, transacting his shipping business at the not far distant town of St Jago de Cuba. He was a friendly, good man, and gave me to understand he was well pleased with his slave Sancho for having taken care of me; but he said I should now go to his caza with him, and remain there his guest until my health got established.

This was a most acceptable invitation to me, and upon the back of a mule I was now conveyed to the planter's dwelling, which was a convenient wooden house of one floor, adjoining the building in which he prepared his colonial produce for the market; but previous to our quitting Sancho's hut, I got the planter to give me change for one of my doubloons, when, as a mark of gratitude, I forced the sum of five dollars upon my black host and his wife, who, however, much to their credit, wished for no remuneration for their kindness shown to me.

The planters in the West Indies, no matter from what country they may have come, are hospitable people. For my part, I was treated as kindly by Senor Fabricious as if I had been a relative. Here I stayed seventeen days, during which I heard tidings of twenty-five of the crew of the Santa Maria, whose lives had been preserved from the wreck. Most of them had quitted the island in trading vessels of other states.

When I had sojourned with him seventeen days, my host had occasion to visit the Havannah to make a purchase of slaves, and the journey being long and tedious by land, he decided on voyaging there in a drogher, which is a little coasting vessel; and I, wishing to see the Havannah, and deeming it the best place to embark at, made up my mind to accompany him. Accordingly we embarked at St Jago de Cuba, and three days afterwards arrived in safety at the Havannah, for several ages famous as the place of rendezvous for the rich galleons and other vessels coming from Mexico and Peru to proud and once-powerful Spain.

The grandeur and extent of this wealthy city filled my mind with astonishment, which elicited remarks from me that a North American Indian or a Castilian would not have exposed his weakness by making, for the American savage and the haughty Spaniard are disciplined in a way which allows them not to betray childish weakness by declarations of astonishment on beholding the works of other men. Great, however, as the Havannah appeared to me, who had previously seen no other town of note except Portsmouth, it had recently suffered a diminution in size by a fire, which destroyed upwards of twelve hundred houses.

At St Jago de Cuba, Senor Fabricious had kindly assisted me in purchasing a suit of clothes, and at the Havannah he became the guest of his factor, who also admitted me into his house, and proposed giving me some employment, thinking I might be useful to him in his transactions with my country people, many of whom frequented the Havannah for mercantile purposes.

The cargo of slaves from which my friend had purposed making his purchases, was disposed of before our arrival; but this traffic was then in a flourishing state, and another slave ship entered the Havannah ten days subsequent to our arrival. She, however, brought into port only one-half of her customary cargo, therefore no reduction took place in the price of human beings. But the story of this ship's last voyage furnishes proofs of the lamentable results attributable to over-strained exertions, where no real power exists to do away with the slave trade. The slaver in question had been chased by a British cruiser, when, to lighten the cargo, the crew cast half of their slaves into the sea, and the other half were destined to follow to prevent the vessel becoming a legal capture to the cruiser; an event which assuredly would have happened, had not the ship of war, by crowding too much sail, carried away her foretopmast, and thus enabled the slaver to escape into the Havannah, while it baulked the hopes of the man-of-war's men regarding the head-money they would have been entitled to for the negroes on board; which large sum of money the British government would have paid to the uttermost fraction, even had the same captured negroes been afterwards given up to the Spaniards at Cuba, and sent into the very bondage for which the English treasury had been drawn upon to save them; this truth, however, is too well known to be commented upon, and misdirected philanthropy has often caused England's gold to be circulated to uphold that slavery in foreign colonies, which Britain has abolished in her own.

Senor Fabricious, who happened to be very short of hands on his plantation, owing to the hooping-cough and the yaws having visited his negroes, and carried off a number of them, was much disappointed at having the full price to pay for the slaves he now bought; and though he was rather a philanthropic character, this circumstance made him become violent in his invectives against the Anti-Slavery Society and its duped partisans. However, as there is no struggling against necessity, and he could not do without them, the Senor purchased five negroes; but the sum he paid for them would have bought eight, had the entire cargo of the slaver reached the Havannah, in place of having had a moiety of the poor Africans thrown into the ocean to perish—thanks to the Quixotic effort of people calling themselves philanthropists.

Senor Fabricious having completed his purchases, prepared to return home; but, as will be seen by the catastrophe I have to recount, he was not destined to fulfil that intention.

The Spanish character has always been remarkable for harbouring the mean passion of jealousy, while, unfortunately, the Spaniards themselves have too rarely shown scruples of conscience in sacrificing the suspected offender to their sanguinary revenge. It might however be thought, that the demoniac passion of jealousy would not be blown into a great flame, even in the breasts of Spaniards, where the Venuses they have to be jealous of are mostly black or mulatto beauties; yet the very contrary is the case at the Havannah, and every person who has been there well knows it.

At the time in question, the green-eyed monster seemed to have found his way into almost every dwelling, but whether it was owing to the good-natured frailty of the ladies, or to the natural character of the Spaniards, or to both combined, that it had made this great progress, is a delicate subject to pronounce upon, and one on which, as I am no casuist, I shall not hazard an opinion.

There was no safety for man in walking the streets, much less in going to places of public amusement, and many were the unfortunate men and officers of the sea service who had recently been assassinated, and whose bodies had been found in the streets. As to any redress being obtained, it was totally out of the question, for the public authorities of the town slighted complaints on the subject, and seemed to consider the revenge taken as nothing more than fair.

Good sometimes will spring from evil, and this absolute lack of morality on all sides gave birth, in my mind, to sound reflections and just comparisons. Indeed, who could contemplate such passing events without marvelling to think how men could be found insane enough to slay others for worthless women, ever ready for fresh intrigue; and who, that like me, had associated with buccaneers, could possibly avoid thinking of their superiority of character for manliness, yea, and for virtue too—to a set of Spaniards who most basely murder each other, as well as strangers, on account of the most faithless of women; they themselves forgetting, while they perpetrate these dreadful deeds, that the basis of liberty is the free disposal of ourselves.

It was considered rather a memorable circumstance, when a day passed over on which one sailor or more had not been murdered; but I little dreamt that the assassin's stiletto, usually employed against sailors, was destined to pierce the heart of my only friend here, who was aged, and not even suspected of gallantry. This, however, it was made to do one unlucky night, when the poor planter and I were on our way home together from the house of a merchant with whom we had dined.

At the moment of the dreadful assassination of my friend I happened to be a little distance behind him in the street, but I saw the assassin come from under a gateway and give him the vengeful stab, when instantly the unfortunate gentleman staggered and fell. The man was now going to search his victim for booty, but I suddenly came upon him, and a most fierce struggle ensued between us, when I was in imminent danger, for he was an active and a determined man. However, though I received several slight wounds from the stiletto of this villain, fortune at last favoured me in the fight, his vindictive fury having somewhat exhausted his strength, and in my own defence, to save my own life, I had no alternative, but plunged my dagger into his body.

CHAPTER XV.

" Despised Jamaica! when thy fate is seal'd
Proud England's degradation shall be peal'd
Throughout the world !"

" I love the beauteous isle !"

THE sanguinary deed I had achieved might be thought an astounding one for a youngster, but the school I had recently come from among pirates, and my own excited feelings at the loss of my benefactor, served to steel my heart on the occasion. I however stood for some seconds by the dying assassin, meditating what I should do, when happily a party of several Spaniards passing along the street, singing a national air, roused me from my reverie, and I hailed them to come to my assistance.

The Spaniards readily complied with my request, when I briefly related to them what had passed, and happily the dying murderer survived long enough to confirm my testimony, and to acknowledge that robbery had been his object in committing the foul deed; after which, assisted by the generous strangers, I conveyed the body of my unfortunate friend to the residence of his factor, where the melancholy sight thus afforded, and the lamentable tidings I had to communicate, filled the worthy gentleman and all his family with unfeigned sorrow and consternation.

The following day, for funerals within the tropics take place soon after life has become extinct, I attended that of my poor friend to a neighbouring church, whence, after the customary ceremonies of the Catholic service had been performed over him, I proceeded with it to the burial-ground, and saw the corpse consigned to our parent earth.

This duty of friendship having been performed, the factor, who was a generous man, called me into his closet to repeat his proposition of taking me into his employ ; but the late melancholy event had prejudiced me against remaining at the Havannah, and I therefore modestly but respectfully declined accepting his offer, and communicated to him the intention I had formed of proceeding to Jamaica, where I thought I might obtain information to enable me to prosecute my claim for prize-money for the West Indiaman's cargo, as it was well understood that its capturers, Captain Quiforga and his crew, were to have shared in the booty with Robertson, who had disposed of the valuable produce. The factor expressed regret at the determination I had come to, and endeavoured to reason me out of it; but on finding I was unchangeable, he pressed me to remain a few days with him, when he said, a lugger was to sail for Jamaica in which he had an interest, and I should pay nothing for my passage. Accordingly I continued at his house until the appointed time, when the worthy gentleman conducted me on board the vessel, and made me a present of twenty dollars as a small token, he said, of the respect he bore to the memory of his departed friend, Senor Fabricious, and of approbation of my gallant conduct in revenging his death, when he wished me success in the world, and bid me good by.

The distance from Cuba to Jamaica is but trifling, and two days from the time of embarkation I was standing on the lugger's deck at anchor near the shore, looking at and admiring the latter island, when I sketched out the following account of it, which I subjoin for the information of such persons as may not have visited this highly-productive, ever-blooming, luxuriant island :—

" The first appearance of Jamaica presents one of the most grand and lively scenes that the creating hand of nature can possibly exhibit. Mountains of an immense height seem to crush those that are below them, and these are adorned with a foliage as thick as vivid, and no less vivid than continual. The hills, from the summits to the very borders of the sea, are fringed with trees and shrubs of a beautiful shape and undecaying verdure ; and you perceive mills, works, and houses, peeping amongst the branches, or nearly buried amidst their shades.

" The sea is, in general, extremely smooth and brilliant, and before the breeze begins to ripple its glossy surface, is so remarkably transparent, that you can perceive (as if there were no intervening medium) the rocks and sands at a considerable depth, the weeds and coral that adorn the first, and the stars and other testaceous fishes that repose upon the last.

"Every passing cloud affords some pleasing variation, and the glowing vapours of the atmosphere, when the sun arises or declines, and when the picturesque and fantastic clouds are reflected on its polished bosom, give an enchanting hue, and such as is only particular to the warmest climates, and which (I have since ascertained) much resemble those saffron skies which so strongly mark the Campagna of Rome and the environs of Naples."

Providence, which must be of close affinity to nature, for she provides for all natural wants and contingencies, has by those inestimable gifts of hers, the land and sea breezes, shown herself peculiarly beneficent to the human race, as also to all other living creatures and things vegetating in the West Indies.

During the day here the solar rays rarify the air on shore, and dry up the moisture on the surface of the earth, and this it is which occasions a breeze on every side to blow from the sea towards the centre of each island. On the contrary, as soon as the sun sets, the heavy dew peculiar to the tropics begins to arise from the earth, and this, during the whole night, keeps driving back the sea air—to which latter source it is we are indebted for the land breeze.

These breezes, except during the time of a hurricane and perhaps an earthquake, are as aithful to their courses as time itself is to its march; only, it is to be observed, that they vary n their strength according to the seasons and the temperature of the air.

At a large island, such as Jamaica, sometimes their influence extends to not more than three or four miles from the shore, while at others the breezes will be felt full twenty miles distant from the land.

For the purposes of navigation they are peculiarly advantageous, inasmuch as they enable the mariner to know the proper time for approaching the shore and for quitting it. Were it not for the assistance afforded by these much-favouring breezes, coasting vessels bound to windward ports would have no way of evading the trade wind, which they do by keeping near to the shore.

The lugger I was on board was indebted to these breezes for getting, in three days, to the place of her destination, an harbour on the south side of the island, celebrated for its great shipments of coffee, and named Alligator Pond.

The wharfinger's house was the only one at the place of landing, and in the first boat which put to shore after we anchored I proceeded there, intending to make inquiries regarding the best mode of proceeding to Kingston, the capital mercantile town of the island.

When I landed, the wharfinger, who was a swarthy, sickly-looking man, was sitting in his varanda, facing the sea, to catch all that he could of the coming breeze; and the captain having introduced me to him, we sat down to table to partake of his second breakfast.

In reply to my inquiries, the wharfinger informed me that Kingston is nearly seventy miles from Alligator Pond, and that to journey there by land would be fatiguing and expensive, as it would be necessary to travel the whole way on horseback, and have my own horse, for no person in that neighbourhood hired them out. He advised me to wait the arrival of a Kingston drogher, which might be expected in a week; meanwhile, he said, I could pass my time pleasantly visiting among the planters, who would any of them show me hospitality. Presently, too, before we had finished our breakfast, several of these gentlemen, who had descended from the mountains to see to the shipment of their coffee, entered the room, and when it was made known to them how I was situated, they invited me home with them; while, as they had spare mules and horses at the wharf, which had carried their bags of coffee that morning, there was no difficulty in providing me with a steed.

Where injuries are inflicted the injured will complain. I now heard a great deal of the rascality of the negro population here, which had begun to set their betters at defiance, and act as if they were assured that the lands and buildings of the country would speedily be their own. One of the planters present had that morning to investigate into the circumstances connected with a robbery of coffee, and he procured evidence, which seemed conclusive, against an Hebrew storekeeper, of his having purchased an entire cask of that prized article from a negro, who had stolen it from his master. However, as it will prove that theft is of all trades the most profitable in this quarter, I shall communicate the almost incredible fact, that receivers of stolen produce are known to ship and sell nearly as great a quantity as the proprietors of estates who grow and manufacture the articles!

When the sun was sinking in the horizon I mounted a good hackney, and accompanied two of the planters on their ride home to the Manchester mountains. The road was almost one continued ascent; but we reached Mandeville, distant fifteen miles, in less than two hours. Here my companions had to separate; but, to use the language of the country, they proposed having a " drink" before they parted, and for this purpose we adjourned to a tavern, then, with the exception of the session-house, the workhouse, and the parsonage, the only building in this assized town. It was named after the second title of a man whose aristocratic consequence has mainly been upheld by the sweets gleaned by him during a protracted term of governorship over this rich island.

To pass over minute particulars it will suffice to say that I remained fifteen days amongst the ever-hospitable residents of Manchester parish, living, as they termed it, " on planters' fare." At some of their houses I was feasted most sumptuously, but everywhere treated with urbanity and kindness. Woodlands, the favourite residence of a great proprietor here, I shall never forget. Its owner was hospitality itself. He was warm-hearted, much-esteemed, a member of the assembly, a major-general of the militia, and. to his lasting honour, a real patriot.

After sojourning here for the term mentioned, at a *dejeune* given at the pleasantly situated plantation of Java, I met the custos of the parish, a gentleman now no more, but who was an excellent orator and an enlightened member of the assembly of Jamaica, and he, having been informed how I was situated, kindly proffered me the use of a spare horse to travel in his suit to Spanish Town. Accordingly with the dawn next morning we descended the hills to Spring Plaine state, seven miles distant, where the party breakfasted with the worthy proprietress, and afterwards proceeded on for Spanish Town. Fortunately there had been no rain very recently; therefore, without inconvenience, we passed across the bed of Dry River, which after rains is impassable. The journey well evinced the hospitality of the country; for, as matter of course, everybody's house was open to us, and the whole party invariably dined at one estate, slept at another, and breakfasted at a third; until, after two days spent in this way, we arrived at Ensom Pen, a sweetly situated villa appertaining to the custos of Manchester, and which stands near a bank of the rapid river, the Rio Cobra, surrounded by extensive and luxuriant grounds.

Spanish Town is the seat of government of Jamaica, and has been so, not only from the time when Oliver Cromwell added this fine island to the British possessions, but it was such under the Spaniards before us, who made choice of this spot when they conquered the aboriginal inhabitants and colonized the isle. Spanish Town, however, is not conveniently situated for commercial purposes, therefore, as a town, it has never throve; and save a few public buildings, the place contains little more than negro huts and a few lodging-houses.

On the other hand, Kingston is the focus of trade. It stands at a most convenient part of the most commodious and safe harbour in the whole island. Until just prior to the time in question, it had, from our earliest knowledge of its history, been a wealthy town. The Spaniards enriched it; the buccaneers enriched it; and the merchants, as long as there was any security for property, trebly enriched it; but when I went there Kingston was a drooping, spiritless, miserable place, overrun by missionaries and corrupted by the cant of methodism. But the West India isles have been scurvily treated by the mother-country; indeed, since she prides herself on the maternal character she may be said to be an unnatural parent. The toiling islanders have long been taxed to uphold placemen and pensioners, but they toiled on in quiet, and bore the taxation with patience. Their miserable fate is precipitated on them by the rule of men totally ignorant of their localities; for what are Colonial Secretaries but statesmen who have just sufficient influence to get the rich appointment, and, to retain it, must act under the mandates of artful brawling demagogues, many of them wearing the cloak of religion, whose fallacies, uttered at meetings of the fair sex, tend to deceive the gentle-hearted, as also to the destruction of happiness, property, and order in the colonies where negroes are employed? And, ye gods of Rome, what is methodism, as also what are some other persuasions ending in *ism*, more than cant terms to facilitate certain impositions upon the mind, which serve to trick the gentle community out of much money?

Oh, ye lovely islands of the west! Nature has been lavish in her gifts to you; but rapacious man has so regulated your affairs, that there is no security left for the estate of the living or the dead. For example, anybody there may throw his neighbour's property into Chancery, which is threefold more expensive than in the mother-country, and

> " Courts of justice understand
> The plaintiff to be eldest hand,"

while, as to the testaments of the departed, they avail but little for the intended heirs when escheats are sought after to further enrich overpaid governors and presiding worthies of the long robe.

The colonies, too, which in the height of their prosperity knew not of such evangelical appointments, are now blessed by having highly endowed bishops, even where the language of the people is unknown to the prelate; but I beg pardon of the right reverend fathers, for I should have denominated them "lord" bishops, as some are regular sticklers for their right to the double title.

CHAPTER VI.

> " Synods are mystical bear-gardens,
> Where elders, deputies, churchwardens,
> And other members of the court,
> Manage the Babylonish sport."

> " He was the mildest manner'd man
> That ever scuttled ship or cut a throat,
> With such true breeding of a gentleman,
> You never could divine his real thought."

THE fatalist maintains there is a fate in everything, and the Turk, though he may run like a madman at sight of the lance of his Cossack foe, is a fatalist in the fullest sense of the word. Occasionally, however, events fall out so strangely, that a person of the soberest judgment is half inclined to be of the Turk's opinion.

I had not long arrived in Kingston ere, in passing along the streets, my attention was attracted to a number of staid-looking personages sallying forth from a meeting-house, and I overheard one gentleman say to his companion, that a synod of Methodist parsons had been in conference there. "Zounds," thought I, "I'll warrant that Robertson's relative is amongst the crew;" when, without knowing the evangelical man's name, much less his person, I looked attentively at the demure characters as they severally came out of the conventicle. A corpulent, glossy black man, and a sickly, yellow-faced Creole, duly habited in sable dresses of a most puritanical fashion, for a time engaged my attention; but presently spying out a squinting, carbuncled-countenanced gentleman, leaning on the arm of another, I turned my eyes to discover what kind of a man was his supporter, when, to my unspeakable astonishment, I beheld in that individual my old friend Captain Robertson. "A bad man may be made still worse by keeping bad company," said I to myself, as I looked at these path-directors to heaven. "The grain, however, shall be sifted from the chaff before I make myself known to my old friend." It was a prudent resolve, and to act up to my resolution, I followed about after the party at a convenient distance, until at length Robertson bid good day to his companions, and entered the door of a lodging-house. I paused for a few minutes, and then knocked at the door to inquire for Captain Robertson, when a black girl made her appearance, who, on learning my business, at once ushered me into the apartment where he was. I had felt dubious how he would receive me, but his reception of me was kind, and he expressed joy at my escape from the wreck of the Santa Maria. Captain Robertson now informed me that he had come to Jamaica expressly to make inquiries regarding the shipwreck and the survivors of the crew; but he said that, in addition to me, he had met with only two, and they were ignorant blacks, who had given a lame account of the dreadful misfortune.

At his desire, I related the particulars of our cruise, and of the prize we had taken; as also, minutely as I could, of the storm preceding it, and our terrific shipwreck, when it became evident to me, from the exclamations and observations that escaped his lips on hearing the sad tale, that he had been a great part owner of the Santa Maria, and he avowed his disappointment at finding we had not disembarked any of the captured treasure; and, moreover, intimated that Quirorga ought to have gone to St Domingo to have done so, for that silver bore a premium there, and good bills could have been procured by him; whereas he had wantonly risked the dangers to be apprehended from discovery, and consequent capture, as likewise those of shipwreck on the coast of Cuba, which last had visited us, to the destruction of our vessel, the treasure on board, and the crew. On the loss of human life, however, Robertson made very few comments, for he was by far too heroic a character to attach much importance to such an event; indeed, my opinion is, that provided our treasure in specie had previously been landed in a place of safety, he would inwardly have rejoiced if every individual on board the Santa Maria had been drowned.

There is nothing like having an eye to the main chance, and I, after having given Robertson all the information in my power, discovering that he was going to dismiss me without saying a word regarding the merchandise taken by us out of the Columbine, ventured to put some home questions to him on that delicate subject; but his answers were vague and unsatisfactory: at length, however, finding me resolved on the subject, he suddenly changed his manner; and, from having been very formal, became affable and friendly; when, after some preliminary discourse, he informed me that he purposed to embark soon for St Thomas's, and would take me with him, and that there I should be paid my quota of prize money: he even hinted, that provided I conducted myself to his satisfaction, he would be the making of my fortune; but cautioned me, above all things, as I valued our lives, not to mention the name of the West Indiaman our prize, especially in Jamaica.

That I might the better delve into the secret views of this extraordinary man, I readily agreed to everything he proposed to me, while, in unhesitatingly promising not to name the Columbine, I consulted my own welfare, as the act of piracy committed in taking of her, and the barbarous action of making away with her captain and her crew, might, if known, have brought my life into the greatest jeopardy. On parting, he presented me with a few dollars, and told me to be with him at an early hour next morning. "Ah, my old governor," added I, as I walked away from the house, "you are wary, I see, as you are rich; but it remains to be seen whether you can come the buccaneer over a youngster such as I am."

I had been recommended to a certain lodging-house, and I now proceeded there. It was kept by a Creole miss, and she received me with the drawled out tokens of satisfaction usually shown by these accommodating ladies to their moneyed customers. She provided a tolerable good dinner that day, of which several lodgers partook as well as myself, and afterwards I went to the theatre to witness the performance of an American company which had recently arrived from New York, to display their theatrical talents to the community of Kingston. The professed amateur of dramatic performances would have derived no pleasure from seeing and hearing Macbeth consult the weird sisters in the way I now saw and heard this ceremony managed; but to a youth like myself, who had never witnessed anything more theatrical than Punch and Judy, as they are exhibited about the country throughout England, even the acting of this, perhaps the most strolling company of the United States, could not fail of being entertaining, and I was vastly amused by it. I also derived pleasure from beholding the costly and, some of them, fantastic dresses, worn by slaves present at this exhibition; but the sight in no manner surprised me; for in Jamaica, the people then denominated slaves, since that time apprentices, and now freemen, have long enjoyed the sweets of the soil, while many of the proprietors of land, at whose charge it is cultivated, perish, worn out by anxiety, in a state of bankruptcy. However, what I witnessed on that occasion was a bagatelle compared with what had taken place a few nights previous at Spanish Town, where the slaves gave a ball, at which ices, and every other luxury that money could produce, were introduced, together with a plum cake of extraordinary dimensions, and six feet in height. There was scarcely a negro in the room whose dress had not cost at least five pounds; while some of the more fanciful of these gentry, more especially among the females, had expended from thirty to fifty pounds upon theirs. This extravagance, however, will not be thought surprising by those who know that a negro can earn five shillings per diem by picking coffee, a task about equal to that of gathering cherries in England. The negro looks with contempt upon a white pedestrian—a walking buckra, as he calls him, and still with greater upon the sailor of a merchant ship; and well may he do so, for when he himself works aboard ship, he gets threefold the wages of that slave of all work, though he is a freeman and a Briton. The merry negro laughs, too, at the British soldier eating his ration of salt meat in a country abounding with cattle of all kinds;

and who is enlightened enough to tell whether the aforesaid ration is issued for the benefit of the home contractor, or to give the soldier an additional zest for the new rum of the country?

When I waited upon Captain Robertson in the morning, he behaved to me even more courteously than at parting the night before, and telling me his breakfast would soon be ready, insisted on my staying to partake of it. At this meal the shrewd captain affected to open his heart to me; and, well knowing the nature of his own species, he baited the lure of deceit with personal flattery and the promise of aggrandisement. I was a fine, handsome young fellow, he said, the very counterpart of a favourite nephew of his, who had been lost at sea in the Guinea trade; and, provided I did everything he wished of me, and served him faithfully on all occasions, he would adopt me in his place; for he had no child of his own, nor any young relative he wished to provide for. This apparently was a golden opportunity for the child of Diana Winpenny, and he possessed too large a share of worldly wisdom to allow of its passing by without returning abundant expressions of thanks to the promiser of so many advantages. In short, matters were now so well understood between us, that after we had done breakfast, and he had given me the cue how to behave myself, the captain took me to the house of his relative—the evangelical gentleman with the carbuncled nose, and introduced me to him as a youth who had come strongly recommended to him from England, and whom he purposed taking under his own care.

This preacher of the gospel was one of those officious persons who never let slip an opportunity for trumpeting forth their own godliness. Accordingly, he seized on this occasion for sermonizing me on the sweets of a religious life, and the grateful duty I should owe my beneficent protector; telling me, in conclusion, especially to observe all good precepts, read holy works, and implicitly follow the orders of the worthy Christian who had taken me under his paternal care; for that the youth who is well trained, never forsakes the path he should go.

Like an apt scholar, I listened with much seeming attention to all the foregoing, and a vast deal more such cant, dealt out in profusion, but with puritanical precision from the mouth of this teacher of the doctrines of Christianity; for well did even I know that attentive auditors make contented preachers, while that to preach and to listen is the main business of the two; inasmuch as the conduct of both the parties almost invariably proves that they neither of them care anything about following the doctrine inculcated, however dogmatic and orthodox it may be.

My conduct on this occasion evidently was gratifying to the lecturer, as, in summing up what he had to say, he was pleased to signify that I was a grave, promising youth, endowed with a sprinkling of grace; one, in short, of whose welfare on earth, and salvation hereafter, he entertained no faint hopes.

No man can compete with a professed swindler in professions of honesty; and to judge by the same standard, the most eloquent preachers are the most arrant impostors. For his part, Captain Robertson affected to receive as so much unerring gospel all that his relative had said, and consequently now looked on me with the soft beaming eyes of complacency; but I, though not yet out of my noviciate in worldly matters, inwardly laughed at them both, and recollecting Diana Winpenny's advice, said to myself, while their attention was otherwise diverted, " Yes, ye pair of sanctified old rogues, never doubt it; the boy before you has been trained in the way he will go."

———

CHAPTER XVII.

" Have I once lived to see two honest men?"

" Oh, who can tell, save he whose heart hath tried,
And danced in triumph o'er the waters wide,
The exulting sense—the pulse's maddening play,
That thrills the wanderer of that trackless way?"

THE Creole miss, my hostess, who in her short career had been cruelly duped by two or three itinerant preachers, was no advocate of the Methodist persuasion, and, finding this to be the case, I ventured to question her regarding my new patron's brother-in-law, whose name I forbear mentioning; though, to avow the truth, not out of regard to the reverend gentleman himself, but in mercy to the feelings of well-meaning persons belonging to the Anti-Slavery

Society, as they would be sadly put to the blush were I to make known this man's name to the world.

The lady unhesitatingly told me that she knew him to be a sad wretch, yet that he was so wary, that there was no possibility of getting him convicted of any one of his crimes in a criminal court; besides, the slave population, she said, looked upon him as a saint, and would not suffer a word to be spoken to his disadvantage.

For her part, she added, it was impossible he could again deceive her, so greatly had her family suffered from his rascality. Her sister Julia, for example, had been seduced by and borne a child to this parson, who shortly afterwards not only forsook her, but gave out that a sea captain had been poor Julia's seducer. Yet, what still more grieved her was, his having so worked upon the feelings of her mother by alternate threats of punishment and promises of rewards in a future state, that to mollify his heart, and ensure, as she thought, a good berth above, the old lady, shortly before her death, and unknown to her family, had made a will, bequeathing to this man the best part of her little property, which he had inhumanly seized upon. He had a wife and a family of children in England, she said, and yet that she knew of no less than four Kingston girls whom he had seduced and forsaken; besides which, he kept a young black mistress, whom he passed off as his housekeeper.

A novice in the knowledge of these sort of evangelical characters might have imagined my fair hostess to have been actuated by prejudice when she complained in this manner; but truths force conviction, and for my own part, I verily believe she spoke nothing more than the truth; yet she charged the reverend gentleman with being an impostor, who made his God's name a tool to work with, and bartered away the Bibles, Testaments, and tracts sent to him to distribute in exchange for marketable goods, such as pigs, poultry, vegetables, and fish. With this divine and Captain Robertson I was now honoured by dining every day, and from being myself constantly on the watch to glean information, I found out that the captain had recently freighted several vessels with goods to this island, which had been disposed of, and he had taken bills of exchange upon mercantile houses at New York for the amount of the sales. His business here being all done, the captain became anxious to get back to Porto Rico, for the time was fast approaching when the slave ship he expected home might arrive from the coast of Guinea; accordingly, that time might not be lost, as there was no vessel at Kingston bound to Porto Rico, he agreed for his passage and mine in a Bermudian trader bound to St Thomas's, from whence we could cross to Porto Rico any day we pleased.

All was got ready for our voyage, and the sea stock had already been shipped, when, from my having suspected something wrong in their intentions, and at a time when they believed me to be employed elsewhere, I happily placed myself in a closet adjoining the chamber of conference of the two relatives, my professed friends, and here I heard amply sufficient to put me on my guard against their machinations for my ruin.

The parson it was who first touched on the theme so interesting to me, which he did by saying, that the safest way to ensure silence of one who knew too much, was to set his tongue at rest in the silence of death; when the captain, encouraged by this hint, said the youth was now off his guard, and therefore might be let live for a time, and if his services were required, sent on a voyage or two to Africa, where most likely he would die; but provided he did not, there would be ways enough to dispose of him. Here the preacher, with a compliment or two to the other's sagacity, declared that no man knew better than himself what was incumbent on him to do; nevertheless that the wisest men sometimes erred, and for his own part, he thought the sooner a dangerous evidence was sent to his resting place, the better it was for the mind's peace as well as the body's security.

There was at all times a something ominously imposing in this clerical gentleman's manner and words, but now both were so much more impressive than I had ever before witnessed them to be, that I was not in the least surprised to find Robertson was moved by his friend's arguments to alter his sentiments regarding me, and made to avow that he would take an early opportunity of ridding himself of the youth.

Here the conference terminated, and the two relatives, much to my satisfaction, took up their hats and went out of doors; when, judging they would go on board the vessel, I hastened there as fast as I could, and so contrived that, when they arrived on board, they found me busily engaged overlooking our stores.

There is nothing like cheating the devil : both the gentlemen bestowed commendations on me for my zeal ; and I, satisfied of the value of their praises, failed not to return due thanks for the same ; yet in my heart I felt satisfied that the youth was trained in the way he would go ; while that, wily as these confederates were, still he would contrive to come the buccaneer over them.

My conduct on this occasion was so satisfactory, that this being the last day of our stay, the parson was pleased, after our dinner, to take me, along with the captain, to pass the evening with a wealthy member of his flock. Here I should observe, as we found some Jews were of the party, that no monopolizer of tithes, however illiberal might be his sentiments, could show more rancour against the Jewish religion than Robertson's relatives always did ; but then, like many such illiberal characters, he was narrow-minded and most prejudiced. He, however, could preach about crucifying his natural feelings, and debasing himself before men, but he was too stubborn to do so.

Our Methodist parson, who was grieved to think that in Jamaica the Jewish citizens enjoy every privilege to which their worth as men, and their tolerating spirit towards other religions, fully entitle them, could not forbear from showing his envious spirit by insulting the Hebrew gentlemen, who had come there for the purpose of conviviality and not that of dispute ; till at length, highly to my delight, an elderly, bearded Jew—a rabbi I believe he was—silenced the troublesome preacher by putting the following interrogatories to him :—" You are extremely free in your abuse of our religion, but do you know, learned sir, that Jesus Christ was a Jew ; that he was born, lived, and died a Jew ; that, as a Jew, he celebrated the passover in the full moon ; that all his apostles were Jews ; that after his death they went into the Jewish temple, as it is expressly written ; and that the fifteen first secret bishops of Jerusalem were Jews ?" Without any other memorable event intervening, Captain Robertson and I embarked in the Bermudian vessel, and his reverend friend had the complaisance to accompany us on board. He sailed with us to the mouth of the harbour, when, after cautioning my protector not to be unmindful of his advice, he departed in a shore boat to land at Port Royal, where he had a conference to hold with several elders of his church.

The Bermudian captains trading between the West India Islands are experienced seamen, who know how to make the most of the trade winds, as also the properest time to get into port to escape those hurricanes which too frequently sweep every sail from those seas. Our captain steered his course for the north side of St Domingo, that he might have the wide Atlantic to work his schooner in, and where, by steering a degree or two to the northward, a little variation from the trade wind is usually found. We continued tacking about here for twelve days from the time of quitting Jamaica, during which we caught an abundance of fine fish, among which may be enumerated the king-fish and the dolphin : we also hooked a large shark and speared two porpoises, which last, contrary to the prejudices of most British seamen, we found to be good eating, the liver tasting like pig meat, and the flesh not unlike beef.

Here I should mention, that my patron, as I suppose, the more effectually to throw me off my guard, now invariably called me his nephew, no matter whether speaking of me to others or personally addressing myself ; the consequence of which was, that every person of the crew believed me to be his nephew.

Great events not unfrequently originate from trivial causes. Neither Robertson, nor any other person not possessing the power of divination, could possibly have foreseen, or even conjectured, that the appellation bestowed on me by this gentleman, when calling me " his nephew," would prove a great means of facilitating my success in getting possession of much unlooked-for wealth. To explain this, I must premise the story by mentioning, that many experienced mariners, who have voyaged in the tropics, pronounce that fish which have been exposed during the night to have the moonshine upon them consequently become poisonous ; but whether this assertion is grounded upon fact I shall not presume to decide, although, to judge from what I have now to relate, it may well be believed as a truth.

We had been fourteen days at sea in the Bermudian schooner, the " Lovely Lass," beating to windward the whole of the time, when Captain Robertson, who, it should be observed, was much of an epicure, and remarkably fond of that great delicacy the king fish, requested of our skipper to have a slice of one which had been taken on the preceding day cooked for his dinner, and according to his desire this was done, and my patron ate extremely hearty of it; but an hour or two afterwards he was taken dreadfully ill with a retching of a violent nature, which nothing we had on board could stop or allay.

It was conjectured that the captain had been poisoned by the king fish, of which no other person on board had eaten freely; but several who partook of it in a more moderate way were more or less suffering from the same poison, and everybody now called to mind the circumstance of the fish having been hung up during the whole of the preceding night, with a full moon shining upon it. In defiance of all we could do for him, poor Robertson's sufferings kept on increasing; the poison seemed to work upon him in the manner that arsenic does. He endured dreadful torment · but at last, seeing all was in vain that we could do for him, and that death was inevitable, he, with a promptness of decision always remarkable in his character, resolved on the latest act of his life. Having ordered every one out of the cabin except the captain, he directed him to write what he dictated; which being done, two of the crew were brought in to witness his signature to the document; he then desired the skipper to clear the cabin, and let me alone be with him, when, on our being closetted together, the poor gentleman spoke as follows:—" He who has but a few minutes to live has nothing to dissemble. I have been a great sinner, who cloaked his crimes under the cloak of religion; but I now abominate those who were associated with me in the Satanic deception. However, Andrew," added he, sighing most grievously, " I feel that I am dying; so, to the point. I have a wife and children in Europe, but there is ample wealth there for them; therefore, as I loathe my late associates, and none more than my deceitful brother-in-law, who advised me to make away with you, I have left you the sole heir to all I possess in this quarter. There is the will," concluded he, giving me the newly written paper; " but be cautious—hasten away with your money to a safer quarter, for soon will it be discovered that you are not my nephew, and every possible effort will be resorted to to dispossess you of the inheritance."

The poison had done its work: my benefactor could say no more, but gently waving his hand to the Bermudian captain, who at this moment entered the cabin, and pointing towards me and the will displayed in my hand, as if in the way of appeal to him to see justice done to me, he fell back on his pillow, and presently, with a great groan, yielded up the ghost.

CHAPTER XVIII.

" 'Tis trick and trickery makes all crafts to thrive;
Starts interests new, and (like the laudanum dose)
Sets the poor dupe asleep! Your governors,
Directors, managers, and other knaves
Who thrive on ill-got wealth, laugh in the sleeve
At those who pay them."

NECESSITY is a stern tyrant. Even the great debt of gratitude I owed my benefactor, in return for the affluence he had so unexpectedly bestowed on me, could not avert the harsh decree of necessity: there was no alternative, the body could not be preserved for interment on shore, and I was obliged to consent that my *soi-disant* uncle should be cast into the ocean—a ceremony which was performed with a double-headed shot enclosed in each end of the hammock wherein was his corpse.

The Bermudian captain, who was an honest, straight-forward sort of a man, used his best efforts to console me for the untimely death of my uncle; while I, to play the nephew's part, put on the appearance of greater sorrows than I really felt. However, although until very recently I had lived in dread of Robertson, and that I well knew him to be a most dangerous, wicked character, yet now his testament made in my favour had so thoroughly changed my sentiments regarding him, that I respected his memory, and felt grief at his lamentable end. By his death, too, I had been taught a good moral lesson for all grovellers after unnecessary riches—namely, that of seeing the small importance they attach to them in their dying moments; and I had also by that event been made more sensible than heretofore of the inscrutable ways of Providence, which had permitted Robertson to go on in a long, prosperous career of aggravated crime; and for what, as far as I could perceive, but to make Andrew Winpenny, a youth until recently unnoticed by him, heir to his ill-gained wealth?

I lost no time in possessing myself of my benefactor's writing-desk, and what small packages were at hand, and two days after his death the schooner reached St Thomas's, when the captain, to whom I presented a good bonus for his services, acted the part of a man of honour, by delivering up to me everything on board belonging to the deceased gentleman's estate. At the time of that event, I much regretted the necessity of consigning Robertson's body to the deep; but after my arrival here, I found it was the happiest disposal of him that could have taken place, as, had I brought his remains to this island, the Danish lawyers would have sifted into the particulars of my declared relationship, and obtained possession of all the property of Robertson's estate within the Danish rule, most likely for ever, as I never could have satisfied the Danish laws and their greedy lawyers on this delicate subject. Indeed, such is the law's rapacity, that, as in some other states, poverty is the only safeguard for those persons who mix with the legal tribe, and I had not been forty-eight hours ashore at St Thomas's, when an Englishman, settled there as a merchant, and who knew something of what was in contemplation, advised me to depart the isle without beat of drum, which accordingly I did, with bag and baggage, in a Spanish fishing-boat, which sailed immediately I got on board for St Juan, Porto Rico. The passage is but a few miles across the ocean from one of these islands to the other, and the trade-wind favouring, we were soon harboured in safety at St Juan, where I proceeded forthwith to the lodging-house of my former hostess, Mademoiselle Delisle, who expressed herself delighted to see me once more, and, at my desire, deposited my baggage in a safe store-room. The good lady proved very inquisitive; she put a thousand questions to me; but Robertson's advice, and the danger I had been in from Danish lawyers, served to make me cautious, and I gave her no more information in return for her questions than what I deemed safe for myself; but I communicated the story of our shipwreck, which much shocked the feelings of the tender-hearted female, and many tears fell from her eyes at the recital.

From Mademoiselle Delisle I learnt that the captain of our slaver was absent from Porto Rico, on a voyage to the coast of Guinea, to procure a fresh living cargo; and a day or two after my arrival, my new friend Jenkinson, whose advice had so essentially befriended me, crossed over by appointment from St Thomas's to Porto Rico, to consult with me as to the best mode of proceeding in the management of my affairs. Jenkinson, I should observe, bears a very high character, both for probity and his great knowledge of mercantile business; and knowing a half confidence to be no confidence, I candidly communicated to him all my story. The intelligent merchant, after listening to me with profound attention, and reflecting for some little time on my critical position, counselled me to act by the deceased Robertson's advice, and get away from the West Indies as expeditiously as possible; for otherwise, he said, unprincipled enemies would most likely prove the destruction of me. "For example," added he, "have you not every danger to apprehend from the slaver's captain when he returns here, and you call upon him for a division of the profits of his voyage? And may not your enemies, to secure to themselves some of your wealth, get you apprehended for piracy, and sent to Jamaica for trial, when assuredly your riches would be an irresistible lure to the great law officers there, and most likely a gibbet at Port Royal Point be the finale of your adventures?"

My friend's advice was excellent, and well knowing that he, in the capacity of my agent, could act far more effectually in my behalf than I could for myself, in a quarter where my person would be in constant danger, while I could command no great respect, from having been known only as a youth in a very subordinate character, I promptly decided on executing and leaving with him a power of attorney to act for me in recovering all and every description of property he could under the will of my supposed uncle, and of myself departing forthwith to the United States of America, there to await in security the result of his endeavours."

The resolve once made, no time was lost by me in executing a power of attorney, whereby I gave the same powers to my confidant to act in my behalf as I myself possessed; and having furnished him with this document, together with a certified copy of my uncle's will, of which I took probate in Porto Rico, and also a letter of general instructions, I engaged my passage in a vessel bound for New York, on board of which Mr Jenkinson and Mademoiselle Delisle saw me with my bag and baggage safely embarked; and the wind proving fair, the brig was well away on her voyage, indeed almost out of sight of the land in little more than two hours from the time of my taking leave of these friends of min

The vessel I was on board of was named the Joachim; she was an hermaphrodite brig or large dimensions ; and as her captain had only three other passengers, neither of whom paid him a price proportionate to what he required for the use of the cabin, he gladly accommodated me with his state-room, in return for the more liberal sum I agreed to give him for my passage-money.

On any other occasion a common berth would have suited my purpose quite as well as this little cabin, but now, for a good reason, I wished to have a place entirely to myself ; and this having a door to it which locked, and being furnished with a table and a chair, suited my purpose to a tittle.

My luggage I got stowed away in my cabin, and as soon as we were fairly out of sight of land, I went below and shut myself up to gratify the furious desire I felt to become acquainted with the actual amount of treasure I had come into the possession of by the demise of my self-constituted uncle, as Mademoiselle Delisle, at Porto Rico, had been too prying into my affairs to allow me a safe opportunity of examining my things, and I was far from desirous of having any one present to witness what I possessed.

It was an enchanting employment, and to this day I think of it with glee, the examining of the contents of Robertson's writing-desk. I found deposited there a great number of gold coins, together with two watches of the same metal, and a variety of diamond and topaz rings. But what most merited my attention—and which, by the by, I was rather slow in finding, for they were stowed away in a secret drawer—were the bills of exchange upon mercantile houses in New York, which the departed gentleman had received in return for the shipments of goods disposed of by him in Kingston.

These bills were well worthy of the search I had to make after them, inasmuch as their amount altogether was for sixty thousand dollars, or, in other words, more than twelve thousand pounds of English money, which, added to the specie I found, amounting to better than four thousand dollars, made an inheritance well worthy of touching ; yet, besides this money, I had to thank the captain's memory for abundance of clothes, as well as the watches and rings already mentioned.

" Ah," said I, laughing with self-complacency as I contemplated this treasure, " the youth has been trained in the way he should go."

Having thus far satisfied my curiosity, I repacked the bills of exchange and what other property I had found in the writing-desk, and carefully locked up the same ; but I put off the task of examining my new wardrobe to some more convenient opportunity.

A good-humoured, facetious little fellow, named Grenville, who had recently been a merchant at St Thomas's, and two Irish gentlemen on their return from Mexico, where they had been employed with the title of managers to superintend a mining concern, were the other passengers on board the Joachim.

The Hibernian gentlemen were great talkers. By their boasting it came out, that, by means of their own great assurance, they had obtained the appointments they held under a company of persons in England, who, having more money than sane brains, had embarked a vast deal of the former in a mining concern, the projectors of which had promised them to procure gold in such abundance in Mexico, that it should be sent home by ship loads at a time.

The projectors of this laudable speculation, it seems, had procured the two Irish gentlemen expressly that they might act the part of puffers, and consequently they had been at the trouble of having them schooled to know all the names of things, as also the terms of art used in every branch of mining ; when, as soon as all this knowledge was attained, as the heroes had long before gained a conquest over their modesty, they talked so very learnedly, and made such great promises, that they not only satisfied the minds of the capitalists engaged in the concern as to their ability, but made them rejoice at having two such able persons to send out as their confidential agents to South America.

The Hibernians had implicitly obeyed the private orders of the nefarious projectors of this concern, and they were now on their way home to explain to their simple capitalists the necessity of raising another loan of money before they could clear the mine of water, and effectually get at the gold there. But for the satisfaction of the mine proprietors, who thereby would get the shares up in price, they carried home with them several beautiful specimens of gold in the crude state, which, they said, had come out of their mine.

Man is a sad scheming animal. Over the bottle one night, when they were more than half tipsy, Grenville, who knew well how to worm secrets from characters of this sort, got one of these adventurers to admit that they had purchased the samples of gold they carried with them ; and, moreover, that not a tithe of the money subscribed by their employers had ever been spent in attempts to work their mine.

In short, it was made evident by what this man said, that the mine was little better than an imaginary thing, but by means of which the projectors trusted they should be successful in mining the pockets of the shareholders.

After a pleasant passage of fifteen days, we entered the beautiful bay of New York, which is said to be second in magnificence only to that of Naples. Having come from the West Indies, we were detained a short time at the quarantine ground, but on the following morning we disembarked at the spacious city of New York—the mart of commerce. With all its advantages, however, it labours under two great disadvantages—the first is the want of pure fresh water ; the second, the great variableness of its climate, which not unfrequently changes more than twenty degrees in one day.

The four passengers arrived in the Joachim put up at that famous inn and boarding-house the City Hotel, where, for ten dollars a week, any decently-dressed person may be lodged and boarded better than many princes are housed and feasted when in the zenith of their glory. But with all this excellent living there is one custom prevalent here, which in Europe would be thought a most unmannerly one—namely, that of bandying the different dishes about the table for every one to serve himself to what he wants, as no person at a public table here condescends to help his neighbour to food.

Nearly a hundred people usually dined at this ordinary every day while I was here ; but then, it should be observed, that only a small portion of these were lodged in the hotel. At New York it is customary for single men to dine at ordinaries, which in consequence are numerous, and varying in price to suit the pockets of all ranks, from the leading merchant to the humblest clerk.

We met with many remarkable characters at our ordinary, not a few of whom had rendered themselves notorious by their frauds. Indeed, good evidence might have been procured among them of the grand truths inculcated in the preliminary chapter of this work ; but I shall not act the part of an informer against people of other countries, it is sufficient that I incontrovertibly establish, to the satisfaction of the impartial part of the community, that the philosophic assertions of the learned sceptic convey nothing more than truth.

Even among the Britons who revelled a part of their time away here, there were characters of whom the vulgar might say " hanging would be too good for them." One of these was a London banker, a superlative villain, who had crossed the wide Atlantic with all the cash in his chest which his unsuspicious customers had intrusted to his keeping. Another, who was, if possible, a still more unprincipled wretch than the banker, had been a famous solicitor in the British metropolis, till at length, having got together several hundred thousand pounds, the purchase and sale-money of estates belonging to his clients, he took advantage of their ignorance of the human character, shown by placing trust in him, and, without beat of drum, marched away with the precious booty. There was also an Englishman here, who, after playing strange pranks in the other three quarters of the world, foolishly defamed his hostess in this quarter, and had been tried, and sentenced to pay a heavy fine for his pains in doing so ; when he, preferring his money to all other things in life, got a Commission de Lunatico Inquirendo against himself ; but the American jury, by their verdict, defeated the gentleman's intentions, and left him no other choice than to suffer long years of imprisonment, or be forthcoming with his money, for they most sagaciously decided that he only laboured under the influence of an ungovernable temper.

The foregoing, it will be observed, were persons accustomed to move in a genteel sphere of life ; but we had also some ignorant and vulgar Englishmen boarding here ; one of whom only will I particularize, which I do in consequence of the novel mode he had taken of realizing a comfortable fortune. This man had recently been a watchman in the metropolis of England, but happening one night to witness an improper intimacy which took place in a churchyard between a senator and a soldier, he turned the adventure so much to his advantage, that he shortly afterwards emigrated here with a good fortune, supposed to have been extracted from the rich senator's pocket.

The bills of exchange I had upon the merchants at New York were all duly honoured, and in due time I touched the large sums they entitled me to receive ; when, having seen all that there was to see at New York and in its vicinity, the love of change of scene got possession of my mind, and I started one morning in the public steam-boat for Philadelphia.

———

CHAPTER XIX.

" Say, what's nobility, ye gilded train '
  Does Nature give it, or can guilt sustain
  Blooms the form fairer, if the birth be high ;
  Or takes the vital stream a richer dye?
  What ! though a long patrician line ye claim,
  Are nobler souls entail'd upon a name?
  Vice levels all, however high or low,
  And all the difference but consists in show.
  Who asks an alms, or supplicates a place,
  Alike is beggar, though in rags or lace ;
  Alike his country's scandal, and its curse,
  Who vends a place, or who purloins a purse."

" 'Tis the temptation of the Devil
  That makes all human actions evil :
  For saints may do the same things by
  The Spirit in sincerity,
  Which other men are tempted to,
  And at the Devil's instance do."

An American steam-ship, with her passengers on board, furnishes a good epitome of human life.

Among the heterogeneous mixture of nearly three hundred persons we had on board, was the President of the United States ; a man, like all his predecessors, worthy of the high and honourable situation his discerning countrymen had appointed him to fill ; one or two of the members of his council were also embarked with us ; but here the taint of aristocracy is mixed up with the constitution, and it is to be apprehended, that unless the fulsome term honourable be detached from the names of those who fill this office, that the taint will spread into vile corruption, till the land has become accursed by the burden inseparable from a real aristocracy of title.   Indeed, it is essential to a people desirous of maintaining their freedom, to permit not of titles and decorations amongst them ; these being instruments of their governors to enslave them, by working on their love of approbation, to make it degenerate to servility, that these baubles and symbols may be obtained.

Two venerable personages, in the garb of Quakers, seated themselves near me, and entered into a dissertation on politics, when the youngest observed that the American constitution was a happy one, but he feared not doomed to continue so, for that the different governments scattered over the world had invariably began by being republics, and ended by becoming monarchies ; as some ambitious wretch always arose to rob his country people of their rights, by seizing upon the sovereign power and basely enslaving them, which is easily done through the medium of long, partially chosen parliaments, amongst the members of which corruption never can fail in its object.

To this the elder citizen made reply, that in the ignorant ages these misfortunes had visited the people in all quarters ; but now, he said, that the people were wiser than in olden times, and, instructed by the press, in countries where the institutions were just and sound, as with them, there need not be any fears entertained of such a lamentable result.   The past, he added, so far from arguing bad for the future, as the partisans of royalty would infer, was the best guarantee they could have against danger ; and this, inasmuch as no class of men knowing anything of history, could be so depraved, or so blind, as to give ear to any upstart who would impose on them an aristocracy, a national church, and septennial senators, to be paid and upheld by all classes of the community.

The Quaker who had first spoken on politics again expressed doubts as to the probable durability of their government, whereupon the most venerable of the two resumed as follows :—

: " The United States of America have profited by the errors of old-established governments, and, therefore, keep themselves free from debt and the grievous taxation it occasions ;

but royalty is incompatible to cheap government, and creates a continued inroad on the people's liberty and property. It requires to be upheld by a long list of pensioners and an all-grinding aristocracy; and for these its bounties to vice are innumerable. The labourers are plundered by every device, under the head of taxation, to grossly pamper the profligate and the idle. In short, steam itself is nothing to it. Steam of a million horse-power would not do the work of execution half so effectually as a despotic royalty. Happily, too, the sunshine of America has commenced at an auspicious hour; and it is reserved for us to be a religious people, without having to uphold what often is its bane—a national religion. Our constitution is excellently framed; it makes the various states of the Union serve as checks upon each other, and compels the government to be economical—perhaps the most difficult point to be achieved. Then, again, the division of property between children is beneficial, for it adds to the respectability of the middle classes; whereas, what is the law of primogeniture in some kingdoms but a state device for upholding one great personage at the head of a wealthy family, while the younger branches eat the bread of idleness, as pensioners or placemen. Our criminal laws also are excellent, for by them justice is promptly administered; and although our judges are exempt from their labours only on the Sabbath, so honourable is public employ deemed in a well-governed republic, that they think themselves well remunerated by salaries of fewer hundreds of dollars than conspiring judges, who sit in judgment only occasionally, receive in pounds sterling, where wide-spreading corruption taints the entire land. But royalty," added this republican citizen, after having paused for some time, "royalty is an expensive government; for what is a king without an aristocracy and a priesthood? and what are any of these unless supported in splendour and magnificence? It is a system in which men are sought to be governed by appearances, and the senses rather than the understanding, and is more adapted to a barbarous than a civilized state. Happily, however, we are no copyists of the institutions of our English forefathers, who, like the Egyptians of old, were the servile and submissive slaves of priests and kings. Pageantry and ceremony, the parade of crowns, coronations, and coronets—of gold keys, sticks, white wands, and black rods—of maces, lawn, and ermine, and of horsehair wigs—these are the chief attributes of monarchy. When men become enlightened, they cease to inspire respect, for the real object of government is to confer the greatest happiness on the public, at the least expense; and it is, therefore, a beggarly greatness—an absurd system that would perpetuate these tom-fooleries amidst an impoverished population—amidst never-to-be-paid debts, all-grinding taxation, and frightful, wide-spreading pauperism."

"The language of truth, uttered from the lips of reason, must carry conviction," said the junior Quaker, "and I see that the pageantry of a court, and the prodigal expenditure in equipages, high living, and in all devisible ways, of those who frequent it, must indirectly be paid by the toiling community; as likewise must the martial troops, the army of policemen, and the unnumbered spies which it entails as essential to its pomp and grandeur."

Thus reasoned the gentlemen with the broad-brimmed hats; for so very ignorant were they on some points, although extremely enlightened on others—as, for example, traffic in all branches—that they knew not that many things which sound remarkably well as precepts, have been exploded in practice, even from the time when the first of the Ptolemies reigned over Egypt; and, probably, to judge from their ignorance of the blessings of royalty, and the many good gleanings to be picked up under that form of government, they took the groundwork of their reasoning from some old barbarous history

From political matters the conversation was now turned upon the news of the day, when our two friends deplored the sad circumstance of there being pirate vessels afloat in their neighbouring seas; which they said, most assuredly there were, as many ships had recently been lost, which were unaccounted for by shipwreck or otherwise. Of these they specified no less than six, in which list, not a little to my confusion, was the Columbine, as also the Carthagena packet, which Captain Quirorga pillaged and scuttled.

The eldest Quaker, seeing I was interested in the conversation, and, mistaking me for an innocent youth about terminating his education, good-naturedly observed to me, that pirates, after the aristocracy and the stipended national church they had been talking of, were the greatest thieves and scourges mankind could be afflicted with; and he added, that he trusted it would always be my good fortune to steer clear of the whole three.

I always possessed much self-command; yet I could not forbear laughing at the worthy gentleman's comparisons, and, telling him I felt thankful for his good wishes towards me, and would endeavour to steer my course in life clear of the dreadful rocks he had pointed out, I made my bow, and proceeded to a remote quarter of the deck; for really I was afraid that in some way I should be discovered, if I staid longer with such shrewd observers of mankind as were these Quakers.

The journey between New York and Philadelphia, though an affair of only ten hours' duration, is remarkable for being made in two steam-vessels, and the voyagers having to travel by coach a distance of six or eight miles midway from one of these vessels to the other, that is, from the North River to the Delaware, by which the traveller reaches the last city.

There are two ways of voyaging between these places; one is by Burdenton, the town wherein Joseph Bonaparte long resided, and freely expended a part of that large fortune his labour never earned; the other road is by the way of Trenton. This it was by which I passed; and at the time in question there resided there a more philanthropic man than ever was Joseph Bonaparte, or than were the whole of the Bonapartes clubbed together. This man, to the shame of both the new and the old world, lived there in all the squalid misery of poverty. He was housed, it is true, but he was without a chair or a table in his house. If shame is more than an idle name, surely the managers of school and missionary societies, who waste money and create jobs in pulling down and erecting buildings at pleasure, will blush when this great man's name is mentioned—it is Joseph Lancaster!

We arrived at Philadelphia in good time for dinner, and after enjoying an excellent one at the States' Hotel, I sallied forth to perambulate the town, in doing which I could not fail admiring the great regularity with which that enlightened citizen of the world, the philanthrophic founder of this great city, laid out its public streets. The city stands between the Delaware and the Schuylkill rivers, which are about three miles apart from each other, and the streets, which cross from one to the other, are at uniform distances, and in lines exactly parallel; while they are named, not from fulsome flattery after men or their battles, but by the names of trees. The streets which intersect the foregoing, and constitute the remainder of the town, are also all of them parallel to, and at equal distances from, each other, and are numbered First-street, Second-street, and so on to the completion of the number.

William Penn, as everybody knows, was a Quaker, and no one disputes his having been a good man. He was peaceable, quite unlike the Quakers of the present day, who are, too many of them, a brawling, selfish, hard-dealing race, with whom even a Jew pedlar can have no chance of making an advantageous bargain. They are a proud hearted set, governed by the weighty friends, their aristocrats of wealth; but, happily, are all agreed upon the subjects of negro slavery, opposition to tithes, denunciation of war, improvement of prison discipline, and the promotion of education. At the period I am speaking of, the public tranquillity was dreadfully disturbed by this race, who had split into factions among themselves, and were frequently to be seen fighting with each other in the public streets. In many respects they furnish bad examples as citizens and men, but perhaps are useful, to show that no other religion than that of adoring God, and acting justly towards man, is called for in this world.

The most remarkable character at this time in Philadelphia was Mr Gerard, a Frenchman, who had emigrated in his youth, and without a friend or any money, commenced his career as a sailor-boy; but, by the force of industry, prudence, economy, and mercantile speculations, he at this period had risen to be the wealthiest private man probably in the whole world. He was an eccentric character, of whom almost innumerable droll anecdotes are related; but, though he knew his own species well, he would place no uncalled-for trust in the honesty of the Gospel-mongers of the times in which he lived. The great proof of which was afforded after his death; for, although he bequeathed several millions of pounds in sterling money to the city of Philadelphia, to be laid out in improvements and the endowing of a college, this unprecedented munificent bequest was made subject to an express condition, namely, that no clergyman of any religious persuasion whatever should ever be intrusted with the management of a single shilling of the money; for he was of that poet's opinion, who thought "that priests of all religions are the same."

The long suspension bridges, covered over with timber from one extremity to the other for the accommodation of passengers, of which I had passed over one at Trenton, and now saw another, which traverses the Schuylkill, at Philadelphia, filled my mind with no small astonishment, and made me contemplate, with feelings of admiration, the enterprising spirit of the people of this well-governed republic, where education is good for the middle and low classes, and the servants of which, alike in the law, the navy, the army, and the state, are well remunerated for their services while they are employed, but afterwards not heavily pensioned to burden the state, or give extra patronage to those persons high in authority.

To conclude.—If the noxious vapours of one spot of corruption could hide the solar light of reason, the vote of parliament that decreed the burning of Priestly's works by a common hangman, would have prevented the dissemination of this enlightened philosopher's writings, which did more to establish the domestic freedom of America than even the valour and virtues of her incomparable Washington; but, thanks to such philanthropic citizens of the world, the profession of religion is an open one in the United States, and therefore it thrives exceedingly; for the clergy must live, which makes them conciliate the people. Yet they join with each other here in teazing those persons who go to no place of worship; and who, rather than be continually harassed by a set of parsons that take especial care of themselves, though they pretend to think of nothing else than the soul's welfare, mostly, after a time of persecution, to enjoy future peace, pay for a seat in some place of public worship.

Thus preaching is made to flourish here, but the preachers are not all of them educated for the pulpit; in proof of which I adduce the circumstance of my having one Sunday attended service at four places of worship, at one of which the sermon was preached by a brown woman, at another by the President's chaplain, at a third by a seaman, and at the fourth by a cobbler, who bore the imposing title of a bishop; and, inasmuch as he received no wages, and possessed no church patronage, indubitably he approximated closer to the chosen disciples of olden days than all the stipended bishops of modern times. But under the blessed sun, which invigorates and gives life to all in this world, there are only two grand systems of religion—one, is that of good sense and benevolence; the other, malice and hypocrisy.

CHAPTER XIX.

"Throughout that clime the feudal chiefs had gained
Such sway, their youthful monarch hardly reigned;
Now was the hour for faction's rebel growth."

"It was too late to check the wasting brand,
And desolation reaped the famished land;
The torch was lighted, and the flame was spread,
And carnage smiled upon her daily dead."

AFTER spending several months in Philadelphia, I became desirous of seeing more of the world, and with this object in view, as well as to ensure their safety, I exchanged most of my valuables for sterling money; when, having reserved for myself what I thought I might require, I invested fifty thousand dollars in the States' Bank here, at six per cent. interest, and procured good bills of exchange, at ninety days, upon the Barings of London, for two thousand four hundred pounds, being the residue of what I had to spare; for as yet, it should be observed, I had received no money, or even tidings, from my agent at St Thomas's. This business done, by the same merchant's advice who had guided me in it I enclosed my bills of exchange in a letter to a celebrated London banker, whom I directed to invest the sum of two thousand pounds in the British Consols as soon as the aforesaid bills were paid, and to open an account with me in his books for the remaining four hundred pounds. My mind being thus relieved of anxiety respecting my treasure, and I having heard a great deal of conversation here about the much-celebrated falls of Niagara, came to the determination of visiting them with a party of gentlemen on the eve of journeying there; and from thence I purposed proceeding to Canada, there to take my passage to England.

Accordingly, four of us set off together on this trip, and a delightful journey we made of it to the Falls, travelling the greater part of the way in steam-vessels, for which the rivers, lakes, and canals, so abundant here, afford every facility. Here I might say a great deal concerning these stupendous cataracts, which perhaps form the greatest wonders of the natural world; but any description I could give is uncalled for, as they have been described a thousand times. It may not be amiss, however, to observe, that the rocks upholding the immense bed of water are found to be wearing away, insomuch, indeed, that the Great Leap is thirty yards further up the country than it was twenty or thirty years go; and, as the rocks forming the bed of the river, from the Rapids upwards, are of a softer nature than at the Falls, they consequently are the less able to resist the action of the current.

Speculative people, from the foregoing causes, may set themselves to work in calculating the time when the bed of the river will be washed away to a level with the bottom of Lake Erie; for then its waters, together with those of the upper lakes, will escape so rapidly, that Ontario must overflow its banks, Lower Canada and the northern parts of the States of America be completely laid waste under water, and the Gulf of St Lawrence turned into another channel.

The sight is a most beautiful one, to stand on the Canadian shore, at the elevation of a hundred feet or more from the bed of the river, and see the vast clouds of white foam ascending high in the air, sometimes tinged with variegated colours caused by the last rays of the setting sun, long after it has ceased to illumine the dark expanse beneath. There are also, at irregular distances, shelving rocks, which appear to have been made of more durable stuff, and which run completely across the river, forming numerous embankments, over which the waters roll and tumble with terrific fury. These Rapids continue battling with the current to the very brink of the Great Leap, a distance of more than a mile, and are divided by Goat Island, a small island whose foundations may truly be said to be laid in the deep. A handsome bridge, about one hundred and fifty yards in length, from the centre arch of which you have a beautiful view of the Rapids, both up and down the river, connects it with the village of Manchester. This island, by dividing the river, makes two separate falls, but by far the largest portion of the water goes down the Canada side; and by far the finest view of the Falls is from this side, for here you have both the Horse-shoe and the American Fall at once before you. This last-mentioned is a most beautiful sheet of water well worthy to hold the rank of the second wonder in the world of the kind, although not to be compared in grandeur and sublimity with the other. It is about two hundred yards in breadth, and either from its rocky bed being composed of harder materials, or from the greater weight of water coming down the British side, and wearing away that channel more rapidly, it is about twenty feet higher than the Horse-shoe. It does not fall into a gulf or caldron as the other does, but amongst huge rocks, where it dashes itself into an ocean of foam, and then rushes with tremendous velocity to join its former companion. The body of waters around here are truly awful; the beholder has reflected before him, on a fine day, when the sun shines full on the cascade, a succession of the most beautiful prismatic colours that can be imagined; it is altogether a lively scene, which, once seen, can never be forgotten.

One of my companions, who was a clergyman of middle age and most staid manners, was walking with me looking at the majestic Falls, when we met an Indian and his family, who, it appeared, were on their return home from Quebec, where they had been to barter away their furs with the English; and as this chief, for such he proved to be, could speak our language, we were enabled to enter into conversation with him; when one of the first questions the parson put to the warrior was, to be informed whether or not he was a Christian?

"A Christian," replied he, "no; I am of my own religion; why should you wish me to be that of another man?"

This reply, short as it was, made the clergyman reflect within himself for a brief space; and then he said, "You have your own God, and your own law, I presume."—"Yes," rejoined the Indian, with an unmoved manner and firm voice, pointing to the heavens; "my God is there;" and, putting his hand upon his heart, "my law is here."

The parson stared with amazement, but I turning to him said, "Religion, perhaps, is a matter of opinion more than of the understanding, for it seems pure unsophisticated nature knows more than all the doctors of divinity in the world."

The warrior was accompanied by his squaw; two sons verging towards manhood; and a daughter, a fine girl of about sixteen. From his discourse, it appeared that he had left behind him his other daughter, a lass of seventeen, to pass away the winter at Quebec with a young British officer, who, entirely with her approbation, had solicited her father to leave her there with him; while this parent possessed too great a share of paternal affection to refuse this gratification to a favourite daughter, and too high a spirit of that honour on which the North American savages pride themselves, to refuse to an avowed friend so simple a request; which, moreover, was held to be complimentary on both sides.

The clergyman betrayed tokens of surprise on hearing the Indian chief's ingenuous confession; and he made an observation, implying that the young woman's conduct was sinful, and contrary to the spirit of Christianity; but the chief, who had calmly listened to him, replied, that his forefathers had held it as their opinion, that the best religions and the wisest men were those which fostered the fewest prejudices; and that for his part, he considered no one was warranted in interfering with other free persons in their enjoyment of natural rights, more than they would be in dictating to them what they should eat at their breakfasts, dinners, and suppers.

It would have been ridiculous to have stood balancing opinions any longer with a man who views all our sublime mysteries of the Gospel as so many fables; therefore, to relieve the parson from his dilemma, at not being able to convince a mere savage by the force of his reasoning on divinity, I invited the warrior to adjourn with us to our place of abode, to partake of refreshments.

A North American Indian, though he is of the learned Jesuit's opinion, that "there is no true religion in the world, nor any satisfactory cause why one religion should be more genuine than another," yet is a man well worthy of the name of man. He despises ceremony too much to make use of it; therefore, as the invitation suited his convenience, he and his family walked our way with us, without even replying to my proposition. At our meal, the Indians did ample justice to the entertainment, for although they can fast uncommonly long, yet they can eat voraciously. In fine, they are not people to live by Cornaro's rules. They neither weigh nor measure their quantum of nourishment.

When my guest the warrior had satisfied his appetite, we held some conversation with him respecting the continued warfare carried on by the United States' government against one or another of the Indian tribes. "Yes," said the Indian, "that nation thirsts after lands which it needs not, and never, while we possess a tract of the extensive country of our forefathers, will its people bring us the calumet of a lasting peace. They deceive us by treacherous promises, and they rob us by means of an overwhelming force. Were they children of the forest as we are, who live by hunting, their numbers would never have increased so as to require our lands from us; but they are ants, who swarm and generate on the same dirty heap, and yet they have fifty fold more land than they can make use of. They talk of honour, and they violate every principle of it. They came here as interlopers, as vagrants, and as criminals, and now they seize upon our persons, which should be free and respected; and imprison and put us to death for crimes they say we commit, although what we do is no crime by our laws, while we know nothing, nor desire to know anything, of theirs. They talk too of a Providence, and their missionaries, who appear to us to be a blind set of bigots, astound our ears with unintelligible tales; but they have not the good manners to listen to those we could tell them. Like so many evil geniuses, they stir up strife and hatred wherever they go. But if there is that Providence they say, if our great Monitor is in the Heavens, why is not the calumet of peace brought to us? and why are we not left in quiet possession of the back country, which is now all that remains to us?"

The parson could make no reply to the questions of this leader of a tribe of persecuted Indians; but the equanimity of this hero himself, who would have defied death in the cruelest shape human ingenuity could inflict it, was not to be shaken by any subject of discourse; and turning to me, he good humouredly asked, how it was that a youth like me, in the bloom of health and the dawn of manhood, could reconcile himself to voluntarily endure the effeminate life of a prisoner, shut up in a pestilential and a smoky city, amongst people whose souls were centred in money, and they consequently incapable of a generous thought.

My eyes quailed before those of the free-souled Indian, while I replied to his heart-searching question. But I now was the master of wealth, which serves as a loadstone to enslave the world, and draw man to the more refined and civilized scenes of multiplied crime. My answer was, that urgent affairs demanded my presence among the busy haunts of men, but that my heart yearned for that enjoyment of liberty of which his more happy stars had destined him to partake, and that yet it might so happen I should shape my course to discover some friendly tribe of his countrymen, to live happily among them.

The pipe of fraternal peace was now smoked by us, and the Indian, with his family, afterwards proceeded on their journey further into the interior of the beautifully romantic country, to travel over large creeks, swamps, and rugged hills, wet with rains and the dew of heaven. His example, however, had impressed this grand truth upon me, that, except health, strength, and an easy conscience, all the comforts and pleasures of life are dependent on opinion.

The day following that of our interview with the Indian warrior, our party broke up, two individuals of it to return to Philadelphia, and the clergyman and myself to proceed to Quebec.

It was a fine morning when we started on this new journey. All nature seemed refreshed, and the dew fell drop by drop from the trees of the forest. The wild turkeys were calling to each other from the lofty branches of the oak; the cardinol was expanding his golden plumage to the sun, the woodpecker was sticking his beak at the worms in the bark of the trees, and the mocking songster with faint carol was hailing the return of day. We prosecuted our journey through forests of oak and hiccory, from whose stately trees hung a long and shining moss: the wood rang with the loud and melodies note of the red bird, and everywhere the woodpecker was heard, though he could not be seen.

About noon we reached an Indian village, where we found the chief warrior on his death-bed. The hoary chief, weighed down with years, lay indulging the retrospect of the enemies that had fallen into his hands, and triumphing over the recollection of the groans produced by the infliction of slow torture. The only heaven he looked to was an imaginary country beyond the trees, where food would await him without the toils of the chase. The grounds of his hopes of reward were the trophies of his cruelties; and he pointed to the scalps that hung around his wigwam, charging the youthful warriors present to emulate his deeds, and revenge him of his enemies.

Having refreshed ourselves at his village, we quitted the dying warrior to resume our journey, and when we came to a halt on the evening, the scene was interesting to an extreme. The bat was then wheeling his flight through the air, and the whip-poor-will was welcoming the approach of darkness; while the sun, which had disappeared among the forests of the west, had not been obscured by a single cloud; but a cooling air shook the foliage of the trees, and the shrill hissing of the locust echoed from the oak. I saw the trees beautifully marked upon the sky behind them, every leaf and branch looking like filigree work, while a breeze was brushing over the grass, and carrying with it the fragrance of the flowers.

My companion, though a little prejudiced by his clerical education, was a man of good understanding and generous sentiments, and, while we journeyed together, he edified me by excellent remarks on the Indians and their country. Particularly well do I call to mind some of his observations, when on the morn following our interview with the dying chief, we sat under a cypress, the tallest of the American trees, on the top of which the crane finds a resting-place, and the eagle builds her nest. "The original savage," said he, "like the Bedouin Arab, regards with disdain and proud independence all other classes of mankind, but especially those of their own nation who have degraded themselves by taking up their abodes within walls: he moves on slowly and reluctantly, while under no particular impulse. He considers ease as one of the greatest blessings of life, and is not readily roused from it but by the force of some potent passion; yet when moved by hunger to pursue his game, by revenge or hatred to destroy his adversary, or by national honour to engage an enemy, nothing in human nature can exceed the ardour of his exertions. When free from these passions, he conceives it useless and ridiculous to labour more than is necessary to satisfy the few wants that he has; such as to procure fish and game for his food; a bark-covered wigwam, which he prefers to a large house, saying the last must be very troublesome; and furs to exchange for spirits, with which to intoxicate himself. The little land appropriated for corn and tobacco is cultivated by the women, for the savage thinks it beneath him to cultivate his rich lands, or to exert any mental talents to become opulent. The same may be said respecting their conversion to Christianity, for which so much money has been cajoled out of the pockets of the credulous by knaves, and by fools who have believed these knaves. It is true a few savages allow themselves to be baptized, and have received a Christian name, but it has been done in the same way; and with similar ideas, as they would (from savage politeness) receive the honour of knighthood, or any other title from their red brethren, as they call Europeans. Reckless of consequences, the Indian is always governed by the impulse of the moment. He keeps up many of his ancient customs, one of which is that of painting black those prisoners he intends to destroy, and mixing red spots on the black with such as he purposes adopting. Another is that of whooping to announce his arrival with prisoners, and when the Indians encamp, they lie around a large fire, wrapped up in blankets, with their faces towards it. Many possess the talent for eloquence, and that of native poetry is found in perfection among them. Every idea, every conception, is clothed in image and metaphor. ' The bones of our deceased countrymen lie unburied,' says an American orator, ' they call out to us to revenge their wrongs ; and we must satisfy their request. Their spirits cry out against us, and they must be appeased. The genii, who are the guardians of our honour, inspire us with a resolution to seek the enemies of our murdered brethren. Let us go and devour those by whom they were slain. Let us console the spirits of the dead, and tell them they shall be revenged.' The North American, however, is inferior to what he formerly was, for much of his undaunted boldness has degenerated into submissiveness, and he has acquired no good quality in exchange ; indeed, it is a melancholy truth, that where the Indian tribes admit free intercourse with, and settlement of the Europeans among them, they shrink and melt away to nothing ; but those tribes who have more prudently retreated. as the Americanized Indians have advanced, retain the primitive energy of savage warriors."

Thus it was that my companion reasoned, and on viewing the immense tracts of uncultivated country lying contiguous to our road, his kindly feelings would often break out in observations upon the injustice with which the aboriginal tribes of people of this country had been treated ; while these remarks not unfrequently led him into dissertations on the fallacy of those political reasoners in Europe, who blindly assert that the human species have a tendency to increase beyond the means given by a boundless Providence for its support. " What dolts, what idiots we must all be," he would say, "to listen to Malthus and such insane writers as he is. What a monstrous absurdity it is to think there is a principle in the economy of Nature, by which population increases beyond the means of support. It is impugning the magnificent designs of the Creator, to call in question his vigilant and ever-sustaining providence. To say that God creates millions of thinking beings, only to put them to death by starvation, is to impeach the grand God of the universe.

" And who is it," he would add, musingly, " that gives vent to these abominations? Is it because eighteen millions of people happen to be spread in Great Britain and Ireland, that these things are uttered? Infamous fallacy! Why the lands of the world have never yet been half peopled. Immense tracts of lands, islands, and even continents, at this time are lying in near their primeval state, with the soil untouched since the beginning of the world. The waste lands could hold the existing population of the earth, and yet not be filled. Canada itself is capable of receiving and maintaining the whole of the people of Europe ; while the eighteen millions of the human species belonging to the little islands which have raised such needless alarm, might be transported to the banks of one of the mighty rivers in the United States, and it would hardly be known they had taken up their residence in the country.

" An American writer has said to us, ' Send over your entire population, the whole of the people of Europe, for we have plenty of room for you all, and for one hundred millions more.' And, moreover, has not Audobon, the ingenious naturalist, assured us that in the back woods of America he has seen a flight of pigeons so extremely numerous, that by calculating their numbers from the space they filled, he computes, that at half a pint a day each, their food must be eight millions seven hundred and twenty bushels per diem, which, whether by weight or measure, would be sufficient to support the eighteen millions of people of Great Britain for at least a week.

" Bedlam is well stocked with lunatics," the parson would add, " but still room should be found there for Malthus' partisans. Even without their emigrating, without sending a single Englishman from his native land, they might be provided for, and provided for abundantly. Nearly a fifth part of the lands of Great Britain are uncultivated, and the produce of more than three millions of acres is consumed by the keep of horses. Why not, then, cultivate the waste lands, and employ fewer horses? For every twenty thousand of which, thirty thousand fat oxen might be kept. Before the firebrand of rebellion blazed abroad, and the savage-painted Indians, with their tomahawks, took the field, prepared for the work of butchery, the sight was a most pleasing one, in passing through Canada, to behold the industrious British settlers, who mostly are neighbourly and kind to each other. They lived blessed with an abundance of food, and were cheerful and happy; but, in the genial seasons of the year, have to toil hard, that they may lay up their winter's supply. This condition of life, with the industrious and the healthy, is perhaps an enviable one; but to the idle and the infirm, it must be quite the contrary. The British government, shortly before I was here, seemed to have lost sight of profit—the legitimate object of colonization—for it had expended vast sums in fortifying the unproductive colony, and had acted an impolitic, and many thought it a cruel part, in giving veteran soldiers and sailors a small sum of money each as a commutation for the pensions their services had earned for the poor fellows, and sending them out ostensibly to become settlers in this country. In a few months most of these men had wasted and made away with all their money, when many of them contrived to get back to their native land, to laugh at the government they had jockeyed, and become paupers on their previously over-burdened parishes."

Without any memorable occurrence on the way, my companion and I arrived safe and well at Quebec, highly delighted and instructed by what we had seen.

CHAPTER XX.

"Is love array'd
In threats like these, and thus convey'd?
Go bind the winds, or bid them veer,
The ocean smooth, the earth unsphere;
But seek not love with force or fear!"

"Money has a power above
The stars and fate to manage love;
Whose arrows, learned poets hold,
That never miss, are tipped with gold."

"He turned to pass away,
But the stern stranger motioned him to stay.
A word!—I charge thee stay."

"'Tis he? how came he thence?—what doth he here?"

My travelling companion and I were so well pleased with each other, that, by an agreement entered into on the journey, we now put up at the same hotel, and both of us having come provided with letters of introduction to highly respectable persons, we speedily became known to most of the leading characters in Quebec. However, as my business is to confine myself entirely to the relation of matters requisite to my memoirs, and many were the discontented republican-principled people at this time resident here, I shall avoid entering into any detail of the society I met with, further than to observe, that among the individuals with whom it was our good fortune to get acquainted, was a lady verging towards her fortieth year. She was the widow of a celebrated dealer in furs, who, on one of his excursions, in the way of business, to the territory of an Indian tribe, foolishly had been induced to take the field with these un-civilized friends of his, on a predatory service against another tribe at war with them, and it was his misfortune in the campaign to get tomahawked and killed; when his heart had been cooked and eaten by the cannibals, his conquerors.

This grievous calamity extremely affected the poor sufferer's relict; insomuch, indeed, that she lost her reason in consequence of it. Time, however, that balmy comforter, which can assuage even a widow's woe, made all things right with her again; and as she was wealthy, for the fur dealer, her husband, was reported to have died worth twenty thousand pounds, which in reality he did, the gentle dame, in due course of time, procured many admirers.

The soundest reasoning is that which is demonstrable by facts; therefore, the better to prove the truth of the Jesuit's assertion made in these memoirs, that "education is everything and crime cannot be greater than the conscience makes it," I think it incumbent to mention that shortly after the widow's happy restoration to reason, the Indian chief, whom it was killed her husband, and had his heart cooked and served up on his board, paid a visit to Quebec;

when, on being questioned upon what they called his inhuman conduct, in having feasted on the merchant's heart, this renowned savage, so far from expressing contrition on the occasion, made a merit of what he had done, by telling his questioners, that they would have given the man's heart as food for the worms, but that he had bestowed a more honourable sepulchre on it. Moreover, this great chief, who most appropriately had been christened "the Wolf," and whose name should be passed down to posterity with those of other famed heroes, proved himself on this occasion to be as philanthropic as he was heroic: inasmuch as, when her friends communicated to him the circumstance of his having made a disconsolate widow, by tomahawking the fur merchant, he spontaneously offered the fullest reparation, by taking the lady to himself in place of a squaw of his who had been captured and allotted to one of his party by the Fox, an Indian warrior of a tribe then at war with the tribe of "the Wolf."

The fair widow, it seems, preferred a state of celibacy to a union with this brave and disinterested man, for he was permitted to return home to his native wilds, unaccompanied by her.

In refined life we cannot boast of finding many such magnanimous characters as "the Wolf." He, to make reparation to a woman, a stranger to him, for having killed her husband in fair combat, freely proffered to take the widow to his bosom, to share his all with her, and make her his partner through the vale of life. He, however, who would accuse "the Wolf" of making this offer because the widow possessed wealth, would wrong him extremely, for this disinterested hero never had heard of, or thought of inquiring into, to him, so trivial a circumstance.

Well would it be for certain quacks, who hasten thousands of their fellow creatures on the great journey of futurity, to cogitate over the conduct of this generous Indian; and to think whether the great David or the wise Solomon ever had such abundantly stocked harems as they themselves would have, where they to take to their bosoms all the fair widows of their making.

A rich widow, like ripe fruit, is sadly beset by wasps. Madam Chinchilla, at the time of my arrival at Quebec, had already wasted away several valuable years of her life in a state of widowhood; but her professed admirers were at this time numerous, and she had refused many offers of marriage. Report now gave out that she was on the eve of being united to a Captain Hardsides, a Bostonian, who had realized a considerable fortune by traffic, and dealt largely with the Indians in furs.

Idle report, like character, goes a great way with the world; yet they may both have been engendered by deceit; and, after all, what more is character than the colouring of a picture by interested parties? and what is report but the offspring of a well-intentioned or a wicked imagination? The philosopher values these fleeting deceivers at a low rate, and wisely judges of men and of events for himself; but the great body, called the world, too often take these false counters for real coin, and consequently join in blasting the characters of the worthy to please the invidiously base; while, by believing in report, they not unfrequently make it the parent of reality. The report now alluded to doubtless had been set afloat by Captain Hardsides and his partisans, and it had spread so generally, that the fair widow was often jeered on the subject of her approaching marriage—for that married she must be to the captain, was almost everybody's opinion. He was a rough sailor, and, as a Bostonian, one of the race of such hard dealing people, that no Israelite to his time had been able to pick up a livelihood in the town of Boston. How this gentleman had got his money no person in Quebec save himself could tell, for he had spent his best days away in remote regions, but how or where formed a tale which he never told. For my own part, from all which I heard, and what I saw of the man, I could come to no other conclusion than that he had been a buccaneer; while so disagreeable a fellow was he, that in my heart this was the only meritorious thing I could find in him.

Captain Hardsides was an indefatigable gallant. He allowed the widow no rest; but whether it was agreeable to her or otherwise, he would be a visiter at her house. Apparently he was of the Quaker Hilkier's way of thinking, when he says,

"He that woos a maid, must seldom come in her sight,
But he that woos a widow, must woo her day and night."

And I make no question, but that eventually his perseverance would have been crowned with the desired success, had it not been for the following circumstances.

Madam Chinchilla, for reasons best known to herself, grew cool in her behaviour towards the captain, almost from the day when I had the honour of becoming known to her; while, for my part, novice as I was in the affairs of gallantry, yet I saw too plainly the many advantages to be attained by securing the affections of a widow lady, with twenty thousand pounds at her disposal, not to exert my best efforts for so laudable a purpose.

The captain, who witnessed my attentions to the widow, and saw that they were most favourably received, while that he and his attentions were ill-requited by her on my account, grew furiously angry; when, in the first instance, instead of striving to gain her over by additional kindnesses, and devising means to lower me in her estimation, he was insane enough to remonstrate with, and reproach the lady, for her unkindness to him; and also tax her with showing partiality towards a mere boy, as he thought fit to term me.

Madam Chinchilla, by judicious management, possibly might have been soothed into the views of the sturdy sailor, but she was not a lady to be intimidated by his threats. She retorted rather severely upon the veteran gallant, on which he grew still more furious, and the result was that she forbade him her house.

Often have I reflected with astonishment on this part of my history: as who, with one grain of sense, could suppose that a rough old sailor, past the meridian of life, would attempt by means of blustering to turn a widow woman's heart about like a weathercock, and compel her to give up a young lover, who was pleasing to her, to bestow her person, her wealth, and affections upon himself. The Bostonian, whose heart was set upon her wealth, felt highly indignant and mortified at being discarded in an abrupt manner by the widow; but he, being a revengeful man, yet knowing no good was likely to result to him from further altercation with her, determined to bring me to book for the conquest I had made, as he thought, at his expense.

Accordingly, he sent me a message by a friend of his, a naval officer of the United States, calling upon me to resign all pretensions to Madam Chinchilla, or otherwise to meet him, at an appointed spot on the ramparts, at the dawn of the following day, to render the satisfaction due to an injured gentleman. The bearer of the challenge was a blustering fellow, much like the challenger himself, and he thought to intimidate me by his arrogant manner, but I treated him with merited contempt; and being very sensible that there was no alternative in a case of this nature, I abruptly dismissed the naval gentleman, saying I should be punctual to the time and place.

He who has served among buccaneers never thinks of flinching from fighting a duel, at least where there is no shorter way of getting rid of a foe, and none such did I desire; therefore I provided myself with a second from amongst my coffee-house friends, and armed with an excellent brace of hair-trigger pistols, at the appointed time we proceeded together to the ramparts. Captain Hardsides was a man of business in this way, therefore no superfluous words passed between us; but I won the toss, and so took the first fire.

I was too good a shot to waste ammunition fired at a man only twelve paces distant from me, consequently I saved the captain the necessity of drawing a trigger on this occasion. He fell, the seconds thought, mortally wounded; when I, with an appetite sharpened by the morning air, proceeded to a coffee-house outside the city to get my breakfast.

The news of this affair spread like wildfire, and, of course, one of the first persons to hear of it was the fair widow. I am told she was absolutely distracted on the occasion, not that she cared a straw about the captain, but from the apprehension of the consequences which might arise to me from having killed him.

By the advice of my confidential friends, I staid away in the country for several days after the duel; but, during this time, I was honoured with many kind messages from Madam Chinchilla; when now, the captain, so far from dying of his wound, was announced to have survived the dangerous crisis; and the person who brought me this grateful news was the amiable widow herself.

To a young fellow like myself, it seemed rather a preposterous thing to get tied in wedlock to a lady much my elder; but twenty thousand pounds outweighed all other considerations, and I now hinted to the fair widow that, after the duel I had fought on her account, I thought marriage was the only way of saving her character from the shafts of scandal; when her sentiments coinciding with what I said, our union was agreed upon.

With fair woman, there is nothing like bringing matters to a close while her inclination is warm. I was not in the smallest degree afraid of any change taking place in the widow's sentiments, yet, as I thought some officious persons might step forward to talk to her of making a settlement of her property upon herself, or else of a dower, or some other such mercenary arrangement, to deprive me of all control over her wealth, and which might have put a termination to our projected marriage, I told the fair, that, to prevent all chance of our happiness being frustrated, I must insist on making it a condition that we returned not to Quebec until after the Hymeneal knot had been tied. She agreed to my proposition; when, at my suggestion, the better to accomplish our purpose, we journeyed to an hotel on the high road, some few miles from the city; meanwhile, my friendly travelling companion, the clergyman, to whom I had sent an express on the occasion, procured a licence of marriage, and, on the following morning, accompanied by the gentleman who had officiated as my second in the duel, and another coffee-house acquaintance, whom he brought to be witnesses to the ceremony, the worthy parson celebrated our marriage in a neighbouring chapel.

My duel with the Bostonian captain, and my marriage with Madam Chinchilla, served as a nine days' wonder to the people of Quebec; but I had now provided an excellent house over my head, and got a large additional fortune placed out at interest, therefore I cared as little regarding the people's opinion as a sailor, when he has retired to bed on shore, cares which way the wind blows.

The jade Fortune cannot content everybody. If I was well pleased, Captain Hardsides was far from being so. He saw his old mistress's happiness and her youthful husband's satisfaction, with sensations of anger and discontent, which increased upon him every day, and served to make him the laughing-stock of those persons who dared to laugh at so formidable a personage.

Money, like manure, is of no utility until it gets spread. This is a truth, of which, thank my stars, I have always been so thoroughly satisfied, that I have ever lived nearly up to my income, whatever it has been. At this time I lived like a wealthy lord, and yet, as most things are cheap at Quebec, my expenditure fell materially short of my rental.

My unhappy rival, who probably would have got more reconciled to his disappointment, had he seen me a miserly fellow, incapable of enjoying the wealth I had not got possession of, could not contain his feelings of anger at witnessing my lavish profusion, but vented them every day, by reporting, in his vulgar manner among his associates, that I was an extravagant youngster, who would soon bring himself and his wife to a mouthful of bread. Some officious person or other invariably brought his remarks to my ears, but their effect was only that of making me laugh, and becoming more ostentatious in my extravagance.

A duellist, like a game bird, is shy of engaging again in mortal combat with his conqueror; consequently the captain, though he was highly nettled at my behaviour, and would not from any other man have put up with such taunts as I wantonly threw out to provoke him, yet showed his forbearance by never sending me a second challenge. But I think his avarice would have stimulated him to do so, had I not, by my marriage with her, have put the widow's cash entirely beyond his reach.

In this manner we jogged on for a few weeks, my lady and I enjoying ourselves in every way to which money and contented hearts could conduce, and the Bostonian continually fretting himself at witnessing our profusion and happiness.

A certain philosopher has said, that happiness is not the child of imagination, but the shadow of content; consequently, where the substance is, the shadow must follow. This philosopher's assertion I believe to be grounded on fact, for, verily, whenever I have been content, I have been happy; for which reason I now strive to avoid discontent, as I would any raging pestilence of the day.

I was youthful, healthy, and rich, and daily heard tell of the pleasures to be enjoyed in Europe, by visiting famed places, and participating in innumerable amusements, not to be found in a city such as Quebec; and in consequence, I became desirous of crossing the Atlantic to visit my native land. Man, however, only rows in the voyage of life; he is steered by Fate, and not unfrequently knows no more where he is going to, than did Adrian of the journey his fleeting spirit was about to take, when he invoked it just before its flight.

A wife of mature years will generally be found ready to humour her youthful husband in any reasonable whim he may form. I found no difficulty in getting Mrs Winpenny into the mind to dispose of our property in America, that we might remove together to Europe, to enjoy the sweets of a finer climate, and the advantages of a more extensive circle of acquaintance than Quebec could afford. But, though the good woman fell into my views, still she entertained certain local attachments to Italy, the country of her birth, which made her extremely unwilling to fix upon England as the place of our future residence; and she adduced so many convincing reasons to show that Italy was in all respects the preferable country to reside in, that I yielded to the force of her arguments, and it was therefore agreed upon that Italy should be the land of our abode, and Genoa, or its neighbourhood, the spot.

The greatest part of my wife's money had been invested in Italian stock, long previous to the time of my becoming acquainted with her; and we now busied ourselves in disposing of several houses, and some other property we had in Quebec, that we might either remit the produce to Italy, or carry it there with us in good bills of exchange.

Those who are earnest in a business of this sort, require not much time to accomplish this object. Ours was speedily effected, and we were only awaiting the departure of a vessel for Leghorn, which my wife was most anxious for the sailing of, as her health had now become alarmingly delicate, when the following unlooked-for event threatened to mar all my bright prospects.

One day I was on my way to the docks, when, to my inconceivable astonishment, who should I meet but the Bostonian captain, walking arm-in-arm with my old commander, Lieutenant Jones, whom I would most gladly have avoided; but he had eyed me before I saw him, and leaving his companion some paces behind, he hastened after me, when having overtaken me, for I was walking away from them, he addressed me by saying most familiarly, " Andrew, my old shipmate, you have given me a precious long cruise in search of you; but here you are safe, and in gallant trim, within gun range of me. I shall now overhaul your lockers, and take into my sure keeping some of the many thousands of sterling pounds which you have got possession of, by heaving our old governor into Davy's locker."

For the ears of a young and wealthy benedict this was a most uncourteous address, and I confess I did not at all relish the salutation; but the want of self-command is not my foible, and I knew better than to show my anger where I could not injure. Besides, the terrific fellow I had to deal with, hitherto I had been accustomed to view with feelings of awe, and they were not to be shaken off without some considerable exertion.

" You are welcome to Quebec, Mr Jones," said I, almost choking with vexation while I spoke the words; " I trust you have made a prosperous voyage to South America."

" Ah, my youngster," rejoined he, " this sort of palaver may pass current amongst landsmen, but we have other fish to fry, and I will go home with you and look at your reckoning.''

" If there is a place of purgatory, I heartily wish you were there," thought I, but I took especial good care not to say so, for I felt that this was an affair where the most able generalship was called for; therefore, assuming as much composure as I could on so trying an occasion, I observed, that what we might have to say to each other, had best be done in private, while that, provided he got rid of his companion, I would accompany him to a retired coffee-house for this purpose.

" An old shipmate and brother buccaneer may be trusted; besides, the man knows all about this business already; howsoever, since you wish it to be so, and mayhap we may then arrange the thing more to our own advantage, I'll propose to him to sheer off," was the lieutenant's reply to my proposition. A few words were now exchanged in conversation between two men whom I would willingly have seen kept from me by the bars of a prison; after which, Mr Jones led me away with him to a retired inn, where, when closeted with each other, a good deal of conversation passed between us.

By what I gathered from his discourse, it appeared that Mr Jones had returned to Porto Rico from his mission to the South Seas shortly after the time when the Spanish captain arrived there with a fresh cargo of slaves; and that this captain, who, like most other speculative men, could not be satisfied with any share of wealth while he thought more might be obtained, had shown extreme inveteracy against me for my having been made Robertson's heir; and because my agent, Mr Jenkinson, had taken some legal measures to make him account for the share of the slaver and her cargo, to which I had become entitled as part of my inheritance. The ungrateful fellow, too, though he stood indebted to my benefactor for the command of the

Saucy Jack, as also numerous other favours, by which he had grown into considerable wealth, yet now sought to monopolize to himself the whole of this vessel, together with the produce of her last cargo; and assuredly he would have succeeded in his object, but for the well-timed steps taken by Jenkinson, who, on my behalf, had got an injunction placed on the property in question. Baulked as he was in his views, still the unprincipled Spaniard resigned not his object; therefore, Lieutenant Jones's arrival at Porto Rico at this critical period he hailed as an auspicious event, inasmuch as he thoroughly well knew the lieutenant's character, and to what lengths self-interest might urge him to proceed against me. Accordingly, Lieutenant Jones had scarcely put foot ashore before the Spaniard made him his confidant, and the lieutenant being almost as indignant as he was, at finding that I, whom he had always looked upon as a youngster dependent on himself, had become master of Captain Robertson's wealth, most readily joined with him in devising measures to rob me of a part, or, if possible, of the whole of the rich inheritance.

With this object in view, it was agreed upon between the well-matched pair, that Mr Jones should follow after me to the United States, to overtake me in my travels; when it was thought that, by his influence over me, he would be successful in making me surrender up a portion of the deceased Robertson's wealth, or where, perhaps, by making away with me, or intimidating me by threats, they might strip me of the whole of it. Moreover, I afterwards found these heroes purposed dividing everything between them, and going into partnership in trade together.

The lieutenant, with more than blood-hound sagacity, had traced me to every place where I had been. The only lucky circumstance on my side was, that he had not found his way to Quebec before Madam Chinchilla exchanged her name for that of Winpenny; for had that happened, most assuredly my old rival, the Bostonian, would then have triumphed over me.

The lieutenant, who cared not a sou in what manner Robertson had met his death, had scarcely put a question to me on the subject, yet showed himself extremely earnest to be made acquainted with the precise sum of money which I had already netted by that event, as also regarding how much more I expected: I, however, waved the subject, and accounted for my present wealth as being most of it the fruits of my happy marriage.

Lieutenant Jones was not the man to credit this tale of mine; consequently, he blustered a great deal, and attempted to frighten me into his views; yet I continued firm in my manner, and at length he pretended to believe me; but perhaps the knowledge he had of the duel I had fought had some effect in making him act so compliantly. Nevertheless, in spite of his concession, we had much conversation on this occasion, and some of it very acrimonious; however, the lieutenant, who had views upon me beyond what he avowed, so mollified his tone, that towards the close of our interview he became somewhat communicative, when in reply to a question of mine, regarding his acquaintance with the Bostonian Captain Hardsides, he gave me to understand that he was an old buccaneer commander, who had for many years been concerned with the deceased Robertson and their Spanish friend, the captain of the Saucy Jack, at Porto Rico, both in the slave trade and buccaneering adventures.

This piece of information opened my eyes to the real character of my old rival, for it instantly brought to my mind that he could be no other than the notorious pirate Martinus, long the terror of all honest navigators in the South Seas, and afterwards in the Gulf of Florida, and whose companions, most of them had been executed for piracy; some at New Orleans, and others at the point at Port Royal, in Jamaica. He himself had been outlawed by several states, and eventually compelled to resign the command he had of a slaver, and to fly from Porto Rico, in consequence of a murder perpetrated by him on a priest in a confessional box of the church there. "Young man," said the lieutenant at our parting, for well he remembered former days, and on the strength of them thought to still arrogate authority over me, "do you see, I mean to let you off on easy terms; but reflect upon it well before we again meet, for, by the powers, I must share with you some of the old commodore's doubloons. Think of it, Andrew, and bear in mind that I am not to be shuffled."

"I know you, Mr Jones," replied I, "you are a man of your word; and, believe me, though I am not to be intimidated, yet I will do what is right."

CHAPTER XXII.

" 'Tis true they are a lawless brood,
  But rough in form, nor wild in mood,
  And every creed and every race
  With them hath found—may find a place."

"'And vengeance vow'd for those who fall,
  Hath made them fitting instruments
  For more than e'en my own intents."

"'Time at last sets all things even ;
  And if we do but watch the hour
  There never yet was human power
  Which could evade, if unforgiven,
  The patient search, and vigil long,
  Of him who treasures up a wrong."

IT was fearful odds for a young man to have to cope against two such desperate characters as I now had to deal with ; for that Jones and Hardsides would lay their heads together to my detriment, to rob or even to destroy me, I made no question ; indeed, I was so thoroughly satisfied on the subject, that it filled my mind with serious reflections during the time I traced my steps home from the interview with Lieutenant Jones. Happily, however, I knew my men. I recollected how readily the lieutenant had obeyed his commander's orders, when he barbarously made away with the captain and crew of the Columbine ; while, as to Hardsides, alias Martinus, I doubted not, from his character and the ill-will he bore towards me, but that he would readily have joined with his friend in flaying me alive for the sake of my wealth. Heathen priestcraft, from those amongst all the motley garbs she wears, would find a difficulty in producing two more determined and dangerous individuals. Had we been living under an Italian sky, in a state where assassination is winked at by the lay government, and encouraged by the crime-absolving, and consequently more tolerating one of the church, my enemy might readily have got rid of me, and thus have ensured to himself a share of the Saucy Jack and her last cargo, even had he not devised means of robbing me of some of the wealth I had in North America ; but, luckily for me, I was not in a country under the dominion of the descendant of that St Peter, who is said to have been Bishop of Rome for twenty years, under the Emperor Nero, who himself reigned only thirteen years ; but I was in North America, where crime is watched with more eyes than Argus ever possessed, and punished with unrelenting severity. I arrived at home in no very enviable mood, and would fain have embarked and set sail for Europe that same day, without giving publicity to my determination, had an opportunity occurred of my doing so. This, however, was impossible, and I puzzled my brains to no good purpose to decide what I had best do regarding Mr Jones, whose avarice I knew was not to be contented by my presenting him with a sum of money, otherwise, for old acquaintance sake, I would thus have compromised the business. I was still deliberating upon this unpleasant affair, when in the afternoon of the same day, Captain Hardsides made his appearance at my house, bringing a message from the lieutenant, whereby he required of me to meet them at a place of my own appointing on the following day, and to bring with me two thousand dollars for Mr Jones, of which he stood in immediate need.

It is folly to despair. The insolence of the message, combined with the arrogant manner of the messenger, at once made me decide on the steps I should pursue ; therefore, the better to succeed in my project, I affected to take in good part all that was said, and in compliance with the lieutenant's expressed wish, made an appointment to meet him and his friend the captain on the following evening, at a cabaret of my naming, a little way outside of the town.

I make no doubt that Hardsides thought all was as it should be, for after he had minutely noted down the time and place for our meeting each other, and given me a caution not to forget the dollars, he departed, apparently highly satisfied with the result of his embassy ; and no sooner was he fairly out of the house, than I sallied forth to prepare measures for ridding myself of these troublesome characters, in a way which I have now to explain.

I had, previous to Hardsides' visit, called to mind the circumstance, that an Indian chief of my acquaintance, named "the Fox," and a party of his followers, were at that time sojourning in Quebec; and I knew that with this chief I could do pretty well what I pleased, but still I had not made my mind up to employ him as my partisan, in getting rid of Lieutenant Jones; now, however, that I saw there would be no contenting the lieutenant, and that Hardsides, alias Martinus, acted in collusion with him, I judged, that if they went on unmolestedly in their machinations, ruin, and perhaps death, would fall to my lot, and, therefore, in self-defence, I decided to act a determined part with them both; with which view, well knowing the usual haunts of "the Fox," I now went in search of him.

Here it is necessary I should explain that "the Fox" was the celebrated chief in whose cause Monsieur Chinchilla had got killed, fighting most gallantly by his side. "The Fox" had for many years been in the habit of bartering away furs to Monsieur Chinchilla, and, like a true Indian friend, since that gentleman's death, had unceasingly done his best to obtain vengeance against the hostile tribe from which he met his fate; but "the Wolf," who was the head of that tribe, and the individual who tomahawked him, was too powerful a chief to be overcome by "the Fox;" nevertheless, this last had so far watched a favouring opportunity, that, on an occasion when "the Wolf" was absent from home, he and his people had not only tomahawked "the Wolf's" mother, but scalped all the children, infirm persons, and women, in the village.

In the arts of war, Ulysses himself was not a more subtle shuffler than "the Fox." He was master of most of the wily tricks for which Homer so vastly extols the divinity Pallas; but in peace, "the Fox" was a perfect Bacchus—a never-flinching, jolly companion. He and "the Wolf," in their native wilds, were almost constantly warring against each other; they each eagerly coveted the other's scalp, and each of them had lost in this warfare his dearest friends and nearest relatives; yet, when at Quebec together, they daily smoked the calumet of peace, and would so laugh and jest with each other, on both olden and passing events, that any one who witnessed their glee, and was unacquainted with the histories of these famous men, would naturally have supposed them to be warriors belonging to the same tribe, who held only one interest, and had the same object in view.

"The Fox" happened to be housed in the first petty inn where I sought after him, and what was a rare thing with him when in Quebec, he was sober as a parson ought to be when displaying his eloquence from a pulpit. "Friend Andrew," said he, on my entrance, addressing me with his accustomed familiarity, "how is your wife? Her first husband was my sworn friend, and he died fighting bravely by my side; say, can I do any service either for you or for her?"

"A faithful friend is a real treasure; Chinchilla was such to thee; and thou wilt prove one wherever thy promise of friendship is given," was my reply.

"Yes," rejoined he, "were it to exterminate an entire tribe of my countrymen, if I had promised as much, I would do it. The leaves should fall one by one, till the tree or I myself perished."

"You are a great warrior, and have a heart as true as it is stout," said I; "your name carries terror with it into the innermost wigwams of your foes; 'the Wolf' himself cannot rest while thou art in his neighbourhood; the scalp of a squaw of his, together with those of many of his warriors, hangs behind your door; but still, my friend, war, however glorious it is, must interfere with your fur trade; you can have little time left you for hunting the beaver."

"Right, you say right," answered 'the Fox;' "I have got plenty of scalps, but I have no rum; and the dogs of merchants here, since I can bring them no skins of the beaver, refuse to give me credit for tobacco and rum."

"I am going to the land of my fathers," said I. "The sun, when it shines upon you, will leave me in the darkness of night; and I have come here, my good friend, to say that I have two puncheons of rum warehoused here, which are quite at your service; and of the smoking weed, I can supply you with as much as you want."

"It is a gift you make worthy of the husband of Chinchilla's squaw. The rum and five hundred weight of tobacco I will myself see borne away to my factor's to-morrow; but say, Andrew, is there no piece of service I can do for you, before you go hence for the land of your fathers?" "Brave chief! there are two scoundrels, two sworn foes of mine living here, who wish to rob me—to strip me of my Chinchilla's fortune. To-morrow evening I am to meet them at an inn beyond the fortifications of Quebec. I ask no other favour of thee, than to forcibly bear them away with thee to thy country, so that they shall be heard of no more in this quarter for at least one month to come." "Take me to the place where you are to meet these men, and point them out to me, and I swear, by the sacred bones of my father, to fulfil these desires of yours regarding them. They shall go with me to my own country, and sleep there to eternity, sooner than regain their freedom before the moon of next month is as old as is now the present moon."

More of our conversation I need not relate, for the mind of man is known to be the same in whatever circumstances the individual may be placed, and, unquestionably, the same motives of action govern all equally, whatever may be their situation. "The Fox," like more civilized men, was open to flattery and a bribe. He loved rum and tobacco too well to resist the temptations they afforded, while the sound of his own praises was the sweetest of music to the ears of this savage.

Besides the spirit of enterprise and the passion of revenge animated his heart, and in punishing my enemies he gratified the former, and persuaded himself that he was revenging Chinchilla's death, by promoting the interests of his relict.

Thus it is that reason is made subservient to education. This warrior had been trained in the way his father wished him to go, and he followed it with filial fidelity. But every nation, religion, and people have their peculiar way of training the youth as he should go, and after making allowance for the customs of all, it would puzzle philosophy, and make sceptics grow more sceptical, to attempt a decision upon which is the best education.

Two puncheons of rum and five hundred weight of tobacco, which I purchased expressly for the purpose, were that same day conveyed by my directions to the store of the fur merchant with whom "the Fox" carried on his dealings; and early on the evening of the following day, by a preconcerted arrangement, "the Fox" and six of his men hid themselves in ambush in the yard of the cabaret, where my meeting with the two formidable buccaneers was to take place.

Captain Hardsides and Lieutenant Jones entered the house in question before I made my appearance there, as, by design, I was a little behind my time. "Well, youngster," said the lieutenant, on my entrance, "you think nothing of keeping your elders waiting for you; but receivers generally are more ready than paymasters; where, however, is the money?"

"Money is a scarce article, and I must disappoint your expectations for once. What say you to a draught upon a merchant at Porto Rico? Will not that suit you nearly as well as ready cash?" "Blood and wounds! what is it you mean, youngster? Has life become a burden to you, that you wish to part with it? Come, none of your shuffling, where are the two thousand dollars?"

"I have come here unprovided with cash, but am ready and willing to give you a bill of exchange upon our friend the Spanish merchant at Porto Rico, who, you know, is my debtor to a large amount, on account of the Santissima Trinidada, or Saucy Jack, and her last slave cargo."

"Villain!" thundered the lieutenant, "make your confession, for you have not ten minutes to live;" and he seized me by the collar while he spoke. "Spare his life, Jones, conditionally, that he signs an order for two thousand pounds on his wife, instead of giving the dollars, and we will keep him our prisoner till we have the money," said the considerate Hardsides.

"Captain Martinus," replied I, "as you well know the people of Porto Rico, you must know that the bill I proffer is a good one; therefore, instead of money, advise your friend to take my bill of exchange."

This last speech of mine stirred the rage of my opponents to a sort of climax; but still they knew better than to slay me, as my murder would have marred their prospects of extorting money from me, and in all probability brought their necks to the halter; their fury, however, was so great, that they threw me down, and began belabouring me with their fists; but I bawled out lustily for assistance, when almost instantly "the Fox" and his followers rushed into the room, and in defiance of their outcries and efforts to prevent them, pinioned my opponents, each with his elbows tight together behind him.

"By my soul," stammered the lieutenant, "this young fellow will prove a master of his trade; he has got us both in his power beyond all redemption, and these Indians, no doubt, are commissioned to slay us." "Would that I myself had thought of employing such people, instead of fighting as I did, like a fool as I am," muttered the chop-fallen captain.

A victory, such as I had gained, was a great triumph. I, however, neither insulted the conquered, nor relieved their minds from the misery attendant on the expectation of being butchered.

The Indians, as had been preconcerted between us, led the captives away gagged and pinioned; but previous to their doing this, "the Fox" took the pistols and everything else he thought worth taking from their persons, which he, hero like, made his own, and agreeable to his education, considered himself justly entitled to.

In this adventure I could not fail admiring the acuteness shown by "the Fox." He performed his part in a most masterly manner; and though his face was hidden in a mask, procured by me for the occasion, yet, not satisfied with this partial disguise, he had clothed himself in an Indian chief's dress, the very counterpart of that usually worn by "the Wolf." Thanks to which, at a future day he would fearlessly re-visit Quebec; while this old enemy of his, who was not likely ever to hear tell of this affair, would hereby have his life and liberty placed in jeopardy in his future visits to the city.

The landlord of the cabaret where this adventure took place was a man I had served, and in whom I could confide, on which account it was that I made choice of his house as the scene for this adventure. He, of course, had taken good care that no individual of his family, save himself, should be at home to witness what took place, and to his heart's content I remunerated him for his services on the occasion.

I have reasons for believing that "the Fox" carried his captives from the neighbourhood of Quebec tied up in sacks; but how far he conveyed them on their way by water, and how far by land, are circumstances of which I am totally ignorant, nor have I ever learnt whether he let them go free at the expiration of the promised month; though, as an American Indian, faithful to his promise, I presume he must have done so. These were things I left entirely to chance, and, indeed, which I cared little about, for my mind was quite made up to bid adieu, not only to Quebec, but to the quarter of the globe to which this city belongs, and that long before another moon could show her bright face to its shores.

CHAPTER XXIII.

"And their baked lips with many a bloody crack,
Suck'd in the moisture which like nectar stream'd.
Their throats were ovens, their swoln tongues were black."

"Ah, mariner! in wayward hour
Ye brav'd the whirlwind's power."

"Long on the ocean tempest toss'd,
At last we gain the happy coast;
And safe recount upon the shore
Our sufferings past and dangers o'er."

THERE is nothing like being prompt in business which really ought to be done. The vessel destined for Leghorn was not to sail for some days after the Indian chief's departure with my two enemies in his good custody, but there was a French brig lying in the harbour, which was to sail for Marseilles the very next day, and to me it was a matter of indifference to which of these places I proceeded.

Very opportunely too, at this critical epoch, I had the satisfaction of receiving most agreeable tidings from my agent at St Thomas's. His letter informed me that he had found it necessary to take legal measures against the captain of the Santissima Trinidada, alias the Saucy Jack, and that he had so far carried his point, as to have recovered a sum of rather better than eight thousand dollars from him on my account, which he held ready to remit to me whenever I communicated my pleasure on the subject.

As to my further claims, he said he feared nothing more could be got on account of the Saucy Jack, for that the captain had concocted strange and many claims against the vessel and her last cargo, which, though most of them evidently unjust, could not be controverted, in consequence of Robertson's death, and the evidence which ought to have been for us having been suborned on the other side. However, all things considered, he concluded by saying he must congratulate me on having recovered what was now got from so unprincipled a man; while that some of my claims for money due at Jamaica, he trusted, would be substantiated and cancelled by payment.

The preceding communication made my mind easy regarding my West Indian affairs, and having written to Mr Jenkinson, to notify that I was on the eve of sailing for Europe, whence he should have instructions from me, I proceeded to arrange my other affairs.

Accordingly, having talked over the business with my spouse, which I did on the same night I so happily had got rid of my two maritime enemies, and she entirely coinciding with me in my sentiments on the subject, at an early hour next morning I engaged for our passage to Marseilles, when, shortly afterwards, I caused my lady and my luggage to be shipped on board the vessel.

Even hot-headed commanders have made the avowal, that a prudent retreat not unfrequently is more advantageous than gaining a fresh victory. On this occasion I was of their opinion, and as soon as I had effected my business on shore, lost no time in hastening on board the French ship, which already had Blue Peter flying aloft, and her cable shortened ready for weighing anchor. The captain alone waited my arrival; therefore, shortly after my embarkation, his anchor was aboard her, and the ship under weigh, sailing from the harbour of Quebec.

"Adieu, a long adieu to the shores of the new world," said I to myself, while taking my farewell look at the land of America. I have run an adventurous, but a prosperous course, in this quarter of the world. My time has not been long here; who, however, can say I have not done more memorable deeds than some men perform in their entire lives? Cæsar, it is said, was prompt in execution. Yet, who can compare that bald-pated old robber, who worked with the hands of others, to a youth such as I am; one that, unaided by partisans, stands indebted to good luck and himself only for having inherited to the wealth of *one*, and got the mastery over *two*, of the most daring and experienced buccaneers, of all whose deeds the pen of history shall put upon record? Who shall compare that vile enslaver of his countrymen, that wholesale butcher of the human species, to a youth who, although born to poverty, and reared up in misery, counselled to by a pitiful-spirited parent, to make his penny how and where he could, has nevertheless, and at an early age, contrived to gather together a sum of sterling money amounting to near forty thousand pounds, with abundance of plate and jewellery besides.

An ordinary voyage at sea is a very common-place occurrence, of which it would ill become a buccaneer, who has suffered the most direful of shipwrecks, to attempt recording the particulars. In short, none except fine-weather travellers, who voyage only that they may write books, but are unprepared to face storms and untoward adventures, when they present themselves, would think of imposing such trash on their readers as it affords.

The La Sybelle, the ship we were on board, had a tolerable good voyage for seventeen days, during which we encountered some blowing weather, which made my spouse very sea sick, but we met with no severe storm. On the eighteenth morning, in latitude 44. 43. north, and longitude 21. 20. west, we came in sight of a wreck, which, as a signal of distress, had an old flag hoisted downwards, on a boom erected beside her broken main-mast.

Monsieur Jaconet, our captain, made sail for the wreck, when, on our hailing her, we were told that she was the Matilda, laden with timber, from St John's, New Brunswick, bound to Liverpool, and that the few survivors of her crew were in a state of starvation; and earnestly implored, for the salvation of their lives, that we would take them off the wreck.

Monsieur Jaconet was a humane man. He hesitated not a moment, but immediately hoisted out a boat, and had the poor sufferers, among whom were two females, conveyed to the La Sybelle. They were all of them in a most dreadful condition. I never before had seen such sad objects; squalid starvation was conspicuous in every face, which sunken eyes, hollow cheeks, and parched lips, combined to impress with a deadly hue. Our surgeon, however, a kind-hearted and skilful man, had the poor sufferers placed in warm beds, and supplied with food and drink in small quantities at a time; by which prudent treatment they were all, save one, gradually restored to health and strength. I shall attempt no particular description of them, but content myself by summing up their truly miserable story as briefly as possible; for, were I to extract it from their log-book, the detail of the protracted sufferings of these unfortunate people would be most heart-rending. The Matilda sailed from St. John's on the 18th January, and on the 1st February she was caught in a dreadful gale, which carried away her fore and mizen-masts, her cabouse, her jolly-boat, and disabled five of her men; the gale continuing, several days after she lost her long-boat, had her rudder unshipped, and a man washed overboard. The crew now cut away the anchors, and endeavoured to save some provision by knocking the bow-port out, for the ship was nearly full of water, and her stern stove in. The quantity saved was trifling; this they stowed away in the maintop, where they also got two females placed, who were on board—the master's wife, and a young single woman, a passenger, and where they themselves slept, lashed in the best way they could secure each other. For twenty-two days this scene of wretchedness continued, during which no less than eighteen out of twenty-four, the original number on board, perished by fatigue or starvation, or were washed alive into the ocean; and what was more horrible and degrading to humanity, the poor sufferers were necessitated to eat of the bodies of their starved companions, to keep life and soul together. At last, though not until after the single woman had partaken of the body of a man to whom she was betrothed, and the master's wife of that of her husband's apprentice—a poor youth, who had been three times wrecked before, and providentially saved, to come to this at last, and that several of the crew, from drinking salt water, had become foolish, crawled upon their hands about the deck, and died raving mad—it was the fate of the survivors to be extricated from their miserable state by the humanity of our good captain.

Monsieur Jaconet showed every possible attention to the poor sufferers, and supplied them with the best food in the ship; yet, prudently, he put them on a short allowance, that they might not destroy the powers of nature by repletion, as innumerable people in their situation are known to have done; and by this considerate care on the part of our commander, all, save one who died on the third day after they were brought aboard us, were happily restored to health.

James Monday, one of the survivors, a young Kentishman, who had been chief mate of the wrecked vesssel, and became disgusted with the sea service, I engaged in my employ; and, happily, after taking these poor people on board us, we met with no unpleasant adventure on the voyage, but arrived safe and well at Marseilles, after a favourable and rather a quick passage.

On landing at Marseilles, I proceeded to one of the best hotels, and the expense being no consideration, my wife and I lived here in splendid profusion. Everything was new to me. It appeared as if I had been transported into another world; theatres, coffee-houses, equestrian and other performances; indeed, all things and places tended to afford me gratification: and as to the French cookery, it was as delicious to my palate as the wines were excellent.

Marseilles, the capital city of Provence, is well worth visiting. Some writers pretend it was founded by the Greek exiles, who were driven out of their country by Cyrus the Great. The Romans courted the friendship of the citizens of Marseilles, and after the fall of Rome, it was governed by four counts; but, ultimately, the inhabitants, finding themselves unable to maintain their freedom, put themselves under the protection of France. The conditions of their submission were very honourable; but, under a Duke of Guise, general of the galleys, their privileges were abolished, and a citadel was erected on each side of the port. The arsenal and the galleys here are well worthy of a visit, yet the latter impress the mind with horror, at witnessing to what a state of degradation human beings may be brought. The vicissitudes of religion, too, are strongly exemplified here; for the church of Notre-Dame des Accoules was formerly consecrated to Pallas, that of Saint Saviour to Apollo, and the cathedral was the temple of Diana. In the last, the body of a Saint Lazarus is kept in a silver shrine, and the true cross of Saint Andrew, seven feet long, is shown. Indeed, the whole city abounds with holy relics; but at Saint Boume, on the road hence to Toulon, is a cave, in the midst of a rock, where lies Mary Magdalen's body, in a coffin seven feet long, and where Mary Magdalen, according to the tradition, lived thirty-three years; notwithstanding which, the place is always extremely cold, from the dropping of water from the impending rock, which fills a cistern below, with what priestcraft has denominated the virgin's tears.

In France, however, few persons, save dotards and children, care about relics or shrines: they have happier thoughts, and they know there is nothing like gaiety. Trouble is only the brooding of a distempered mind, and, happily, the French are not much afflicted this way; but *gai, toujours gai,* is a maxim followed by many of them from the nursery to the grave. They are a joyous people, and so are all others who set care at defiance; for care is a canker-worm to the heart, which none save a lunatic would nourish. Youthful as I was, and blessed with a light heart, the manners of the people here were exactly such as I should have been desirous of finding among persons I had to associate with. The men were all excellent companions; and the women, to do them justice, were all of them kind—aye, and the fair sex of Marseilles are pretty too; yet, notwithstanding my opinion, I know there are persons in the world, who presume to find fault with the Frenchman's character, saying that he is insincere, and professes a vast deal more than he means to perform; I, however, maintain that these people are partly in error, for that the Frenchman is about as sincere as his neighbours. He who doubts this, would do well to consult a few of his old acquaintances; and if any experienced individual of them should tell him that in his career he has found mankind to be sincere, no matter in what clime or country, he himself needs only to reside there for a short time to discover that this friend of his is a romancer.

There are exceptions, however, to all rules, for deformity is to be found even among the fairest productions of nature: and that which I now have to recount, furnishes a ludicrous instance of the variety in the Gallic character.

Among my acquaintances here, there was a certain chevalier, named Bruges; he was a dashing young fellow, the very pink of fashion, and the life of society wherever he moved; but, notwithstanding all this, I soon suspected that at bottom he was one of those enterprising characters known as *les chevaliers d'industrie.* This personage, whose society was courted everywhere, related to me how he had formed an intimacy with a very remarkable character—a nobleman living in the vicinity of Marseilles, who, like many great and distinguished persons that have lived before him, from a disease of the imagination, had fallen into unaccountably strange notions regarding his personal identity and character. The nobleman, the chevalier said, was an hypochondriac, who had been brought to this state from over-study, and whose cure could alone be hoped for by setting him to toil as a ploughman, or at some other sort of hard labour, where good air, strong exercise, and the sweat of his brow, might, by their combined powers, restore him to a sane sense of his condition. Gaspard Barlaas, a physician and poet, it is related, was deranged by study, until he fancied his body was converted into butter, and, in consequence, feared to approach the fire; but the nobleman, of whom I am speaking, was subject to many different delusions of the imagination: like a celebrated prince of the house of Bourbon, he would believe himself to be a woman, which, my informant laughingly added, was no very unusual thing amongst the aristocracy and the clergy of that country; but his most usual fancy, the chevalier said, was to suppose himself the Arcadian Silenus, when, in imitation of him, he would ride over his pleasure grounds on an ass, and conclude the exploits of the day, by getting gloriously inebriated.

Sportive mirth is often the parent of frolicsome adventure. There was a something so ludicrous in this noble person's insanity, that the chevalier and I laughed most heartily about it; until at length, from laughing, we began to devise whether we could make his diseased imagination the source of some humorsome adventure.

The chevalier was fertile in expedients. He also had been well educated, and consequently knew much of the nonsense of the heathen, as well as of certain other absurd mythologies. After a little consideration, he told me he thought he had hit the right nail on the head, and that provided I would personify the King of Phrygia, he would persuade his insane friend that he would take him to a feast in the Elysian shades, at which Midas should be present to entertain him, as he once did Silenus's foster son Bacchus.

Of Bacchus I had frequently heard tell, but of Midas and Silenus knew nothing; and I'll take on me to warrant that my old companions the baccaneers knew as little; nevertheless, I took on myself the task of acting the part of Midas, for the purpose of deceiving silly Silenus; but with this proviso, that the chevalier was to dress me in a way suitable to the part, and give me my proper cue how to act.

The nobleman not only readily fell into the snare we had laid for him, but was in raptures of joy on the occasion, and in the warmth of his heart declared the chevalier to be the best friend he had in the world, for ensuring to him a feast in the Elysian shades, with the ghost of Midas as one of his festive companions.

The farce we had projected was performed to admiration. In a cellar lit by torch lights, fumigated with brimstone, and hung around with curious old goblin tapestry, a costly supper was laid out, to partake of which the chevalier brought the hypochondriac nobleman blindfolded to this Elysian shade; when, on having his eyes uncovered, they were dazzled by the brilliancy of the light, and his senses bewildered at beholding the imposing scene; but most especially me, seated as Midas, at the head of the table, habited in a grotesque satin dress, with long asses' ears attached to my head, which hung dangling over my shoulders.

We made a jovial feast of it, well worthy of Bacchus's foster father, who enjoyed himself to his heart's delight; but, when the juice of the grape began to operate, was rather troublesome in his attempt at pulling my borrowed ears, the length and hairyness of which entirely gained his admiration; and he was inquisitive concerning my celebrated verdict in favour of Pan against Apollo, in their trial of singing, till I silenced him by the assurance that I had been too severely punished for my error by the unnatural growth of my ears. The two servants in attendance wore masks, so their merry countenances were hid, though, occasionally, they found it impossible to smother their rising laughter; of this, however, Silenus took no further notice than once or twice to hiccup a rebuke at their want of manners. Ultimately, the imaginary foster father of the jolly god was made as immortally drunk as ever Silenus is represented to have been, and in this state carried out of the cellar, to be borne home in a carriage we had ready for the purpose.

This frolicsome adventure soon became the talk of the town, and every body of our acquaintance passed their jokes with us upon it; but the best part of the story is, that several days after the supper, the noble dupe waited upon the chevalier to express his regret at not having got Midas to turn some silver into gold for him; when Bruges, who was always on the *qui vive* to make the most of circumstances, fell into the humour of the thing, and promised to get an application made to Midas on the subject of his noble friend's desire. The result of all which was, another supper party assembled in the well-lit perfumed cellar, at which, when Silenus was half-seas over, he was called upon to produce six bars of silver, which had been procured by, and brought with him, for the express purpose; and I produced my wand, with a touch of which, and certain accompanying sleight of hand tricks practised by the chevalier, the bars of silver apparently were transmuted into the like number of golden bars; and in due time, the happy Silenus was borne away from the feast, thoroughly inebriated, to be conveyed home, with six shining bars of gold-like looking metal as his companions in the coach.

I remained not at Marseilles to witness the *dénouement* of this adventure with regard to the apparent transmutation of the precious metals, for on the morning after the last feast in our Elysian shades, my wife and I departed for Genoa; but, certainly, should the hypochondriac not have attempted to turn his yellow bars into money, much time may have elapsed before his eyes became opened to the baseness of the metal.

———

CHAPTER XXIV.

"On the rankling soul
  The gaming fury falls, and in one gulf
  Of total ruin, honour, virtue, place,
  Friends, families, and fortune, headlong fall.'

"Accursed game! thou wring'st the bitter drop
  From gentle eyes that never saw thee play'd,
  And oft the stinted meal, the empty cup
  Mock hungry hearts thy raven waste hath made."

"Religion, virtue, morals, all give way,
  And conscience dies, the prostitute to play;
  Eternity ne'er steals one thought between,
  Till suicide complete the fatal scene."

WE journeyed at a pleasant rate through the picturesque country between Marseilles, one of the richest cities of a pompous monarchy, and Genoa, once the seat of government of a famous republic—the mart of commerce, and mistress of the neighbouring seas. The country about Genoa, however, is barren; but nothing tends more than want to sharpen the wits of man, and the Genoese are esteemed a cunning, industrious people, more inured to hardships than the rest of the Italians, which was the character of their ancestors, the ancient Ligurians.

At Genoa, as I have already said, we intended to sojourn for a time, if not to fix our permanent abode; but had our design been different, still we must have come to a halt here, as, unfortunately, my poor wife's health, which had been declining for months, had got so much worse since commencing our journey, that it would have been impracticable for her to have proceeded further, without first enjoying some repose.

After spending a few days at an hotel, we suited ourselves with an elegant and most conveniently furnished house, the property of a young nobleman, who, owing to losses sustained at play, had found himself under the disagreeable necessity of hiring out the mansion of his forefathers, in less than two years from the time of its becoming his; and here we lived in a style every way suitable to my ample income.

He who has sufficient wealth, everybody knows may by hospitality command the best society, and I now lived on terms of intimacy with most of the leading characters of the place; but of balls, dinner-parties, pic-nics, and other such amusements, I soon grew weary, and, in consequence, turned my attention to those diversions from which an adept may derive profit as well as pleasure. Horse-racing, the billiard-table, and private gaming-houses, now engaged much of my time; for, as to public play-rooms, none, save the proprietors, make any profit there. They it is who, with more than Midas's power, turn everything they touch into gold, but, less liberal than Chevalier Bruges, leave their dupes no kind of metal in exchange for departed treasure.

My acquaintance the chevalier paid this town a visit shortly after I had fixed myself in it; and, as a matter of course, we, who had quaffed our nectar together in the Elysian shades, with the foster father of Bacchus, resumed our intimacy. Besides, to a man employed in the avocations I must plead youth and temptation for now following, this knight of the post promised to be a valuable associate—one who could well back all my undertakings for gain; or, if he was not allowed to participate in them, to often mar their success.

Chevalier Bruges may be said to have stood almost unrivalled in his profession. He could shuffle or pack cards so as to insure the object he had in view; and, when necessary, would pare the skin from his thumb and fore-finger, in a way which enabled him, from certain little marks he put on them, to ascertain what cards he held by their feel. Moreover, at all times he was provided with packs of cards, in which the honours were either a shade thicker, broader, or longer, than the other cards; while, as to dice, he never went abroad, not even to church, without carrying loaded ones in his pocket; and, when a party had been made, at which he might risk detection, he would attend it with dice about him, which on one side had been soaked in water, and, with a proficient like the chevalier, this answers nearly as well as when they have been loaded. In fine, he was a complete master of his trade—one who knew how to turn into certainty those gambling transactions which the uninitiated believe are dependent on chance. From the shuffling game of the thimble-rig, to the unprincipled mysteries practised in horse-racing, all black-leg transactions he could successfully manage, even to the planting of a false tail upon a racer, which, however, was not his invention, but borrowed by him from a certain well-known English sporting lord, who, although sometimes a placeman, and always a pensioner, was of his honourable fraternity.

My heart now became contaminated by the gamester's vice—the love of gain; and with such a colleague as the chevalier, assisted by his professional friends, can it be wondered at that I added something to my wealth? But the fraternity the noble knight introduced me to won very largely, which I, who played on the square, could not be expected to do. I now saw that games of chance may be artfully managed, and the most apparently casual throw of the dice be made subservient to the purposes of chicanery and fraud. The nature of cards must be mixed, most games having in them a portion of skill and of chance; since the success of the player must depend as much on the chance of the deal, as on his skill in playing the game. But even the chance of the deal is liable to be perverted by all the tricks of shuffling and cutting, not to mention how the honourable player may be deceived in a thousand shapes by the craft of the sharper during the playing of the cards themselves; consequently, professed gamblers of all denominations, whether their games be of apparent skill or mere chance, may be hustled together, as being equally meritorious and equally infamous.

When loan contractors, or other persons in the confidence of their government, make a good use of the information confided to them, by securing large fortunes to themselves at the Stock Exchange, at the expense of those not in the secret, the time-bargains and other transactions by which their object is effected are termed speculations; therefore, notwithstanding that the business I now performed to add to my wealth was less dishonourable than what is usually done by the aforesaid personages, yet, as appropriate to its nature, I shall term mine a successful speculation.

My success filled me with ardour for new adventure, and many persons became the dupes of Chevalier Bruges and his party, in successful speculations of theirs. Indeed it was a profitable game we all played; however, the sun of good fortune does not always shine, and he who plays at bowls must sometimes meet with rubbers.

A party for play had been assembled at my house, at which various maritime officers of different nations were present, from whom the chevalier calculated on gleaning no small gains; but unluckily, from imagining these gentlemen were novices at games of chance, he acted too unguardedly in performing one of his sleight of hand tricks, and was detected in the unfair speculation. Instantly all became uproar and confusion, nor could it well be otherwise, for a large sum of money lay deposited on the board, and its fate was dependent on the turn-up card, which the chevalier had so mal-adroitly managed. Human life hangs by a thread. Several of the maritime officers were accustomed to have their own way, except when under the rod of naval discipline; consequently, it is not to be marvelled at that they almost simultaneously seized upon the offender, when a dreadful scuffle ensued, and he was thrown, or else fell accidentally, from the veranda of the apartment. It was a bold measure this, which would have done no discredit to a crew of buccaneers. The veranda from which the poor speculator fell was at a height of twenty feet from the street, and he, unfortunately pitching upon his head, had his neck broken. I wished the whole party far away, and the deuce only knows where they went, for every one disappeared like lightning; and, what was very unaccountable in gamblers, such had been the confusion, that some left money on the table.

Let the statue of honour be erected to the man whose actions merit it. By hollow liberalism, and mad hunting sophistries, and the creation of uncalled-for place, did not a certain state minister (always notorious for his jobs) completely juggle a great nation, and consequently after death have his statue erected opposite the place, where, by means of his oratory, he imposed fallacies upon the people as so many truths? And do not nations too often erect statues to the memory of defaulters and the unprincipled? Since, then, there is a fashion in all things, and gaming is no bar to honours of that description, should there be a subscription entered into, to erect a granite column or a marble statue to his memory, I hope I shall be pardoned for contributing handsomely towards that of Chevalier Bruges. He was a *chevalier d'industrie*, it is true; and I have since learnt, defrauded the hypochondriac Silenus of his bars of silver; but in vindication of my character, be it observed, that at the time of our feast I believed the transmutation of metal to have been meant only as a frolic; yet *malgre* all this, the chevalier was a pleasant companion, probably too as deserving of a statue as half the conquerors and monarchs of olden times. The manner of Bruges's death was a bad affair, which might have brought a slur upon my character had I not circulated money to buy the services of the journalists; and although a sort of inquest was held on the body, thanks to the newspaper accounts, the world was made to believe that, notwithstanding this catastrophe had happened at my house, I was myself one of the most virtuous and best men in the city.

There is nothing in life helps a man on more than character, and yet as all men are actors, character must invariably be false. The worse the man, the better the actor, and consequently the higher will his character stand. This great truth was known to Augustus Cæsar, for he, after murdering friends and foes with a ferocity which would have disgraced Sylla and Caius Marius, thought fit to leave a character behind him for humanity, and made his courtiers greet him by loud plaudits, at the moment when his soul was about taking its flight to futurity.

After this, let none asperse the character of Chevalier Bruges; no, nor that of a buccaneer. The famous Teach, surnamed Blackbeard, was a virtuous man when brought in comparison with Augustus Cæsar; yet no historian has passed encomiums upon the renowned pirate, who, to his lasting praise be it mentioned, though he was a common slayer of man, a bigamist with thirty wives, a violator, and a robber, yet was he no impostor!

The moral character I had made a purchase of, although it was of a nature to procure me advancement in a public situation under a government where the sceptic thinks a man can do no great good for himself, unless he be an arrant impostor, served as an impediment to success in my way of life, and I could well have dispensed with it.

"Confound the character I have got," I would often say to myself, "did a man ever before throw money away to so foolish a purpose as I have done in buying it? Character, indeed; what have I to do with character? It is fit only for a tradesman; but, if it was transferable, I would willingly take quarter price for it."

There is no resisting fate. I set no value on my new character, yet, by a sort of infatuation, acted as if I was desirous of preserving it, insomuch as I gave up holding card-parties in my house, and carried on my gambling transactions elsewhere; but the more gaming is decried, the better it thrives; and as the chevalier's lamentable death afforded matter for the gospel-mongers and sectarians to descant upon, so proportionately it brought more novices to try their fortunes at games of chance, and the greater gains to the fraternity of gamesters.

A rich vineyard was now before them, and I took especial care to gather as full a share as I could of the prolific harvest it afforded; some professional playmen, however, I discovered, are not such proficients or so successful as others, and that these persons are extremely addicted to the practise of borrowing. I lent small sums to many distressed characters, but after a time left off the injudicious custom; for I found that no fortune would be large enough to satisfy the wants of such claimants, and that when men so conquer the sense of shame, as to become regular borrowers of money, the supplier of their wants must be worse than insane if he expects in this life to be repaid. My soul was narrowed by avarice, yet rational men must applaud my conduct; for it was squared by that of bankers and merchants, who lend no money without proper security. Security forms all the links of the chain of credit, without it no business could flourish.

A Spanish don, who had come to Genoa on his travels, well supplied with the needful, in an evil hour found his way among our fraternity, and as he was but a novice at play, who prided himself on his high principles of honour, the result was what might have been expected, he lost to the last coin of his money. His donship, who was a rigid Catholic, appealed to all the saints in the calendar to help him out of his difficulties; but they either did not hear him, or must have felt no compassion for so improvident a character, for certain it is they brought him no relief; yet the wits of the place said the saints were so selfish as to let their wretched votary burn away at their shrines all the wax tapers he could procure. A god, if he were poor, would be despised in a gaming-house; and knowing this, the gentleman's pride, backed by the hopes he entertained of deriving assistance from the saints, kept him above dependence for a considerable time; but during this ordeal his appearance gradually altered for the worse, till from being hale, portly, and well-dressed, he sunk into a wan-visaged, lank personage, who wore threadbare greasy old garments.

I saw he had sunk into a deplorable state of poverty, and when his spirit was debased to a level with his condition, so that he asked me for assistance, on several occasions I befriended him in a pecuniary way. The don's applications, however, became too numerous, and I ceased administering to his wants; but one evening, when I was present in the play-room, his despe_ration became so great, that, on seeing a professed member of the gaming fraternity pocket a handful of gold which he had just won, he whispered pretty loudly in his ear, that money he must have, and provided he did not instantly accommodate him with the loan of five gold pieces, he would publicly expose him.

No gamester chooses to have his honour called in question, and the speech just made certainly implied nothing favourable to the gamester's honour; therefore, considering it necessary to publicly notice the insulting insinuation of his opponent, he gently waved his hand towards him, saying, he had best go home and sleep himself sober, before he again came among honourable company. "Honourable company!" repeated the Spaniard with emphasis, and trembling with passion while he spoke. "Infamous scoundrels! dishonourable ruffians! ye of this fraternity all are. Heartless villains! every man of you deserving of the scaffold!" Several young heirs who were present stared with astonishment at the uncourteous address, and happily for them them lost no time in pocketing their money; but the gamester who had aggravated the don to make his invidious philippic, rising from his chair with the calmness of a judge going to pronounce an extreme sentence, told the offender, that provided he was a man of honour, he would bring a friend with him, and follow into the next room, which said, he himself quitted the apartment, accompanied by a notorious duellist. The Spaniard was in much too angry a mood to listen to the language of prudence, had any one been disposed to preach it to him; but we had no preacher of this sort here, consequently no attempt was made to prevent him following the challenger into an adjoining apartment, which he promptly did, accompanied by another broken-down Spanish gambler.

The challenger's second in this duel was the master of the house, and he was never without proper arms by him, therefore, as soon as the pair of dons had entered the apartment, he, in a most business-like manner, without wasting a word in conversation, locked the door, and laid a brace of pistols and two swords on the table, when the Spaniard being offered his choice of weapons, selected the latter, and the parties set to fighting with great determination; but the Spaniard was too angry to combat well, consequently he soon exhausted his strength, and his antagonist taking advantage of the circumstance, made a furious lounge, by which he passed the point of his sword through the don's body.

The laws at Genoa were severe against duelling, and every one else fled the scene of action, leaving me only of the party with the apparently dying man, whom feelings of humanity would not permit me to forsake in his melancholy situation; but my philanthropy led me into a scrape, inasmuch as the officers of justice entered the house while I was rendering service to the wounded gentleman, and made me their prisoner. I, however, deeming liberty too great a treasure to be wantonly sacrificed, bribed the chief policeman with a purse of money, and he consequently winked at my escape, when I at once quitted the town, to stay retired in a neighbouring village, without even revisiting my own mansion previous to my departure

" What's the use of a good character to a man like me?" said I, apostrophizing while I was quitting the city; " there will be no possibility of retaining it after this new affair, unless, indeed, by making my purse bleed in the way I did before." The don, though he lingered for some time in a very precarious state, eventually recovered of his wound. But the officers of justice during this period of suspense, strove to secure my person, and all the busy characters of the town said I was highly deserving of blame in the affair, and ought to be put on my trial.

My good spouse, who, I have said, was in a delicate state of health, took to heart the catastrophe attending this new adventure, and as every one who is in trouble seeks to alleviate it in the best manner they can, she, poor woman, sought consolation during the time of my retirement from home in the sweets of converse with several staid ladies of her acquaintance.

There is danger in everything. One of these dames, a delicate, nervous lady, who imagined she could not exist without having recourse to the use of medicine, but whom the learned disciples of Galen knew to be a good annuitant to them, whom it would be ruinous to their interests to lose, in the fervour of her zeal was constantly recommending a medical practitioner to my wife, who, she affirmed, would infallibly restore her to health.

The firmest mind is liable to be shaken by persuasion; but in sickness, resolution usually departs from us, and we become the creatures of fear. Poor, weak, objects, ready to receive the doctor's potion. Mrs Winpenny was an example of this, for teazed by the importunity of her well-meaning friend, in an evil hour she consented to call in a medical practitioner.

The professional gentleman speedily loaded the shelves of my wife's chamber with his mixtures, and continued to send more even when she was on the verge of the grave; but at length, finding her case desperate, he called to his assistance a most famous physician, and this scientific character summoned another still more renowned, when, as if in defiance of their learned conferences and joint endeavours to prolong the amiable woman's life, nature gave way, and she unfortunately breathed her last.

CHAPTER XXV.

" The picture 's as it first was drawn,
    I've varied neither shade or form,
    And it will please, I'm not afraid,
    When Time has mellow'd every shade.''

" How thick and friendly lie the mingled groves,
    Distinguished only by some sculptur'd guide."

" Fatal effects of luxury and ease !
    We drink our poison, and we eat disease."

I FELT sincerely grieved at the death of my wife, who certainly was an excellent woman, and had acted with uniform kindness towards me.   By her decease I became absolute master of all her property, and what appeared to me surprising, although she had distant relations living in the neighbourhood of Genoa, she never by word of mouth, or written document, had expressed a desire to me to bequeath them anything ; however, on reflecting upon the circumstance of my having possession of the whole of her estate, I resolved, in honour to her memory, to divide a certain sum amongst her relatives.   Accordingly, I invited them to the funeral, and afterwards distributed three thousand ducats, in sums proportionate to their consanguinity, giving them to understand that in doing this I only fulfilled her wish.

The funeral being over, and my affairs in Genoa satisfactorily settled, I called upon the Spanish gentleman, mentioned as having lost his money at play, and been wounded in his duel with a gamester, and proffered him pecuniary assistance—an offer he availed himself of, which afforded me much pleasure, as happily I had now become a changed man, inasmuch as the detestable passion of avarice had lost its hold on my soul : this was a reformation for which I partly stood indebted to my altered feelings, occasioned by the loss of my wife ; yet, what may seem strange, I was still deeper indebted for it to the perseverance of my Kentish servant, in forcing upon me his excellent advice, however disinclined I might be to receive it.

My conduct with regard to my wife, to whom I gave a superb funeral, made me become a favourite with the fair sex, and my generosity shown to her relatives, and also to the unfortunate Spaniard, entirely changed the public opinion regarding me ; insomuch that I, whose character had been thought disreputable, suddenly grew into considerable favour ; notwithstanding which, I considered it the best policy to quit the republic of Genoa, the country of the great Columbus ; and I decided that my next place of abode should be the city of Parma.

My servant Monday, who had often gone to great lengths to break me of my growing inclination for play, I found to be a young man of determined probity, who had been well educated by his father—a poor curate ; therefore, now that I was a single man, I made a complete alteration in my establishment, by promoting this deserving person to the office of my secretary, and discharging the rest of my establishment, except one lackey.   By the arrangement now made, I relieved myself from much trouble, for what are unnecessary servants but so many plagues ?   Ah, and so many masters too, when the proper master relaxes in his authority : this the famous Lord Chancellor Bacon, who could himself so well lay down rules for the guidance of others, to his cost found to be the case, when to pamper his menials he had stooped to take bribes, and, consequently, got himself turned with ignominy out of his high office ; and that a single servant is better than a host of them, was the opinion of that keen observer of his species, commonly called Old Elves, the miser, when he declared that the man who would have his business properly done, must keep only one domestic, for that if he has two or more it will be badly done.   Besides, in promoting Monday to be my secretary, I secured to myself a pleasant and facetious companion, who was very capable of giving me instruction in many things ; and this last was a grand point, inasmuch as I felt very desirous of obtaining knowledge, and being sensible of the want of education in my juvenile days, was always indefatigable in my endeavours at learning, having constantly engaged masters, and devoted several hours a day to study, wherever I lived, from the time when I resided in New York to the epoch in question ; and, thanks to my perseverance in study, and aptitude at acquiring languages, I could now speak something of Italian and French, as well as Spanish.

We had a delightful journey to Parma, and highly was I gratified in viewing the Alps, from where they begin to rise near the mouth of the Var, on the Gulf of Genoa—these truly majestic mountains, which terminate near the Adriatic, after running a course of nearly seven hundred miles. At Parma I took lodgings at the house of a staid matronly lady of fifty, and had the great good luck to form an acquaintance with a justly celebrated Dutch physician, named Von Drick, who likewise lodged in the house. He had come to Parma for the benefit of his health, and had been sojourning here several months; his brother physicians having recommended the mild Italian air as the best auxiliary to the old gentleman's constitution, after a recent attack of illness, brought on by cold caught in an observatory, when watching the planets on a winter's night; for, besides being a physician, this enterprising scholar was an adept in astronomical knowledge, and, what was of more consequence to me, he was an admirable companion, who undertook the office of showing me what was remarkable in and about Parma. A day or two after our arrival, my secretary and I being out perambulating the city with him, he, after having made the observation that he felt fatigued, as his legs were not so young or powerful as they had been a quarter of a century before, proposed conducting us to an exhibition of pictures, where, he said, he should be enabled to rest his jaded limbs, at the same time that he gratified his sight by viewing some highly esteemed paintings, as excellent, he added laughingly, as some which were baptized by Pope Benedict the Third.

 " The proposition was readily agreed to, and our party proceeded to the place in question, when Mynheer Von Drick, stopping just within the exhibition-room door, invited our attention to a cluster of four persons, who stood intently engaged in examining a picture, at a remote part of the gallery.

 " There," said he, " you behold one of the genuine pictures of life."

 " With the primest spy-glass ever manufactured by Dolland, I couldn't make out which of these many pieces of handicraft is better than the one alongside of it ; for d'ye see, sir, paints and patchwork make a crazy old frigate look new and handsome to the eye," observed Monday, with a smile.

 " You mistake me," answered the physician, " I spoke of a picture of life, not a painting upon canvass.   Yonder group consists of three rogues, who call themselves connoisseurs of paintings, together with their dupe, a man in all respects as roguish as the connoisseurs— although, in this instance, deservedly the victim of his own avariciousness; but indubitably in this world there is a moral principle at work, which sooner or later makes injustice the parent of its own punishment : however, to bring a long tale into narrow bounds, it will suffice to tell that this dupe is an English tutor, who, after practising innumerable tricks at the expense of his country people, contrived to take French leave of his native land with no less than five thousand pounds in his pocket, belonging to a charitable institution, of which, by his devout conduct, shown in regularly attending divine service at a dissenter's meeting-house, he had got himself appointed the treasurer.   Besides which booty, he crossed the British Channel with two thousand pounds' worth of jewellery in his possession, the property of divers tradesmen, who had unhesitatingly intrusted this saintly character with it, on his promise to show the same to an old dowager of title, one of his patronesses, and exert his persuasive powers to get her to purchase a part or the whole of the jewels; in which case, the honest traders were to allow this agent of theirs a commission of twenty-five per cent on the produce of the goods vended by him.

 " With a heavy pocket, but a light heart, the conscientious tutor arrived in Paris, where, by means of tricks practised in gaming, he, after playing for two years, succeeded in more than doubling his property ; but the hero being now detected in the act of cheating, was kicked out of a numerous company, and in consequence of this insult and exposure, found it requisite to quit the metropolis of France, without venturing to show his face again among the playing world.

 " He who possesses wealth in abundance, and keeps himself out of the clutches of the law, may set the whole world at defiance.   This gentleman's company has been much courted ever since he has been here, and to this city it was he came immediately after his flight from Paris; but over-covetousness will soon be the means of stripping him of his wealth, when he will have nought save unavailing regret to remember it by.   In fine, after gathering a fortune together by fraud, he has become a dupe to the scoundrels standing around him; they have succeeded in getting him to lay out his money in pictures, purchased on the strength of their judgment, and, moreover, made him believe that on the sale of them he will realise a profit of two or three hundred per cent.

"Almost the whole of the ci-divant tutor's capital is now invested in this way, and, however incredible it may seem, he is taught to believe his paintings are the works of the best masters; indeed, such is his weakness on this head, that thinking they cannot sufficiently ornament the walls of their palaces without having recourse to him, he lives in hourly expectation of receiving tenders of large sums for some of his daubs from royal and other illustrious personages of Europe; yet, in plain truth, most of his paintings are so bad, as scarcely to be worth the frames which contain them, and assuredly, if they should be brought to the hammer, they will produce only a small per centage on the cash he has expended on them. The connoisseurs," added the physician, "have done their work à merveille, in return for the douceur of twenty per cent they receive on the purchase money of pictures bought by their dupe; however, now that I've given you an insight into the art and mystery of connoisseurship, we shall do well to go and seat ourselves near to the party, that we may benefit by their critical observations on paintings."

Accordingly we seated ourselves on a bench, at a proper distance, to overhear what the connoisseurs might say, and were gratified by listening to the following discourse:—

"See the exquisite beauty of this attitude," said one fellow, pointing with a pencil to the limbs of a male figure; "how plainly it shows the action in which the man is engaged; how perfect must be the painter's knowledge of ponderation, and all that refers to the centre of gravity. He has not departed from probability, but supported the character of his figure, and diffused wonderful beauty over its action."

"See the casting of the draperies," observed a second connoisseur; "do not the folds appear rather the result of chance, than of labour, study, or art? This style of painting, with truth, is denominated the grand; the folds of the draperies are great, and few as possible, because their rich simplicity is more susceptible of great lights. Good heavens! what an error some painters fall into by designing draperies heavy and cumbersome, when they ought to suit the figures with a combination of grandeur and ease. Contrast, order, and variety of folds and stuffs constitute the elegance of draperies; and diversity of colours in those stuffs contribute to the harmony of the whole."

"How admirably the chiaro-scuro is contrived," said the third puffer; "by what artful management the lights of the several objects are thrown on one side, and their darkness on the other."

"The picture is charged," said the first; "the excesses somewhat adulterate the truth; yet they cannot but be commended, for they soften many things to the eye."

"The contour is judiciously managed," observed the second.

"It has marks of age equal to pictures done in distemper," said the third, "and yet it exposes none of the dryness of the early painters in oil."

"The costume shows the action to have passed at Athens, and the people to have been barbarians," said the first.

"On the whole, the design may be pronounced elegant, and the perspective good," observed the second.

"The painter is happy in giving grace to his picture," said the third.

"Although the artist has adhered to nature and truth in most parts of his fine picture, yet there is a touch of the grotesque in yon distance," rejoined the second, pointing with his finger.

"This painter has all the elegance of Correggio, without a touch of his incorrectness of design," said the first.

"What expression is shown in that female face," exclaimed the second.

"'Tis incomparable; agitation is strongly marked there," said the third.

"I much admire the contrast in the position of those figures," observed the first connoisseur, pointing to two of the group.

"The painter may be said to show correctness," added the second.

"The colours are local," said the third.

"The linear perspective is excellent," remarked the first.

"The site well chosen," said the second.

"The outline is admirable; 'tis fine as it can be drawn," observed the third.

To relate more of this conversation is unnecessary, it being sufficient to say the connoisseurs carried their point. They even alarmed the tutor's fears, by telling him an English nobleman was desirous of purchasing the picture, and, in short, so worked upon him, that he deputed one of his fraternity to make an offer on his part of two-thirds of the price asked for the painting; or, in other words, to make it his, in return for one thousand pounds.

This was the last thousand this speculating gentleman had to dispose of, for fourteen had been already paid away for pictures; and though the owner of the one now bid for had put the nominal price of fifteen hundred pounds upon it, the intrinsic value, or rather market-price of the same being only somewhere about fifty pounds, caused the tutor to have his princely offer accepted, and the painting consequently added to his other purchases.

In concluding may be mentioned here some events which subsequently befel these picture-dealers, and also their dupe on the present occasion.

The connoisseurs, after achieving this successful feat, in all Parma were unable to procure another wealthy dupe to their snares; therefore, after making vain efforts in several other towns of Italy, they proceeded to that never-failing mart for designing characters—the British metropolis: There they speedily found employ for their ingenuity. A sort of an old woman, a military baronet, notorious for ignorance of his profession, exemplified at the expense of his country, by his blundering mistakes when commanding an army, but who possessed more money than wit, engaged them in his service, that he might benefit by their advice when enlarging his collection of pictures, and by their assistance this job was executed so very judiciously, that the general's heir-at-law deplores the hour his weak ancestor became known to our wily connoisseurs.

As to the tutor, his buoyant hopes soon gave way to despair. Disappointment and poverty opened his eyes to admit the light of truth, and he became thoroughly sensible that the potentates of Europe could sufficiently adorn the walls of their palaces without having recourse to his pictures. Unfortunately, however, for him, the restoration of reason on this point was accompanied by a return of his inclination for gaming, and he visited the tables of play in the hope of gathering together, at the expense of persons less designing than himself, a sum equal to what he had lost by his pictures. Fortune, true to her accustomed way of treating distressed mortals, proved inimical to his views, and our tutor got stript of the last shilling of his money, when, as a dernier resource, he sent his paintings to an auction, and in conformity to Mynheer Von Drick's prophecy, received back somewhere about one shilling in the pound of what they cost him.

This supply disappointing the gentleman's expectations, he made a desperate effort at the gaming-table, and, to use the language of a gamester, "got cleaned out;" after which, he contrived to get himself conveyed to England as a pauper, where settling himself in a country-town, his psalm-singing countenance and sanctified air so won upon the hearts of the congregation at a meeting-house, which he never failed attending, that they appointed him their clerk; but further honours certainly await him, as several wealthy dowagers have voluntarily offered to be his securities, and the whole of the congregation promised to support him on the ballot at an approaching election for the office of tax-gatherer; some other good dames, however, insist upon it that our tutor shall become a preacher of the Gospel, for they say they know he is born to be a shining light to the people.

Monday had no sooner retired from the picture gallery, than he broke out in violent invectives against the connoisseurs and their dupe. "What a lubber the chap must be to give a thousand pounds for a bit of daubed canvass," exclaimed he, shrugging his shoulders. "An old wooden head of a ship is better than his. Who in his senses would be bamboozled out of his money by four common puffers? However, after all, it cheers the honest heart to see the rascal paid in his own coin. He had a Roland for his Oliver. He bamboozled the public charity, as well as the jewellers, out of their property, and now he is properly bamboozled himself." "You have justly remarked," said I to the physician, "that the characters we have so recently quitted, furnish a genuine picture of life."

"Over-covetousness, sir, generally bursts the bag," remarked my secretary with a smile. On the following day, Mynheer Von Drick, accompanied by a farmer of the neighbourhood, his acquaintance, took my secretary and me to visit an Englishman, residing several miles from Parma; and, as the weather was beautiful, and the old gentleman thought walking exercise would be beneficial to him, we were induced to make our little journey on foot.

We had not proceeded far from the town, ere the farmer, pointing to a yew tree, in a burial-ground, said, "Beneath yon tree sleeps my worthy uncle, and there, my friends, at some future day, shall I near to him be taking my lasting repose." "Ha, my friend," observed the physician, "even so must it be with us all. Death, then, is a suitable subject for meditation; in the royal palace and in the poor-house, in the hall of festivity and in the dwelling of wretchedness, in the prison-house and in the bed of down, it is an oft-recurring object; the perusal of gravestones affords the best check for a fit of ambition." "Yes," remarked my secretary, "death shows the vanity of human projects; blasts man's fondest hopes, and cuts off his career in the sunshine of his glory. Like the liquid tract left behind her by a vessel sailing on her course, so the grave of man smooths over, and the life of the one and the tract of the other are alike forgotten." "Death is the universal doom," rejoined Von Drick; "its empire extends over every class, denomination, and sex; its summons demands prompt attendance, and its edict is irrevocable. Of all tyrants, it is the only one mortality finds no possibility of hiding itself from. Death, however, is just. He who longest escapes from its embrace, is doomed to the greatest portion of misery; yet death, in its perfect justice, spares no class of mortals; but, as the Latin poet quaintly says—

> ' With equal pace, impartial fate
> Knocks at the palace and the cottage gate.

"Happily for the broken-hearted, the incurable sick, and many other sufferers, it is even so," said the farmer. A silence of some minutes followed the last observation, when our party having approached near to the churchyard, beheld a young man, seated upon the ground, at the head of a newly sodded grave. "The grave is a test of affection," now observed the physician; "it is the ordeal for trying the sincerity and fervency of our passions. That young man, in all probability, is a lover, and his mistress, who late was blooming and kind, lies beneath yon turf food for loathsome worms. In fine, the grave makes manifest whether the soul really cherishes a fond regard for the memory, or feels cold indifference at the loss of the departed." "Right, my friend, is your conjecture," replied the farmer. "Yon youth loved a fair maiden, the belle of a neighbouring village; he courted her, his vows were accepted, and the day was fixed upon for their marriage, when, unfortunately, his betrothed caught the scarlet fever, which soon numbered her with the things that have perished. The poor lad has been inconsolable ever since the maiden's death, and the whole neighbourhood feel pity for him, for he is one of the few persons that are beloved by every body; moreover, he is a youth of respectable talents, and has written various pretty sonnets to his mistress, which have procured him the title of the village poet." "If this be the case," rejoined the physician, "we have only to substitute the word mansions for that of nations, to say of him, as of Orpheus—

> ' Love, strong as death, the poet led
> To the pale mansions of the dead.'

Just as the farmer, who led the van, was in the act of stepping over the stile into the churchyard, the youth arose from off the grave, and first casting a look denotive of anguish towards us, intruders on his melancholy visit, abruptly turned round and departed with a hasty step, by the opposite of the burial-ground,

"Go, poor youth," uttered the physician, "words of comfort intended to afford thee consolation, would only add to the bitterness of thy regret, which time alone can subdue. The budding rose, snatched from thee by unsparing death, may yet be replaced by a lovely flower. Youth has everything to hope for." Sweetbriar had been planted over the maiden's grave. "There," said the physician, pointing to the prickly bush, "there is the true emblem of love: the flower is temptingly sweet, but the thorn piercingly sharp!"

From respect to the farmer we all paused for a short time at the grave of his much-lamented uncle, and while we did so, the worthy man picked several stones from off the grass growing over it, and threw them over the burial-ground fence. The party of us now proceeded on our road, and, engaged in rational conversation, beguiled the time away. "Age steals upon man like a thief, and infirmities march in its train; but, in spite of them all, a good conscience is a continued feast," said the physician, musingly, as he trudged along. At length, pointing out a neat cottage, almost embosomed in trees, on a beautiful slope of ground, he exclaimed, " That is my friend's residence."

" It stands on a lovely spot," observed Monday; " Virgil nor Cicero could have chosen more appropriately for the place of their studies." " The learned men you mention stood in high favour with the great of their days, and enjoyed ample shares of the rich gifts of fortune; but my friend, who is a literary character, as were those famed Romans, and moreover was born and bred a gentleman, possesses only a bare competency to exist upon."

While Von Drick was yet speaking, a gentleman, apparently verging on his fiftieth year, from behind a cluster of shrubs made his appearance, when bowing to the party, he assured Mynheer Von Drick that he felt great pleasure at so unexpectedly seeing him and his friends at his humble retreat.

" My friends here," said the physician, introducing Monday and me to Captain English, "readily quitted the city this morning to enjoy a country walk, and have the pleasure of making your acquaintance.'

" This humble threshold is not often crossed by a strange footstep," replied he, " therefore the honour conferred on me by your bringing friends here, will be the higher estimated; but ceremony damps welcome; come, let me show you into the cottage."

His residence was literally what the captain had denominated it; even that arbitrary minister who first taxed the windows through which heaven's light finds its way into the the abode of men, could have made no more of it. It was but a cottage; yet, in its mistress, who was the wife of a gentleman then away from home, who joined in housekeeping with Captain English, it held a treasure worthy of any palace.

" Madam Susan," said the captain, introducing his guests to this accomplished lady, " I must leave it to your good offices, to show such hospitality, as may induce these gentlemen to visit us again."

" The best this humble cot affords shall be at the service of your friends," said the lady, curtseying. Captain English now gave us so hearty a welcome, that the party accepted of his invitation to dinner, and while the meal was being prepared, we all accompanied our host in taking a rural walk, which proved highly gratifying, for it was over a country beautifully intersected by the varieties afforded by agriculture, intermingled with wood, and enriched by a meandering stream.

" His humble abode and narrow circumstances brought no disgrace on Fabricius," said our host, while his guests were seating themselves at his board, " therefore, surely I need make no apologies, when I place before you the best refreshments this cottage affords."

" History allows no credit to Fabricius for epicurism," said I, smiling, as I viewed the neatness of the dishes displayed on the board, and scented the delicious odours arising from the choice viands.

The fair housekeeper smiled at this indirect compliment paid to her; but the physician added to it, by saying, that at Captain English's home, by culinary skill, the good things of life were made the most of. " This is the handywork of a good housewife, I'll take on me to warrant," observed Monday, in a half-whisper to me.

" By Uranus, and all the celestial planets, I vow these delicious viands endanger my life," soon as he had dined, exclaimed Mynheer Von Drick, thrusting his plate further from him with one hand, and unbuttoning the bottom button of his waistcoat with the other.

" A bumper of Burgundy will assist the gastric juice in digesting your food," said his host smiling, and filling his friend's glass.

" Professed gastronomers would not be satisfied with paying a single visit at this table," was my remark to the hostess; " your cookery, madam, would create fresh zests to their palates."

" The gluttons would destroy themselves by eating; I'll warrant they would make a Norwegian dinner of it," said my secretary, laughing.

" Permit me, sir, to inquire in what may consist the peculiarities of a Norwegian dinner?" asked the lady.

" In extreme gluttony, I am sorry to say, madam. However, the better to satisfy your curiosity, I will, provided it is agreeable to the company, give you some little account of a Norwegian dinner, at which, when a stripling, it was my luck to be present."

Here the gentlemen of the party expressed a desire to hear what the sailor-secretary had to say, and the lady assured him she should feel herself much his debtor for the promised relation of what happened at his northern feast, after which he resumed as follows :—

" You must know, madam, that when I was a youngster, learning the art of seamanship, I was 'prentice to Captain Bowling, of the Water Lily ; and one voyage, when we were on our way home from the frozen regions of the north, after we had been drove about by gales from every quarter, and had our bowsprit snapt away by an iceberg, all the crew of us were made happy as so many princes by our reaching Norway, for there we found safe anchorage and good shelter from the gale.

" Now, madam, to give every country its due, I must inform you that the Norwegians are an hospitable set of people, none more so perhaps on the face of our globe.   Captain Bowling was invited to dine with the governor of the place as soon as we had got safe into port, and he thought proper to take me with him to this noble commodore's house.

" The governor, as they call him, received us very courteously, and, according to the custom of the country, made us partake of some brandy and cheese, as a whet to strengthen our appetites for dinner.   The cloth had been laid for our meal before we arrived, and on it was displayed a plate, knife and fork, and a wine-glass, with a bottle of claret beside it, for each individual of the company, while in the middle of the table there stood a large handsome glass castor of sugar, ornamented with a magnificent silver cover.   Every nation has its peculiar customs, and the Norwegians, I should observe to you, madam, are not in the habit of drinking either malt liquor or water with their meals, nor is it customary with them to have salt or mustard on the table.

" Soon after we had done whetting our appetites, dinner was brought in, that is to say, one dish at a time.   The first was a large tureen of cherry soup, which is well known to be a favourite addition to the dinners of the richer people, and, besides, a profusion of cherries and milk ; this had in it sago, claret, and raisins, all boiled together, so as to have made a complete mucilage of the mixture.

We were each of us helped to two brimming full soup-plates of this mess, which we ate without knowing if anything more was to come ; but no sooner had the tureen disappeared, than two large salmon, boiled and cut in slices, were brought upon the board ; and, as an accompaniment, came melted butter, mixed with vinegar and pepper, which looked the very counterpart of oil.

" Though it was a queer mixture to look at, the sauce served well to make us relish the salmon ; yet when we had with difficulty cleared our plates of the large messes of fish the governor had given us, we began to think we had taken cargo enough on board, and so we hoped we had seen the end of our dinner ; but there we were wofully out of our reckoning.

" There was now introduced a large tureen, filled with eggs of the goose or great tern, boiled hard, almost as bullets, of which, to our discomfiture, half-a-dozen were placed on each of our plates ; and for sauce to them, there was a large basin of cream, mixed with sugar, in which spoons were placed for the whole party, so we all had to eat it out of the same measure.

" When I had distressed nature by forcing upon my stomach the grearer part of my eggs, I begged to be excused eating any more, and in consideration of my being a youngster, was allowed to give in ; but the captain petitioned in vain to be spared eating the whole of his monstrous eggs.   ' You are my guest,' said the old governor, ' and this is the first time you have done me the honour of coming here, therefore no excuse can be admitted, you must do as I would have you ; in future, when you visit me, you may act as you like.'

" The captain, finding there was no remedy for the evil, put on as pleasant a countenance as he could under such circumstances, and with some difficulty contrived to force the remainder of his eggs and a portion more cream down his throat ; but no sooner had he accomplished this feat, than half a well-roasted sheep was brought in, with a mess of sorrel, dandelion, and scurvy-grass, which was boiled, mashed, and sweetened with sugar.

" Poor Captain Bowling at sight of these last dishes made sundry wry faces, and to be excused partaking of them pleaded his age, and declared he had already eat more than could possibly do him good ; but, in spite of all he could say, he was doomed to see his plate crammed with mutton and sauce, and he was made to get through it as well as he could ; yet each person's allowance of any one of the dishes we had partaken of, was amply sufficient for the dinner of a healthy man.

"A large dish of *gauffres*, which is a sort of pancake, made of wheat-flour, flat and baked in a mould, succeeded to the mutton: these were about half an inch in thickness, and the size of an octavo book. The governor said he would be content if Captain Bowling eat two of them, and he, poor fellow, was obliged to comply. Norway biscuits and rye-loaves served as the bread for our repast; the sole drink was claret, of which the captain was forced to empty two or three bottles, put in succession beside him.

"Coffee was served up after the pastry had been demolished, and this gave us hopes that the feast would terminate here; but it was not so; much to the captain's consternation, all was not over yet.

"A plate of apples and a large bowl of rum punch now appeared, when three large apples were forced on each of us, and the punch was handed round pretty freely, in long ale glasses, and a toast given each time they were filled.

"By the time the bowl had got drained of its contents, the captain was hard up, chock and block, as we sailors say, madam; indeed, he would not have then known which way the wind blew, even though the compass had been put before his eyes; and yet the unmerciful old governor threatened him with another bowl. Luckily, however, at this time one of the boat's crew made his appearance, to say the boat was ready, and the rest of her crew aboard waiting for him; but notwithstanding this agreeable summons, and that he felt he was nigh bursting with repletion, my commander was compelled, by his over-hospitable host, to swallow three cups of tea before he departed. 'I can't help compassionating your gorging aldermen, whenever I think of the misery a man may bring on himself by over-eating,'" now said the sailor, laughingly. "Captain Bowling, for example, was so greatly inconvenienced by his debauch, that we had no little difficulty in conveying him to the boat, and we were absolutely forced to hoist him aboard ship. Three days elapsed before he recovered from the effects of his involuntary intemperance, and during this time he loathed the very sight of food; but the captain took especial good care never to venture putting his foot ashore again at that place, and soon as the gale lulled, for fear of being honoured by another invitation to dine with the old commodore, he weighed anchor and put to sea, declaring, at the same time, that he would much rather be caught in another gale, than undergo the misery he had endured by going ashore."

His female auditor thanked Monday for the description he had given of a Norwegian dinner, and smilingly remarked, that his story afforded a convincing proof that hospitality is best evinced by leaving visitors to act according to their pleasure; when, in reply, Monday said that he heartily concurred with her; and in his opinion, the old proverb of "enough being as good as a feast," was a crazy one, inasmuch as "enough is a feast."

When the fair housekeeper had adjourned to prepare coffee, and the gentlemen were enjoying themselves over some fine flavoured old wine, Captain English, in reply to a compliment the physician paid him on the snugness and comfort pervading this sylvan establishment, of which he made one, observed, "that the life of man is a kind of dream, subject to this remarkable peculiarity, that it depends mainly upon man himself whether his dream shall be a pleasant one; therefore," he added, "schooled as he had been to the knowledge of this truth by adversity, reverses of fortune, and innumerable disappointments, it behoved him to take a page from the book of wisdom, and make the best of things; following Epictetus's wise maxim, 'to bear and forbear.'"

"Yours, my good sir, is the true philosophy," observed my secretary. "Practise at all times is preferable to theory. Out of the multitudes who preach from pulpits, or deliver discourses in senate-houses, few are to be found who practise their own precepts: even Seneca, by his conduct, belied his."

"Your observations on philosophy are rigidly true," rejoined our host; "but as my history may not be altogether uninteresting, I will, provided the good company think fit to hear it, now relate the tale of my misfortunes."

We all thanked Captain English for his agreeable offer, and expressed ourselves desirous of hearing his history, on which he related what follows.

CHAPTER XXVI.

"I long
To hear the story of your life, which must
Take the ear strangely!"

"I'll deliver all."

"Innocence, alive to shame,
Sinks down oppress'd by guilt's mere name.
Thus, when the orb of day doth rise,
Flooding with light, earth, sea, and skies;
While less pure objects 'scape the glow,
Yielding though spotless lies the snow."

"Aw'd into patience by fresh scenes of fate
We live too soon, and learn to live too late."

Zoroaster says, "An opportunity for doing mischief offers a hundred times a day—for doing good only once in a year;" therefore he advises man to make an early reparation for the wrongs he has done his fellow-man.

"The parentage of an humble individual can be interesting to no persons save his kindred, therefore I shall say no more concerning mine, than that my father was an English gentleman in easy circumstances, whose pride it was to declare not one of his ancestors had been a sinecurist, a parson, or a law officer, nor in any way fingered one shilling of the public money.

"This parent, however, unfortunately for me, died while I was a child, and a kind mother had me educated for some few years at a collegiate school; but this I quitted at the early age of fourteen, to proceed to Africa and the East Indies; of the latter, I visited the chief city of each of the three presidencies, as also two of those of the island of Ceylon; but bad health compelled me to return to my native land, at the expiration of two years. Of my travels in Africa, I recollect nothing worthy of being made mention on this occasion.

"The war carried on between France and my native country at this time was waged with vindictive fury; and after I had got restored to health, to gratify my wishes, which were speedily to serve the state in a military capacity, a commission in a regiment serving in Egypt was purchased; but, before I could join it, the preliminaries of a peace were signed, when shortly afterwards, by purchase, I obtained a lieutenancy in the army, and was soon reduced upon half-pay.

"The peace proved of short duration, and eager for military service, soon as war had been proclaimed, I paid a round sum of money as a difference to get replaced on full-pay; when, now under the command of the noble-hearted Sir John Moore, and other favourite officers of the day, I passed some of the choicest years of my life. Promotion to a company in a light infantry corps fell to my lot after six years' service; but to this corps I was destined to belong for half-a-score years, and then, as will be seen, to be juggled out of active service in the army.

"With my last regiment I served at the taking of Copenhagen, in the Spanish peninsula, the Netherlands, and in Holland, and while belonging to it, I was selected on several occasions to take charge of the depôt companies, and manage its recruiting service—duties I fulfilled so highly to the satisfaction of the Duke of York, the commander-in-chief, that he several times notified his approbation of my conduct, and frequently promised me promotion.

"The cup does not always reach the lip for which it seems intended. This was verified in my case; deceived by promises, and long compelled to remain in charge of the regimental depôt, I was doomed to see sundry junior officers promoted by brevet over my head; but there was no redress to be obtained, a military man's business being only to obey.

"Little minds are the most vindictive. A tyrannical officer, whom I served under, the major of a light infantry corps, used frequently to exclaim, 'O that mine enemy had written a book.' This now became my case. I committed this egregious act of folly; insanity, it may be called, in a military man who aspires to promotion. In a word, a soldier's intellects his military companions estimate according to his rank; therefore, for a junior officer to execute any performance that can be construed as arrogating to himself more knowledge than is professed by his superior, is a crime too heinous to be forgiven. I sinned twofold; I wrote a book of poetry, as also one in prose; the latter, too, was a military one, and dedicated, by his sanction, to the commander-in-chief.

"A military expedition, which called for the effective soldiers under my command, being ordered to Holland, I gladly seized the opportunity of embarking; and yet my health was unequal to the undertaking, for I had only recently recovered from a severe attack of dropsy. The campaign which followed was made in the severest winter known in the memory of man, and though I weathered it, my sufferings from the cold were most severe.

"Man lives in blindness to the future; yet my reward was such as I anticipated. Nothing was achieved on this campaign worthy of winning the corporal's stripe to a soldier's arm; and yet such is interest, that a captain under my own command, many years my junior in rank, got himself promoted, by brevet rank, over my head.

"I complained not of this grievance, for complaint against injustice, inflicted by the hand of military rule, I knew to be unavailing as the wind wasting its strength against a granite rock; but that no fair effort of mine might be wanting to gain promotion, I volunteered my services to lead a storming party, and was in consequence employed to command a detachment of troops intended as such. However, just as we were on the eve of assaulting a certain fortress, the news of Buonaparte's abdication of his throne reached our army, and thereby spared me the mortification of then seeing another favourite officer or two promoted over my head.

"Napoleon's abdication having restored peace to exhausted Europe, I obtained a few days' leave of absence, and presented myself at the Horse Guards, thoroughly disgusted with the service, where I signified my intention of retiring from the army; but Sir Henry Torrens, the military secretary, reasoned me out of my purpose, by an assurance that the commander-in-chief felt warmly inclined to serve me, and waited only a fair opportunity—an assurance backed by his advice, for his words were 'for God's sake don't retire, you little dream of the honours awaiting you!'

"I rejoined my regiment in Flanders, and remained with it until Napoleon re-appeared in France, and, like the god of light, broke through the clouds enveloping him. At Menin, a fine opportunity was afforded me for contemplating the contemptible weakness of monarchic power, unsupported by the goodwill of the people. Louis the Eighteenth of France, who, like the rest of his family, could not be taught that the more merit prevails over titles the more flourishing is the state, and who only a few days previous had appeared firmly seated on his throne, here entered the Netherlands a fugitive, with a heart wrung with grief and tears streaming from his eyes. Forsaken by all his leading officers of state, who, apeing sunflowers, turned their faces to the invigorating deity of the day, the decrepid monarch had learnt the melancholy truth, 'that courtiers are friends, who inwardly swear only to flatter power.'

"Every British soldier that could be spared from other quarters was now hurried away into Belgium, there to be united in one army with the Dutch, Hanoverians, Brunswickers, and Flemings, to be commanded by fortune's favourite, and supported by armies of Prussians, Wurtembergians, Austrians, Poles, Russians, Swedes, Danes, and hordes of Cossacks, all preparing for the field to unite their endeavours for hurling Napoleon from the throne on which he had unmolestedly reseated himself.

"Among the troops wafted over the British Channel into Belgium were the three battalions of my regiment, therefore the provisional one, with which I had been serving, being formed of companies belonging to the others, was now broken up; but instead of joining my own battalion at Brussels, which was commanded by a court favourite, who, to judge by his conduct towards me, is illiberal and narrow-minded, I was unexpectedly sent to a frontier town, to officiate there as a judge-advocate.

"He who suspects not is easily overcome; like an unskilful swordsman he guards his head and receives a death-wound at his heart. In few words, to sum up a tale of complicated grievances, it is only necessary to add, that while I was on detached duty, Napoleon made that rapid advance into Belgium, which precipitately brought on the battle of Waterloo; and that I, misled by the erroneous information given me by every superior officer I fell in with on my route across the country, respecting the head-quarters of an army, known perhaps to no mortal away from them save only those immediately to the rear, proceeded to the divisions of troops in position near the town of Halle, instead of to the main army, with which my regiment happened to be serving.

"This untoward event prevented me from participating in the honours of this famed battle; but though I was no more deserving of blame on the occasion than I should have been if away in the East Indies, it gave my malignant enemies a glorious opportunity for persecuting me, and this was so effectually done by promoting officers over my head—refusing me every kind of justice—and deceiving me by means of a false, though an official assertion, made in the name of my regimental commanding officer—a man whom I had met retiring from the battle's din with a slight wound—that unfortunately I became their dupe, and in a moment of indignant anger signified my willingness to quit the corps and retire upon half-pay.

"Injustice always finds a pretext to palliate her actions. And my case affords a memorable proof that he who has to contend with a party or individuals more powerful than himself, should not evince fear of them; for truly (as the pastor of Isaorens asserts) people in power act like dogs, biting those who retire before them, and only barking at such as pass on without changing their pace. I was not permitted to recall the declaration wrung from me by fraudful misrepresentation; but with a constitution materially injured in the service of my country, I now quitted a profession wherein long and faithful attention, active zeal, good conduct, and talent, too often serve as subordinate recommendations for obtaining promotion when brought in competition with the favour of commanders enjoying their temporary sway. In fact, the system acted upon since the unavailing battle of Barrossa, of granting brevet rank at the recommendation of capricious officers in command over troops in the field, is of a nature to destroy the military spirit by creating well-grounded dissatisfaction; indeed, such had been my feeling on this subject, that had this rank been proffered me out of my proper turn, I should have spurned it as an insult on all senior unbreveted officers of my own rank.

"A man who, confiding in his own wisdom, deviates from the straight path to travel on one he thinks points more direct to his wishes, generally blunders on that which leads to his disappointment. None of my many memorials to royalty and commanders-in-chief have been of any avail in getting my wrongs investigated; and almost immediately after my quitting the army, from a circumstance purely accidental, I was led into speculations at the Stock Exchange, where I was doomed to learn that a man to thrive at that sink of iniquity, ought to commence his operations without a moneyed capital. Success at the Stock Exchange rarely rewards openness and honour, but usually is the follower of selfish misrepresentation and other low artifice.

"Indeed, of all the species of gaming, that of 'time bargains,' by which the great fortunes are lost and won at the Stock Exchange, is the most destructive. In its effects it is even more deadly than the infernal game of *rouge et noir*: at the latter, the wretched victim can lose no more than the money he has ready to expose on the gaming-table; but 'time bargains' precipitate him into losses which oblige him to sell, not only the property he is in possession of, but that also which he is entitled to in reversion; and when all has been done, they leave him a defaulter on his speculations, and pennyless for the residue of his miserable life. This is one of the many frightful consequences of a national debt; and let the culprits be who they may, glad shall I be to record my opinion that the administration which creates a never-to-be-paid-off national debt, like Erostratus, should be mentioned in history amidst flames, ruin, lamentations, and tears.

"At the time I was deprived of my military situation and right of promotion, I learnt the value of military friendship; from that day old brother officers and I affected to have forgotten each other's faces. A novice in worldly affairs might have imagined we had all taken hearty draughts of the waters of Lethe; for even a politic general officer, who dined with me only a day or two preceding our last sanguinary contest, though among courtiers famed for his *coup d'œil*, after this event could not discern me when we ran against each other in the streets.

"Misfortune or loss seldom comes single, but one succeeds another, like the billows of the sea; and in the tide of misfortune, men are in a few days more overwhelmed by the waves of trouble and danger, than they can in the ebb of many years free themselves from. This was my case at the Stock Exchange; I was speedily stripped of all my funded property, and then, in the vain hope of recovering my first loss, I disposed of my land; the produce of which, it is almost superfluous to say, passed into the same hands as my other property. Now, I was taught that misfortune is the thermometer that marks the coldness of friends. My moneyed acquaintances suddenly became short-sighted, precisely in the manner my military friends had been stricken with that deplorable failing. Fortunately, the voice of reason now whispered me that the more a man is ill-treated by the world, the greater is the necessity of his loving himself, to enable him to soar above it and its prejudices; consequently, although the grievous losses and disappointments I had met with could not be otherwise than distressing to my mind, yet, notwithstanding I felt them as a man, I sunk not under them, but bore them as a man ought to bear the galling burden imposed by trouble. The door of death I knew was open to me by suicide, and my opinion was that man should either live contentedly or pass its portal; but though I doubted my ability to exist as that wise man did, to an extreme old age, under an accumulated load of pain, affliction, and penury, yet I reverenced, as I still do, the advice of the stoic Epictetus, where he recommends patience and forbearance under all pressures; and, therefore, animated with the hope of closing the drama in a more laudable way than by forcibly ejecting the vital spark, I departed not out of life.

"Patience not unfrequently is rewarded with unlooked-for success, and after I endured my misfortunes for more than the ordinary term of an apprenticeship, a new era broke upon me, when my private affairs, owing to the death of a relative, were somewhat amended; but they called me across the Atlantic.

"I now passed away several years of my life amongst the most hospitable, although the most persecuted class, of British subjects—the planters of the West Indies. The jaundiced eye of prejudice is levelled at them, through the misrepresentations of designing sophists, who represent them as barbarous, for employing their well-paid labourers about six hours a day; yet these same sophists are resolutely deaf to the bitter complaints of their own factory children, toiling sixteen hours per diem in rooms at fever heat, for a few pence. Plenty of good land, and liberty to manage their own affairs in their own way, apparently are the two grand causes of the prosperity of thriving colonies; but the erroneous system now pursued is, gradually to take the liberty away, and deprive the colonist, the only good judges of their own affairs, of their management; and for what? why, to place all under the guidance of an obstinate place-hunting oligarchy, thousands of miles distant, who know not how to manage their own poor, and are compelled to act as overwhelming petitioners dictate to them. Nor have they yet discovered, that if the spirit of the slave emancipation act be good, their new poor law must be atrocious.

"I quitted the planters with painful sensations, for I felt that their equals for generosity I should never again meet. By way of the United States of America I returned to my native land; but, after sojourning at home for a time, grew weary of compassionating the condition of the numerous blind, who, as if in mockery to the name, had once termed themselves—my friends; when (like Xerxes, the famed Persian monarch, while reviewing his army), being unable to look at them without having my heart rent by feelings of pity, I came to the resolution of traversing the British Channel, to live as a ratioual man, in peaceful content; and this humble cottage, in which you listen to my tale, is the place which I fixed upon for my residence. Adversity, it is said, blunts all the fine feelings of the heart, and leaves us strangers to that sympathetic tie and tender commiseration which glows in the bosoms of those who are strangers to its pangs; but this assertion is falsified in my case, for I am ever ready to compassionate the unfortunate, and relieve them to the extent warranted by my means.

"Heaven be thanked! the precepts of philosophy have fortified my mind, so as to render powerless the sharp arrows adversity has shot against me; and literary pursuits, combined with rational conversation, serve to make my days glide rapidly away. It is almost incredible what man may accomplish by system and perseverance; I myself, in my retreat here, of poetry, dramatic writings, and prose, have composed more than fifty volumes for the press.

"To sum up—I have thoroughly satisfied my mind, that fortune consists in happiness, not in wealth; and I honestly avow, that if I have an earthly wish ungratified, it is that, like Gelimer, the dethroned monarch of the Vandals, I may receive my bitterest foe at my gate, and afford him hospitality and assistance, when the heart-cutting blasts of adverse fortune have driven him from the pinnacle of grandeur to the extremity of misery and want."

Captain English having concluded this story, was thanked by his visitors for the pleasure it afforded them.

But the physician, when thanking the ill-used veteran, declared he must have been born under a most chequered configuration of the planets, and he cheered him by the declaration that he had more to rejoice over than deplore in having been made the victim of deceit and injustice ; for had this not happened, in all probability he would not have exerted his energies in the manner he had as an author. " In short," added he, " your misfortunes have ennobled you as a man ; they have taught you not only much valuable knowledge of the world, but have occasioned you to erect a temple to the goddess of fame ; one which may prove more lasting than the honours bestowed by royalty on your illiberal enemies."

" Yes," said the physician, resuming the discourse after a pause, " fortunately for mankind, the pen effects more than the sword. It sometimes unsheaths that weapon, and directs it to a righteous cause, conveying an energy almost supernatural to the heart that uses it. It unveils those mysteries of church and state, which sear and blast all hope and happiness ; it inspires nations with the enthusiasm requisite for conquering priestcraft and crushing tyrants ; and it establishes freedom and her spontaneous blessings without robbery, or the shedding of human blood."

The persecuted officer now said, that although his friends had been pleased to overrate his poor talents when foreseeing for him a niche in the proud temple of fame ; yet his writings, if they were of no other utility, unquestionably had proved valuable to himself, they having made his time fleet happily away, fortified his mind in the principles of sound philosophy, and for a companion in life given him content.

Truth is omnipotent. His guests were thoroughly satisfied of the injustice with which Captain English had been treated ; but we forbore making further remarks, as we felt that the less he was reminded of his wrongs, the better it would be for his peace of mind. However, after our taking leave of the ancient soldier at his domicile, we could not avoid, while we walked on our way home, expressing our feelings of regret to each other, that public characters, high in office under a government, should be permitted to hermetically seal the door of inquiry into the conduct of minor servants of the same public they themselves serve, who openly and ardently claim redress at their hands for wrongs inflicted on them by the iron hand of power.

CHAPTER XXVII.

" He folded the fair maid to his breast,
'Thou art my lady-love,' said he,
'And I never loved another but thee.' "

"Oh, Pleasure ! you're indeed a pleasant thing,
    Although one must be damn'd for you, no doubt :
I make a resolution every spring
    Of reformation, ere the year run out,
But, somehow, this my vestal vow takes wing.
    Oh, Love ! thou art the very god of evil,
    For, after all, we cannot call thee devil."

" And what has wrought this woful change ?
Fiends wrought it—Av'rice, Hate, Revenge !"

THE affectation of sanctity is a blotch on sanctity itself. My landlady was a Roman Catholic, but being thought a rigid one, was allowed to read the Bible ; with this proviso, however, that she was to admit no doubt in her mind of the consistency and morality of all things asserted therein ; and she availed herself of the privilege in a way which made me think her an arrant impostor. The devout dame never sat down, except at meals, without having the sacred volume displayed open on her table, usually with her spectacles extended upon it, and she would descant on the great truths contained therein with enthusiasm.

The ghostly confessor of this sanctified lady was a corpulent divine ; fond of high living, and so great an admirer of the fair, that it would have been a satisfactory circumstance for some of his fellow-men, if the Jewish economy which was to last for ever, had at this time existed ; as by it, celibacy was deemed infamous, and the priests were expressly commanded to marry, that the tribe of Levi might not fail.

Idleness is the parent of evil. Having little to employ me, my attention was attracted towards a beautiful brunette, about seventeen years of age, who came almost daily to pass away an hour or two with my landlady, who I was given to understand was her aunt.

To gain the old lady's favour now became necessary, and I accomplished that object by making her presents of liqueurs and little delicacies, as also flattering her in no measured strain ; thanks to which generalship, my hostess was thrown off her guard, and I had the felicity of having some private conversation with the fair niece, who, in the simplicity of her heart, told me some odd things of their father confessor, by which I augured that he entertained improper designs on the young lady.

Rosa Matilda, the fair girl in question, was innocence personified ; and, as I loved to indulge myself in a *tete-à-tete* conversation with her, and sought every possible opportunity of gratifying this wish, there is no calculating what might have been the result of my growing passion, had it not so happened that a very remarkable character, a gentleman who had been one of our gaming fraternity at Genoa, at this critical period came to lodge at our house, and speedily gained the maiden's affections. This much-celebrated personage was an Englishman ; but his name, from regard to the feelings of his home connexions, I decline mentioning, and shall content myself by denominating him the Bigamist, a title to which no one can justly dispute his right, inasmuch as he had taken French leave of five or six loving ladies, all of them resident in England, and united to him by the tie of wedlock. Some truths are startling, and those of our bigamist's many marriages are not a little so ; but when we examine into the history of other persons, we shall not deem him one of the superlative characters in immorality. Par example, Bayle, the philosopher, emigrated from his native land for the love of a married woman ; and her husband, though a gentleman renowned for his discoveries in the Apocalypse, was very tardy in seeing what passed in his house between the philosopher and his own wife ; but, when he made the notable discovery, instead of using his influence, as he had promised, to get Bayle another professorship, he denounced him as impious, and procured his expulsion from those of philosophy and history, which had been instituted expressly for him. Unlike Bayle, our bigamist interfered with no man's connubial bliss, but he was an advocate for having a plurality of wives, and often would he say, that his love, like the candle of Amiens, was always burning. Compared, too, with the famed Marshal de Bassompiere, who, when he was shut up in the Bastile of France, occasioned his enemies the trouble of examining seven thousand of his love letters, mostly from married women, our bigamist decidedly was a moral man.

The most sagacious are sometimes imposed upon, and it so happened that Father Le Querque suspected me of being the favourite swain of fair Rosa, and never dreamt of the victorious bigamist having won her affections ; consequently he always looked upon me with the jaundiced eye of suspicion, and bore me much secret hatred. The lodgers used occasionally to take coffee with our landlady, when the priest was always present, and sometimes very aggravating arguments were fomented, which tended to increase the reverend gentleman's acrimony. One evening in particular, when we were all assembled in the *Salle à manger*, I recollect the following conversation as having taken place :—

" Signor Winpenny," said the staid matron, " will have the complaisance to allow me to hear the remainder of what you, reverend father, may have to edify me by saying on the subject of that wicked race, the Jews."

" Madam," replied the priest, " the Jews, according to the best historians, were guilty of the grossest cruelties in Egypt, in Africa, and in Cyprus, when they revolted against the Emperors Adrian and Trajan."

" The Jews," said Mynheer Von Drick, interrupting the propounder of the sacred volume, " the Jews to whom you stand indebted for your religion, which changes about like a weathercock, and, comparatively speaking, is only of yesterday—the Jews, bad as you make them out to be, are far more excusable for what they did than the Roman Catholics for the execrable deeds wantonly performed by them in America and elsewhere ; for the Jews were a conquered people, tributary to the Romans, but the Catholics held sway where they tyrannized ; and, moreover, were they not conquerors of immense possessions in America, who revelled in abundance of all esteemed things, with great nations lying prostrate before them?"

" Young man," now exclaimed the malignant father, unable to contain himself longer on perceiving me to smile, " it behoveth you to remember that your days may be few in this land of trial, and that hereafter your punishment may be lasting. Leaving you, however, to reflect on these things, and charitably hoping that both you and your more aged adviser there may, by repentance and prayer, purge yourselves of all blasphemies and heresies, I now challenge Signor Von Drick to prove his calumnious charges against the Roman Catholics for their conduct to the heathens of America."

" Reverend father," rejoined the physician, " the Jesuits say crime cannot be greater than the conscience makes it ; therefore, make your mind easy, for mine sits lightly upon me ; but, to answer your challenge, the Spaniards, who were called good Catholics, landed upon the coasts of two great civilized nations who had begun to enjoy the sweets of peace, when they massacred twelve millions of their people, and hunted men with dogs; moreover, Ferdinand, King of Castile, assigned pensions to the dogs who tore their flesh for their good services.

" The heroic conquerors of the New World, who massacred an unarmed, naked, and harmless people, had haunches of men and women, buttocks, arms, and calves of the legs, in ragouts, served up at their tables.   They roasted Guatimozin, King of Mexico.   They entered Peru fired with the zealous design of converting King Atabalipa.   A priest called Almagro, son of a priest condemned in Spain for a highway robbery, came with a certain thief, named Pizarro, to signify to his Majesty, by the mouth of another priest, that a third priest, called Alexander the Sixth, a monster in the shape of man, polluted by incests, assassinations, and murders, had given not only Peru, but half of the New World, to the King of Spain, and that Atabalipa should therefore immediately submit, under the pain of incurring the displeasure of the Apostles St Peter and St Paul, of whom he had never before heard.   And as the king did not understand Latin any more than the priest who read the bull, he was immediately declared an unbeliever and an heretic.   They burned Atabalipa, as they had roasted Guatimozin.   They massacred his nation—put the next inca to a cruel death—and all this to rob them of hard yellow earth, which has served for no other end but to depopulate and impoverish Spain ; for it has made them neglect the true earth, the provider of all that is good here, and which, when cultivated, employs and subsists mankind.

" Confess now, holy father," added he, with emphasis, " that had that chimerical being, the devil, been inclined to make men after his image, he could not have made them more abominable, or more infernal, than were these conquerors and rulers, lay and clerical, but who, nevertheless, are denominated good Catholics."

During this discourse ungovernable fury was conspicuous in every feature of the priest's face, and his eyes sparkled with the fire of anger ; but he was incapable of speaking.   For my part, I expected that a visitation of apoplexy would have been made to the reverend gentleman, which might have saved him the trouble of further controversy ; but I was deceived, he was made of tougher materials than I had given him credit for.

My hostess, who best knew the character of the evangelical gentleman, laying her hand upon his arm, while his paroxysm of rage was great, calmly observed to him that the Lord Jesus himself reproved Peter for cutting off the man's ear, therefore no disciple of the church ought to give way to violence.

" Yes, madam," stammered the furious priest, " I allow that St Peter was reproved by our Lord, but it was not until after he had taken revenge on the offender.   Christ let him use his sword before he replaced it in the scabbard, and thus it is the foes of the church should be dealt with by the priesthood."

" Hush, dear learned senor," rejoined the dame, " you know you can excommunicate, and do what you please, to heretics ; but we are all heated.   Let us forget this business, and, as a proof of forgiveness, drink together of a generous cordial from my cupboard."

The matron now opened her cupboard, and took from it a small stand of cordial bottles and glasses, together with a plate of biscuits, when we went through the ceremony of drinking "oblivion to past unpleasant feelings ;" but, while he drank the toast, malignancy was depicted in the priest's countenance, freed from every particle of Christian humility ; and that revengeful feelings were harboured in his breast, no one who beheld him could doubt.

While things were going on thus at our lodging-house, where numerous were the arguments and altercations we had with the vengeful father, the bigamist was slily undermining the affections of fair Rosa, who believed all that he said, and trembled with horror whenever he touched on her confessor's love towards her ; consequently, with so smooth a path before him, that experienced character soon persuaded the maiden to take clandestine leave of her parents, who were people in poor circumstances, partly dependant on her worthless aunt, herself under his protection.

When a maid blushes consent to her gallant's tender proposition, no time should be _ him in carrying his plans into execution. The bigamist was very sensible of this, and acc ingly so managed the business, that at an early hour of the morning, following the fair one's acquiescence, a post-carriage was in readiness outside of the city gate, with his bag and baggage packed thereon, and shortly after pretty Rosa Matilda, with her little bundle in her hand, came tripping along to join her anxious gallant, when they stepped into the carriage, and away they went as fast as a pair of good horses could convey them, bound for fair Florence, the garden of Italy.

Our bigamist decidedly was a great sensualist, and also a most designing character, where cunning could avail in administering to his sensuality, but then almost all his desires centred in love. Even learning he made subservient to the tender passion, and from his not having acquired a thorough knowledge of Italian, I verily believe that his chief motive in stealing pretty Rosa Matilda away was, that she might become his tutoress in the soft Italian language, which an experienced monarch of Spain pronounces the fittest to be taught from the lips of beauty. The bigamist's cavalier departure was almost instantly known at our house; but as he had taken the precaution of leaving a letter for me, enclosing money to discharge the land-lady's account, it created no particularly unfavourable sensation, though the landlady failed not to pronounce his way of departure as a shabby transaction. When, however, the day was more advanced, and the parents of Rosa Matilda had missed their fair daughter, great became the outcry and confusion, until at length it was fully understood in what manner she had taken her departure, with the bigamist as the companion of her flight.

The poor girl's parents were now distracted, and my hostess most furious; and as a thing of course Father Le Querque was immediately sent for to be consulted. I was present when he came, and never can I forget the imprecations he uttered against the bigamist. Indeed the reverend gentleman entirely lost sight of the precepts of Christianity, and displayed only the feelings of ferocity, swearing most dreadful vengeance. However, to pass from this la-mentable instance of the weakness of human nature displayed in an evangelical preacher, I shall mention, that under his counsel and direction no time was lost in sending people after the fugitives; but their endeavours proved futile, as they could not overtake them, though they were near doing so at Placentia, having literally entered that city just as the pair of lovers quitted it in an opposite direction. The officers of justice even followed them to the frontier of the duchy; but the wily Bigamist, who knew when and where he might consider his prize of beauty safe in his possession, never came to a halt until he had passed this barrier, and thereby triumphantly achieved his object, laughing, no doubt, with the fair one, at the disap-pointment and rage of the ghostly father.

Happy love is a great dulcifier of life, and to judge by what their pursuers heard, Apollo himself could not have been more enchanted with the fair daughter of Admetus than was the bigamist with the beautiful girl who had chosen him for her protector. They journeyed together delighted with all they saw, and no doubt the world appeared to them a wide spread-ing garden of fruits and flowers, where from storms or thorns they had nothing to apprehend. Variety too, which is coveted in all ages of life, is doubly pleasing to youth, and therefore to Rosa Matilda, a lass in her teens, and our bigamist who was yet a young man, the journey could not be otherwise than a delightful one; indeed, the bigamist was always of the phi-losopher Martin's opinion that this world abounds with good things, and he is a mere dolt who neglects to enjoy all that he can of them.

But leaving the happy pair to journey on mutually enraptured with each other, and find fresh delights awaiting them at every new stage, it behoves me to mention, that the holy confessor and his friend my hostess, after ascertaining there was no chance of their recovering the fugi-tive maiden, or obtaining satisfaction of the man who had stole her away, turned all their ven-geance against me, and secretly confederated together on the best method of visiting me with condign punishment, and, if possible, enriching themselves at my expense.

One evening, as I was on my return home alone from a private concert, much to my con-sternation, I was arrested in the public street on the charge of treason against the state, and instantly hurried away to prison, without having any opportunity of seeing or sending for my secretary or any other person. On our arrival at the gaol, I was delivered into the custody of a ferocious fellow, its governor, who had no sooner given a receipt for my body than he conducted me to a strong airy cell, situated at the upper part of the building. The cell was lit by a small window next the street, which no captive could well hope to escape by, as it was secured by a strong iron grating, which passed the whole length over the window.

I put several questions to the gaoler, but the surly fellow would give no direct answer to my inquiries, but locked me up, and departed as expeditiously as he could, leaving me to my own meditations, which were not the pleasantest; indeed, the more I reflected on the subject of my being apprehended on a charge of treason, the more was I bewildered at the unaccountable strangeness of the event. The gaoler, however, had left me no light, and wearied with forming vain conjectures, I soon stretched myself on the bedstead, and after an hour or two spent in painful contemplation fell fast asleep.

I awoke not until one of the gaolers entered my cell next morning, bearing my allowance of food. Scarcely had he set down the ration before he glanced his eyes around the cell; looked under the wooden stretcher; and next mounted on the stool, to satisfy himself that all was right at the grated window; when muttering something in a low voice, he commenced examining the bolts and lock; which done, he departed, bolting and doubly locking the door.

"If I am to augur from this fellow's conduct," thought I, "he must have received strict injunctions regarding me; and certainly, the charge of treason on which I have been apprehended, justifies the adoption of strong precautionary measures to secure my person. However, knowing myself to be innocent of any offence committed or premeditated against the government of this duchy, it follows that my captivity has been occasioned by the agency of some vindictive enemy or enemies; but who, I am at a loss to conjecture. When the gaoler next visits me, I will ask him for pen, ink, and paper, that I may invite friends to see me, by their means to find out the cause of my imprisonment."

In many cases it is easier to form resolutions than to put them into execution. The gaoler who probably was desirous of leaving me ample time for contemplation, made no second visit that day, therefore writing letters or dispatching messages were acts not to be performed.

"Confound the fellow," muttered I, after some hours had elapsed, and I had well pondered over the circumstance of my captivity! "confound him, why doesn't he come to see what may be wanted here? Does the rascal suppose a prisoner feels no wants? However," added I, raising my voice, "it is high time to prepare and send off letters, so that prompt measures may be taken by my friends to get me released from this disgusting place, when I hope to obtain full and honourable satisfaction for the indignity and wrongs heaped upon me."

Having thus terminated my soliloquy, I instantly, by thundering at the door and calling aloud, commenced my endeavours at obtaining what was necessary for the accomplishment of my wishes; but all my noise availed not, although it was made loud enough to disturb an entire street, and was reiterated for better than half an hour, the gaoler not choosing to make his appearance, nor allow any of his turnkeys to answer the summons made upon them.

"Pretty treatment this," muttered I, seating myself upon the bed, tired by the futile efforts I had made. "This is conduct to provoke a saint; but I must not forget, that he who would triumph over difficulties must keep himself cool and collected;" then, after humming a tune for a few seconds, I remarked, taking up my allowance of food, that the adage, of hunger being the best sauce, came very home to me; when, without more words, I set to and demolished the day's ration.

I had ample time afforded me for the display of my patience; for, after I had devoured my ration of food, day gradually waned away, until the shades of night darkened my cell, yet no gaoler made his appearance.

I now wrapped the coverlid of the bed around me, and extended my limbs once more on the wooden stretcher to take my nightly repose; but although I possessed one of the happiest of constitutions, and that my body was habituated to hardships, it would be asserting an untruth to affirm that I enjoyed my ordinary night's sleep; in fact, my mind, in spite of philosophy, continued feverishly active for hours after I had laid myself down, and I obtained no sleep. Powerful nature, however, afterwards asserted her prerogative, and I slept soundly until awakened on the following morning by the unbarring of my cell door.

The uncouth savage of a turnkey, who had come to pay his morning visit, said nothing upon entering, but looked about the cell to satisfy himself that all was as it should be, when he was on the eve of taking his departure; but I, who had hitherto eyed the fellow with silent contempt, mentioned to him my want of writing materials.

He condescended not to reply, but after regarding me in a supercilious way, turned himself towards the door, the lock of which was already under his hand, that he might depart; when, overcome by feelings of anger, I suddenly sprung from off the bedstead and caught the fellow by the neck, when, by the violence of my grasp, I forced him to let go the lock, and raise both his hands, with the design of saving himself from strangulation. "Wretch," now said I, casting the man upon his back on the bedstead, "let this lesson teach you how to behave to a prisoner another time, and deem yourself fortunate in being so leniently treated; some men in my situation, with their feelings excited by your brutality, would dash your brains out against the stone-wall."

"Mercy," ejaculated the terrified ruffian, raising himself upon his breech on the bed, and staring with awe and wonder, "if I have offended, I ask pardon; but pray, signor, whatever you do, let me go away; for if you detain me here, I shall lose my place, and be a ruined man."

Fear enacts wonders. The advantage I had gained over him had completely tamed the turnkey, and I availed myself of this circumstance to propose terms, which otherwise he would not have listened to; but, as a bribe was the basis of my conditions, he was brought to consent to them. Accordingly, that same day writing materials were brought to me, and I wrote and dispatched away an epistle to my secretary, as also one to Mynheer Von Drick, which the now accommodating turnkey undertook should be delivered into their hands.

CHAPTER XXVIIL

"Well I know how treachery works;
Still near his prey the tiger lurks
Conspiracy, still dark and deep,
Silent on bloody claws doth creep."

"With languor to his mat he crept,
And, whatsoe'er his visions, quickly slept."

"Let's not be dainty of leave-taking,
But shift away; there's warrant in that theft
Which steals itself when there's no mercy left."

THE brutal ferocity with which men destroy each other in open warfare, serves to impress the mind with a disadvantageous idea of human kind; but the insidious arts practised in private life to overreach, ruin, and bring misery, want, and disgrace upon others, inspire us with still more bitter, more melancholy reflections. In times of peace, innate depravity is the main source of wicked actions; but when war takes place, the animosity of individuals being freed by designing legislators from the restraints imposed by civil laws, affords them a pretence for the display of demoniac passions.

The contemplation of truths like the foregoing, degrading to our species, cannot be otherwise than painful to the mind; consequently I felt highly pleased when at length I was interrupted in a chain of such unpleasant thoughts by the unbarring of my cell door. The gaoler had come to give entrance to a friend of mine, and this was Mynheer Von Drick. He expressed joy at seeing me, and said that he had lost no time in coming to the prison after the receipt of my note; but that the captain, for this was the title he usually gave Monday, was out when he left their lodging, and public report had bruited it abroad that very treasonable papers had been discovered in my trunk.

"It is inexplicable; the whole business is inexplicable," was my reply; "the charge is ungrounded; I am innocent of any offence against the government."

"The captain," resumed the physician, "is indefatigable in your behalf. He has allowed himself no rest since your apprehension, but has already been with several great personages of the duchy, who, however, decline interesting themselves in the cause of one charged with the crime of high treason. But these men," added he indignantly, "are the children of prosperity; believe me, on a levee day, at this paltry court here, I could point you out scores of these reptiles."

"You are a plain, straightforward, honest man, friend Von Drick," said I, smiling; "but honesty and truth have long been out of fashion at court, therefore you have no business to go playing the spy there."

"I go there, indeed!" rejoined the indignant Hollander; "it would be an insult to suspect me. No; give me a last and a cobbler's awl—let me mend shoes, rather than be that viper—a courtier. The cobbler's is an honest trade, and the cobbler may be an independent man in his humble way, but the courtier's trade is a dishonest one from beginning to end. The syco-phant reaps what he never sowed. His idleness must be upheld by the industrious part of the community."

Here the worthy gentleman's philippic was put an end to by the appearance of my secre-tary, who, on entering the cell, expressed his joy in unqualified terms at having found out my place of anchorage; though, he added, he was sorry to see it was in shallow water, among the land sharks. He now acquainted me with all the vain efforts he had made to trace me out, and concluded by declaring his opinion that the intention of my persecutors had been to keep the place of my imprisonment a profound secret.

"But, captain," asked my Dutch friend, "have you made no discovery concerning the treasonable papers alleged to have been found in Monsieur Winpenny's baggage? For my part, I am most anxious to learn who is the author of this mischief; indeed, I would bet two to one that some Jezebel of a woman is at the bottom of the affair."

"Avast heaving there, commodore," rejoined the sailor, laughingly.

"Who ever heard tell of the bottom part of a ship's cargo being discharged before a clear way was made for hoisting it out of her hold? However, after all is said, you sail with a fair breeze on this tack, for a brimstone hatched the conspiracy; but then, d'ye see, a Jesuit put his hand to the helm, to carry her through with the management."

"A brimstone and a Jesuit may sail in the same boat without fear of their honesty over-loading her: they are suitable mates for each other, no matter whether in a convent or a conventicle," was my Dutch friend's observation.

My secretary now informed me, that having suspected my valet as a party implicated in causing my misfortune, he had locked himself in a chamber with him, and closely questioned the fellow, who, however, stoutly denied every thing, until, eventually, he clapped the muzzle of a pistol to his head, and threatened him with instant death unless he atoned for his in-gratitude by making a full confession as to his own conduct, and all he knew of the plans of his employers; but, provided he did this, had promised him not only pardon, but a handsome pecuniary reward; when, fear and hope operating together upon him, the man, who was a Roman Catholic, avowed that Father Le Querque had persuaded him that his master was a confirmed heretic, unworthy of being suffered to be at large, and that as there could be no virtue without the true faith, his best deeds were no more than shining sins; after which he had promised him full absolution for all his crimes, however black or numerous, on condition that he put certain papers, which would be given to him for the purpose, into his master's trunk, and acted in other respects according to instructions he would receive. The valet was thus induced to become a party in the confederation against me, and from what he had further stated to my secretary, it appeared that not only our hostess was concerned, but that a married lady of title and expensive habits, who occasionally visited her house, had, under the hope of sharing in my property, been brought over to fabricate a fresh charge against me of a violent attempt upon her chastity, which the priest and our hostess would be ready, by false evidence, to help to substantiate, so that, should the charge of treason fall to the ground, I might be convicted of this last crime.

Monday's statement caused me much surprise. I could scarcely credit the circumstance, that a female of title could stoop to act so black a part, and I remained for some time wrapped in silent meditation on the subject. The Dutchman, who had become disgusted at the relax-ation of morals witnessed by him among high classes of the Italian ladies, was the first to break silence, which he did by declaiming against women, and aristocratic honours entailed on their issue.

Did I not prophesy," said the now animated old gentleman, holding up both his hands in the manner of a genuine orator — "say, for I appeal to you both, did I not prophesy that a woman was at the bottom of all this mischief? Verily, verily, it could not have been other-wise, for women are the root of all evil. The genealogist is an impostor, as no man can be sure of his wife's virtue; neither can any man say with certainty, 'that is my father.' Let me then ask, why are fools proud of their ancestry? of that of which they are ignorant! Aristocratic rank should descend only in the female line, for on that of the male there may not remain one gout of noble blood. Truly fortunate was it for Louis the Fourteenth that his happened to be a white face; as, had it not, like the negress, his sister, he must have spent his days in a convent; and this, forsooth, as the courtiers would have said, because his virtuous mother, in her freakish moments, had looked too intently on her glossy African dwarf.

I could not refrain from smiling at the vehemence of my learned friend in delivering his philippic against the fairest work of the creation; but my secretary heeded him not, for he was too deeply absorbed in reflecting upon what might be the most advisable way to employ himself to get me promptly liberated from prison, to allow of his attention being diverted to another channel.

After some further conversation, it was agreed upon by the trio of us that my friends should bring an able lawyer on the following day, that we might consult with him on what was to be done, when they from necessity departed, leaving me to another night's solitary imprisonment. Next morning, however, they came punctual to their time, with a legal gentleman as their companion, who had already sifted, as far as was practicable, into my affair.

Where there are most laws there is least polity, and this gentleman, being a thorough lawyer, has discovered there would be no possibility of rebutting the evidence against me, and that for the most potent of reasons, namely, because the said evidence was entirely founded on falsehood, and therefore could be enlarged and strengthened to any point requisite for ensuring the prisoner's conviction; a sort of evidence which Parma lawyers, in the cant of their profession, style the invincible.

"The countess, Signor Winpenny," said this enlightened counsellor, "has positively sworn that you made a forcible attempt on her chastity, and, moreover, that you have communicated to her a plan you have formed for subverting the government of this duchy; while, unfortunately, the Jesuit priest, Le Querque, circumstantially confirms her testimony by deposing that she communicated these things to him at the confessional, and he admits that it was by his advice your crime of treason was made known to the proper authorities, by whose order your baggage was seized, and your person taken into custody. Unfortunately, too, full and corroborating proofs of your guilt have been found deposited in a trunk of yours. Indeed, seignor," added the counsellor, with peculiar emphasis, "it appears the clearest law case I ever gave professional advice on; you have not a loop-hole to escape by."

"Heaven preserve us," exclaimed Mynheer Von Drick; "yes, Heaven preserve us from the machinations of such a terrible woman; she is more to be dreaded than plague and pestilence." "And Heaven preserve us from the disciples of old Dominick," observed my secretary. "The symbol on their flag is a mad dog, bearing a lit torch in its mouth. They are all precious rascals; and as Mynheer properly says, a Jesuit and a brimstone may sail in the same craft without fear of their honesty sinking her."—"In most cases of common law," resumed the counsellor, disregarding the observations just made, "alibi's and false swearing may be resorted to with success, to mislead a judge and confound a jury; then, again, provided it was a case of debt sworn unjustly against you, we could ensure a nonsuit by bringing witnesses to prove payment of the amount, though you had never owed it, or had a transaction with the perjured claimant. In a Chancery suit where affidavits are received as sterling testimony, the wealthiest man bringing most of these documents, no matter how false they are, may almost to a certainty ensure to himself the estate of any poor wretch, especially when he has previously got possession; though sometimes it will happen that he has to throw his untold folios of affidavits overboard, and resort to common law for his verdict. But, Signor Winpenny," concluded the learned man, sorrowfully shaking his head, "this case of yours seems altogether hopeless and desperate."

"Your opinion is extremely unfavourable," replied I, "yet, learned signor, I must request you will once more consider over this business surely there must be some way by which an innocent man's conduct may be justified from false charges made against him."

"Innocence has no claims upon the law—evidence is all we lawyers look to," replied he, with profound gravity. "If, indeed, these damning papers had not been found among your baggage, something perhaps might be done to rebut the charge of treason. Then, again, was the countess a poor woman, we could procure certificates of insanity, as also that of her colleague, the father confessor, for medical gentlemen run no risk on such occasions, as it is an established truth in law that *nemo mortalium omnibus horis sapit.*"

"Many," resumed my legal adviser, after a few minutes of reflection, "yea, hundreds of our fellow-creatures, who are no more deranged in their intellects than I am, are annually incarcerated within the walls of madhouses by means of this expedient; but then, the lady in question being wealthy, it follows that there would be a commission established in her case, and from what information I have gathered, her husband is not as yet sufficiently tired of her to join with us in our plan, consequently we should be defeated. Indeed, I must once more repeat, this is a bad cause; a cause in which every art can be practised against us to impose upon judgment, and to defeat the ends of justice : we have everything to fear, and little or nothing to hope. In short the cause is so very bad, that I apprehend I must throw up my brief."

The learned lawyer, though he was burdened with rather too great a share of honesty for a Parma advocate, yet prudently took further time to determine whether or not he would throw up his brief; and during this interval of suspense he obtained an interview with my treacherous valet, as also with the still more treacherous father Le Querque.

From the former he heard a confirmation of all which that person had confessed to my secretary; while, by his conference with the priest, he satisfied himself that he was to be bought over, but then the bribe must be enormous : considering, therefore, that the Jesuit was too unprincipled to be relied on, even although bribed, at our next meeting the counsellor again candidly confessed that he knew not what course to recommend. I thanked the learned gentleman for the zeal he had displayed in my cause, and after making a suitable pecuniary compliment, dismissed him, saying I would take a day or two to consider over the business, when I would make known to him my determination.

Scarcely had the door been closed on the long-robed gentleman, after his last visit, ere my secretary broke forth in invectives against the Jesuits. "For his part," he said, "he didn't believe any young woman could long retain her virtue, nor any man his honesty, who had a Jesuist for their ghostly confessor. In short," added the worthy sailor, "villany and Jesuitism go hand-in-hand together, and so closely, that should Old Nick take a spell upon earth among the Jesuits, no matter whether he assumed the sex of man or that of woman, or came in a black or a white skin, he would inevitably be caught in their traps, and fall a victim to their machinations."

The worthy physician, notwithstanding the prejudice he had imbibed against certain Parma dames of fashion, with the kind hope of softening thereby her evidence and serving me, now departed to pay a visit to the dashing countess, who had thought fit to institute a grievous charge against me, and at the expiration of a couple of hours the good man re-entered my cell, almost breathless with agitation, when some time elapsed before he could compose his ideas sufficiently to make known the grounds of his fear; a fear growing out of his apprehensions from her threats, and the conversation which had passed between them, that the countess, as a punishment for his officious interference in her affair with me, might swear an attempt at rape against himself. Fear has many eyes; yet this conceit of the good gentleman appeared so ridiculous, that I could not forbear smiling when he made the communication; but my secretary laughed for several minutes at the idle apprehension, as he termed Mynheer Von Drick's conceit, and then told him to keep a light heart, and should the worst happen, defend the action, either by establishing an *alibi*, or pleading corporeal infirmity.

The astronomer bore my secretary's jokes with good humour; nevertheless he shuddered on contemplating the character of the fair countess, and certainly could not have mastered his antipathy sufficiently to have paid the lady another visit in my behalf. After his departure, my secretary, having cautiously closed the door, in a half whisper asked what I purposed doing to get out of that vile gaol; for his part, he said, if I would be guided by him, he'd warrant I'd soon hoist my anchor apeak, and make sail from the foul berth I was in.

"Since you tender your advice so freely, my friend, and that I well know your sincerity, let me hear what you have to propose," said I.

"A crow bar, in your honour's hands, may be made to clear away a part of yon grating, and a sound inch rope might serve to lower you into the street below."

" I understand you," replied I. " Flight you think preferable to captivity, and in this case, where personal honour is not concerned, I am of your way of thinking; be it therefore your office to provide the articles you have mentioned, and it will be my fault if I don't make a proper use of them."

" Enough, enough has been said ; the craft which has many reaches to work through before she floats in good sea room, should, with the turn of the tide, commence her voyage down the stream ; therefore, your honour, I'll sheer off, without waiting to hoist up Blue Peter."

As he had spoken so he acted. My secretary departed at the termination of his speech ; but, before two hours had elapsed, re-entered my cell, when, having closed the door, he extracted several fathoms of rope from under his coat, where it had lain snugly coiled round his body. Moreover, the zealous sailor repeated this feat. so often during that and the ensuing day, that the pieces which had been brought by him, when spliced to each other, formed a rope of sufficient length to extend from my cell to the pavement of the street beneath ; after which a crow bar, smuggled into the gaol under his trowsers, served to fulfil this part of his engagement. It should, however, be remarked, that in all probability the gallant sailor would not have been able to accomplish this task, had it not been that the gaolers were grown less vigilant in their care of me than was usual for them to be with prisoners ; but whether this relaxation had been caused by the free circulation of my money amongst them, would be ungenerous, and perhaps imprudent, to promulgate. Whatever it arose from, the negligence was favourable to my views, insomuch as it enabled me to get the crow bar and coil of rope, and to keep these things apparently undiscovered beneath my bed.

Two o'clock of the morning, after our arrangements were completed, was the time fixed upon for attempting my escape, and punctual to the minute, my secretary was at the appointed spot, where I soon had the satisfaction of joining him ; but extremely to his surprise, instead of descending by the rope from my cell window, as he calculated on my doing, I made my exit from the prison by the identical door through which I had been conducted into this place of incarceration.

" Your honour," said the astonished sailor, while we were jogging fast along the street, "your honour must have come the old soldier over the rogue of a gaoler, for apparently you have made no use of the rope which I smuggled into the prison."

" Gold has mollified a pair of hard hearts and opened a strongly barred door," replied I. " The rope and the crow bar, however, are not without their use. The gaolers will make it appear to the world that I escaped by these means ; and although the artful fellows knew these things were under my bedding, and notwithstanding that the turnkey himself saw me pass safely out of the prison, yet by masking their treachery, they, like some villains of a high grade in society, who effectually cloak and mask their iniquitous deeds, will continue to retain their situations."

CHAPTER XXIX.

" Much my tale would swell,
Might I the war-horse virtues tell ;
Yet trace him through but one day's chance,
A whirlwind in the first advance—
A fury in the battle's heat—
A guardian angel in retreat,—
Who bears the loser from the fray,
And saves him for a luckier day ;
By whose good help, when fortune's down,
Full many a king hath saved his crown."

" Enough, good Hylas, we each other know,
A truce to compliment, 'tis friendship's foe."

" THE horses are standing ready rigged just without the city gates, and the passport is snug in my pocket," said the sailor, soon as we had passed a street or two ; " so, your honour, let us bear a hand and push ahead while the breeze favours, and the enemy has no frigates abroad."

" Show the way, Monday, with the best speed you can," was my laconic reply.

It was a dark morning, and a drizzling rain fell; but these were circumstances favourable to a fugitive. We passed through the town without meeting more than two or three straggling persons; when, by virtue of Monday's passport, which he had procured in the names of two of his acquaintances resembling us in age and size, we found no difficulty in satisfying the guard, and getting egress at the city gates. Having now proceeded a short distance, we came to a cabaret, in the stable of which, thanks to the sailor's arrangement, three post-horses were standing ready bridled and saddled.

My secretary directed the attendant courier to bring out his horses, and the landlord, who seemed half asleep, his dram bottle, when recommending me to take a *gout* of *eau-de-vie* and a mouthful of bread and Parmesian cheese, to fortify my stomach against the damp of the morning air, he himself, contrary to the custom of medical advisers, enforced his own recommendation by taking a double dose of the liquid prescribed for another.

"Foul weather befal the rascally old Jesuit, and the letter out of this overgrown garran besides," say I. "Would that his reverence the priest was here, riding between us, mounted on this restive jade, and that I was aloft on a smoother goer; that's all I've to say," observed Monday, after his horse had started off, kicking and plunging at every step.

"Riding, I perceive, is not your fort, and you are mounted on a vicious animal; therefore let us change horses," said I.

"Never fear me, sir; I'll keep my seat, I warrant," replied the sailor, whose maritime pride forbade of his dismounting.

"Pride!" says one of our adages, "generally meets with a fall." Before we had proceeded far, the sailor was thrown headlong from his horse, and thereby punished for his obstinacy, which is the name for persevering courage when misapplied. Fortunately, as it prevented him from being maimed, his head pitched on the thickest part of a mud-heap scraped on one side of the road; but, jumping up as soon as he could extricate himself from his uninviting bed, he bawled in a loud voice that he was overboard, but trusted I would take either his or the postillion's horse in tow.

The advice was not thrown away. Finding the loose charger had galloped to the rear, and that our attendant was on the eve of following after him, I promptly stopped the fellow from executing the retrograde movement by seizing hold of his horse's bridle; when Monday, notwithstanding his woful plight, stepped to the opposite side of the steed, and in coarse terms ordered the rider to dismount and go on foot after his beast; for he and his friend, he said, should employ their time better than in searching after vicious runaway horses.

The man, evidently dissatisfied at the order, commenced starting objections to complying with it; on which the sailor, unwilling to waste time in useless discussion, caught hold of him round the waist, and lifted him from his horse, when he himself mounted the animal, and saying that the pair of hacks and money for their hire should be left with the postmaster at the next stage, he put spurs to his charger and galloped away, leaving our late attendant, thanks to the fraternal embrace he had received, in nearly as muddy a condition as himself.

We now proceeded on our way at a brisk rate; till, after a time, checking my pace, I jocularly said, "The Jew, when he takes in his neighbour with a bad article, declares that a fair exchange is no robbery; and you, my friend, by your late bargain, show yourself to be much of the Jew's way of thinking."

"Why, sir, to own the truth, the capsize I have had has taught me that he who rides post on a bad horse, when his postillion is aloft upon a good goer, is but a ninny for his pains."

"You are a gainer more ways than one by this exchange," observed I; "but, joking apart, 'tis well you were not hurt by the fall."

"A sound hull, your honour, receives no injury by running foul of a mud bank; yet I'm in a pretty pickle I must own, and the sooner I get scrubbed down the better," rejoined he, looking at his own dirty condition.

We put to proof the good bottom of our horses; for aided only by several short delays at cabarets on our route, to bait the generous animals, we managed to reach a large posting village on the road to Placentia, to which, after our cavalier treatment of the postillion, we deemed it advisable to proceed, instead of going in an opposite direction, under pretence of which we had hired the post-horses.

"*Ah, mon Dieu,*" exclaimed the ostler, who was a Frenchman, when he received charge of our cattle at the inn door here, "these horses belong to old Deranzy, of the Pewter Pot, in the faubourg of Parma old city."

" You think yourself a shrewd fellow, no doubt," said the sailor; "nevertheless you may be wrong for once in your life."

" Ha, ha, ha!" laughed aloud the ostler, "wrong for once in my life, did you say? Yes, senors, mayhap I may, for who can be always right? Howsoever, by Saint Benedict, I am not in the wrong box this time. Here, too, are my evidences, and they shall bear me through the truth of my story. This, gentlemen," added he, patting one of the horses, "this is Whistling Meg, as good a goer as any mare that travels the road; but then she has got a string halt, and is a little thick in the wind or so. Then, again, here's Old Boreas, as noisy and hard trotting a gelding as rider ever crossed; but I'll tell you what, senors, you were in luck's way not to have had the old trooping horse hired out to you, for if you had, depend on it you would not have forgotten him in a hurry."

" Why," inquired the sailor, "what is there remarkable in the animal you allude to?"

" Why, master, to let you into a bit of a secret, you must know, it is not long since I lived ostler at the Pewter Pot, and the old trooper there, I can assure you, is a rum one. How Deranzy managed to train him, I am sure I don't know, though this is certain, he keeps him to let out to strangers; and as soon as the old devil gets some little distance on the road, he kicks off his rider, and gallops home to his stable, where a feed of corn, he knows, is in the manger ready for him.

" Deranzy, who on these occasions stays on the watch for him, now sends the trooper away to work at a farm he has some miles from the Pewter Pot, and pretending the horse is lost, he frightens his unfortunate customer by threats of a law-suit to recover its value, until at last the poor fellow is glad to compromise the business by paying money to advertise the lost animal, and make up for a week or two of his hire."

" If what you say be correct, this Deranzy must be a precious rascal," observed the sailor, rather angrily.

" 'Tis as true as that I stand here," rejoined the ostler; "howsoever, provided your honour misgives my word, you have but to ask among the sailor chaps of Genoa, who sometimes travel this way, whether or not they've heard talk of Deranzy's trooping horse, and I'll take on me to warrant you'll hear enough about him."

" Why would you have me inquire among the sailors, more than any other class of people?" asked Monday, somewhat pettishly.

" Lord bless your honour," replied the grinning ostler "anybody may take in a sailor; a sailor scarcely knows a horse from a cow—you may believe it or not, as you please; but, on my oath, a Dutch skipper bought a mule of my old master for the purpose of keeping her to breed; and another spoony of a skipper took a great fancy to an aged nag, almost past his work, because he had very long grinders, which this sailor captain said would give him a good start at an inn stable, by enabling him to eat two allowances of hay and corn to another horse's one. Pincher was the name of this horse, and it was lucky he hadn't been bishoped, that master might palm him off for a young 'un, as he got more money for him than he would have got for a six year old gelding."

" These were lubberly bargemen, and not sailors, who were taken-in in this foolish manner," said Monday, evidently annoyed by the conversation.

" Ha, ha, ha!" again laughed the ostler, disregarding the last observation, and then adding, "Deranzy has gathered lots of shiners from the sailors; the old trooper is kept on purpose to accommodate such flats, and they have paid him her value twenty times over."

" Come, my friend," said I, smiling, and drawing Monday aside, "the ostler pushes you too hard; you will do well to call to mind the words of your own inimitable bard,

" Let the stricken deer go weep,
The hart ungalled play;"

for, rest assured, when we have the free choice left us, no matter whether we may be stricken in mind or body, the wisest course is to play like the hart, and not suffer affliction like the wounded deer."

" Would that I had the lubber aboard a-ship. I'd soon teach him the difference between a sailor and an ostler fellow," muttered Monday, walking away from his unintentional insulter.

From feeling apprehensive that news of my flight would speedily be spread throughout the duchy, and considering the circumstance of the horses my secretary and I had journeyed on being well known here, I deemed it prudent immediately to decamp, and resume our journey, in such a way as would attract the least notice, and leave reason for the people of our hotel to imagine we were still in the village.

Accordingly, after having given directions that the horses should be taken good care of during the time of our absence, we quitted the hotel, and on foot proceeded on our journey towards the frontiers of the empress-queen's rule. It was our intention to get into the first diligence that might overtake us; and after we had marched at a brisk pace for several hours, that of Placentia came up, but, to our disappointment, had its full complement of passengers. Presently afterwards, a courier, who also overtook us, stopped his horse to mention that, when he left Parma, search was making there after a runaway traitor, and provided that either of us should be the man, he said he would advise him to get out of sight of people on the high road.

The well-meaning courier was no sooner lost to our view than we profited by his good advice, and taking a distant hill on the road for our guide, directed our course for it; but walking over a pathless country, where hedges, ditches, trees, and newly-ploughed land obstruct the way, admits of little comparison, in the fatigue it causes, to journeying on foot upon a smooth road; and of this we were soon made sensible. Besides, sailors are not remarkable for being good pedestrians; and Monday, for example, had not exercised his legs more than two hours in walking over the broken soil before he declared that he could get on no longer, but must come to an anchor, to take a short spell of rest.

"Yonder is a shepherd, tending his sheep; we will seat ourselves beside him," was my smiling reply.—"Willingly, willingly, sir," rejoined the sailor, and the pair of us trod our way over the greensward, to the bank upon which the shepherd was seated.

The four-footed guardian of the sheep boldly confronted us, to oppose our further progress towards his master's seat ; and, with the hair of his back bristled up, and his long white teeth rendered furious by his snarl, looked no contemptible opponent; but his master's word and whistle in an instant tamed this faithful slave, who, obedient to his duty, at the shepherd's order turned to his daily occupation of lording it over the fleecy flock, and left us to pursue our path in quiet.

The shepherd was a silver-headed, lame old man, yet he cheerfully rose from his seat to salute us, and shortly afterwards the whole three were comfortably seated beside each other, under a shady tree, on the verdant bank.

The complimentary expletives resorted to, to mask truth in more fashionable life, were not called for at this meeting; but, pleased at the unsophisticated manners of the shepherd, after some little conversation had passed touching his fleecy charge, I thus addressed him :—

"Your days, my friend, must be passed away rationally. The struggles of men after the gewgaws of life disturb you not; but nature, in all her luxuriant simplicity, constantly grati fies your sight."

"You say true, worthy sir," replied the shepherd, "I have grown old amongst my sheep; and, God be praised, am well satisfied with my lot."

"'Tis an enviable one to a man who can divest himself of ambition, which few in the busy world know how to do," observed I.

"Ha, this is what Strephon has taught me," said the shepherd. "Till Strephon came home from the wars, I was not so content. He it was taught every one in our village to be satisfied with his lot; but mayhap, sir," added he, looking earnestly in my face, "you have read or heard talk of Strephon and Hylas, for we have been sung together in a book called the ' Belgic Pastorals.'"

"Ha, worthy shepherd; is it you then, is it Hylas that I see?" said Monday, extending his hand to take that of the old shepherd. "I have read the ' Pastorals' of which thou speakest; but so far was I from ever expecting to meet Hylas, that really, until now, I entertained doubts whether Strephon and Hylas were real characters."

"Real to be sure," exclaimed he, with emphasis; "but the night is drawing in, and I am going home with my flock; therefore, if you are not better engaged, prithee, kind gentlemen, satisfy yourselves we are so by accompanying me to Strephon's abode, where, depend upon it, you will be welcomed as worthy guests ought to be."

"We accept of your invitation with joy," answered I, "and believe me to be sincere. kind shepherd, when I say, I would rather be the companion of Strephon and Hylas this night, to witness their happy friendship, than the guest of a monarch."

The lame shepherd now arose from his seat to collect together his flock, when I, who had never perused the ' Belgic Pastorals,' and consequently knew nothing of the story of Strephon and Hylas, availed myself of this opportunity for satisfying my curiosity by questioning Monday on the subject.

Hylas rejoined us, holding the bridle of a pony, which he had caught up from grazing among his sheep; and observed, that lameness, added to a touch of the infirmities of age, he trusted would sufficiently plead his excuse for riding home, when accompanied by foot companions far his betters in every respect.

The party of us proceeded on our way to Strephon's house, the lame shepherd seated on his pony, which walked between Monday and me, and the faithful dog taking the management of the flock.

"That was a rare happy day," now remarked Hylas. "Ah, that was a real happy day, on which the companion of my boyhoood returned home in safety from his arduous campaigns. His warlike tales, his music, and fine figure, soon won the hearts of some of our village lasses, and got him wedded to the richest of them all; since which, however, the house of Orange lost its rule over our native land, and sooner than remain living there under the new dynasty, Strephon and his family quitted the country of their birth, having sold all their property there, with the produce of which my friend bought an estate in this beautiful duchy, and I came here with his family, still to tend my friend's flocks. The clime is congenial to us all, and the way Strephon came to fix on this spot was from his having campaigned here when a soldier in the French army. What Strephon possesses I know is at my service, but I abuse not his confidence; and although Hylas is the envy of all shepherds who see him riding before his flock, yet, were it not for lameness, I would scorn to ride at this employ."

A spacious farm-house, surrounded by lofty elms, was Strephon's place of abode; and when our procession entered upon the lawn fronting his mansion, the worthy farmer came out to meet it. He was a tall, military-looking man, apparently verging on fifty, but athletic, and handsome for one of his age. He met us in the courteous pleasing manner peculiar to men trained in that great school the world, yet said nothing until Hylas had notified that we were travelling gentlemen, who, at his invitation, had come to pay him a visit; but then he welcomed us with great cordiality, and leaving Hylas to house his flock, himself led the way into his house.

In the snug parlour into which Strephon conducted us was his wife, a good-humoured buxom woman, about forty years of age, two of their sons under sixteen, and a daughter more than midway advanced in her teens; and, in addition to the family party, a benign-looking middle-aged man was housed there, who I was given to understand was the celebrated Signor Albini, well known in that quarter as the hermit astrologer.

"Friend Strephon," said the hermit, soon as the ceremony of introduction had taken place, "with these good signors' permission we will resume the conversation we were engaged in."

"Most willingly, for I always feel pleasure and derive instruction from hearing you discourse," replied Strephon; "and here," added he, "comes our friend Hylas most apropos for the subject, as astronomy is this honest shepherd's delight."

"Your last question," said the astrologer, soon as Hylas had seated himself, "regarded the signs of the zodiac, which apparently you think astronomers attach great importance to; but, my friend, here I must undeceive you, for in this opinion you are altogether in error."

"Why, then, do they make use of the signs?" asked Strephon.

"For the reasons why medical men write their prescriptions in Latin; why religion is involved in deep mystery; the law encumbered with useless words, foreign to the language of the country where it is practised; and that students are made to waste the best years of their lives in learning a smattering of dead languages, as is stated by pedants, to prepare them for the study of living tongues."

" If," rejoined Strephon, " I may venture to draw an inference from your observations, the signs of the zodiac are neither more nor less than mysterious symbols, invented to shade over astronomical ignorance."

" Precisely so ; every trade, profession, and religion has its mysteries, differing in degrees only proportionately to the clearness or obscurity of the rules and principles of the craft, or faith itself, and the relative degrees of knowledge or ignorance of its professors : thus, for example, the business of a carpenter, though of the highest utility, does not abound with mysteries, because almost every man is competent to judge of what he sees done. It is those things of which the great majority of mankind are incapable of judging correctly, such as the drawing up of law papers, or the exact proportion of drugs required to be mixed in a sick person's medicine, which leave most room for the practice of craft in those who prepare them."

" I feel the full truth of your remarks," observed Strephon. " In my campaigns, many is the fine fellow I have seen suffer—the victim of a wrong medicine."

" It will generally be found," resumed the astrologer, " that the most ignorant practitioners, as well as those professions which are of the least real utility to mankind, are the most remarkable for their frauds—that which is clear and simple being sound and good, and that which is complicated or veiled in mystery dangerous and worthless."

" Far as regards individual merit, I strongly feel the truth of these remarks," answered Strephon. " In my military career I could not but discover that the most silent, guarded characters generally are most shallow in capacity, and show themselves to be the worst principled where self-interest is at stake."

" Evidently so," said the astrologer. " Justice needs no veil, and genius ever casts mystery aside. Hence it follows that little-minded men, being incapable of feeling generous thoughts, are perpetually on the watch to aggrandize themselves, and consequently they rise to the higher stations among mankind."

" The days of Fabricius are long since gone by," observed Monday, with a smile. " Dare to be poor, and emulate a god, is not a maxim for this age."

" So much the more unfortunate for the age," observed the astrologer. " But to return to the subject of empiricism, which must ever be a thriving trade, inasmuch as the world love mystery, or, in other words, to be imposed on ; else, why so many religions, or why so many impostors ?

" A quack doctor, simply to become rich, should adopt a mode of practice ridiculous in itself, and contrary to reason in all its essential points ; but if he would amass a prodigious fortune, he must profess doing things in his practice which it is impossible can be done. Thus, for example, one man imposes his worthless mixture upon the world as a balm of Gilead, or vegetable pill, endowed with virtues to cure all complaints ; and the impostor, in due time, accumulates ample riches. Another designing knave starts up to out-Hector this quack by professing the power of divination ; and this wonder of the world, this more than Delphic oracle, speedily secures to himself a princely revenue : he pretends, by extracting what he calls the acrid humour from them, to prevent certain dreaded disorders afflicting his patients, who, to make the absurdity doubly glaring, usually are persons in sound health, until their bodies get mutilated by the cutting and maiming practice of this destroyer of his species."

Here Strephon's good dame interrupted the discourse by an exclamation of horror, and asked the astrologer if what he had stated really was fact ?

" Yes, signora," smilingly replied the sage ; " when man loses sight of reason, nothing can be too absurd for him, and this is as true as that the mud of the Ganges, stuffed into the mouth and nostrils of the dying, is the Hindoo priest's extreme unction."

" To return to the first subject," said Strephon, disregarding his good woman's question, at which the astrologer had smiled. " You acknowledge to us that the zodiac signs are but mysterious symbols, invented to veil over astronomical ignorance ; but you have not told us whence these symbols originated."

" To be brief, then, as I see the supper is being put on the table, I will content myself by quoting a passage from the tragedy of ' King Murat ' which, I think, will sufficiently elucidate the subject :—.

History tells,
A shepherd of Mount Caucasus 'twas framed
The zodiac—a geograpuic sphere—
Suiting his native land.'

I shall merely add, that what this ingenious shepherd devised as fit symbols to represent the petty state wherein he resided, astronomers, since his time, have but altered and enlarged; they not having been able to devise a more mysterious system than what these symbols afford for amusing the credulous readers of their almanacs."

Excellent food and a hearty welcome were given Strephon's guests at their supper, and choice wine constituted their beverage; compliments there were none shown, for Strephon had learnt in his travels that they serve as a drawback on hospitality

The meal over, cigars were introduced, when the kind host, after telling the sailor he was acquainted with the customs of England, mixed a large flowing bowl of punch, and ladled out a glassful of the generous liquor to each individual of the company.

" Here is prosperity to old England and her navy," said Strephon, drinking off his punch.

" Thank ye, thank ye, sir," cried the sailor; " it seems that you know something of my country ; mayhap, friend, as you so kindly toast the navy, you may have been aboard a king's ship."

" I've been aboard many ships in my time, but of all the decks I ever trod upon, that of an old English frigate is the freshest in my memory."

" Bless me !" exclaimed the sailor, evidently delighted at what he had just heard ; " I didn't know you had been aboard a British ship of-war; however, 'tis a charming place for passing away the younger part of a man's life; isn't it now, sir ? "

Strephon smiled at Monday's observation, saying, different men had different ways of thinking, and the merits of everything were dependant on comparison.

" Odd's blood," asked the astonished sailor, " what can be compared with a British man-of-war ?   Tall and straight, tight and buoyant, clean and neat, she walks through the water; a man-of-war is the best of homes for a seaman in all climes he may visit."

" Two dreary long years passed at Sheerness on board an old frigate, fitted up as a hulk, might serve to cool even the warmth of your zeal," drily remarked Strephon.

" It would serve as a cooler to any man living," replied the sailor, " howsoever, I hope you've not undergone it."—" Indeed I have," rejoined he ; " nor can I think of my sufferings without saying, 'twas a cruel system of the government there to punish unfortunate soldiers, their prisoners, by shutting them up in loathsome ships, to linger life away almost in hopeless misery.'

Monday now looked somewhat abashed; but I, feeling for him, changed the conversation ,by asking Signor Albini if he attached importance to the predictions of his brother astrologers.

" No man in his senses, and acquainted with astrology, can doubt the influence of the stars," replied he.   " I myself can cast nativities, so as to foretel a man's ultimate fate, and the great events of his life; but let the doubter examine the predictions of Adam Müller, the Maestrich prophet—for they have become famous as those of the famed Nostradamus—and astrology bear out these prophecies.   Alexander of Russia and the King of Prussia received Müller most favourably in the year 1808, and seeing some of his prophecies had been fulfilled, they acted on his advice, and made many happy political changes.   Amongst the unfulfilled announcements of this great prophet are these—that many of the German states will change their places—that armies from the west and from the north will cleave the threefold lily; or, in other words, will divide France into four portions — that her monarchs will give way, the old to the young, the young to the younger, and the younger to him who will be their monarch, but is no monarch.

" In the east of Europe there is to be a struggle between two monstrous females — one a heathen Christian, the other a Turk, and each will conquer the other; and then they shall unite in bearing a large book, scented with the richest perfumes, and surmounted with a massy golden crown; which book shall be universally read when Britain knows and keeps her true place, and after a year of universal opposition.

"Müller, who was ignorant of astronomy, looked for this universal opposition on earth, whereas he should have sought it in the sky.   He would then have known that his predictions pointed to events subsequent to the year 1830, for in this year all the superior planets, including the new ones, were in opposition.   Let us watch, then, the unfolding of events, and endeavour to decipher honest Adam Müller's half written words, Bera—, Beae—, Bona—be."

Hylas looked wildly around him at the termination of the hermit's discourse, and endeavoured in vain to repeat the words Bera—, Beae—, Bona—be.   Meanwhile the hostess sat bewildered by the astrologer's allusion to a struggle between two monstrous females.

Till the time came for retiring to repose, friendly instructive conversation passed around among the happy company assembled before Strephon's cheerful fire.   This may truly be said to have been a feast of reason ; and yet the circumstance communicated by the hermit astrologer of his being able to cast nativities, inspired a great portion of the company with strong feelings of awe towards him, and caused their hostess to express a desire that her daughter's nativity should be cast by the learned man.

Comfortable beds in a double-bedded room awaited Monday and me, and after we had bid good-night to the company, our kind host escorted us to our chamber ; when, having closed the door, he communicated that one of his labourers had recently returned home from a neighbouring village, bringing the news that search was being made there after an Englishman, who had escaped from prison at Parma, and was accompanied by a young countryman of his ; both of whom, it was reported, had been seen and spoken to by a courier, travelling *a-pied* on the high road, not more than three leagues off.

With an enlightened man, such as Strephon, I deemed it best to place implicit confidence ; and therefore frankly communicated to him that I was the party sought after, but explained how unjustly I had been imprisoned.

In return, the worthy farmer remarked, that it would be imprudent for us to travel any further upon the high road, and unhesitatingly offered himself to be our guide over the country until we had crossed the frontier ; however, on second thoughts, he said, it appeared to him that the safest course to pursue would be for me and my friend to travel in company with Signor Albini, whose intention was to depart in the morning the same way that we had to journey, to go to his hermitage ; adding, that his highly respected friend was reverenced everywhere, and as he made his journeys across the country on foot, he knew all the by-ways, as well as the most retired cabarets ; therefore, if in his company, there would be little or no danger to apprehend of our getting safely over the frontier of the duchy.

We highly approved of this salutary advice, and thanked Strephon for having given it, when the worthy man quitted us to communicate his little plan to the astrologer, so that he might be prepared to depart with his fellow guests at the dawn of day.

Young healthy persons, who have contented their appetite after they have undergone much bodily fatigue, seldom require the aid of narcotics to drown their senses in oblivion, and I enjoyed one uninterrupted sleep from shortly after Strephon's departure, to when that worthy farmer awoke me on the following morning.   "My worthy guests, the cock has crowed to proclaim a new day ; now," said he, "the day too will be fine, for my never-failing barometer proclaims as much."

"These barometers of yours must be choice ones," observed the sailor, rubbing his drowsy eyes ; "for my own part, I never could meet with one to be depended on."

"Mine are the barometers of nature," rejoined Strephon ; "I mow and I reap ; I plant, I gather in my grapes, and am guided in all agricultural pursuits by them, for they never fail me."

"Bless us !" exclaimed the sailor, raising his eyes with wonder, "these are rare compasses to steer by.   "What! no variation in them?   But pray, my good friend, explain their nature, for who knows but they may prove a fortune to a sailor?"

"The shepherd, the grazier, and the farmer who would thrive, must attend to these barometers," replied Strephon.   "I repeat, they are the barometers of all-bounteous nature. The spider is busied weaving his silken snares in the open air, and the horse-leech lies quiet at the bottom of the stagnant pool ; therefore, depend upon it, for these are unerring prophets that fair weather is before us."

The astronomer was a true republican in his ideas, for he detested oppression, and loved to see a proper equality among mankind; and also a philosopher, enlightened by the inestimable gifts of learning, without wearing the yoke, too often attendant on it, of pedantry : therefore he rejoiced at the opportunity afforded him of aiding a fellow-citizen of the world in escaping out of a country where he had suffered unmerited persecution, and was being sought after to be made suffer still greater injustice, which made him signify to me the pleasure with which he undertook the office of my conductor.

The members composing Strephon's family may be said to live all their days, for they rise with the sun ; consequently, when we were about to depart, the family all made their appearance, and by its loved mistress's direction, bowls of warm milk, and white wheaten cakes of her own making, were presented to the departing guests.

" Bena—, Bona—be, and the good company of last night, will be fresh in my memory while I am tending my sheep to-day," said Hylas, when taking his leave of the hermit astrologer.

" Remember my wishes regarding Augusta's nativity," were the last words of their hostess to the same.

" I've sailed out of fairer ports, but I never left honester people behind me," exclaimed the sailor, taking a farewell look at the mansion he had just quitted.

CHAPTER XXX.

" In spacious subterranean room,
Capp'd by a lofty form of dome,
By viewless chain, hung moon-like ball,
Shedding its ghastly light o'er all.
Things stuff'd of every kind were there,
That live in earth, in sea, and air ;
From frightful monsters of the deep
To smallest tribes that fly and creep :
All which, the hermit said, were store
For works of scientific lore."

" This region surely is not of the earth,
Was it not dropt from Heaven ? Not a grove,
Citron, or pine, or cedar, not a grot,
Sea-worn and mantled with the gadding vine,
But breathes enchantment."

STREPHON accompanied us a short distance on our way, when he bid us good bye, to return to his peaceful abode. " Adieu !" said the hermit astrologer, smiling and shaking hands with his pastoral friend ; " when the lion roars, and the scorpion spits forth its venom at my hermitage, I shall again seek the rural abode where Mars lives in the clothing of a lamb." —" Adieu, worthy friend," was my observation ; " believe me, in whatever thorny path I may tread, the remembrance of the happy evening I passed at your cheerful hearth will ever be soothing to my mind.   He who should quit your house in search of felicity elsewhere, would be insane as a lunatic, who weds a scold with the view of enjoying domestic peace."—" Adieu, friend and messmate," said the sailor ; " the navigator who sails round the globe will not find a snugger port to put in at than the one in which we lay anchored last night.'—" Farewell to ye all, my good friends ; but let me entreat of you, when you can, to revisit me ; for at no time does my wine look so bright, or my heart feel so buoyant, as when kind guests enliven my house with their presence : to Strephon friendship is a blessing which cannot be defined ; a treasure, without which the world would appear to him a blank."—" There," remarked the hermit, soon as the warm-hearted farmer had got out of hearing, " if happiness be a resident on this earth, with our excellent friend there it is that she resides.   Fortune favoured him with some of her choicest gifts at a time when he had learned their value ; and experience has taught him that rich wisdom—content."

After Strephon had quitted us, pleasant discourse, interrupted only by occasional halts to refresh ourselves, served to lighten the fatigue of our journey until such time as an homely supper, and a few hours of sound repose at the humble abode of a peasant, closed the events of the day.   Next morning we arose with the lark, when, after drinking a draught of new milk, and eating an oaten cake each, we proceeded on our journey, which, as on the preceding day, was enriched by the hermit's conversation, so as to be made a constant intellectual feast. Signor Albini was a native of the duchy of Parma, and in his younger days had filled a high office in the government there; but disappointment in a love affair, and disgust engendered by seeing his countrymen put under the rule of any foreign state or personage whom it might please certain great powers to nominate, had driven him to seek for happiness away from the busy haunts of man, and a cave in a mountain between Parma and Genoa was now his usual residence. But this enlightened personage was no misanthrope; for, though denominated a hermit, he not only loved his fellow-men, and would frequently journey about the country bent on deeds of benevolence towards them, but he well knew how to enjoy with moderation all the rich gifts of Providence; and, when at home at his cavern, he was always willing to share these gifts with his visitors, while the study of astrology, and the vast wonders of nature, afforded him constant occupation, and served to make him the most instructive and agreeable of companions.

As we trudged along, the hermit amused my secretary and me by his account of the little court of Parma, presided over by the great Corsican adventurer's imperial widow—the arch-duchess of different husbands. "Her pageant court," said he, "apes the great one of Paris, and constantly affords an harlequin exhibition, at which the titled and subordinate grades admitted there, habited in embroidered coats, the breasts of which were bedizened with stars, medals, ribands, and other badges of servility, serve to show the grossest want of manners, which disgusts the man of refinement. In fine, this insignificant court, with its birth-days, drawing-rooms, and levees, exhibits the frivolity of a great one, placemen and pensioners herding to it to grin thanks for favours, and solicit fresh ones, to more grievously burden the state. However, contemptible as we are, we have not yet acted the insane part of some states, which have banished the ablest citizens for publishing matter not offensive to truth or to religion, but offensive to their courts.

"Monarchs, ministers of state, and aristocrats, would do well to bear in mind, that those who quarrel with truth, merely because truth is unpleasant to them, can make no pretensions to the wisdom of philosophy, or the knowledge requisite for legislation; they should also recollect, that when the press swerves from truth, it loses its influence. Moreover, truth will shame the page of falsehood, and reconvince those who have been momentarily deceived. But here I shall conclude the sad subject," added the hermit, smiling a sarcastic smile; "therefore we will leave the head governing powers to the gentle mercy of ministers and courtiers, whose study it is to keep truth from entering their ears, and honesty from approaching their persons."

We arrived at the hermit astrologer's place of residence on the third day, without any memorable adventure. It was a monstrous cave, divided into several compartments, the largest capped by a lofty form of dome, which abounded with stuffed or petrified bodies of almost every description, and also skeletons. Specimens, too, were here of many kinds of stone, metals, plants, and earth, some, as the hermit told us, of his procuring, but that the greater part he had found here; while, as to the skeletons and petrified bodies, he considered them to be of animals, reptiles, and birds, which had found refuge in the cavern, in times of devastation, from storms, inundations, and rancorous foes. The furniture of the large compartment was of a character suitable to the place; the legs, for example, of stools, chairs, and tables, being shaped in bone-like fashion, and the little looking-glass was framed in the extended mouth of a huge skeleton of a man. Bars of iron, in imitation of human bones, were fixed in the spot allotted for the grate; and a row of skulls, set in blackened metal, ornamented a shelf, as the drinking cups of the chamber. But although everything in the large division of the cavern was of an appalling character, such was not the case in the smaller chambers—there all was neatness and propriety; the furniture, too, plain and good, and the signor kept two elderly servants—a man and a woman.

It was evening when we reached this extraordinary place of abode, and our host, after ushering Monday and me into his grand sepulchre for all things, smiled the smile of welcome when he contemplated our countenances, whereon astonishment must have been forcibly depicted. He, however, was well bred, and therefore made no uncourteous remarks; but briefly observed, that this wonderful cave was his own, and that he possessed lands on the Alps, with vineyards, sheep-walks, and a fair share of gold and silver besides.

A lamb, which in that cheap country is worth about one shilling, was now cooked for our supper, and with rich wine as its accompaniment, a most hearty meal we all made; but not in the grand sepulchre, for we preferred a smaller apartment, and wine glasses, to the skulls displayed in that great place of mortality. Good beds were prepared for our accommodation, and on the following morning I proposed departing; but my host so warmly invited me to spend a day with him, to view the rich scenery of the neighbourhood, that I gladly availed myself of his hospitality, when my secretary and I, accompanied by our hermit friend, much enjoyed a delightful walk, and the magnificent views of the country which it afforded us. In the evening, after our dinner, my enlightened host was pleased to cast my nativity, as also that of my secretary; but as I attached little importance to astrological predictions, I took not much notice of what he foretold, though this much I can call to mind, that he said fortune promised me an aristocratic title and a wealthy young wife, with whom I should live long and happy. But how could I do otherwise than laugh in my sleeve at the idea of Andrew, the son of Andrew and Diana Winpenny, living to be ennobled?

As our route to his wondrous place of abode had diverged from the road I proposed journeying for Florence, but my host so strongly recommended me to proceed there by the circuitous way of Lucca, that I could not but agree to follow his advice; and this I did the more readily, as he voluntarily engaged to go to Parma, where he possessed some influence with the government, purposely that he might interest himself in my affair there, and, if possible, get my seized property restored to me.

It was with feelings of real regret that I took leave of this truly good man, and I thoroughly believe that Monday felt similar sensations. He himself saw us depart in a hired carriage from a neighbouring village, after explaining how I was to write to him at a given address at Parma as soon as I came to a stationary halt, and how, in return, he would write to me, and, if possible, transmit me my baggage.

Everything tended to make our journey to Lucca a delightful one, inasmuch as we ourselves felt an inclination to be pleased. The weather was beautiful, the roads in good condition, and our fellow travellers were agreeable companions.

The independent-spirited man feels enlivened, when, having quitted a territory where idle forms and ceremonies predominate, he enters into that of a well-governed republic, where diligence, enterprize, and bustle, mark the prosperity of the people. What a happy contrast! —Instead of satiating the sight with the equipages of sloth, and tax-gatherers at their unceasing employ, gathering revenue for the support of profligate idleness, to glad the eyes with beholding the vehicles of traffic, and the great community zealously labouring for the general good!

The diligence of the people of the city of Lucca has given it the name of Lucca the Industrious. Their manufactures consist chiefly in silk, and gold and silver stuffs. The olives and oils produced in their territories are very much esteemed. They have also plenty of wine, but not sufficient corn for their subsistence; therefore the common people eat chesnuts frequently instead of bread, as they do in many other parts of Italy. In olden times, Lucca republic usually followed the fortune of the neighbouring cities of Tuscany. Happily, however for them, in 1279, the people purchased their independency of the Emperor Rodolph for ten thousand crowns, and by this purchase escaped a multiplicity of wars, inevitable under the ambition of sovereign rule, as also the payment of more than five hundredfold the sum given for their liberty, which would, sure as that the sun should ripen their vintage, have been extracted from the people for the extravagant ends of Italian pageantry.

Anxiety is a bad companion. I felt anxious regarding the fate of my baggage; and, therefore, although I was extremely well pleased with this little republican city, hastened away from it after a three days' stay. My secretary and I departed post for Florence, denominated by many people the Athens of Italy, and supposed to have received its name from the goddess Flora (for no other spot abounds like its neighbourhood with fragrant flowers). The ancient town was destroyed by the Goths, and Charlemagne built a handsome city on the site of the old one; but instead of its being a record of arts, sciences, and learned men, the history of Florence consists of little more than the wars of the Florentines against Rome, Venice, and Milan, together with the deeds of the Guelphs and the Gibellines, and the remarkable events which happened during the reign of the Medici family.

Scarcely had my secretary and I got housed in this city, after a most pleasant journey, ere I proceeded to pay my respects to a well-known prince, who had hired the palace of a cardinal, to deliver to him a letter of introduction with which I had been favoured by my friend, the hermit astrologer, who knew the prince intimately, and had been honoured with his company for several days as a guest at his cavern.

I found his highness at home; and he received me most courteously, making many kind inquiries after Signor Albini, for whom he avowed a sincere regard; but the prince being engaged out to dinner that day, yet wishing to pay immediate attention to me on the senor's account, proposed my accompanying him to the Hon. Mrs O'Shufflewell's, where he was to dine, and afterwards accompany her party to a masquerade. This, to me, novel scene in high life, promised much amusement, and I thankfully accepted the offer; and accordingly, in due time, had the honour of accompanying his highness to the mansion of the distinguished dowager.

—◆—

CHAPTER XXXI.

Sir David.—Now for the catastrophe.
Sir Roger.—What catastrophe?
Sir David.—Why, the catastrophe of all this long story.

I HAD just written the foregoing quotation from the Loggerheads, and was, with my grey goose quill in hand, and all the glee and good will imaginable at heart, intently occupied in the task of showing the humours of a masquerade, to finish the third number of my Memoirs (the portion I propose publishing every spring), to transmit it to England from my villa near Naples, when my servant disturbed me in my reveries by entering the apartment with a letter in his hand, which I eagerly broke the seal of, on discovering that it came from the publisher.

Authors in general, like parents, are most partial to their youngest bantling, and blindest to its faults, while I, having a fair share of this weakness, now expected pleasing tidings of my two first numbers; nor was I disappointed, and with them came a report of the present literary taste of the British public, which may not be deemed unworthy of commenting upon.

My honest publisher tells me 'Andrew Winpenny' is liked and sells well, notwithstanding that I have mistaken the public taste by professing to expose roguery; as, to use his words, the lantern of truth must not be suffered to show much of its light; and this enlightened gentleman complains that we give too much for the money, remarking, that should a Johnson and a Goldsmith arise, the one to publish a new 'Rasselas,' and the other an improved 'Vicar of Wakefield,' they would mar the sale of their works, should they vend sixty-four large close pages for one shilling.

"Yes," says he, in concluding his epistle, "you give twofold too much for the money, while, as an honest publisher, I must inform you that it is customary to force the sale of new works by the puffery of bribed reviewers, aided by newspaper advertisements more numerous than those of a successful quack; whilst even then, to ensure a great circulation for those which are brought out periodically, and make them fashionable works to quote from for thrice told jests, quaint sayings, and *bon-mots*, it is essentially necessary to embellish these with childish illustrations, make them replete with slang words, abound with Joe miller jests, and be almost one continued dialogue."

Having read the publisher's letter, I laid down my pen and bundled up my papers; when, soliloquising, I said, " Aye, be it so; the British public has an undoubted right to please itself, and if it takes interested reviewers' reports on trust, instead of judging for itself, that is not my affair. I would fain have related a few more things, but since truth is not in favour, I will light up no more of its bright beacons. Let the world of fashion amuse itself with Joe Miller jests, slang terms, petty dialogues, and pretty illustrations; meanwhile the Count de Deux Sous will consider how far he can make his history accord with the fashion of the times, so that the public may find a work to its taste in the Second Part of the Memoirs of Andrew Winpenny "

PART THE SECOND.—CHAPTER I.

" Palaces, where song
Re-echoes nightly through its splendid dome,
And the light dance invites the courtly throng ;
Where vice too wears the matron's stole,
And sinful pleasure looks divinely fair,
Whilst mad intemp'rance fills the frequent bowl,
And even beauty smiles but to ensnare."

" A new Democritus we see on earth,
With cheerful wisdom and instructive mirth,
Who laughs at life in motley trappings dress'd,
And feeds with varied fools th' eternal jest :—
He has discovered, what we all should know,
The world is masked, and every mask our foe."

FLORENCE at this time abounded with distinguished visitors, of whom the wealthiest were
natives of Great Britain and Ireland, where they had left their tenantry to bear the galling burden
of home taxation, while they themselves squandered their lordly revenues among foreigners,
who regarded them only for their money ; and of all the strangers sojourning here, perhaps,
the most remarkable was the prince to whom I had come recommended. From what Signor
Albini told me, I knew he was extremely wealthy and though but a little past the meridian of
life, that he was in a state of mental imbecility almost as deplorable as Chevalier Bruges' dupe, the
imaginary Silenus ; while on the turf and in play-rooms he had been most egregiously duped
by more designing men, and it was notorious his highness had sunk into so contemptible a
bigot, that his weakness was now played upon by the whole of his servants. *Par* example,
the domestic chaplain, who in reality was a jovial fellow, when in his highness's presence acted
the sanctified priest to admiration ; for, as the servants shrewdly said, he had an eye to a
bishopric. But of the sly rogues on the establishment, the butler made himself the most
amusing, for although he was a thorough *bon-vivant*, unflinchingly devoted to his bottle, and
as free from a belief in christianity as Pope Leo the Tenth showed himself to be, if he really made
the celebrated remark to Cardinal Bembo, which is recorded of him, on what he pronounced a
fable in religion, yet the merry fellow knew his own interest so well, that, when at home with
the prince, he always assumed a sanctified look, and rarely came into his master's presence,
even to attend at table, without a huge bible tucked under his arm. Sacred music was invariably the order of the day at the palace, and the professor of the harmonic art, who inwardly
abominated the monotonous tunes he was called upon to play, was compelled to attend on all
occasions dressed out like a lord in his holiday suit ; but this performer's salary and perquisites,
all extracted from the prince's purse, netted him nearly a thousand pounds every year, and
this afforded a sweet source of consolation to the otherwise outraged musician.

Persons of weak intellects not unfrequently are very discerning as to the faults of others ;
and on our way to the honourable Mrs O'Shufflewell's mansion, his highness was pleased to
communicate to me that she herself was an enormously pensioned lady, who had been the
chere amie of an illustrious personage, but withal so bigoted a Roman Catholic, that she would
live in perpetual terror of heaven's vengeance, should she unwittingly eat of proscribed food
on a fast day. The prince likewise mentioned several other remarkable characters in high
life whom we should meet at our dinner party ; for example, the Marchioness of Slyham, a
lady, he said, whose virtues ought to be recorded on *very white* marble, for that, in addition
to trafficking her own fair person to great advantage, she had, if report merited credence,
bargained away for her own exclusive advantage numerous titles of the aristocracy, together
with an infinity of places in church and state. But his longest tale related to the celebrated
Marquis of Derrymine and his lady. This nobleman, he said, had been one of the wealthiest
of the aristocracy, and filled a public office of importance : nature too had shaken hands with
fortune in favouring him, inasmuch as even now, though he was upwards of fifty years old,
his constitution was hale, and he a handsome man. The fair marchioness, my informant
stated, had been one of the richest heiresses of the northern part of her native land, and was

still a lovely woman, though Time had marched on as her companion almost forty winters. By the prince's account, these choice favourites of the capricious dame lived in a sumptuous style, and were considered subordinate to none figuring in the proud list of fashion ; but their conduct, nevertheless, furnished a memorable instance of the deceitfulness of outward appearances between some married people, for so bland were they together, that although they bore little or no affection towards each other, yet a superficial observer might well have imagined them to be two of the happiest of persons among those long riveted in the chains of Hymen. The marquis, it appeared, had received an excellent education, and been endowed with a fair share of good sense, but unfortunately, owing to his associating only with the higher classes of society, he had imbibed the gross prejudices widely disseminated among the noblemen of his country, and his judgment was consequently warped from the standard of reason. In fine, he was now one of those pitiable characters who verily believe themselves endowed with superior talents to all persons moving in a subordinate grade of society to theirs, and who, like Madame la Maréchale de Meilleraye, imagine that the Great Judge at his assizes hereafter thinks *twice* before he damns such greatness. Were it not for visitations of sickness, persons of this sort might believe themselves formed of more valuable materials than others—moulded from clay sent purposely from a better planet ; but it was this nobleman's dire misfortune to add bigotry to pride, and therefore to be an egregious dupe to the priesthood.

By his highness's account, the marchioness, in addition to her fat, fair, and forty years of growing recommendations, was affable, sprightly, and accomplished. She was conversant in three languages, and moreover a proficient in music, drawing, and dancing. The fair lady, too, prided herself on being a patroness of certain amatory bards, several of whom had celebrated her as a poetess : one inspired genius sung her as Daphne, another compared her to Sappho, and a third eulogised her as a beauty equal to the Cyprian goddess ; but no poet coupled her name with that of Diana, for every one knew such a comparison would be unjust, as she possessed no portion of the iciness of character or constitution attributed to that superlatively chaste goddess.

"Poets are artful sinners," laughingly said the prince. "When they deify their fair ones, it is with a view of winning a spice of divinity for themselves : the bards, for example, who have sung the marchioness as a Venus, profess themselves emulous of becoming Cupids to the goddess of their creation, thinking, perhaps, that her heart is a target of sufficient dimensions to receive the whole of their arrows; and indubitably, though she has been sweetly sung as a goddess, this fair one is a *woman* to the uttermost sense of the word ; for sometimes she is endearingly kind, yet at others agitated by the very reverse of a *gentle* passion. The marchioness's conduct," concluded the prince, "gives birth to no jealous feeling in the breast of her noble spouse, for he, good man, being scrupulously religious, and seeing a crucifix constantly suspended from his wife's neck, with a string of beads hanging by her side, cannot possibly dream of impurity lurking under such sacred symbols ; besides, he knows her confessor to be an austere priest, one who, though young in years, standeth high in the order of the Jesuits. However, who shall read the heart of a devotee, who deliberately crosses herself, and telleth over her beads, preparatory to and after every piccadillo she commits ?"

My princely companion was interrupted in his relation by the arrival of his carriage at our hostess's mansion, where we were received with the greatest urbanity, and shortly afterwards comfortably seated with a numerous party at a splendid dinner, when the opportunity was soon afforded me for witnessing how greatly personages in high life can be delighted with wit and humour, displayed at the expense of others.

A pedantic-looking man, named Syntax, who had come to the Mediterranean as the schoolmaster of a ship of war, and quitted the vessel off Italy in consequence of his captain's tyrannical conduct towards him, being in Florence, and extremely distressed in his circumstances, had awaited upon the honourable Mrs O'Shufflewell to solicit her patronage and assistance, when she, on discovering him to be an off-handed, extraordinary person, for the frolic's sake invited him to our dinner party, thinking, no doubt, to have some amusement with him at the masquerade which was to follow after that scene of conviviality.

Amongst our dinner company was a Welsh baronet, Sir Watkin Morgan, who, on the fish being removed from table, slily winked to another individual of the party, while addressing

Syntax, he said, "Have you any objection to join me in drinking Lady Caroline Sophia Bramble's health in a glass of sparkling champagne?"

Syntax widely opened his large eyes on hearing the invitation, then bowing to the young lady in question, who was an orphan protegé of our hostess, gravely declared that he who could hesitate at drinking the lovely Lady Caroline Sophia's health in champagne, sparkling less than her bright eyes, merited having his name obliterated from the long list of mankind.

Most of the company laughed at the pedagogue's unlooked for compliment, but Lady Sophia must have been pleased with it, as she declared she had not of late heard anything half so gallant.

"Pray, reverend sir," said a dashing young officer of dragoons, now addressing himself to Syntax, and at the same time looking intently at his rusty coat, "may I, without giving offence, ask what is your religious persuasion, and in what tabernacle you edify the sheep and lambs of your flock by the delivery of orthodox sermons?"—"Orthodoxy is your doxy, my doxy, and everybody's doxy," replied Syntax with a smile, "but, my gallant friend, if the ladies and the cloth were withdrawn from the table, I would answer your question by toasting Mother Church in burgundy or champagne."

"Good exhilarating wines," rejoined the dragoon, "they are fit for the rich pluralist to quaff every day, till such times as the gout brings the old boy to a sober reckoning; but, reverend sir, from the spareness of your person, I presume you can be no monopoliser of tithes: indeed, to the disgrace of church patronage, many of the names of our most zealous divines remain during their lives in the list of ill-paid curates."—"True, sir, true; your remarks are very correct; therefore, when I turn preacher, it shall be to hold forth in a tabernacle, where love-gifts serve as the substitute for tithes."

A general laugh followed Syntax's reply, but the bold dragoon, who loved jokes only at the expense of others, felt nettled at the laugh raised against him, and in a half whisper said to the gentleman next him, "What the plague can the fellow be? I would have betted five to one on his being a half-starved curate."—"For fifty double ducats, he is a disciple of Esculapius, regular or irregular, was the reply.—"Done, 'tis a bet, Sir Peter," rejoined the dragoon.

"Pray, sir, allow me to ask, is not the pure air we inhale here extremely beneficial to the constitution?" asked the sporting knight of Syntax, after a little pause in the conversation, and then added, "it certainly provokes an appetite, which you medical gentlemen usually consider a good symptom."—"An admirable one when dinner awaits us," replied the pedagogue, who had overheard the wager, and was desirous of keeping the sporting characters in ignorance of the employment by which he had thriven so badly; "hunger is a savoury sauce: the stomach affords a good criterion of the health of the patient. Galen of old, and almost all the intermediate doctors, down to the great Abernethy of modern times, looked to the stomach as the barometer of the constitution."

"Come, captain," whispered the knight, "two to one that the fifty ducats are mine."—"I'll give you twenty to let me off the bet," answered the dragoon.—"I'll take ten, sir; I'll relieve you of it for ten double ducats," said Syntax, who had listened to all that had been said on this sportive occasion.

The captain mused for a moment, perhaps from a feeling of shame at this indirect avowal from one of the party of his having overheard him say all he had pretended to whisper; but with this gentleman modesty formed no characteristic feature, and presently he replied, "'Tis a good hedge; ten to secure fifty; done, sir; I take you at your word."

"I am neither a quack doctor, apothecary, surgeon, accoucheur, chemist, nor physician," replied the delighted pedagogue, "and this, my brave sir, if necessary, I will prove to every gentleman's satisfaction, soon as the ladies have withdrawn their fair persons from the society."

"Pray, sir, what should prevent us ladies from being present on this interesting occasion?" asked the honourable Mrs O'Shufflewell, and then laughingly added, "Come, come, if you act thus, Mr Syntax, Lady Sophia will have to retract her assertion in favour of your gallantry: however, that I may act a friendly part, and from my knowledge of your avocation in life, settle the point at issue to your satisfaction, I take upon myself to assure the betting gentlemen that you are not a member nor practitioner of any branch of the medical profession, and consequently to pronounce that Sir Peter has lost his wager to the captain; while being sporting characters ourselves, the gentlemen present must be satisfied that it will afford us ladies pleasure to witness its being settled."

At the conclusion of the dowager's speech, Sir Peter, bowing to her, pulled out his purse, and handed fifty double ducats to the captain of dragoons, who in his turn paid ten of the glittering pieces to the schoolmaster; and he, however pleased he may have felt at his good fortune, had the presence of mind to receive them with great affected nonchalance.

The curiosity of both the knight and captain of dragoons to know who and what Syntax was had been so thoroughly aroused, that although they had been foiled in all their attempts at ascertaining these points, still their inquisitive spirit towered predominant over other passions; but the dowager felt resolved to withhold this knowledge from the company, because from this person's extraordinary appearance, and the great self-possession she discovered in him, the honourable lady promised herself considerable diversion at the masquerade, and therefore she thought the less was known of him the better. For the reasons specified, and also, as Syntax himself, though plied with wine, evaded returning an explicit answer to any one of their questions, and, with skill comparable to that of an able diplomatist, was guarded in what he said, all their experiments at sifting him proved so abortive, that when the company broke up from table, none of the inquisitive visitors knew more regarding this worthy than that Syntax was his name.

Although he was honoured by making one of our party at the masquerade which took place at a splendid palace, the schoolmaster was left unprovided with masque or domino, for our fanciful hostess promised herself more diversion from exposing him before the masqued crowd in his own unfashionable habiliments than she could expect him to afford her if he assumed a character.

The Honourable Mrs O'Shufflewell's party had scarcely made its appearance at the masquerade, before masks, in various characters, strove to amuse themselves, and the spectators of their wit and adroitness, by making a butt of our pedagogue; but the coolness, equanimity, and readiness of repartee displayed by him, completely foiled their efforts, and left those persons who practised them debtors to their masks for hiding the blush of shame which must have suffused the cheeks of the most confident among them at being conquered, and having their own weapons made to recoil upon themselves.

To attempt enumerating the futile efforts for turning our schoolmaster into ridicule is unnecessary; but still several of these may be mentioned. For example, one person, whose misfortune it was to be knock-kneed, and who personified a chimney-sweeper, taxed our hero with having been a parish clerk; in return for which courtesy, Syntax, extremely to the individual's annoyance, gravely declared, in a stentorian voice, that this conjuror was a real chimney-sweeper, whose barbarous mother had sold him to the soot trade at so tender an age, that mounting the chimnies occasioned the urchin's legs to grow crooked, and what was even more to be deplored, steady application to the practical duties of his calling had weakened and contracted his intellects.

Another mask, a physician, made very free with our pedagogue, whom he charged with following the sorry trade of a stay-maker. Fortunately one of his hostess's party whispered to Syntax who this mask was, and the schoolmaster, profiting by the information, retaliated on the disciple of Esculapius. He gravely assured a crowd of masked persons, that the gentleman who had spoken so lightly of the business of the never-to-be-forgotten Thomas Paine, whose writings were unanswerable, was himself a veterinary doctor, notorious for making away with his patients, and charging thundering long bills; but, he added, it was his duty, as a citizen of the world, to caution the public against entrusting, dog, mule, ass, or horse, to the care of so general a destroyer.

A third mask, a notorious and unprincipled radical, not worth a single shilling, and who had emigrated to avoid his creditors at home, declared that Syntax had been the leading man of a select vestry, which charged whatever sums they thought fit against their parish, and when called upon for an explanation, talked of their own infallibility, and smothered the voice of complaint by employing a proctor of a similar character to the one whose conduct gave rise to the famed Rochester charity, to prosecute parishioners with their own money for defamation of their vestry gentlemen.

One of his party whispered to the schoolmaster's ear who the disinterested gentleman was, when he profited so well by the information that he outranted the radical, to whom he recommended economy in his own private affairs, and counselled moderation and good temper, as beneficial for mind and body; after which our pedagogue eulogised public employment in the management of secret service money, thanks to which, he said, preachers of charity sermons, humane collectors for the poor, and missionaries, by the blessing of Providence (as they term their management), thrive tolerably well; as far preferable to the sour grapes attendant on the labours of a radical, who applies himself to the affairs of the public, only because he has none of his own worth attending to.

A fourth personage, the son of an Irish peer, who owed his fortune to trade, apostatised to sit in Parliament, and deceived the freeholders who gave him the seat which paved his way to the peerage, taxed our pedagogue with being a petty dealer and chapman; but Syntax, who promptly received his cue from the mischievous dowager, sarcastically complimented the child of young aristocracy on his good fortune in being blessed with a father, whose honest labours, aided by his all-accommodating conscience, had insured him against the necessity of being a dealer and chapman himself.

Soured by the schoolmaster's remark, and the general laughter it occasioned, this lordling, who personified a fop, protested that the clothesman from Monmouth street ought to be taught better manners by being kicked out of the company; and very unpolitely concluded his aristocratic speech by a string of virulent observations against trade and those persons who pursue it for a livelihood.

Syntax listened to the young lord's discourse with a smiling countenance, and on its termination, standing upon a form, looked sapiently around him at the crowd, when, pointing his finger to the imprudent scion of nobility, he spoke thus:—" Composure and dignity mark the empire of godlike reason; but, ladies and gentlemen, although yon fop, whose sentiments you have just heard pronounced from his own lips, may possibly possess some smattering of book knowledge, yet I take on me to prove that he lacks wit and discretion; and this is a task easily achieved, for he loses his temper and abuses trade; but a prudent man, before he vented an opinion unfavourable to the most ancient, most essential, and most honourable of all employments, would reflect well upon what trade really is.

" The gentleman's forefathers, for at least half-a-dozen generations, I presume, have been noblemen, or independent persons; as, had any one of them been engaged in avowed trade, he, of course, would not have delivered his sentiments against this ancient calling in the arrogant terms he has just done; yet it signifies not, for prejudice, like the spider, makes everywhere its home, and the flimsy assertions of ignorance carry no weight against truth.

" With regard to trade, it may not be pronouncing too much to say that every great and noble institution owes its origin to it. The exchange of the produce and manufactured articles of different countries enriches every nation, and affords the industrious inhabitants of a poor soil equal comforts to those enjoyed by the resident natives of more genial climes.

" The gold dug from exhaustless mines of the New World increases in value from being circulated in Europe; and does not the herring caught by hardy northern fishermen serve to flavour the yam of the African and South American, scorching in tropical climes? The freezing European, too, warms and invigorates his blood by partaking of a beverage produced from the berry, or the blossom of a shrub, or a tree, growing only in far distant regions, and from this cause the value of land in China and in both the Indies becomes dependent on the quantity of tea and coffee that is consumed in Europe.

" Iron of the north is of inestimable value to people of the southern parts of this planet. Indian colonies furnish Europe with luxuries, and Europe, in return, supplies luxuries to the colonies. In short, trade is but another name for wealth, enterprise, and industry, considered in their most extensive and happiest sense.

" But giving the young man credit for descent from a long line of nobility, let us now inquire why this advantage is to turn his imagination from the true source whence not only his own. but all honours are derived.

" The thrones of monarchs, from the remotest page of history to the present day, have been upheld by trade those monarchs having been the most powerful who afforded the greatest encouragement to this universal enricher. Egypt, for the seventeen hundred years she flourished under the Ptolemies, stood indebted to trade for her preponderating wealth. Carthage, and then Venice in her turn, commerce made the richest of states. Rhodes, Tyre, and Genoa, owed their proud days to the same golden source. The riches of trading Crœsus must not be thought fabulous, and even Jason's much vaunted voyage in search of the golden fleece was but a commercial adventure.

"However, to pass from remote to more modern times. Is not the wealth of Holland dependent on her trade? and do not some of the wealthiest of the nobility stand indebted for their honours and their property to common traders? In a word, trade is honourable; conquest is robbery.

"Those persons who rise to the highest honours by means of trade, are benefactors to the human race; these are men who disseminate the bountiful spirit of industry wherever they move; but conquerors, such as William the Norman and those followers of his, ennobled and enriched by the successful adventurer, as barons with baronial manners, were but so many infamous robbers, and he who boasts of his descent from one of these, prides himself on an ancestor who was a leader of murderers and thieves.

"I feel sensible that I have too long trespassed on your patience; therefore, ladies and gentlemen, knowing brevity to be the flower of oratory, I shall make the best amends in my power for the indulgence you have shown in listening to what I have said by resorting to it in what I have to say. To sum up then, in a few words, where an oration worthy of Demosthenes might well be made, I cannot be too pithy or concise.

"The man who buys or sells a house is a trader; as also is the man who purchases or vends the produce of the soil, whether living or dead stock. The man who cheapens an article of raiment, or a thing of any description, is a trader; as likewise is he who cavils respecting the marriage settlement of an intended wife, or the portion to be given with a daughter. In fine, more or less, we are all traders, from the monarch and his queen down to the scavenger and milk-maid; consequently he that abuses trade rails against himself and against all his forefathers, is a defamer of his sovereign, of the aristocracy of his country, of the clergy, of the representatives of the people, of the learned professions, and of the whole of the world's population, male and female; therefore, for these potent, these unanswerable reasons, I can entertain no doubt but that my kind auditors will coincide with me in opinion, that the man who rails against trade, even though he may be a nobleman, a courtier, and a fop, ought, as base metal, *una voce* to be cried down."

Shouts and the clapping of hands proclaimed the general approbation with which Syntax's speech was received; yet the young lord, stung to the quick by the vigour of talent, depth of observation, and jest in the style of this speech, indignantly muttered something about treating the impertinent orator to a good horsewhipping, though so far was he from attempting to execute his threat, that he had scarcely given it utterance before he was observed sneaking away from the merry crowd.

Fun and frolic was now the order of the night and a crowd of masks thronged around the pedagogue, boisterously signifying their desire to crown him with a crown of laurels and honour him with a triumphant chairing; the schoolmaster, however, who knew that danger and glory are near neighbours, and a fall from his elevated seat might very well happen to him, with some difficulty, and partly by means of the following speech, diverted his merry admirers from their design. "Give, oh my friends," said Syntax, "give the laurels of glory to those who, like Cæsar of yore, lack hair to cover their brows; for my part I need them not. Nature has furnished me with raven locks, even to profusion. Laurels would sit loosely on my head; crown me, if crowned I must be, with wreaths of blooming roses, or clustering bunches of delicious fruit, gathered ripe and luscious from the vine. Love and jollity sweeten the cares of life, and public honours are but so many plagues, which Dioclesian knew, when, to be a gardener, he abdicated his imperial throne, though, to obtain the sceptre, he had worked his way through every grade of society; but the ever successful Dioclesian had now learnt that one philosopher, and he too an heathen, was of more use to the world than all the conquerors that ever existed."

The great self-command Syntax had shown at the masquerade, as also the ready wit and quickness of repartee displayed by him there in turning the tables upon his assistants, afforded no small diversion to the Honourable Mrs O'Shufflewell and her party of friends, but most especially to the lady herself. On their return from the assembly, she gave a decided proof of her approbation of his conduct, for she invited the willing pedagogue to take a bed at her mansion ; and on the following morning, after having indulged herself in immoderate laughter during their breakfast at what she termed Mr Syntax's masterly conduct, the considerate lady had some private talk with him respecting what could be done to serve our pedagogue, when, having been made acquainted with a part of the schoolmaster's history, she actually promised to exert her influence in the proper channel for getting him re-appointed as school-master to a ship of war.

Fortunately for Syntax, the honourable dowager had no occasion to give herself any further trouble on his account, nor had he the misery to undergo of dancing attendance for months, perhaps, before a vacant unpromised situation could be found for him, as it so happened that a rich wine merchant, named Macdonald, who had been present at the masquerade and heard the whole of the schoolmaster's oration in honour of trade, was so highly delighted with it, that when he had subsequently learnt some particulars of Syntax's history, he caused himself to be introduced to the pedagogue, and at their meeting the schoolmaster rose himself still higher in the merchant's estimation by the judicious observation that trade tends to promote the intercourse of distant nations, increase the useful stock of knowledge, and reward industrious enterprise ; in short, Mr Macdonald was so extremely pleased that, after some preliminary conversation with him, wherein Syntax's facetious humour not a little aided his good sense in impressing the merchant with a favourable opinion of his understanding, this worthy gentleman made our *ci-devant* schoolmaster over unruly tars one of the happiest of men, by engaging him in his service, as his secretary, at a handsome salary.

CHAPTER II.

" By those that deepest feel is ill exprest
The indistinctness of the suffering breast;
Where thousand thoughts begin to end in one
Which seeks from all the refuge found in none
No words suffice the secret soul to show
Nor Truth denies all eloquence to woe."

" The righteous pow'rs that mortal lots dispose,
Decree us to sustain a length of woes,
And from the flow'r of life, the bliss deny
To bloom together, fade away, and die."

" In life itself she was so still and fair,
That death with gentlest aspect withered there."

SCENES in high life among the affluent, who, could riches and power achieve that desired object, would be monopolizers of the world's pleasures, afford a scantier harvest for the gleaner than those created by persons in a more humble sphere ; for which reason painters and writers prefer depicting the latter ; nevertheless, examples are to be found which form an exception to this rule ; and the following tale, which is related here because it bears upon a subsequent adventure that will be found recorded in these memoirs, may be considered one in question.

Rosetta, a lovely young lady, the daughter of an ancient baron, whose income was inadequate to the support of his aristocratic dignity, had for some time been the leading toast among the fashionable beaus at Florence, and her extreme beauty, combined with the many virtues for which she was deservedly extolled, had procured her several very eligible offers of marriage ; but the baron, clinging to the hope that Rosetta's charms might obtain for him a son-in-law, from whose wealth the mortgage on his domain might be redeemed, and the old baronial castle put in a state of repair, had long refused his sanction to her union with any one of her suitors, and this because no individual among them was wealthy enough to spare the large sum requisite to enable the noble baron to execute his selfish intentions. However, blind love and the fickle goddess, Fortune, two deities who make laughing stocks of mankind, at length procured what her parent deemed a fit suitor for Rosetta's fair hand, yet he was unsuitable to the youth and inclination of the lovely maiden.

The gentleman in question was an ancient, grave counsellor, named Hezekiah Gotschalk ;

a widower, who had twice participated in the joys afforded by Hymen. Pecuniary matters had brought Baron Florimond acquainted with the counsellor, to whom he had mortgaged his castle; but scarcely had the usurer beheld the lovely Rosetta before her wit and beauty captivated his heart; when, notwithstanding the snow which covered his head, and the chillness of sixty winters, which had benumbed his flesh and weakened his pulsation, the old gentleman found the ice begin to melt which the frost of age congealed about his heart, and the fiery passion of a youthful lover gambol in his breast.

The hoary counsellor strove to the utmost to conquer his growing passion, for which end he summed up all his philosophy, and from morn till night quoted stoical maxims and moral adages; but he might have spared himself this trouble, as all his endeavours proved unavailing against the potent artillery of young Cupid. Day or night, a-bed or up, the venerable gentleman, save when asleep, could find no rest; for juvenile thoughts, such as pierced old Vulcan, when he betrothed Venus, in spite of the exertions of philosophy, would spring up in his bosom, while the image of the lovely, blooming, virtuous Rosetta, remained perpetually in his sight. The worthy counsellor was like a loadstone attracted by the magnet. He perseveringly continued his visits to the conquering fair, till at last his passion burnt so furiously, that he felt himself irresistibly compelled to declare it to her father. This he did, accompanied by a request to be permitted to pay his devoirs to the maid. The baron, though inwardly rejoiced at the counsellor's proposition, yet had the address to dictate terms on which he would grant his only child to the embraces of the fiery old lover and these being complied with, he commanded the damsel to entertain him as her intended husband.

The grave counsellor now become a child again, ridiculously re-acted at three score and six all the follies of a youthful lover, and made his court to the blooming virgin, by discoursing about love, fire, and flame; yea, he scribbled verses in praise of her wit, beauty, graces and other accomplishments; and he talked, as have other mad lovers, even before the wise David with Balshebar, of her eyes being suns, and her flesh comparable to alabaster. To his mortification, however, Rosetta was to him a perfect stoic—a female philosopher. In reply to his gallantry, she represented the ill effects springing from unequal marriage, and foretold that his flame would speedily evaporate, or else precipitate him into a fit of jealousy; while, she said, no matter how innocent might be her conduct, or vigilantly circumspect, the contrast between his advanced age and her youth would inevitably afford the malignant a pretence for aspersing her character. Besides, the maid candidly declared to the dotard that she could not entertain a passion for him, and gave it as her opinion that marriage devoid of love must be an intolerable double yoke; but still such is the phantasy of love, Gotschalk remained obstinate. His heart was fixed on obtaining the maid, and he turned a deaf ear to her arguments; while as he persisted in his views, and vehemently urged Baron Florimond to forward them, the commands of the father became terrible to the poor daughter.

Here must be mentioned that among the conquests Rosetta's virtue and beauty had obtained for her, was Lieutenant Blucher, a young Prussian military officer of a noble family and good expectations, yet owing to his being the cadet of his house, he possessed little or no fortune. Subsequent events fully proved the sincerity and constancy of this gentleman's affection for Mademoiselle Florimond, and also that she was impressed with reciprocal sentiments.

By Rosetta's consent, her father's approbation for her marriage with the young Prussian had been solicited, but the baron was not of the Grecian's way of thinking, who preferred a *man* without a fortune for his son-in-law, and rejected the one who had only wealth to recommend him to a woman's affections; therefore he peremptorily spurned the needy soldier's suit, and as resolutely assisted that of the rich counsellor, his rival, whom the jade Fortune seemed to have brought at this critical epoch to make his overtures expressly to mar a fond couple's happiness.

Rosetta, until the detestable proposition of old Gotschalk was made to the baron, had entertained hopes he would relent in his severity, and consent that she should bestow her hand on the man whom she loved and was loved by; but when she found her covetous parent resolved to sacrifice her happiness to his private interest, she prudently and virtuously intimated to her young lover, that duty and obedience to her father forbade of her longer cherishing the soft passion and delusive hopes which delighted his heart, for that she had the sad tidings to communicate of her parent's having determined on her marriage with Signor

Gotschalk, and even fixed on the day for its solemnization, which he had warned her to be prepared for.

Poor Lieutenant Blucher, whose hopes were thereby annihilated, was driven almost to madness on the receipt of Rosetta's letter, containing this melancholy information; yet, when reason had resumed her sway over him, he wrote to her, earnestly entreating that, previous to her marriage, she would grant him a farewell meeting.

By her father's consent, Rosetta complied with the request, and their meeting took place in the baron's house, on the night previous to the fair maid's marriage. The scene which now passed between the lovers, is represented to have been moving to an extreme; but to pass over its detail, poor Blucher, at their separation, received Rosetta's farewell with an emotion of spirit, comparable to what a criminal does his sentence of death. The young lover posted away from Florence at an early hour of the day which was to make Rosetta an unwilling bride; but the counsellor, infinitely more happy than his rival, after subscribing to certain documents that had been prepared by the baron's lawyer, escorted the blooming maid to the altar of Hymen, and thence carried her home, his third spouse, to the identical country chateau, to which he had triumphantly borne her two predecessors on, to him, similar happy occasions; and here some merry scenes and pastimes among the villagers were made to take place, in the hope of thus diverting a bride's sorrowful heart.

The counsellor's flame, as his charming bride had foreseen, burnt too furiously before marriage, to leave fire enough for it to endure long with a man of his years. Satiated with the enjoyments of love, he soon after the hymeneal knot had been tied, returned home to his town house.

The chaste Rosetta now set a pattern for all youthful females who wed aged partners. Faithful to her church vows, she comforted the old man, her husband, to the utmost of her ability, declaring it was her delight to contrive by every method to afford him pleasure, and that she desired not to visit at any place, or partake of any amusement, at which he was not present.

The benefit of treasure should be felt in the enjoyment. Gotschalk could not be otherwise than sensible of his wife's amiable conduct; yet avarice, the deep-rooted passion of his heart, speedily ejected that of love. He now secretly bemoaned the price at which he had purchased a husband's right to his incomparable lady, and his regret at what he conceived an unprofitable bargain daily increased, until it so mastered his prudence, that frequent half-smothered exclamations betrayed, even to his lady, the dissatisfied state of his mind.

Rosetta, with a prudence beyond her years, appeared not to notice her spouse's discontent, but she redoubled her attentions to him, and submitted without repining to all the mean ways he had recourse to for saving money. In short, her patience astonished every person who knew anything of Gotschalk and his domestic arrangements; yet unkind fortune, not propitiated with these trials, shortly after her marriage put to proof also the virtue of our heroine. To explain this, Lieutenant Blucher, owing to his eldest brother being killed in a duel and his second perishing at sea, had fallen into possession of a handsome estate and a viscount's title; on which the young nobleman, actuated more by love than discretion, returned to Florence, where, passing under an assumed name, he contrived to obtain an interview with Madame Gotschalk, when he told her of the wealth and title which had devolved upon him, and offered to share both with her; proposing she should bless his love by eloping with him, as a preparatory step to that of obtaining a divorce from the counsellor.

The lady's purity of mind triumphed over the seductive temptations of true love and exalted rank. She reproached her faithful lover for the art he had practised to gain an interview, and not only spurned at his proposition, but insisted on never more hearing from him on a subject so insulting to a virtuous married woman.

The viscount, though baffled in his views, yet could not but respect Rosetta for her great virtue, and he endeavoured to move her from the resolve she had come to, but virtue was stronger implanted than even love; therefore, after all his exertions, he was under the painful necessity of parting from his beloved, with an understanding that he was to see her no more; for the virtuous lady not only forbade him to cultivate her husband's acquaintance, from apprehension that the former sparks of her affection might rekindle in his presence, but she rendered his case hopeless by declaring it to be her fixed resolution to meet no man without the sanction of him whom the viscount was forbid knowing.

Viscount Blucher's affection for her was too sincere to allow of his disappointing Rosetta in her wishes, therefore he quitted Florence, leaving the fair one satisfied with his departure, for she hoped it would leave her to the enjoyments of repose ; but, alas! her hopes were delusive, and her virtue had to undergo a new and severe ordeal—to withstand the fury of a libertine's desire ; one who was sullied by every impurity, and assisted in his base views upon her by the man that, at Hymen's altar, had sworn through life to be her protector. The bud of dissatisfaction, unless it be destroyed, will ripen into the fruit of danger and trouble. Prince Swarthyburg, whose fortune was prodigious, and who himself stood high in favour at a certain imperial court, from beholding her at church unfortunately became enamoured of the charms of Madame Gotschalk ; when having made himself acquainted with the character of her husband, the crafty prince, under pretence of negotiating a money loan for a friend, got introduced to the usurer ; after which he often invited him to his palace, where he designedly lost money to him at cards, and by this *ruse de guerre* his highness won the miser's heart and gained such influence over him that, in all things not injurious to his finances, his will became law with the counsellor. Gaming is said to be a magical stream. Monsieur Gotschalk found it a profitable one, and therefore was always ready and willing to try his fortune at cards with the prince for his opponent. It soon followed that his highness expressed a desire to visit the counsellor, who gladly availed himself of the opportunity for becoming more intimate, and no doubt but the counsellor now expected to ensure two tides of good luck where hitherto one only had offered. Be this as it may, his doors, which were shut to almost everybody else, were readily thrown open to Prince Swarthyburg, who, when fairly admitted into the fortress which held the treasure he lusted after, was by no means tardy in acquainting the fair object of his desires with the love he felt for her, and he solicited her acceptance of some valuable presents, little doubting but that she would surrender her lovely person after a short siege. This unfavourable opinion of Rosetta was formed from the misconduct of some court ladies he had met with, and which, were women all of one character, might have justified him in surmising that her youth and beauty, contrasted with the advanced age and extreme avarice of the counsellor, would play the part of traitors within doors, to obtain a place for him in that fort—the heart of his mistress ; for, libertine like, he thought such guards as honour and duty could make only a feeble defence against the assaults and stratagems of a prince of his great qualifications, assisted by the traitors just enumerated.

The most sanguine are not always the most successful in their pursuits. The prince soon discovered he had calculated on too easy a victory ; and woman's sweetest attribute, modesty, he little knew the strength of, because the artificial distinctions of court rank, which give her a bold, forward manner, and mix the modest, immoral, and unchaste with the virtuous and the refined, had misled his judgment. He knew that public virtue is not a concomitant feature with an hereditary government, and that under a monarchy the main object is not to preserve the purity of woman's manners, but to punish her crimes and irregularities without endeavouring to prevent them.

Aristocratic titles are great seducers of female virtue, and from this cause women in a republic are more virtuous than under a monarchy, where the pomp and pageantry of a disgusting court is of a tendency to corrupt them. In a republic, where fulsome titles exist not, woman is man's dear companion, equal to him in everything save physical strength and political power. The prince, counting on his high-sounding title for a victory, was astonished at finding his addresses treated with disdain, his presents refused, and his company sedulously avoided. What was now to be done became the consideration with him, as although checked in his object, yet, while a chance remained of success, he felt determined not to relinquish his views on the lovely woman.

" What !" said this potent aristocrat, when ruminating on the subject of Rosetta's virtue, " what madness can have got into the foolish woman's head ? Disdain my person, indeed ! Refuse my costly presents, and resolutely avoid my society ! The woman's brain must be turned, or 'tis impossible she could act thus, to prove true and faithful to a superannuated, ungrateful, curmudgeonly miser. She is mad ; stark staring mad. This is not the way other ladies treat my overtures; married or single, noble or plebeian, they meet my advances, of which my conquests over the fair, and the crim. con. cases I have been a party to, furnish incontrovertible testimony; however, she shall be mine, I swear to heaven she shall be mine; her affected virtue shall not preserve her from my embraces; yea, to mortify her pride and make my triumph most conspicuous, her covetous husband shall himself bring her blushing to my arms. I will bribe the wretch; from him I will purchase the dishonour of his wife.'

With Prince Swarthyburg, in matters of intrigue with the fair sex, his actions followed close on his resolves. He now lost no time in inviting the counsellor to his mansion, where, after they had partaken of a delicious banquet, at which he plied the usurer with champaign, he proposed their adjourning into his cabinet, where, he jocosely said, he would gratify his eyes with a most tempting sight. The wily prince having thus raised the miser's curiosity, conducted him to a small chamber, which he entered by means of a key taken from his pocket, when having fastened the door, he gently lifted a baize cloth from off a table it had been spread over. Heavens, what a sight for an avaricious man! On the table were displayed five thousand pieces of gold, laid out and sorted in lots.

" My friend," now said the prince, drawing a chair for the astonished miser, "prithee seat thyself, and examine whether these coins are of genuine gold, and of a just weight; good money scales lie on the table before you, with which you may prove a sample from each lot." ¡

The miser's eyes had been fixed upon the god of his heart, but on being requested to essay the shining metal, he gazed alternately at the prince and the money, then, after his surprise had somewhat subsided, weighed and examined various pieces of the gold, which done, he gravely declared his thorough conviction that the coins were all of full weight and pure gold; while for his own part, he added, he desired no better fortune than that the rich treasure should be his.

" My good friend, whether this gold shall remain mine or become thine, depends on thy pleasure; you have only to will it so, and the shining metal shall be transferred to your coffers," eagerly rejoined the prince.

· Gotschalk's heart leaped with joy. He was highly delighted and wonderfully surprised by his highness's declaration; yet was he by no means backward in asking by what service the gold was to be purchased; for he knew the world too well to imagine that a prince accustomed to deal with the minions of corruption would bestow such a sum as lay before him without receiving an equivalent. In answer, his noble host candidly confessed that he was passionately in love with the counsellor's wife, and as openly avowed that he had made tender proposals and offered costly presents to her, all which, he said, had been spurned with contempt.

The artful prince, after his avowal, hinted suspicions that Madame Gotschalk was in the habit of privately meeting some youthful gallant, for he said it was too much to suppose that a beautiful young female should be true and constant in her love to a man who had weathered near seventy winters; nevertheless, he added, though possibly the lady might indulge herself in propensities suitable to her years, still he was willing to pay a high price for the gratification of his whim, therefore he had to propose the exchange of a substantial weighty substance, namely, the gold spread out before them, for the transitory pleasure to be enjoyed by familiar converse with Madame Gotschalk; and provided this was to be obtained with the consent and through the management of his good friend the counsellor, he declared one moiety should now be paid over to him, and the remainder of the money as soon as the affair had been happily accomplished.

Counsellor Gotschalk, whose eyes were still dazzled at sight of the golden idol glittering before him, and whose heart throbbed with rapture at the bright prospect of making it his own, made answer that his highness had now resorted to a fair, though an unusual course, to obtain the gratification of his wishes; for that, unquestionably, since the wife, her honour and chastity, are the husband's own proper goods, it was a better and more lawful way to gain possession of them by his consent, than basely to purloin these things by means of corrupting the wife; which, if done without the husband's acquiescence, would be underhand dealing, and not a legal purchase. Moreover, he said, his highness had bid him handsomely, and therefore he was willing to close with the offer, but conditionally that their treaty should be kept a profound secret, not only from the world at large, but also from Madame Gotschalk, whose foolish scruples might otherwise defeat their project; and he further added that, provided his highness agreed to these preliminaries, he on his part consented that the prince should accomplish his full desire with his juvenile spouse; and promised he would assist him to the utmost in carrying into effect this condition of their agreement.

At this termination of their discourse the two worthies, in the joy of their hearts, embraced each other, and the prince solemnly promised to perform his part of the engagement; when the bargain being concluded, the mean-souled usurer speedily returned home, triumphantly as a hero after gaining a glorious victory, with two thousand five hundred newly gained pieces of gold in his possession; but in his sleeve laughing at his noble friend for his egregious folly in having given him the money. Indeed, so great was the miser's felicity on the occasion, that it deprived him of prudence, inasmuch as he displayed his gold before his spouse, boasting that he had gained it by his adroitness.

A day or two subsequent to that of their amicable negotiation, Gotschalk visited Prince Swarthyburg, when all things being in readiness, he, at a late hour of the day, sent his ring to Rosetta by a trusty person, together with a message, informing her that he had been taken alarmingly ill, and requesting to see her without the smallest delay.

The obedient wife, soon as she had received the ring and heard the message sent her, concluded that her husband must be in a dangerous state, and anxiously hastened away with the messenger, that she might perform the kind offices duty required towards him. On her arrival at the palace, Madame Gotschalk was conducted to a stately chamber, in which there was a superb bedstead furnished with gold and crimson curtains; when the servant having ushered her into the room, withdrew unnoticed; meanwhile she hastened towards the bed to seek her husband, and Prince Swarthyburg entered the room behind her and closed fast the door. The light of truth now burst upon her, but the heroine, finding she was betrayed. and seeing the amorous prince was hastening towards her with open arms, precipitately seized hold of a small Turkish dagger hanging at the bed head, and flourishing it, warned him not to approach her person, but show respect to her honour by permitting her to retire.

Love is deaf to the voice of prudence. Prince Swarthyburg, blinded by his passion and thinking her threat an empty bravado, and that he could easily overcome so fair an antagonist, laughingly approached and rudely seized upon her person, when Rosetta, after struggling for a time, finding that her assailant's brute strength would inevitably overcome her, yet feeling resolved at any price to protect her honour, plunged the dagger she held into the prince's body, and hastily withdrawing it, lodged the gory steel in her own bosom. The noise made by the struggling pair, and the fall and groans of the wounded sufferers, alarmed the servants of the house, who from all directions came running to the chamber door, but finding it locked, while groans and cries for assistance issued from within, they burst open the door and rushed into the room, where they beheld the frightful sight with horror and amaze: in short, such was their confusion that for a time nothing proper was done by them to assist the unfortunate sufferers. The butler was the first person to recollect himself, when he caused his master, who was nearly insensible from the loss of blood, to be laid on his own bed. But poor Rosetta, who appeared to be dying, he had conveyed to a bed in an adjoining chamber; meanwhile a messenger was dispatched to communicate to Gotschalk the sad catastrophe which had befallen his wife, and others were sent to procure medical aid.

The officious domestics called at every medical man's house they came nigh, and the doctors of the neighbourhood consequently thronged to the Swarthyburg palace, but unfortunately their efforts to succour Madame Gotschalk were altogether unavailing: she, poor lady, breathed her last in little more than an hour after she had inflicted the deadly wound in her bosom. With the prince these scientific characters had better success: he gradually recovered; for the fact is, that although he had fainted from excess of hemorrhage, his wound had never been dangerous. However, to give science its due, it must be mentioned that these learned men held a protracted consultation on his case, and issued a bulletin, pronouncing that his Highness Prince Swarthyburg, if kept quiet, and provided no unlooked-for bad symptoms should arise, in their opinion was likely to do well.

The messenger dispatched to the counsellor found him at home; indeed, on his wife's arrival at the palace he had quitted it by a back door, to hasten to his own abode; but whether he took this step from scruples of conscience stirred up by the apprehension of hearing his wife call for assistance against her ravisher, when he had resolved to afford her none, or that he felt eager to minutely examine if his last moiety of gold was pure in quality and correct in amount, does not appear, yet the messenger found him locked up in his cabinet, whence he was so tardy in making his appearance that he judged it expedient to communicate his distressing tidings through the key-hole, when the jingling noise of money, as if being tost into bags, reached his ears before the door was opened for his admittance.

The usurer's curiosity had not been sufficiently roused to make him ask any questions while he was in his cabinet, but when the servant and he were posting together along the streets, he expressed much anxiety to learn all the particulars attending his wife's calamity. From the tenor of his questions evidently his chief object in evincing this curiosity must have been that of satisfying himself, whether he was legally entitled to the last half of the precious metal for which he had bargained away his wife's honour. However, some compunctions of conscience seemed to disturb the gentleman when, on his arrival at the palace, he was made acquainted with the circumstance that his spouse had just then expired; but weak must these compunctions have been, for upon a question being put touching the poor woman's funeral, he sneaked away after intimating his expectations that his highness, who had occasioned her death, would take on himself the charge and management of her funeral.

By the inquest on the body, it was made to appear that Madame Gotschalk, in a paroxysm of insanity, had mortally stabbed herself and severely wounded Prince Swarthyburg; but as this politic prince gave her a costly burial, the journals of the town extolled the nobleness of his conduct, in showing such forgiveness and respect towards a maniac, who had placed his prized life in imminent jeopardy.

Prince Swarthyburg's cure verified the prognostications of the learned doctors. He got completely well, but owing to the many precautions taken by his medical attendants his highness was made to suffer the mortification attendant on being confined to his palace for three weeks, although he felt sufficiently recovered, and ardently wished to have gone abroad, at less than half that time.

A true lover glories in avenging the wrongs done his mistress. The prince had scarcely made his appearance abroad, ere he was disagreeably surprised at receiving a hostile message from Viscount Blucher, who had posted to Florence on hearing the foregoing sad tidings, and now called on the lamented woman's aggressor to give him personal satisfaction for his infamous conduct to Madame Gotschalk, whose death he affirmed had been caused by him.

His highness, indignant at the foul charge, yet unwilling to incur the danger attendant on a duel, threatened the viscount with a visitation from the police, as also an action at law; and the noble Prussian's second, with these threats resounding in his ears, departed from the prince's residence without obtaining any satisfaction on the behalf of his friend.

Happily, the resolute man holds a rod over his enemy. The prince had not long got rid of his unwelcome visitor before he sallied out of doors habited in a splendid uniform, but scarcely had he put foot in the street to step into his carriage, before the Prussian viscount, who had come there attended by some friends, to prevent the possibility of his servants protecting their master, suddenly grasped hold of his highness by his coat collar, and snatching his sword from the owner's side, broke it into two pieces, when disdainfully throwing the weapon into the street, he told the prince he was no better than a common murderer, while that to his cowardice he now stood indebted for the prolongation of his wretched existence; which having said, he deliberately spit in his highness's face and gave him an unmannerly kick or two on the seat of honour.

After he had thus gratified his revenge and shown his detestation of Prince Swarthyburg's conduct, the spirited viscount turned from his discomfited antagonist, and followed by his partisans, quitted the scene of action, without casting a look behind him.

E

CHAPTER III.

"Ah me! what perils do environ
The man that meddles with cold iron!
What plaguy mischiefs and mishaps
To dog him still with after-claps!
For though dame Fortune seems to smile,
And leer upon him for a while,
She'll after show him, in the nick
Of all his glories, a dog trick."

"In all courts of justice here
A witness is not said to swear,
But make an oath; that is, in plain terms,
To forge whatever he affirms."

THE viscount's assault on the prince having taken place in the public street, in presence of the prince's servants and other persons, it naturally became a subject of general conversation among the gossips of Florence, and every one formed their own surmise as to what might result from the unusual affair. Some asserted it as their opinion that a sanguinary duel would take place between the noble parties; others said they thought the viscount's person would be seized upon and he have to endure a tedious imprisonment; while not a few of these anglers in the stream of futurity hinted their apprehensions that his assassination would be the result of his temerity.

From this point of conjecture the busy reasoners would travel back to the cause of the gross outrage committed by the Prussian; and on this head sundry reports were industriously circulated; some of which were grossly slanderous of poor Rosetta's character, and framed to move compassion for her unfortunate spouse; but others were severe against the prince and prejudicial to the character of the counsellor, whose diabolical conduct in bartering away his wife's honour for gold got noised abroad, and many believed the report founded on fact.

The characters of living men depend much upon fortuitous circumstances, yet the most designing are usually represented as the most honest. The creatures of Prince Swarthyburg, finding that their patron's influence stood in need of propping, made it their special business to extol him in the newspapers, coffee houses, and all public places, for great virtue, and as much to decry the character and conduct of the nobleman who had assaulted his person. This ministerial course for hood-winking the crowd was pursued during some days, when the public mind having been prepared for the event, Viscount Blucher was arrested and taken out of his bed at a lone hour of the night, to be incarcerated in prison. The parasites even carried injustice beyond this act of the government, as they were guilty of the unpardonable crime of slandering poor Rosetta's spotless character, thereby to cast a false lustre on that of their depraved patron. The viscount's apprehension naturally set the gossips to work anew, when the character of Gotschalk was made to suffer in no slight degree; and assuredly, to the virtuous mind his crime appears unpardonable; nevertheless there were people in Florence who took the melancholy truth into consideration, that greater personages than the counsellor have grown rich by pandering with their spouses, and these liberal-minded gentry, with a generosity worthy of commendation, considered that all degrees of vice and virtue ought to be pronounced upon by comparison.

Now it so happened that, on the day following after the noble Prussian's arrest, I was engaged to dine with a lady of quality whom I had met at Mrs O'Shufflewell's, and Monday took his dinner at a famed restaurateur's, where it was his luck to get seated at a table adjoining to one occupied by a party of four military officers, whose conversation was one continued abuse of Viscount Blucher, intermixed with hyperbolical praise of Prince Swarthyburg.

The sailor, whose ideas of liberty were more enlarged than general report allows those of Italian soldiers to be, listened to these remarks in contemptuous silence, till at length, the subject having exhausted his patience, he attempted to divert his attention from it, and amuse himself in a manner more congenial to his feelings, by whistling a sea tune; but scarcely had he commenced upon this innocent recreation before it became evident, from the fierce looks assumed by the officers, that his pastime was not pleasing to them; Monday, however, regardless of the consequences, most perseveringly kept on whistling the old nautical song—Rule Britannia; and whenever the officers recurled their mustachoes, or otherwise attempted to look fiercer than before, he whistled proportionately louder. The sons of Mars, from time to time, exhibited fresh symptoms of their disapprobation, yet as none of these were personally offensive to the sailor, he took no cognizance of them, but calmly cracked filberts, and sipped Burgundy, when he was not engaged in whistling.

This was the state of affairs between the parties, their angry feelings being ripe and ready for combustion, when an officious character, one of those persons who make it their business to pick up acquaintances at taverns, that they may partake of good cheer at their expense, and who had become acquainted with Monday in this way, entered the room, when, spying out his convenient entertainer, he approached his table to salute him, and was invited to a share of Monday's Burgundy. The sailor, who in his hazardous career had frequently felt the want of generous wine and was of an hospitable disposition, having seated the parasite near to him, filled his glass, which was emptied in a trice; but the second bumper not going off so glibly, he said, " Come, clear off your heel-tap," which being done, he refilled both their glasses to the brim, and gave for a toast, ' The Prussian count, who brought the stiff-necked, buckram-rigged prince to his bearings.'

" To the last drop will I drink off that toast," rejoined the Corsican guest, as he lifted the glass to his lips; when having quaffed off its contents, he turned the measure upside down, resting the rim on the back of his thumb nail, and after noticing that not a *gout* of the liquor remained, laughingly observed, that having done justice to the toast of his entertainer, he should return the salute, by drinking, ' Perdition to all such cowardly rascals as Prince Swarthyburg.'

" Bravo," returned the sailor, refilling their glasses until they ran over, " your toast merits old wine and overflowing measure."

" Zounds," exclaimed one of the officers, who was a terrible looking man, with mustachoes projecting from his face, like a cat's whiskers, " who, in the name of perdition, have we here, that dares calumniate the character of Prince Swarthyburg in my presence?" then addressing himself pointedly to the sailor, he added, " you, sir, who have presumed to couple the terms, stiff-necked and buckram-rigged, with this noble prince's name, answer me these two questions, and with sincerity, if you possess the requisite courage,—are you one of the partisans of Viscount Blucher? and do you approve of his infamous conduct to his highness the prince?"

" You, mister hairy-mouth, are free with your questions, but suppose I may not choose to answer them; then, I'll warrant, you would soon clap your helm about and sheer off, before your insolence made me fall foul of your craft; howsoever, all things considered, I will answer your first question, by telling you I know no more of the viscount you palaver about, than you do of Paul Jones or Jack Hatfield; who, d'ye see, are both hard up in Davy's locker; but as to this Prussian's conduct towards the lubber of a prince, you may take your Davy I'll clap no stopper on my mouth; and thus much will I say, no matter who comes athwart my hawse for doing it, that he is a brave hearty fellow, and acted in this affair like a true man; yet, though I mean no reflections on him, for doubtless the thought never crossed his mind, had it been my case, I would have ploughed a few seams on the prince's back, just to have given the doctor a job in caulking and paying them."

" You are a low, vulgar fellow, I find, unworthy of a gentleman's notice," superciliously observed the officer, reseating himself at table.

" Words don't kill nor capsize, else you would sink all before you, Mr Tinselcoat, or whatever is your name," retorted the sailor.

" Hell and fury, what's that you say," cried the martial hero, starting up from his chair and seizing hold of the hilt of his sabre. " You are an impertinent rascal to speak contemptuously of the imperial uniform; but, by all that's sacred, you shall eat your words, or this steel make room for heaven's light to find a passage through your body."

" Let go your toasting fork, or I'll wipe down your back with this oaken towel," replied the sailor, flourishing his large stick.

Instinctively the officer stepped back several paces, and drew his glittering blade, the sight of which set the whole room in a ferment; every chair was now vacated, and every person was hurrying towards the scene of action.   Monday, however, undaunted at the hostile preparations of his enemy, pressed upon him so fiercely, that the gaunt soldier found it necessary to make a further retrograde movement, as many greater heroes have done, without awaiting the ceremony of beating a retreat ; till at length, being pent up in a corner of the room, with the blade of his sabre lying shivered to pieces on the floor, he could neither escape, nor longer protect himself from the merciless blows dealt him by the gallant sailor, who, highly to the diversion of many civilians of the party, kept bawling out, while he was employed chastising the martial hero, " So, mister hairy mouth, you mean to make the light of heaven shine through my hull, don't you ?"

The disconcerted gentleman's brother officers, whom astonishment at beholding Monday's impetuosity of attack had prevented from acting sooner, now interfered in behalf of their distressed comrade, and, by seizing the conquering hero by the shoulders and skirt of his coat, made him in his turn retrograde from his foe ; but the Corsican, although he was a common parasite, to his honour be it mentioned, was a valiant fellow, nobly stepped forward at this moment of necessity to assist his entertainer, and by sharp kicks and keen blows, dealt out with great good will, soon succeeded in convincing these soldier officers that active interference in a private quarrel of others is a service much more likely to be rewarded with blows than by honorary medals.

Monday had struggled to the utmost to save himself from making the retrograde movement his foes had compelled him to resort to ; and now, as soon as he was freed from his rearward assailants, he bravely faced about, reflourishing his stick, and called aloud upon his partisan to back him, while he, he said, would beat the dust out of a few uniform coats.

" Corsica against Florence," was the reply, and pell-mell, helter-skelter, went to work both the sailor and his supporter.

" British oak for ever," bellowed out the former at almost every blow he made tell ; while " revenge and old Corsica," was the cry of the latter hero, when he performed similar martial exploits.

Open warfare is highly extolled and admired by the heroes who are victorious in it ; and the more sanguinary the battle, so proportionately is the pride of those personages inflated by empty air, foul as that blown from the trump of Fame, for, notwithstanding what the tongue of sophistry may assert, honour and glory, dishonour and shame, are mere names, dependant for their effect on report and the fashion of the times.

The sailor and the Corsican had hitherto carried on this warfare much to their advantage, and three or four prostrate antagonists bore conclusive evidence of the severity with which their blows had been administered ; but treacherous Bellona, who alike favours just and unjust causes, and changes about from side to side, to retain her warriors the tighter in their leading strings, now infused an additional stock of courage and sagacity into the most numerous party, and they, consequently, being assisted and guided by a divinity, simultaneously fell upon our two sturdy champions, and by their united strength overwhelmed and forced them to measure their lengths upon the sandy floor.

It would have fared badly with Monday and his colleague had the conquerors been left to treat them according to their sovereign pleasure ; their hopes and situation would then have been somewhat on a par with those of citizens in a besieged town, at the moment of a triumphant enemy's entrance through a breach on its wall.   In short, to judge of the brutality shown in their assaults on the prostrate pair, there can be little question but that, had it not been for the waiters and some other persons who forcibly interfered to separate the conquerors from the conquered, the former would have sent the souls of the latter, unprepared, on the great voyage of futurity, before they had fully satiated their vengeance upon their bodies.

A stout heart is not to be dismayed.   The sailor was scarcely on his legs after his overthrow, ere, rubbing his eyes, which were considerably swollen and blackened by the blows which had just been inflicted on them, he exclaimed, " Cowardly lubbers as ye are, would that I had the handling of you, one by one at a spell, I'd teach you to give a wide berth to your betters ; I'd make you glad to dance from the presence of a brave man ; I'd put metal into your legs, as Boney did to those of the Austrians, when they capered away, while he took Vienna from them."

" Sacré dieu," stammered the Corsican, feeling over his mouth, where several teeth had been forcibly ejected from their places, "this comes of meddling with other men s quarrels; this is the way we poor Corsicans get treated by Florentine and Austrian soldiers."

"To the guard-house with these disturbers of the public peace, these vagabond fellows," said the senior of the officers, addressing a serjeant who had just entered the room with half a dozen rank and file of soldiers at his heels. "I take on me the responsibility of the measure; it is my order that you take these fellows into custody."

"Your honour's commands shall be obeyed," replied the obsequious serjeant; "is it your honour's pleasure, colonel, that they shall be locked up in the black hole?"

"Should they prove obstreperous, but not otherwise," rejoined the officer; "but away with them, serjeant."

"My lad, give the chaps their hats now," said the serjeant to one of the waiters; when this having been done, he turned to his prisoners, saying, "come, my lads, march away to your new quarters."

"This comes of meddling in other men's quarrels; this is the way that poor Corsicans get treated here," ejaculated the Corse.

"This is a sample of liberty," observed Monday, looking disdainfully at the armed soldiers: "'tis a pity these worsted-laced gentlemen have not something better to employ them than boarding unarmed vessels and taking defenceless prisoners."

"Away with the ruffians," shouted several of the officers; "put handcuffs on them if they resist."

By the serjeant's command the soldiers now pushed their prisoners towards the door; but as the sailor evinced some backwardness to move in that direction, he was goaded, à posteriori, by the point of a bayonet, which acted more forcibly than any wordy argument could have done, and convinced him that resistance would be downright madness; therefore, making a merit of necessity, my secretary marched away peaceably among the escort. But still, when quitting the chamber he had dined in, he further insulted his enemies by proclaiming aloud that Prince Swarthyburg was a good-for-nothing humbug, and it should go hard with himself, but he'd find some way of obtaining satisfaction for the treatment he had met with on the lubberly rascal's account.

The Corsican, who, by woful experience, had been taught that the miracle of a poor man's obtaining redress for wrongs inflicted by a great one is not performed every day, marched along the streets leading to the guard room in no small tribulation, which the pain and melancholy reflections, occasioned by the loss he had sustained of several teeth, tended not a little to aggravate.

Monday made occasional attempts to rouse the sufferer out of his doldrums, as he termed his depression of spirits, sometimes telling him not to be taken aback so, but cheer up, for that he would take on himself to warrant one day or other they would have their revenge; and at others, advising him not to take so much to heart the loss of his masticators, for that he would hand him over some shiners, by way of a compliment, for his services in the fight they had maintained together.

Language meant to condole a sufferer, unless it be baited with the lure afforded by affection, or that of profit, as may best suit the occasion, usually fails in effecting the desired object; but Monday's well-timed hint, regarding the present he purposed making his companion in misfortune, seemed to afford that individual some consolation.

The subaltern officer of the guard received his prisoners from the serjeant in a contemptuous manner, scarcely condescending to honour two such ragamuffins, as they appeared to him, with a single look. "What are these fellows sent here for?" was the question of this redoubtable ensign.

"Please your honour, they are sent here by Colonel Hofflemans, for creating a riot at Bonvoison's, the restaurateur, where they ill-treated four or five of our officers, and the colonel amongst the number."

"You must be dreaming, serjeant," rejoined the ensign, "these fellows are fit company for a petty cabaret, and nothing better: at Bonvoison's such ragamuffins are not admitted. However, to the guard-house with them, and see to it they don't escape."

The ensign's suspicions, though not of a flattering nature to the prisoners, were quite pardonable, as neither of the heroes bore the smallest appearance of being gentlemen. The one, in addition to black and swollen eyes, exhibited a pair of pantaloons much torn in front, and a coat stripped of one of its skirts; besides which, it was rent up the back, to the very collar. The other discomfited hero's appearance was still more deplorable. In addition to his disfigured mouth and a frightfully scratched nose, owing to his cravat having been torn in pieces in the struggle, he exposed a bared neck, and through the holes cut in his small clothes protruded his naked knees: moreover, the garments of both these combatants had got miserably dirtied in the conflict.

When they had got themselves seated amidst the soldiers in their guard-room, Monday and the Corsican had ample leisure time for meditating upon the mutability of human affairs; but the sailor's reflections not unfrequently were interrupted by the groans and lamentations of his companion. "What a wretch am I become," the chop-fallen hero would involuntarily exclaim. "My handsome teeth knocked out of my mouth, my best suit of clothes torn to rags, and my person imprisoned in a common military guard-room; while I, unfortunate man as I am, stand threatened with a still more deplorable fate; and for what am I brought to this misery? merely for partaking of a pint or two of wine with a quarrelsome Englishman. Alas! alas! see what my love of good fare has brought me too. Oh! that I had been satisfied to earn my bread by the sweat of my brow, as my good, honest, hard-working parents have done before me.'"

"Come, cheer up, messmate," the sailor would say at the termination of each soliloquy of the foregoing nature, "a light heart is a man's best companion through the stormy voyage of life; it serves, like a lit candle in a binnacle, to show him which course he should steer to keep clear of rocks and breakers, in reaching the port of his destination; besides, it brightens the countenance and keeps old father care at a wide offing: in short, a light heart is better than a weighty bag of money, for the latter may get canted overboard and buried for ever in Davy's locker, while, d'ye see, messmate, the former stays snug in a man's own keeping, and provided he parts company with it, he has none but himself to find fault with."

The sailor's reasoning, though straightforward, and sufficiently clear to be understood by any one, apparently made little or no happy impression on the discomfited Corse; on the contrary, when he made mention of the heavy bag of money, that unfortunate gentleman sighed and lamented more grievously than before; but grog, that solacer of a sailor's heart, proved successful in effecting a purpose which reason, with all her much-vaunted powers, had failed in accomplishing. To persons unacquainted with the soldier's character, it may be difficult to conjecture how this balmy comforter could be made to find its way to prisoners confined in a military guard-house; but the mystery lies in a narrow compass. Soldiers love the dear creature, therefore they are at all times ready to tolerate the indulgence afforded by tippling, and underhandedly to render their assistance in procuring the loved article of drink, provided, at least, they are permitted to imbibe an honest share of it.

The drummer of the guard was the individual who performed the notable commission of purchasing pipes, tobacco, eau-de-vie, sugar, and a lemon, for the sailor; but from prudential motives, well understood by his serjeant, he brought these articles into the guard-room at a time when one of the corporals was absent with the relief of sentries, and the other busily employed assisting the serjeant in handcuffing a black-hole prisoner, who was doomed to this extra punishment for having disturbed the ensign by the loudness of his singing.

The mysteries of guard-keeping should be passed lightly over, therefore I shall content myself by saying the party enjoyed themselves over their punch during two-thirds of the night, when the Corsican, having drunk himself into a comfortable state of inebriation, forgot all his troubles in sleep, and the sailor, not sorry to see his friend in this condition, wrapped a soldier's coat round him, then habited himself in another, and extended his frame on the wooden stretcher, to take his night's repose near to his fellow combatant. As to the serjeant, liquor rarely affected him more than by making his nose assume a somewhat redder hue, and his eyes become brighter than ordinary: both which effects were wrought to admiration by the sailor's exhilarating mixture.

Wisely is it ordained that excess of pleasure shall be the parent of the opposite extreme. Were it otherwise the world would abound with drunkards and gormandizers; but the gout, headache, apoplexy, palsy, and some more of the mementos of the weakness of the human constitution, have a wonderful great tendency to check and prevent these, and some other such inconsiderate characters, from indulging to an excess in their propensities, and sometimes they turn jolly fellows into milksops and teetotallers.

Our Corsican next morning, after a yawn or two, awoke to a thorough sense of his woes, aggravated by a miserable sick headache, arising from the fumes of the punch he had so freely partaken of overnight. "Oh! that I was dead," he was heard to exclaim in the best manner his mutilated mouth permitted of his articulating the words, at the same time glancing his eyes at his rent garments, and the whole of the novel scene around him—"Oh! that I was dead, rather than be exposed to all this misery."

Indeed the poor gentleman's exclamations, denotive of his sufferings, were many and lamentable, yet they extracted no pity from the soldiers, who were busily employed furbishing their arms and putting their accoutrements in order, preparatory to the relief of guard; therefore, had our prisoners been disposed to have indulged themselves longer in sleep, they could not have done so, for they were called on to strip themselves of the great coats Monday had hired for the night, and which their owners required, that they might get them rolled up and strapped in parade order; while the morning was too cold to permit of their sleeping without this covering.

On the preceding evening Monday had intrusted the drummer with a letter for me, and this noisy child of Mars, at the time he took the piece of money meant as a remuneration for the trouble he would have in going to the post-office with the epistle, most solemnly promised to execute the commission, and afterwards told his employer, with a staunch oath to back his assurance, that he had done it; consequently the sailor, being under the impression that I should shortly pay him a visit, on beholding the desponding condition of his companion, slapped him on the shoulder, saying, "Messmate, cheer up, for presently a friend of mine will put into port here, who, I'll warrant, will be an overmatch for our enemies, and get us safe out of limbo."

Monday, like the dupes to Pitt's sinking fund, was egregiously out in his calculation, for the drummer, who considered no promise binding, unless made to his military superior, and with whom assertions weighed lightly, as they do with most Chancellors of the Exchequer and diplomatists, had deemed it unnecessary to deposit the letter in a post-office, but having a sudden call for a morsel of paper to light his pipe, he had unscrupulously made use of the letter.

"Your friend is very tardy in making his appearance," was the oft-repeated observation made by the unfortunate Corsican, till at length came the new guard, but no tidings of me.

"I never passed a pleasanter time on guard than I have now done," the sailor overheard the red nosed serjeant say to his successor on duty; "I've been treated to as much good swill as I could barrel up under my belt; and I'll tell you what, comrade, provided I could be sure that the two guard-room prisoners were to remain here so long, I'd volunteer, or change a turn of duty, to relieve you in the morning, and so get another pleasant day of it to-morrow."

The new serjeant felt quite enlivened by the hint he had received, and soon as the old guard had been marched off, he hurried to the guard-room, when, wishing to commence his turn of duty in the pleasant way he anticipated, he smilingly addressed his prisoners, saying, "Comrades, if 'tis agreeable to you, I shall feel no objection on my part to take a glass or two with you, to drink to our better acquaintance."

"Yaw!" ejaculated the sick Corsican, "I wish to my soul that I was dead."

Complaint excites contempt, and the serjeant, on hearing the preceding apostrophe, stared at the disconsolate prisoner with astonishment depicted in his countenance, till at length he muttered, loud enough to be heard by those near him, "A pleasant guard, indeed, with such a spoon of a fellow for a companion."

"Yaw," again ejaculated the Corsican, groaning aloud, "I wish to my soul that I was dead."

"You may be dead and damned into the bargain, for what I care," said the serjeant, unstrapping the pack from his shoulders.

Monday, unable to contain himself longer, burst into a hearty fit of laughter, and soon as he had given vent to it, he told the serjeant that his hint was by no means a bad one, and despatched the drummer away with money to replenish the bottle and procure a fresh supply of polonais sausage and bread.   To be guarded against any charge of a breach of military duty, the serjeant now took his two corporals out of the guard room, under some specious pretence, and thus afforded the drum boy an opportunity of bringing in unwitnessed the *eau de vie;* when, having returned, and finding everything prepared for the repast, the brave serjeant seated himself at the board, and filling his glass from the bottle of *eau de vie,* which, that his soldiers might not by any accident bear evidence of its name against him, he thought fit to call holy-water, he said, " Comrades, this is now the way to carry on the war.   Talk of being dead, indeed, while a man can drink holy-water and feast on polonais sausage.   He who can do this, as the saying goes, may live all the days of his life ;" then having spoken thus, he happened to perceive that the state of the Corsican's mouth prevented his eating with any pleasure to himself, when musingly he added, that mercury was a bad companion for the mouth, and to judge from the loss of his teeth, he supposed the poor gentleman had taken too much of it; but then, he said, every man had his particular fancy, though, for his own part, added he, refilling his glass brimming full, he loved to stick to the bottle.

In the midst of his repast the gallant serjeant was disturbed by a message from his officer, directing him to send a corporal and four rank and file as an escort to convey our prisoners before a certain magistrate, and he being a wary old soldier, was well aware that military orders cannot be too promptly complied with, and therefore merely drank off his glass of *eau de vie* and refilled it, which, by-the-bye, was the fourth time of going through that ceremony, before he let his prisoners know what instructions he had received regarding them.

" A man does well to keep himself sober and have all his wits about him when summoned to appear before a magistrate," observed the serjeant, while his prisoners were engaged brushing their dirty garments; " then," resumed the considerate soldier, after some pause, " these civil magistrates make no sort of allowance for a man being a little fresh or so with liquor, but they commit him to prison, or squeeze money out of him as a fine, for being a rogue and a vagabond, when they would let a sanctified-looking scoundrel get his discharge, in return for a teston or two, handed over to the magistrate's clerk."

" Yaw," ejaculated the Corsican, with an attendant groan, at the same time examining his phiz in a morsel of broken glass. which served as part of the shaving apparatus of one of the corporals.

" Comrades, I suppose you won't venture to take any more of the *eau de vie,*" said the serjeant, grasping a tight hold of the corked bottle, when his prisoners were on the eve of being marched out of the guard room.

" No, serjeant, it is extremely at your service," replied the sailor.

" You are a gentleman," rejoined the non-commissioned officer.   " I hope you'll get well out of this scrape.   Bad luck to the magistrate if he commits you for trial."

" Did gentlemen ever before suffer such an indignity as this," muttered the Corsican, at a time when the sailor and he were being marched along the public street, laughed and hooted at by a set of rabble, in consequence of their vagabond-like appearance.

" After a gale, a gallant craft may be seen under torn canvass," remarked the sailor, laughing and pinning together the cloth of his pantaloons, so as to hide the linen beneath, and make the rent there less conspicuous.

The distance to the magistrate's office was not very considerable, and as Colonel Hofflemans and the rest of the witnesses had arrived there before them, our prisoners were not long detained waiting before their examination was commenced upon; but the witnesses against them made it appear that our heroes alone were in fault, and what they themselves said was totally discredited, consequently the magistrate's clerk whispered his worship that the evidence against the prisoners was conclusive, and the magistrate accordingly directed that their mittimus should be made out.   The Corsican endeavoured to remonstrate against this unjust decree, but the state of his mouth prevented his being well heard.   However, this signified little, as, had he possessed the lungs of a Stentor, and the eloquence of the corrupt turn-coat Burke, the exertion of their powers could have answered no salutary purpose, in pleading against the enforcement of a sentence given to make friends of the great.   Monday was sensible of this truth, therefore all he did was to utter violent philippics against his assailants, the soldier officers, and their patron prince, Swarthyburg, but this tended only to aggravate the case, and occasion the magistrate to have them carried away to prison.

CHAPTER IV.

"The world is full of strange vicissitudes,
And here was one exceedingly unpleasant."

"He saw some fellow captives, who appeared
To be Italians, as they were in fact;
From them at least their destiny he heard,
Which was a sad one."

THE prison to which Monday and his companion in misfortune were conveyed, was not far remote from the magistrate's office; and as the civil officer employed to take them there permitted his prisoners to hire a coach on the occasion, they were speedily housed in their new place of incarceration, without having again been exposed to the mortification attendant on being marched like felons through the streets. The gaol was crowded with a rare motley set, but perhaps there could not have been selected from among the number any other two, disfigured in their persons and habiliments so greatly as were our heroes. Misery, however, can point the finger of derision at greater misery, and their fellow prisoners, although familiarized to the sight of ragamuffins of all descriptions, yet laughed and indulged themselves in many rude remarks at the appearance of their new companions. The Corsican not feeling pleased with his lodgings, or the reception he met with, frequently gave utterance to exclamations denotive of his wretchedness, and when jokes or inuendoes from those about him reached his ears, he involuntarily ejaculated his favourite word *yaw*; but Monday, though he could scarcely forbear smiling at the deplorable state of his associate, being more accustomed to meet untoward reverses of fortune, knew how to philosophize in a prison, and could borrow a portion of Momus' mirth, to clear away the vapours which find their way to the unwilling inmates of such places.

"Variety," now said the sailor, laughing and tapping the Corsican on the shoulder, "variety, my friend, in all countries and climes is most charming: the same food every day becomes very palling to the palate; and, d'ye see, a perfect saint for a messmate would soon be thought but a lubberly sort of a companion."

"Yaw, what's that you say?" ejaculated the Corsican, with a vacant stare and his mouth half open.

"Possession," humorously resumed the sailor, "long, secure possession, would make the face of a Venus look altered and unalluring: it would cause spots to be seen on the whitest skin,—on a skin previously thought spotless; and even Diana, with all the much vaunted graces of her figure, would, in the eyes of a satiated swain, appear not a jot better than an old Indian squaw or a dumpy woman."

"Yaw," once more ejaculated the Corsican, fixing his eyes on Monday, with his mouth wide open.

There was a something irresistibly ludicrous in the Corsican's appearance, wildly staring, as he did, with his mutilated mouth stretched open. Monday could not command himself, but burst into a loud fit of laughter, and many of his fellow prisoners who beheld the sight, laughed as heartily. The Corsican, on witnessing this display of feeling, looked angry, but the sailor, without appearing to notice his discomposure, provokingly resumed his discourse.

"Yes," said he, "variety indisputably is charming. Variety is to be admired even in a prison: for example, we have companions of all sorts to-day, but yesterday we had only slaves of soldiers for our messmates."

"Yaw," whispered the Corsican, "we had best say nought to the disparagement of the troops, else we shall get into still more grievous trouble."

"I care not a rope's end for the lubbers," resumed the sailor; "all I mean to infer is, that a seaman is better off, imprisoned in a common gaol, amongst a mixture of people, many, no doubt, jolly, good-hearted fellows, than shut up in a guard-room, with soldiers only to keep them company."

"Yaw," muttered the Corsican parasite, significantly placing a finger on his mouth. Meanwhile several of the prisoners were seen to grin at Monday's last observation.

" It doesn't signify yawing a man's speeches," continued the tar, smiling and apparently resolved to continue the subject; " I'll take on me to warrant there are more clever fellows to be found, in proportion to their numbers, in any gaol of the four quarters of the world than in any regiment; for, d'ye see, messmate, none save the most booby-headed of lubbers would make a voluntary slave of himself, to have his back wiped down with a cat 'o nine tails for any trifling offence, and be shot at, right and left, fore and aft, and exposed to be blown up by mines of gunpowder, of the enemy, or abused worse than a negro by Jackanapes of officers placed over him, and all for what, let us ask ?—why, a few pence a day, a little worsted to imitate silk on his garments, and the prospect of getting a bit of ribbon, or some trumpery cross or medal, hung out, sign-like, on the breast of his livery coat; which, no doubt, makes the mountebank think himself a gentleman don of no little consequence."

Many of the prisoners laughed at the sailor's observations, and some few cheered him, or otherwise signified their approbation of his declared sentiments. " However," resumed he, soon as the laughter had subsided, " although it displays no sign of a man's wit or talent to enlist himself, yet I maintain there are many good fellows in the army, and some few lads of talent also; for, d'ye see, messmates, a vast number are made to take service by the conscript, alias the militia laws; while not a few get themselves enlisted when the fumes of grog, or the juice of the grape, have fired their brains and turned their understanding adrift."

" One would think, sir, that your understanding was adrift, as you call it," whispered the Corsican, alarmed at his companion's pertinacity in continuing to discourse in this manner.

" It doesn't signify palavering;" resumed Monday, " here we are, sure enough, in close limbo, with a few ounces of bad bread and as much water as we can swill for our day's allowance; then, let me ask, what have we to dread? They can't well do worse by us—therefore, messmate, lighten your heart of its heavy cargo, and cheer up; for depend on it, after foul weather comes fair; and never fear, though we ride at anchor in a foul berth, but that, when the wind shifts, we shall swing round to a better station."—" Swing," muttered an ill-looking fellow, to whom Monday's technical terms were unintelligible; " who the *diable* is it that talks of swinging. It shows bad breeding to prate about what we are all likely to come to? The drop, as every one knows, has been erected for our accommodation."

The Corsican, with fresh symptoms of alarm in his countenance, stared at the last speaker in silence; but the sailor, after having mused for a few seconds, exclaimed, " Confound such accommodation I say."—" Keep your tongue to yourself, and provided you have got the needful, pay your garnish before you preach," rejoined the first speaker.

" Right," said the sailor, looking sternly at him, "garnish paid or not paid, a wise head holds a silent tongue, in company such as we have got here."

The ruffian who had shown himself fearful of the gibbet, and desirous of participating in the garnish money expected from the newly arrived prisoners, clenched his teeth and grinned with anger at Monday's last remark, but threatening mischief was now averted by an elegant, well-dressed man, who, leading the sailor and his companion away from the scene of contention, thus addressed them :—

" Gentlemen, it ill becomes me, who have been the occasion of your present trouble, to stand by a passive spectator, and see you insulted in your misfortune."

" You are extremely courteous and polite," answered the sailor, " but, sir, you need not have given yourself any concern about my being insulted by yon lubberly landsman, for depend on it I should treat him to as good as he brought. However, I must observe that I think you are altogether wrong in your reckoning, as how can you have been the occasion of bringing me into trouble, when this is the first time I ever cast eyes on you ?"

" Your conduct, worthy sir, affords proof that a generous heart may instigate its owner to brave danger and despise imprisonment in upholding the character of a perfect stranger," replied he.

" Your speech is a perfect riddle to me," said the sailor, looking fixedly at the stranger, " I've neither braved danger nor suffered imprisonment on your account, and he who has told you I have done either, has been speaking you under false colours."

I can undeceive you in a moment merely by telling my name; I am Viscount Blucher, the Prussian, on whose account you have undergone every indignity, and are now suffering imprisonment."

"Then you are a hearty good gentleman," rejoined he, shaking hands with the nobleman, "and I don't value a rope's end what I've suffered; howsoever, on the word of a British sailor, here's my messmate here, and a brave man he is for a fair fight, though just now a little cast down in spirits, as you see, on finding himself hard up in limbo here, who really deserves well at your hands, for he upheld your character at the expense of his person, which has been battered and bruised in the combat ; and, moreover, he deserves well of me, as he did his best to help me out at a dead lift, and I should be false-hearted not to stand forward and avow it."

"Let us adjourn, my good friends," said the viscount, "I have a small apartment to myself, and there we shall be retired and more at our ease than we are here."

"Willingly, willingly, noble sir," replied the sailor. Meanwhile, as they walked away, the Corsican's countenance brightened up at the prospect of his having made a rich, powerful friend.

"So, my friend," said the viscount to the sailor, soon as the three were seated by a good fire with refreshments on a table before them, "I have been given to understand it is your opinion that I ought to have inflicted a severe horsewhipping on Prince Swarthyburg, in addition to the chastisement I bestowed on him."

"'Tis true, I did express myself rather freely about your honour, but, on the word of a straightforward sailor, I meant neither harm nor reflection—my remarks being intended more as a return fire to the insulting crew of officers than anything else."

The viscount laughed at the tar's honest warmth in his behalf, and having signified his sense of the obligation he felt under to him, communicated the circumstance that one of the corporals on guard where his guests had been confined had, some years before been a soldier under his command, in a Prussian corps, and that this man had related the whole story to his servant, of the quarrel at the restaurateur's, as also many particulars concerning the prisoner's behaviour while they were confined in the guard-house; in reply to which Monday acquainted the viscount with his suspicions relative to the letter he had entrusted to the drummer, which, he said, could not have reached its destination; for that, provided it had, he felt satisfied his friend and patron, to whom it was addressed, would ere that time have honoured him with a visit, preparatory to exerting his influence to procure his and the Corsican gentleman's liberation from prison.

Viscount Blucher now made an offer of dispatching his servant with a letter or message, which Monday availed himself of, and instantly wrote to me by that person, detailing what had befallen him; but the man soon returned, saying he had left the letter at my hotel for me, as I was absent in the country, and in fact that was the case, for I had gone from home to keep an appointment a few miles from Florence.

The servant having stated what he had to say, Monday addressed the viscount as follows : "My lord he, who in the same cruise has had to beat five hundred leagues to windward, in the very teeth of a trade wind, may be supposed to carry a good cargo of patience on board his craft. Besides, after all, it signifies little whether a man is a day or two more or less jambed up in limbo, provided he is accommodated with excellent rations, society and quarters, such as, thanks to your lordship, we have found here. However, our rigging is a little shattered, and our hulls are a little battered; therefore it is to be hoped we may get safe into port in a day or two, that we may lie up to repair and refit, after the damage we have received."

At the preceding hint for change of raiment, as he supposed it to be, Viscount Blucher pressed Monday and the Corsican to select clothes for themselves from his wardrobe, instead of wearing the torn ones they had on ; but the latter gentleman did not think proper to act differently from his companion, who, for his part, obstinately refused to change his raiment, saying he had seen far worse squalls than what had brought him into quarantine there, and that he didn't doubt but the wind would veer round, and he get under sail again in a few watches, when his old shivered canvass would serve to carry him to the port where he kept his supplies.

A good friend, a cheerful fire, and choice wine, are great soothers of care; and, combined together, may make a prisoner happier in a gaol than some spendthrift princes are in their sumptuous palaces. This would literally have been the case with the sailor and his fellow combatant, had it not been that their persons were extremely sore and tender from the bruises they had received in battle, and moreover, that the latter gentleman could not help lamenting the irre-trievable loss of his teeth; yet, notwithstanding these drawbacks upon felicity, the day passed away with them tolerably well, and on the night succeeding it, they slept together on a straw mattress, spread over a wooden bedstead, when, in defiance of their bruises, the god of sleep favoured them with hours of uninterrupted repose.

After their breakfasts next morning, the viscount and his guests adjourned to the court-yard of their prison, where Monday joined a party at tennis, which was played against the lofty wall that divided them from the free part of the town's community; but the Corsican, feeling less inclined than the sailor to use violent exercise, made one at chicken hazard, the party's cards being dealt to them upon an old target fixed on props for this purpose, and round which the anxious players seated themselves how they best could.

The viscount was desirous of avoiding much intimacy with strangers of a very inferior rank to himself, and therefore he declined playing either at tennis or cards, but entered into conversation with a sturdy old gentleman, who, it appeared, was a Bohemian captain or infantry. He had served better than forty years, and lost a leg, an eye, and an arm, fighting for the Emperor of Germany; in return for which he had obtained the grant of a trifling pension, but not until after he had been long suing for it; and unfortunately, the hoary soldier was now suffering imprisonment for a debt incurred by him in feeing certain well-known official characters, whom he had found it necessary to bribe ere he could get his hard-earned pittance.

The captain, although he was poor as the usher of a parish school, and ignorant as a junior schoolboy of the pauper race, yet was opinionated, and obstinate as a mule. Rendered proud and fierce by the rank he held in the Austrian service, he considered himself a personage of no small importance; and, as such, that it would be derogatory to his dignity to yield up his opinion to that of any living mortal whatever; consequently, force of argument and superiority of knowledge, or of talent when opposed to him, carried no conviction, for this veteran and his opinions, like an aged tree and its roots, were so inseparably united that they could only live and die together.

The viscount, when he first entered into conversation with this crusty veteran of the Aus-trian old school, had no further object in view than that of whiling an hour away, experience having taught him that men who have been much more buffeted about the world, whether by sea or land, are usually intelligent, and remarkable for a certain peculiarity of character, which renders their society agreeable. This veteran, however, completely disappointed Blucher's expectations, as, besides the mulish obstinacy shown by him, he was garrulously precise in praising all the military tactics of Austria's old school, and unceremoniously abusive of the tactics of Prussia, which last theme could not be otherwise than offensive to one of its officers.

The viscount having taxed his patience to the utmost to listen with complaisance to the thrice told heroic deeds of numerous Austrian soldiers, the human butchers of their day, ever ripe and ready for pillage and slaughter, from the time of the wily field-marshal Louden and the infamous Francis Trenck down to the days of General Mack and the renowned Archduke Charles, had at length, but nearly at the expense of a coat button, so tightly was it held by this veteran, to force himself away from him, completely astounded and wearied by the strength of lungs and unceasingly provoking conversation of the white-headed hero, and after all he followed after him, to renew the discourse; consequently, the marquis, wishing to avoid hearing more of his conversation, was under the necessity of returning to his apartment.

The nobleman had not been long in his chamber before Monday and the Corsican joined him, the former having had his waistcoat pockets picked and his coat purloined, at the time he was displaying his skill at tennis, and the latter gentleman being cheated of the few coins he possessed; for sharp as he was and eager to win money, the rooks with whom he played proved too knowing for him.

The vexation and mishaps they had experienced at first made the viscount and his guests indifferent company for each other; yet after the sailor had got accommodated with the use of a laced military coat, which he selected from the clothes tendered for his service, as he said for the novelty of the thing, for that his old comrades would not know him under such colours, the party become facetiously merry, insomuch that many jokes were bandied about ; nevertheless, from time to time, a half-smothered sigh would arise from the Corsican's breast, and more than once he was heard to exclaim, " Oh, my money."

This was the state of things with the prisoners, when towards night, while they were enjoying their wine, I entered their apartment. An involuntary smile played on my countenance, as I glanced my eyes at my sailor secretary, in a Prussian hussar dress. He now introduced me to his companions in captivity; and I, who on receiving Monday's letter, had posted away to my noble friend the duke, and got him to use his interest with the proper authorities in the behalf of my secretary and his fellow combatant, was so far from affording empty condolence only, that I had the gratification of notifying the successful result of my endeavours in their behalf, by the production from my pocket of an order for their discharge from prison.

" Huzza," shouted the sailor, slapping the Corsican's back, "did I not say the doors of this gaol would soon be open for us."

The Corsican, however, who naturally expected the viscount would speedily be liberated, and had been made an offer of being taken into his service, now signified a desire of remaining with that nobleman; but before my secretary and I quitted the prison, I presented the Corsican with a purse of ducats, which had a talismanic effect in cheering his spirits and brightening up his countenance; insomuch, indeed, was his heart elevated by the gift, that he laughed aloud on the sailor's saying to him, " Lighten your heart, messmate, and try to stow those ducats safe away from the light-fingered gentry who rooked you so cleverly at cards."

CHAPTER V.

" How sweet the moonlight seems to sleep,
    In yon azure cloudless bed !
No ruffian murder now awakes,
    To rear his fearful head !
For midnight rapine hates to view
    The glories of the skies:
And when the living sapphires burn,
    He turns him round and flies."

" By Arno's tide !
Lady, I swear, as sure as thou
Reject'st the love I here avow,
So sure shall blood of man be shed,
So sure that blood be on thy head."

THE morning following his liberation from prison, Monday accompanied me in paying a visit to Viscount Blucher, whom we found ready prepared to quit Florence, the order for his liberation having been sent to the gaol; but it was coupled with the condition that he instantly quitted the Austrian and Tuscan dominions in Italy; while so eager was he to get out of the power of his vindictive foe, that his carriage was standing at the prison door, with the nobleman's luggage packed upon it, ready for departure. The scene was now made diverting by Monday's friend, the Corsican, who, highly to his own satisfaction, was equipped in a new and most fashionable suit of clothes, with a watch displayed in his fob, and a row of beautiful teeth, set to admiration, in his head.

" Adzooks," exclaimed the sailor, as he scanned him over, " the craftsmen have been busily at work with you, messmate : if it were not for the build of your hull, and the cut of your jib, an old shipmate would not be able to make you out at a fair offing."

The Corsican laughed on hearing Monday's salutation, and by doing so, made a full exhibition of his mouth's new inmates ; after which the viscount remarked that his friend had been abroad shopping, and no doubt, he added, it would afford him pleasure to find that his purchases gave satisfaction to his nautical friend.

" Yes," said the Corsican, " I have visited the streets here to furnish myself with some of the handy works of a famed dentist, as also to fit myself with clothes and other articles necessary for the comfort of man's person ; but Viscount Blucher has done more for me than these characters united. To his lordship's kindness am I indebted for a valuable gold repeater, chain, and seals; and moreover, what is of infinite greater advantage to me, his lordship has taken me under his patronage, and I am on the eve of departing with him for Berlin."

"A friend who has proved himself such, ought not to be forsaken when he needs a return of service, and as this gentleman has voluntarily fought for, and suffered bodily injury in supporting, my character, he shall accompany me to Berlin, and there I shall make it my affair to get him provided with a situation, to make him comfortable in life. Captain Monday, happily for him, requires not my services; but, provided he did, it would delight me to render them; still, as a token of grateful remembrance of his zeal in my behalf, I must beg him to accept of this," added he, presenting to my secretary a handsome gold watch.

"Thank'ye, thank'ye, viscount," exclaimed the sailor; "I am bad at compliments, else I might spin a long yarn of thanks; howsoever, thus much I must say, that although I shall ever esteem your gift, I am made happier by your promise of getting a snug berth for my messmate here, than I should be at your lordship's giving me a box of presents."

The Corsican now commenced a set speech, which from its formality was likely to have been tediously long, but the sailor interrupted him by exclaiming, "Avast, brother; avast heaving; least said the soonest mended, as, d'ye see, there's no hoisting in what has been thrown overboard; and mayhap a man, in his hurry, might cant a part of his cargo out of a port-hole, which it would grieve him to see picked up by an enemy."

"Captain Monday gives seasonable advice," said the viscount; "we too frequently have cause to repent of speaking; but very rarely of keeping our own counsel. The old proverb relative to the wisdom of a still tongue is as true as 'tis good."

"Your caution is dictated by wisdom," replied the Corsican; "without secresy success is not to be looked for; but the memory of the heart—gratitude, shall forsake me only with my last breath."

The party of us now hastened out of the prison, the head gaoler respectfully accompanying us, as we surmised, to act the part of a spy. A few words were now exchanged by Monday and me with the pair on the eve of starting on their journey; after which they entered their post carriage, and away it went rattling at great speed along the streets.

"Probably you may feel somewhat dull, now that you have lost the society of your friendly fellow-prisoners," observed I, as we walked towards our hotel; "therefore the best thing you can do, is to accompany me to a dinner party, at which I am engaged, at the mansion of a fair widow, who gives a concert after her dinner."

"Willingly, willingly, sir, I shall be proud to bear you company anywhere; howsoever, I must be plain to say that, although I love a good old English tune, I have no ear for the refined music practised at many musical entertainments. Even a boatswain's pipe sounds sweeter to me than the notes of an opera singer."

"You are as bad, Monday, as a bagpiper, who delights only in the sounds extracted from his drones; but, joking apart, your taste would not be thought refined by the company I shall introduce you to."

"Depend on it, your honour, I shall not promulgate it among them. They may believe me to be as much enamoured of the music, as many who have dull ears for such harmony affect to be on these occasions, that they may fall in with the tide of fashion."

The proper time having arrived, and my secretary and I being attired in the height of the fashion, we stepped into an elegant carriage, in which, by moonlight, we crossed a bridge over the Arno, and proceeded to a superbly elegant mansion, beyond the suburbs of the capital: Here we were ushered into a magnificent apartment, the walls of which were of wainscot ornamented by richly-gilded pannels, which being reflected from numerous mirrors, that were illuminated by the wax lights, burning in costly glass chandeliers, gave the apartment, or rather suite of apartments, a truly brilliant appearance. A lady, about thirty years of age, the mistress of the mansion, received us with marked attention, and on my introducing my friend, she was profuse in her civilities to him; consequently Monday had now to undergo the ceremony of introduction to nearly a score persons of high fashion.

The most exalted personages invited to our entertainment, and these usually, to show their consequence, make their appearance the last, having arrived, the dinner was announced; at which the seat allotted me was at the upper end of the board, next to our fair hostess, while on the other side of me sat a youthful Neapolitan duchess, whose noble spouse, it appeared, was absent from his court, on a mission to a northern state. Monday's lot was to be seated between a youthful lady, the wife of a military officer, and an elderly dowager, the wealthy widow of a baron of the German empire, who had enjoyed a profitable post and sundry distinguished honours under that ancient government.

A plain man, not in the habit of frequenting the tables of the great, cannot feel otherwise than at a loss when he happens to be at a feast where almost every sort of made dish that can be named is on the board, and where ladies of fashion are seated near him, to whom he is desirous of showing himself complaisant and well-bred. " Madam, or my lady, will you permit me to serve you to a little of *this?*" sounds as a stupid invitation to the ears of a person conversant with the name of the article of food alluded to; yet how is it possible that an individual, unacquainted with the fashionable culinary art, and unaccustomed to frequent tables whereon these delicacies are displayed, can be acquainted with choice dishes, *à l'allimande, à l'espinole, timballe,* or *à salpicon;* indeed, this is not only morally impossible, but it is also extremely unlikely that he should know anything particular regarding *truffles, entremits, genevoise* sauce, fowls *à la condi,* or even that more ordinary dish, denominated *potit puits d'amour.*

My secretary, to use his own expression, was out in his reckoning on every occasion when he attempted to name any one of the made dishes at table. His question of " Will you please to take a little of this soup?" was invariably replied to by a request to be made acquainted with the name of the soup; while, with regard to the *truffles,* he was still more unfortunate; for having only imperfectly heard their name pronounced, he mistook it for the English word *trifles;* and, to the diversion of the company, persisted in calling the article of food by this name.

" Confound the trifles, and other outlandish dishes," repeatedly thought he, when vainly puzzling his brains to recollect their proper names. " One would imagine," he told me he was once on the very eve of saying, " that these messes had been brought here only to bewilder a man." However, though the sailor bestowed no benizon on the cook in return for the delicacies of his dishing up, he may be said to have made amends for his lack of courtesy by the hearty manner in which he feasted from the choice things of this scientific man's preparing: he was also assiduous in his attention to the wines; the sparkling champagne, the old burgundy, and the bright claret, being highly approved, and repeatedly partaken of, by our son of Neptune.

That wine cheers the heart, enlivens the countenance, and adds flippancy to the speech, was now verified in its effects upon Monday, who laughed heartily, joked freely, and said an abundance of pleasant things to the ladies seated near to him; but the youngest of these fair ones being a novice in high life, although proud, was timid and shy, which occasioned her to receive his attentions with hauteur and apparent indifference; therefore the sailor's self-esteem being hurt by this conduct, he after a time retaliated upon her by bestowing undivided attention upon the dowager baroness, who in return for the compliment listened to his speeches, and laughed at his double entendres with great seeming satisfaction.

An affair of gallantry is soon made up in Florence. The antiquated dowager, flattered by the attentions paid her in public by a handsome young British captain, made no kind of difficulty in overlooking his ignorance of the names of soups and dishes of eatables; but this lady's liberality is in no way surprising, when we take into consideration that widows of a certain age, and sailors of all ages from the verge of manhood upwards, are generally allowed to possess no very extraordinary delicacy in affairs of love; indeed, vulgar report allows these characters to be the easiest to content of all Cupid's votaries, and this to an extreme, where the widow's gentle bosom begins to be disturbed with doubts as to the efficacy of her charms; as also when the sailor entertains fears that spinsters and widow ladies may have grown scarce since he departed on his last cruise; in short, judging from their conduct to each other, the company, long before it broke up, considered this affair of gallantry between Monday and the baroness as having commenced under promising auspices.

The fair mistress of the mansion, who, it must be mentioned, was the widow of one of the wealthiest bankers in all Italy, was still a most lovely woman, marriage nor time having materially sullied her beauty.   The banker had wedded this rose of loveliness when it was a mere bud, and scarcely had the bud expanded itself before the envious fates, jealous of his happiness, summoned the man of business to close his account, when he left behind him one of the fairest and wealthiest widows to deplore his loss.

Selina, for this was the fair one's name, while she was habited in her widow's weeds, had been the focus of admiration, and many were the sly aspirants after this great and lovely prize ; but when the year of Her mourning had passed away, and men could presume to address the chaste widow in the seductive language of love, open hostility towards each other was declared by many of the pretenders to her affections.   Various duels were fought on her account, and on more than one occasion the weapons of war were made to weaken the stream of life ; still, however, the lady's heart was not to be won by the gallantry of any brave cavalier, and of this they became so satisfied that, in succession, her admirers resigned their hopeless pursuit after the widow.

Much to the astonishment of the fashionable world, two or three . years fleeted away after Selina had got freed from her importunate gallants, during which more staid and wealthy gentlemen offered themselves to her, and yet the blooming widow was not to be won over to marriage.   The Florentine beaus were bewildered in conjecturing what could be the cause of this extraordinary conduct ; some declared it as their opinion that she was a prude, while others pronounced her a coquette ; but the female gossips, after having formed a thousand idle con-jectures and successively abandoned them all; ultimately came to the ill-natured conclusion that she laboured under some grievous bodily infirmity, of a nature to prevent her embarking in wedlock, and some prying dames mysteriously pretended to know all the particulars of her malady.   But after the latter insidious and false report had got into general circulation, the discovery was made that her passion for music absorbed her entire thoughts, and shortly after-wards it got bruited about that she had declared to a confidant her determination was never to marry, unless she should meet with a man she could love in a first rate musician, when to him she would unconditionally yield up her liberty and her wealth.

This declaration, so flattering to gentlemen musicians, having got spread abroad, inspired a crowd of these admired characters with the sweet hope of revelling in all the ecstatic delights which happy love and abundant wealth can produce.   Moreover, all-conquering time, though with its vast power it cannot lessen a musical professor's opinion of his own skill, taught the musical gentlemen who visited her that they had no chance of triumphing over the banker's widow, and yet, disappointed as they were, excellent dinners, choice wines, and good company had the effect of making them flock to Selina's gay parties.

The handsome and accomplished musicians of Florence having failed in making their solos produce the much wished for duet of hearts, musical gentlemen on the wings of hope came flocking from surrounding states, armed with the sweet instruments requisite for captivating the female ear, if not making a conquest of the female heart, and still Selina could not be moved to the passion of love.   She not only admired, but she was absolutely captivated by the sweetly passionate airs and cantatas of many of these imitators of Apollo ; but whether it was that the performer was not sufficiently handsome, or that his music did not come home to her feelings, is not to be ascertained, yet assuredly her heart remained frozen to all their fiery professions of affection. After a time, however, one of her musical swains, a Polish noble-man, of a diminutive person and mean appearance, gained an ascendancy over the widow, but he was indebted for this advantage to his extraordinary fine tremor voice, coupled with the inimitable manner in which he sung his cantatas, and not to any softer passion lurking at Selina's heart.

This was the state of affairs at the time I became acquainted with the fair widow, but there was a something in my person or manner which, even at our first meeting, seemed to afford pleasure to the hitherto fastidious lady ; and though I was no musician, it soon became evident that her heart could no longer be deemed impregnable, but in all probability would be surrendered at discretion, should a proper summons be sent.

Soon as the company had broke up from our dinner, the concert was commenced, but in mercy to others, I shall not attempt an account of the indescribable grimaces and vocal noises that were made by the several performers ; indeed, I verily believe that the distorted faces and screaming sounds seen and uttered at a first rate concert, with Lucifer's sonata, as described by Portini, for an accompaniment, could not distress an unmusical person much more than our concert distressed my unmusical secretary.

The baroness, who sat next the maritime hero, occasionally distorted her countenance by joining in chorusses; but Monday, whose musical abilities extended no farther than to enable him to sing a sea song, never once disfigured the face bountiful nature had given him by straining his voice and mouth in attempting to warble in chorus to the screams so inordinately admired in singers of the Italian school. "Oh! how exquisitely fine is that note," the noble lady would exclaim, while apparently she was lost in rapturous delight, "it really deprives me almost of the power of breathing."

"Why, as to that, my lady, it may be very fine to those who understand it; but, in honest truth, I am unable to fathom so deep," was the sailor's not unfrequent reply, when the titled lady made remarks to him of this kind.

To procure love we must please; and the baroness, who, it might be conjectured, would have felt shocked at the unfashionable honesty of the sailor's answers to her, never once evinced the smallest symptom of disapprobation of them, which can alone be attributed to the facility with which people accommodate themselves to any customs, manners, language, or character, however uncouth, in one of the opposite sex, whose favourable opinion they feel desirous of retaining. This condescending dame, who, to encourage the sailor in his gallantry towards her, had overlooked his ignorance of the names of made dishes at their table, with like sagacity was pleased to turn a deaf ear to his unfashionable remarks on music and its professors, both vocal and instrumental.

"You will at least admire the performance of Signor Violini," remarked the baroness, tapping Monday's arm with her fan. Not a breath was now heard: even the asthma of age was smothered, that no interruption might arise to the exquisite harmony.

"What a performance," exclaimed numerous voices, soon as the sound of Violini's Cremona fiddle had died away, after having filled the company with delight. "Was ever solo so singularly beautiful? with what taste and precision it has been executed: surely it surpasseth all the music of the violin before heard of or conceived."

These and other such strong declarations, denotive of admiration of Violini's solo, resounded from the tongues of the assembled dilettanti; but though the voice of all proclaimed his unmatched excellence as a musician, envy, with her myriad of stings, was busily at work in the brains of many, with whom she made thought act as an antithesis to speech.

"Selina's heart is lost for ever; her person and possessions are at your friend the signor's disposal whenever he chooses to ask for them," said the baroness in a half whisper to Monday, on her observing the widow's eyes to be fixed on me. "A more gallant prize was never taken in tow, let whoever may carry her," answered he: "howsoever, baroness, something whispers me that the signor is not bound for the land of matrimony."

"A beautiful woman, with a princely fortune, is a prize not to be obtained every day," rejoined she; then laughingly asked, "suppose now that a large fortune and a wealthy lady should fall in your way, should you then consider the voyage of matrimony, as you facetiously term wedlock, a desirable one to embark on?"

"'Tis a voyage there is no considering, or foreseeing the end of, nor yet telling what goods may suit the market when a man gets snug into port, to lie wind-bound there; therefore, my lady, all I can say to your question is, that should such luck befal me, I would take time to reconnoitre the coast and learn the qualities of my intended consort; when provided all was right above-board, and I approved of her cargo, trim, and build, then, baroness, d'ye see, I would not hesitate to man her, fair weather and foul, through the voyage of matrimony, taking all chances, whether it might prove stormy or only breezy, a long or a short one."

The baroness now simpered and smiled like a young spinster, but extremely *mal á propos* for her, she had only sufficient time afforded her to say that Monday was master of the drollery of his profession before she met with an interruption in her *téte-á-téte* conversation by being called upon to make one in singing a duet.

The god of love is a jealous deity. I was happily seated between Selina and the fair duchess, who both of them possessed charms sufficient to captivate a bashaw's heart, and doubtless every rival of mine in the room felt jealous of my good fortune; when the diminutive nobleman mentioned for the excellence of his tremor voice, actuated by his evil genius, was moved to ungovernable fury at witnessing the fair widow's freedom of manner towards me, and under the influence of his blind passion, he approached close to this lady's ear, in a whisper to tax her with fickleness of conduct in listening to a man who was almost a stranger, when a lover well worthy of her affections was present.

Perfection is not a human attribute. The lovely duchess felt delighted at witnessing the check given to her rival in the midst of her gaiety, and was mischievous enough to smile to the company in a way strongly denotive of her feelings; but the fair widow, although at first she was embarrassed by the strange interruption to her discourse, speedily recovered her self-command, when, turning to the arrogant musician, she asked him whether she must attribute his impertinence to insanity or inebriety.

"Madam," rejoined this nobleman, in a voice even more tremulous than usual, "you ladies know not the value of a lover until you have lost him. You can cast substance away for shadow. A stranger, though he may be of no man's land, is now preferred by wilfully blind beauty to a nobleman, great by birth, rich in acquirements, blest with wealth, and tried in the sincerity of his affection."

There was a something in the Pole's speech too cutting to her feelings for Selina to pass it over in silence; but being a lady of much discretion, she bridled her passions; nevertheless, in spite of the refinement of education, which makes dissimulation sit easy on a thorough paced votary of fashion, the more than ordinary sparkling of her eyes, the convulsed motion of her lips, and the nervous agitation of her playful fingers, of which she was unconscious, plainly evinced that she was agitated by feelings of anger; and yet, in the hope of disguising them, she spoke the following speech more placidly and slowly than it was customary for her to speak.

"If, my lord, you allude to yourself when making your coarse remarks on the value of a lover, your vanity is extremely to be admired; but if in your comparison between shadow and substance you infer that you are the substance, and Signor Winpenny is the shadow, then of all mortals your vanity must be the most inordinate. Bring you, indeed, a frightful abortion, a mere apology for a man, into comparison with the signor, who stands six feet high, and is generally admired for symmetry of make and fineness of countenance! the very idea is preposterous. High blood, rich acquirements, and tried affection, attached to one like you, are laughable recommendations. You are contemptible in my eyes! I despise you, and desire to see you no more at my house."

"Madam, when your temper cools, you will regret the precipitancy of your conduct," rejoined the baron; then addressing me, he said, "you, signor, whatever may be your name, who have occasioned this lady to act so foolishly, you shall be made to repent of your temerity."

"Away, begone; go, Baron Cantata, to strain your voice elsewhere;—the ladies are tired of its squeaking noise," was all the retort that I made to the hero's threat. The little baron, spluttering with rage, too great to allow of his articulating what he wished to say, now retired from the apartment without even noticing the ladies; but, shortly after his departure, a noble friend of his approached to whisper in my ear that Baron Warsac waited in an adjoining apartment to take satisfaction for the insolence of my behaviour.

"He is welcome to wait," rejoined I, without turning my head to the nobleman I addressed. "But, signor," said he, "surely you don't intend this reply should reach the ears of my friend the baron."

"I have spoken, sir, and I have no more to say," was my answer.

The baron's friend wisely attempted no further altercation, but instantly quitted the apartment, when, quite indifferent to what had passed, I turned to the fair widow, who was intently engaged relating anecdotes of a certain songstress, who had that evening warbled some sweet ditties to delight our company.

"Good character," said the widow, for I take her discourse up from this time, "is considered a drawback upon a female's claims on the public as an actress or vocalist; yet I grant that in the other sex this rule usually is reversed. If we inquire into the characters of actresses and singing women of olden times and the present day, we shall find that the depraved have met with the greatest share of patronage: for example, one actress has been known to fill a theatre to crowding with enthusiastic admirers whenever she was known to have jilted a gallant that she might replace him by a wealthier dupe, and the more numerous became the living fruits of this woman's amours, so proportionately the voice of fashion and a corrupt press extolled her the higher for morality and the virtue of chastity, till ultimately, when she had carried depravity to its most terrific length by utterly ruining and bringing to madness a simple youth who would have married her, as if it was thereby intended to stamp the true spirit of the age, she was rewarded for her heartless infamy by marriage with a count.

"A second courtezan, called by the name of an actress, after becoming remarkable for her depravity, engages a barn for the stage to exhibit herself upon, and then all the leading theatres are forsaken, that fashion may show its discrimination by sending its votaries to this barn until it be made to overflow. Meanwhile the fascinator is ever busy with her paints and patches, and every artifice, to lure the young and the old into her snares, while such are her expensive habits, that a gaol becomes the general resort of her ill-starred dupes.

"Again, a fair siren of the stage captivates the ear of a nobleman, who, fancying himself in love, marries the vocalist; but she, being incapable of estimating the advantages attendant on high life under a monarchy, where the toiling crowd live for little else than to uphold the nobility, like Lais of Corinth, prefers a life of freedom to nuptial bondage, and therefore breaks the hymeneal tie; when, by flying to the protection of another man, she becomes a new heroine to the stage of spouters, and her voice is now deemed more harmonious than it was before her matrimonial *faux pas.*

"Of these sort of precedents, hundreds might be quoted; many where the folly of matrimony has been consummated between peers of the realm and harlots of the stage, and not a few where lords and wealthy idiots have got themselves bullied by fiddlers and buffoons, until forced to fight duels with them by way of reiteration for insults offered to their wives and mistresses, who encouraged, sought for, and courted every liberty; but it is not my object to enter into the merits of public taste, nor should I have specified the cases I have, had it not been that I sought some explanation necessary to vindicate my own conduct to my friends for having invited, or rather hired, the depraved character to sing here for their amusement, whose siren notes have given birth to the present discourse."

Selina had scarcely concluded the last sentence, before Baron Warsac, from behind my chair, where he had posted himself unobserved by me, taxed me with pusillanimous conduct in having refused compliance with his message, to which, without altering my position so as to see my adversary, I replied, by saying that the baron would act wisely in taking our fair hostess's hint before he hazarded an opinion on what might be gentlemanly conduct.

My speech proved too galling to the petulant baron, who, without allowing himself a moment for reflection, seized hold of my ear; but almost instantly after, as if actuated by a sense of his own rashness, strove, as fast as his diminutive legs could carry him, to make off from the field of his exploit.

The noble Pole had roused the lion. I started from my seat, and in a few strides came up with his lordship, when seizing him unceremoniously *à posteriori*, I hoisted him at arm's length in the air, and, highly to the diversion of the company, bore the captive triumphantly through the crowd; till having carried him into an anti-chamber, I suspended the nobleman by the waistband of his pantaloons on a large hook projecting from the wall, and then proclaimed that any person who relieved him from his position would make an enemy of me; which done, I retraced my steps to the concert room.

The terrified Pole, when left to his own reflections, strained his tremor voice in singing a cantata of a different nature to those with which he was accustomed to delight his auditors; but though he roared and screamed to obtain assistance, exclaiming that a nail was penetrating to his back bone, which would be the death of him, still no one ventured to incur my displeasure by relieving him from his perilous situation.

The banker's fair widow had not yet forgiven him for his insolence towards her, therefore she felt no compassion for the baron; but at length, when his agony was nigh causing him to faint, and every person in the house had gratified their eyes with a sight of the sufferer, I, at the lovely duchess's intercession, extricated him from his painful position, when, setting the little Pole down on the floor, I cautioned him to be more careful how in future he made use of his tongue and his hands.

Practice is better than precept. On a former occasion we have seen how contemptuously Baron Warsac treated good advice, but now that he trembled in the presence of his counsellor, he made no scruple in attending to his recommendation. Indeed, without uttering a single word in reply to me, he contented himself with feeling over his bruised back, and then, ruefully glancing his eyes around the room, shuffled away as fast as he was able.

After this little exploit, I was looked upon as the hero of the company, and every lady present became solicitous to engage me in converse ; but this attention, however highly I might prize it, evidently baulked the young duchess and the fair widow in their views, inasmuch as it prevented those ladies monopolizing my conversation to themselves ; therefore, after a time of tantalization to them, the fair duchess, rather than afford an opportunity to rival beauties to ensnare the gallant she felt desirous of insuring the attentions of to herself, called for her carriage, and by this movement of the leading personage, broke up the assembly.

CHAPTER VI.

" Doubt not my fitting answer to requite
    The unsought courtesy of such a knight."

" 'Tis a dread state for luckless wight,
    When tired and overcome in fight,
    To spy foes on his left and right,
    And close behind, with all their might,
    While breathing enmity and spite,
    Pressing on him in the dire flight ;
    They well may make him wish for night,
    And loathe the rays of solar light."

WHILE we were riding home after the concert, Monday laughingly remarked that the little Polish baron, musical as he was, had learnt some new quavers that night, when cutting capers in the air for the diversion of his mistress.

" Few men," said I, disregarding my secretary's remark, " are favoured as Captain Monday is in his amours. His reception by the ladies disproves the old saying relative to the first comer having the best chance with them. My friend, like Cæsar of yore, has only to show his face, and conquest awaits him."

" Your honour, I find, is in a jocular vein," rejoined he. " Talk of my good fortune, indeed, in coming athwart of an old hulk, a crazy catamaran, not worth taking charge of."

" You are a dainty gentleman, perhaps a little over-fastidious," observed I ; " but probably you may not yet have reflected on the circumstance that a life passed on the ocean, through a long and prosperous career, would not in old age leave you master of half the property that the widow lady in question can bestow on you by pronouncing a few words at the altar of Hymen."

" Mayhap not, your honour ; but then, what young fellow, able to steer a free course in life, would willingly get grappled to such a weather-beaten old craft? For my own part, I would rather pick oakum and eat junk in freedom than man such a crazy frigate ; 'twould be comparable to going to sea in a worn out Nore-light vessel, with barnacles three inches deep sticking on her hull."

I laughed at the oddity of the comparison, and then inquired whether he had yet made the discovery that money was the sheet-anchor, as well as the loadstone, of mankind.

" Why, as to that, sir," answered he, " I can't say but it is, and moreover, I am of opinion that I should have been for running bump alongside the ricketty old girl and trying to grapple with her in the voyage of matrimonial life, had it not been for the cantata she sung ; but, Lord bless us, what sailor, tight in wind and limb, would lash himself to an old siren who makes ugly faces, and blows away like any porpoise, while she is squalling bravuras and other such balderdash sounds? No, no ; let me only steer clear of ancient singing women and the frightful faces they make, and I don't care a pinch of oakum with what widow or lass I may come to close quarters ; whether she may be black, tawny, or white ; for I'se warrant we should make headway together, braving the rough storms of life ; in short, any woman but a songstress might do for James Monday.'

I laughed at the tar's description of an elderly lady's appearance when she is engaged entertaining the world by her talents as a vocalist, yet reflection brought to mind the distorted countenances of even the loveliest females when they are in the act of singing, and I consequently felt there had been some truth conveyed by my friend's observations.

"It doesn't signify preaching more on the subject," resumed he, after a pause, "but if old dowagers must sing, why, your honour may depend on it, they should do so behind a screen, as then people might listen to the song without seeing the distorted countenance of the songstress; indeed I think I may stretch further on this tack, and say that, young or old, neither man nor woman's face should be seen in the act of singing, or playing upon a wind instrument; for d'ye see, sir, they make baboon faces and always spoil the cut of their jib, while they are blowing or screaming to bring forth musical sounds."

"The eccentricity of your opinion," said I, "will ensure my recollection of it at all times when I witness the performance of vocalists, or players upon wind instruments."

"Your honour may take your spy-glass and quiz them, but never need fear putting them out of countenance, as depend on it, they can't look uglier than they do when blowing their wind instruments or singing; besides, folks of this character carry an abundant cargo of assurance, else they could never muster resolution to stand up making monkey-like faces before crowds of people."

The carriage had now arrived at the door of our hotel, therefore Monday's illiberal remarks were put an end to, and we entered the house to retire to our pillows.

"Your honour was merry with me on our way home last night," remarked the sailor at our breakfast. "A rich old baroness giving a small matter of encouragement to a youthful sailor, seems to have inspired you with feelings of surprise."

"Not at all, Monday; the thing's quite natural; I am by no means astonished at the lady's conduct; but when January weds May, interest must be paid for the disparity of age."

"'Tis all well what your honour says, and provided the wind always blew soft and fair, mayhap it might be better for a mariner to become the husband of a crazy old craft, with a rich cargo on board, than for him to undertake providing for a spanking new vessel, carrying more sail than ballast; but then d'ye see, sir, the ancient vessel would strain at every puff of wind, and so become leaky, and be a constant trouble to her owner; besides, she might require more manning than her freightage would pay for; therefore, all points fairly overhauled, if I am to sail with a consort of my own choosing, she shall be well built, fair to look at, and not strained in her timbers."

"Such, for example, as the fair Sophia Bramble," observed I, with a smile.

"A seaman might sail far and wide round the globe, and cast anchor in many a port, before he came athwart of a more compact little frigate than the one your honour alludes to. With that lovely lass a man might think himself lucky to swing in the same hammock until Father Time cut the suspending cords, and they foundered together."

"Bravo!" exclaimed I; "you are in the heroics, my friend. However, to the bold seaman no vessel is too rich to be boarded, and when boarded, surely she may be carried: favouring opportunity is all the gallant heart requires, and the prize must be carried. But, Monday, should this be the tack you want to sail on, we must watch for a favouring breeze."

Here the conversation was interrupted by the entrance of a military officer, who with due formality notified that he was the bearer of a letter from Baron Warsac, calling upon me to make a full apology for my unwarrantable conduct on the preceding evening, or in default of doing this, to meet him at the next dawn of day, armed with a sword and pistols, and attended by a friend, to render the satisfaction due an aggrieved nobleman.

"He who prizes life ought not to be the first to violate peace," replied I, "it is the baron who should apologise to me: but long stories impede business. I have no more to say than that I shall not fail meeting the baron at the place and in the way he has requested; so, sir, our business being over, I wish you a good day."

The martial gentleman apparently was disappointed at my declaration, for he made an attempt to prolong the conversation respecting the quarrel; but I stopped him in his remarks by repeating that I had no more to say on the subject, and once more bid him a good day; upon which the officer made his bow and departed.

Punctual to my appointment, I was on the ground betimes in the morning to render satisfaction to the Polish baron, while Monday, who on the preceding night had furbished up my sword and pistols, accompanied me in the capacity of second.

" 'Tis a hazy morning," said the sailor, after we had been kept waiting, cooling our heels in the wet grass for upwards of a quarter of an hour ; "so, mayhap a signal may be wanting, to enable the enemy to make out our station ; therefore, your honour, here goes ; I'll fire off a pistol, which I'll warrant will bring him abreast of us, if so be he is within hearing of the shot."

" Stop," cried I, catching hold of the cocked pistol, for there was no time for reasoning, as Monday with Hibernian promptitude was suiting his action to his words, " you forget what you are about : do you wish to alarm the country and collect the police around us, to prevent the duel taking place, and thus bring a reflection upon the character of your principal in this affair ?"

" Odd's blood !" exclaimed the sailor, " I never thought of the matter in this light : how-soever, be he who he may, I should desire no better sport than to come athwart the man that dared in my presence cast a reflection on your honour : still, on second thoughts, it matters little what I could do ; an enemy might as well expect to harm a church steeple by firing swan shot at it as to injure your character for courage by anything he could hatch or invent to its disadvantage."

Presently after this discourse the little baron and his second made their appearance, when Monday, stepping forward to the latter, inquired which of them it was should measure the ground, and whether the distance should be six or eight paces ; on which the martial gentle-man very judiciously turned himself about to consult his principal, when their conference led to a proposition that the duel should be fought at twelve or fourteen paces, as might be decided by a toss-up.

" 'Tis a lubberly distance this," said the sailor, when he was employed measuring off fourteen paces after the toss had taken place ; " however, it matters little : I'll bet two to one with any man that at twenty paces my principal hits the bull's eye of a fair-sized target two shots out of every three that he fires at it."

" *Le diable* ! 'tis murder to fight with such a man," muttered the baron, looking altogether aghast at this piece of information.

" All's ready," now exclaimed the sailor, " the gentlemen may as well take up their ground at once ; while, d'ye see, brother," added he, speaking to the other second, " if so be that your pistols are not so good as ours, that all may be right and square, for I know Signor Win-penny wouldn't desire to take an advantage of his enemy, you shall have one of our barking-irons, and I'll warrant 'em as pretty a pair as ever did the work of execution ashore or aboard ship."

The military second declined profiting by the sailor's offer, saying he and the baron were quite satisfied with the pistols they had brought with them ; and now the nobleman, to whom Monday's recommendation of his pistols seemed to afford no kind of satisfaction, seeing that his antagonist had taken up his position for the combat, slowly advanced to perform the like ceremony, and duly received a loaded pistol from his second.

On seeing the principal performers had taken up their ground, Monday inquired whether he was to give the preconcerted signal for firing, but Baron Warsac, whose fury, or else his fears, made him tremble violently, called aloud to the sailor not to be in such a tre-mendous hurry, for that there was plenty of time before them for the signor and he to kill each other, should they be so bloody-minded ; to which Monday, shrugging up his shoulders, replied, " Why, as to that, baron, a man can be killed but once ; and for my own part, I think, when two gentlemen are met together to settle a quarrel, the sooner one of them dispatches the other's soul aloft, the better it is for them both."

Monday's observation was intended to try the baron's mettle, and assuredly it did not accord with that nobleman's sentiments, for so far was he from declaring his approbation, that he thus addressed the officious sailor, but in a voice nearly inarticulate.

" The dispute, sir, between Signor Winpenny and me, needs not your interference, and I desire to hear no opinion of yours regarding it."

" Your lordship wants to sheer off with a sound hull, that's all," retorted Monday.

"Fellow," stuttered the baron, "is it befitting such as you to dare make vulgar remarks on a nobleman?"

"Gentlemen," now said I, addressing the seconds, "why do you permit this unnecessary procrastination of business? I call upon you to bring our affair to a conclusion."

"Soon as I have counted ten, I shall let drop my handkerchief as the signal for you both to fire," said Monday, placing himself in a position suitable for the purpose."

"Take up your ground, gentleman, and look out sharply for the promised signal," said the other second.

The Polish nobleman, who manifested great uneasiness, so far from complying with the instructions just given, now retrograded some three or four paces in an oblique direction, and placing himself in a line with his second, called out to me that the quarrel was between us only, and for his part, sooner than blood should be shed, he would waive his intention of receiving satisfaction, and be content to shake hands with me and make up the business."

"He who prizes life ought not to be forward in challenging others," replied I; "nevertheless, make me an apology, baron, and your temerity shall be looked over; you may then depart quietly in a whole skin."

"It is enough," replied he, making a merit of necessity and courteously walking up to me. "I regret all that has passed, and hereby own my error, and make the fullest apology for the assault I committed."

"Enough, baron, I am content," rejoined I.

We duellists now shook hands with each other, after which the whole party walked over several fields to the high road, where the horses and servants were detained waiting; but it so happened that while we were engaged talking on the way, the baron, who, so far from being a prudent man who says less than he thinks, unfortunately was a passionate man who says more than thought or prudence would dictate, somehow grossly insulted Monday on account of his conduct on the field of warfare; and that hero, who made no sort of allowance for the aristocratic superiority of his companion, in consequence called upon him, noble as he was, to retrace his steps to the ground he had quitted, that he might afford the tar personal satisfaction for the insult just given. The baron replied to the challenge by telling the sailor he was totally unworthy of his notice, and therefore, he said, he had no alternative, but must positively refuse accepting his challenge; on which Monday observed that he'd warrant to bring him to before he stretched far on that tack, and then commenced whistling an old sea-song.

The noble Pole paid little attention to my secretary's remark, but our horses being in readiness, the baron and I were on the eve of riding back together to Florence, and had already mounted our steeds for the purpose, when Monday, suddenly and unceremoniously clapping a pistol to the nobleman's head, desired his lordship to bring to, as he must overhaul his bill of lading. The Polish nobleman's second seemed inclined to interfere, but I made the observation that my friend had been insulted and refused honourable satisfaction, and therefore he was entitled to take it in the way he thought fit. This declaration caused the gentleman to change his tone, and when I proposed we should ride home together, he contented himself by saying, that on reflection he must avow that Baron Warsac had no claims to his support on an occasion such as the present, and having said so he mounted his horse and rode off in my company.

Insolent boldness and base fear are inseparable companions. Monday still pointing a pistol at the baron's head, so terrified him, that he compelled him to dismount, when he commanded the disconcerted nobleman to strip off his coat and waistcoat, but he showing reluctance to obey the order, the sailor administered a few strokes of his horsewhip with no little effect on his person, upon which his lordship, after cutting a few graceless capers and calling in vain on the groom who was holding their horses to assist him, made a merit of necessity by disrobing his august person of the before-named articles of raiment.

"There's no knowing what a man may come to in the voyage of life, for, d'ye see, I must turn valet de chambre without having served an apprenticeship to the business," said the sailor, snatching the nobleman's coat and waistcoat from his hand, and turning them inside out; which being done, he restored them to the owner, telling him to re-rig himself and be ready to make sail, unless he wanted to have his back seasoned to the whip, to make him more handy.

The baron, disgusted with his own coat, would fain have evaded wearing it in its present state, but the sailor's horsewhip and threatening attitude inspired him with so great a degree of terror that his disgust gave way to his fears, and he clothed himself in the now unsightly garment, the courteous sailor telling him he was not the only turn-coat in the world, and bidding him mount his charger and make the best of his way home, unless, as he jocularly said, he had occasion to go visiting first.

While the noble Pole was engaged in the performance of the ceremonies of his toilette, my companion and I had made some progress on our way home; but shortly after Monday's compelling the discomfited hero to remount, our ears were astounded by the noise of horses on the gallop, and loud shouts made by the sailor; till presently the baron passed by us at full speed, with Monday and a groom galloping in his rear, though without any prospect of their overtaking the nobleman, whose high-mettled horse, it was now evident, had run away with him.

" 'Tis a noble craft that, she cuts along like the wind," shouted the sailor while he was passing along the road near to me; but so great was the velocity with which he journeyed, that no time was afforded me for hearing more of his remarks.

"Johnny Gilpin himself rode not more furiously," thought I, on seeing the baron's hat blowing far behind him along the highway.

" Sacre dieu, haste, pick up your master's hat," called the military gentleman to the baron's groom.

"Old Mazeppa, the baron's countryman, somewhat like your friend here, was taught to ride by an uncourteous master," said I, smiling, and then putting spurs to my horse, added, " good sportsmen ought to be in at the death;" when away we went, galloping along the road, until having arrived at a suburb of the town without seeing anything of our advanced guard, we pulled up our horses and entered at a foot pace.

After we had rode along several streets the military gentleman quitted me, and shortly after I had reached home, Monday entered, in a very dirty condition, when laughing, he told me he had frightened every bar of music out of the whipper-snapper baron; " and," added he, " we had as merry a ride into Florence, as your honour or any one else could desire to see. The road near to the city was covered with people who hurrah'd us to the top pitch of their voices, which well they might, for the race was a prime one, the baron not being many lengths a head of me; but then, your honour, d'ye see, I should never have gained ground on him as I did after being so far astern, had it not been that his horse by shying had unshipped the little fellow from the saddle and thrown him forward on his charger's neck, around which he clung like a monkey, and thereby afforded diversion to every one that beheld him, rigged out as he was in turned clothes, with his head uncased and his hair standing upright.

" After we had galloped through five or six streets, the baron's ill star so ordained that we came upon a crowd assembled about a dancing bear, and there being no way of stopping his horse before the people could get themselves out of the way, the urchin noble rode bolt against them, when his steed fell to the ground, and he himself was precipitated over the heads of many persons and fell upon the bear, whose dancing he spoilt, for he knocked Bruin completely over.

" The general confusion was now great, yet every one tried to get at a wide offing from the bear, who roared at a tremendous rate: but luckily he was muzzled or it would have been all over with the baron, for Bruin no sooner had recovered his footing than he seized his assailant in his rude paws and prepared to press him to his breast in a warmer embrace than lover ever contemplated receiving.

" It would now have been soon over with the noble Polish baron, as his tremor voice had already got stilled, but fortunately the pole of his keeper, by being administered with powerful effect on the beast's carcass, compelled Bruin to relinquish his hold of the little great man, when some kind-hearted folks of the crowd having dragged him legs foremost to fair anchorage ground, I stepped forward to finish the job by putting the baron into an hackney carriage and taking him to his home, where I left him in as pretty a pickle as any lord need to be."

" Really, Monday, you are a pretty fellow to treat nobility in this manner," remarked I, and here the conversation terminated.

CHAPTER VII.

"Her tongue run round like a wheel, one
Spoke after another, there was no end of it."

"A tigress robb'd of young, a lioness,
Or any interesting beast of prey,
Are similes at hand for the distress
Of ladies who cannot have their own way."

I HAD not long returned from the duel before a letter was brought me express from the Duchess of Malvedo, in which she stated an earnest desire to see me immediately at her mansion on particular business, and I hastened away to meet the fair challenger, whom, on my being introduced into her drawing room, I found seated on a sofa, habited in a most costly dress.

"Oh, Monsieur Winpenny," she anxiously exclaimed, "the scandalous world have been busy traducing my character, and I have been impatient to see you that I may benefit by your advice: come, take a seat on the sofa, while I lay before you proofs of the world's wickedness and my own imminent danger."

I seated myself as directed, when the duchess handed me several anonymous letters. "See," said she, in an impetuous, agitated manner, "see, my dear Winpenny, the perilous situation in which I am placed; and tell me, O tell me, how to satisfy the world of my innocence."

I perused the letters, three in number, which were worded differently, but they all breathed the same sentiments. In each the duchess was charged with too great an intimacy with me, and threatened with having her conduct exposed by letter to her absent partner. "Madam," said I, soon as I had examined the letters, "fear not the effects of vindictive threats; your innocence will triumph over your calumniators; you have nothing to apprehend from their malice; the shield of virtue is invulnerable to base weapons."

"Oh, dear signor, you see not the extent of my danger: accused, and from various quarters, of an improper intimacy with a foreigner—pardon me for saying it in your presence, —the handsomest man in all Florence; what is to become of me? I shall be repudiated, abandoned, and ruined."

"Pardon me, your grace, but really you allow your fears to get the better of your judgment. I pray you quiet your groundless apprehensions and re-examine these letters, which you will find have all been written by the same hand. Yes, I see through it; 'tis a scheme of some worthless person to extort money from you."

"Truly," rejoined her grace, after an affected scrutiny of the letters, "truly there appears to be grounds for your observation; but, my dear signor, character once blown upon will never again be thought pure: it is comparable to a full blown flower, which cannot shrink back into bud."

"Your character, fair lady," said I, "will not suffer from the arrows of defamation; but prudence, the irresistible buckler of virtue, must remain your shield in the duke's absence. Cæsar's wife must leave no opening for suspicion."

"Telemachus had not such an adviser as thou art. The Fates have only to spare your life to old age, that you may serve as a Mentor to teach prudence and the sister virtues to young females," laughingly said the duchess.

"May I ask you, fair lady, do you recommend me to wait until grey hairs have disfigured my head, and deep wrinkles furrowed my brow, ere I attempt speaking words of prudence to the loveliest part of the creation, when such vouchsafe to appeal to me for counsel?"

"Yes, my dear signor, such shall be my recommendation; there are times and seasons for all things; and believe me prudential advice breathed from lips such as yours can only lead to an effect the reverse of that contemplated by you: it would make giddy the previously sage dame."

"If I thought that honest advice would have such an effect on your grace, it would be my duty to fly your presence," said I, rather gravely.

How this scene would have terminated had we remained *téte-à-téte* much longer, I pretend not to determine; but at this critical epoch our mutual friend, the banker's widow, was announced, and on entering the apartment she started, apparently with surprise, at finding me closeted with her grace; when I, seeing the ladies were far from being at their ease together, soon made my bow and retired.

In due time to participate in the pleasures of the table, Monday and I made our appearance together at the fair widow's mansion. No other company than the antiquated baroness had been invited to meet us; as the cause of which, the fair hostess declared that the crowd of the preceding day had fatigued and harassed her spirits ; therefore, she said, she now sought, by the sweets of conversation with two or three rational friends, to solace and restore them to their accustomed vigour. The baroness professed herself to be much of the same way of thinking, observing that when she was engaged in converse with a sensible, entertaining companion, time never appeared too long with her; but that among a crowd of people, she invariably found the very reverse was the case. However, the sailor, to whom these remarks of the noble lady were chiefly addressed, either did not sufficiently feel their force, or else he himself must have been of a different way of thinking to what she expressed herself, which was made evident by his lukewarm manner of assenting to the baroness's observations.

A small select party possibly may not be so merry a meeting as is a larger assemblage of company, but then their real enjoyment is greatest. The sailor, for example, was quite at home on the present occasion, as he felt no vexation arise from his ignorance of the names of made dishes, but laughed heartily and joked freely with the ladies whenever his attention was diverted from the excellent cheer before him. The ladies also made themselves extremely agreeable, their behaviour being divested of that ceremonious etiquette so generally resorted to in polished society, but which, indubitably, is of a tendency to mar social intercourse.

When we adjourned from the dining to the drawing-room, the sailor's lot was to be seated on a settee next to the baroness, and being exhilarated from the effects of wine, and spared the mortification of seeing his gentle companion distort her countenance by the grimaces attendant on Italian singing, he began to form a more favourable opinion of the lady than what he had heretofore entertained. For my part, seated as I was on another settee, with the banker's lovely widow as my companion, I had either to answer, or waive replying to, numerous artful interrogatories put by this fair one. She was extremely inquisitive regarding the duchess; but although she threw out numerous hints, and freely declared her suspicions relative to that noble lady's entertaining a partiality for me, yet from my lips she could extract no information, but merely heard a repetition of that which I had previously said; when, however, the cunning widow positively found she could glean nothing of a satisfactory nature, to help gratify her ardent curiosity, she gradually changed the subject of conversation, until she brought it upon the subject nearest her heart.

"After all has been said, my dear signor," now observed the fair widow, heaving a low sigh, and looking most tenderly, "there is nothing in this life comparable to happy marriage. What, for example, is wealth to a single woman more than an endless source of care? It exposes her to all the insidious arts of the fortune-hunting adventurer, to the chicanery of the law, and to gross impositions of every denomination; in short, such are the snares laid for them, that the wealthy spinster and the well-endowed widow need possess the eyes of an Argus to watch over and provide for their own safety."

" Generally speaking, my fair friend," answered I, "your observations convey no small portion of truth ; nevertheless, madam, there are to be found many single ladies who can manage their worldly affairs quite as prudently as the sagest of men, while of these, permit me to add that the Phœnix is now before me."

" And so even the sage Signor Winpenny can stoop to be a flatterer," said the widow, smilingly ; "would, however," added she in a whisper, "that he would take the burden from weak shoulders, and place it on those of the strong. Would that he would ease me of my load, and thus make me the happiest of women.

" If, my dear madam," said I, after bowing thanks for her compliment, " if your riches are a burden to you, there are many ways of benefiting the community by their distribution—for example, contributing money to charitable asylums for orphans, the blind, the deaf, the dumb, the poor, and the helpless."

"Would Signor Winpenny have me resign my money up to the mercy of rapacious governors, treasurers, trustees, and stewards of these charities—to men who, in many instances, themselves contribute nothing towards their support, but who, most of them, flourish in their private affairs, after they obtain office under these institutions?"

"I admire your sagacity, madam: the greatest rogues are usually sanctified fellows, who chatter about divine aid and divine providence while they are committing their infamous robberies, and such it often is who worm or preach themselves into the management of charitable funds; honest men seek not the office; they would feel compunctions of conscience arise to disturb their digestion, when enriching themselves by salaries and perquisites extracted from the funds gathered for the orphan, the decrepid, and the blind; nor could men whose hearts had a spark of honesty or charity unquenched in them for an instant tolerate the tricks resorted to for wasting money intrusted to their stewardship in unnecessary buildings and repairs, from which they themselves reap a share, nor allow tradesmen to give short weight and measure, and act nefariously in their charges, that they may pay these unworthy servants a per centage as hush money to wink at and pass over their villany."

"Experience, my dear signor, of which, young as you are, you have attained a princely share, has taught me that charity should be her own almoner, as who can be trusted when religion itself is made to cloak over robbery, and when public meetings are got up for fraudulent ends?"

"Yes, my dear madam," observed I, "you are quite correct in your observations; and, believe me, the most pious in profession are generally the most profligate in practice. Could you imagine that there are bishops in the world who, while they pretend to follow in the steps of the fisherman apostle, compel people to pay fees for the burial of the dead to the covetous priest of the parish wherein they died, although they have to be buried elsewhere, and fee the rival parson? But these time-serving bishops are so extremely mercenary that they will not even consecrate a place of worship unless for a fee of about six thousand ducats; however, for my part, I value the Indian mode of consecration with cow-dung at as high a rate as that of these priestly worshippers of mammon."

"Where you attained it I know not," said the smiling widow; "but I well know you have a strange opinion of the goodness of a certain priesthood. However, as to charitable institutions, does not Rochefaucault say, they would not be carried so far unless pride kept company with charity? But, my friend," added she, "are we not wandering from our subject, and, like the duchess of your acquaintance, becoming somewhat inconsistent?"

"It is the abuse of charity—a subject which would warm an anchorite—has led our tongues into this labyrinth; but, dear madam, unless my memory is unusually treacherous, we were discoursing upon the best mode of easing you of a part of your golden burden."

"Yes, dear signor, you are right, that was the subject of our conversation; still you misunderstand me; I feel no sort of desire to cast away my wealth, burdensome as it is; all I covet is an affectionate companion, one who, through life, would direct a feeble woman how best to conduct herself, and take on himself the management of her possessions."

"Your desire, madam, is no longer to be misunderstood. You feel inclined to enter into the tie of wedlock; and, inasmuch as the suitors for your hand are numerous, you have ample scope afforded you for pleasing yourself in the selection of a husband."

"There is only one man on earth I could be happy with, and that individual is wilfully blind to my favourable opinion of him," said the fair widow, fixing her eyes intently on me.

"Are you quite sure you are correct in the opinion you have formed of this person?" asked I.

"If you doubt the accuracy of my judgment, you shall decide the question yourself," said the widow, blushing, and, after a little hesitation, adding, "to use scriptural language, as Nathan said unto David, 'Thou art the man.'"

The whole of the conversation just related had been carried on in a low tone of voice, and hitherto free from interruption, a circumstance to be accounted for by the baroness and Monday having been equally intent on their *tête-à-tête* conversation; but just as I was about to reply to the fair widow's puzzling observation, the sailor appealed to me respecting the corectness of some information he had been stating to the baroness, and by doing so afforded me an opportunity for evading making a reply to Selina's question.

The fair widow evidently felt nettled at the ill-timed interruption to her discourse, and no doubt wished the sailor had been elsewhere on his travels, but pride and delicacy forbade of her resuming the subject of the discourse again that night, and I cautiously forbore touching on the tender theme.

For the reasons now specified, our party passed over without any *éclaircissement* taking place; but the lovely widow was so much disconcerted at what had passed, that when I took leave of her for the night, formality and constrain' were very discernible in her manner towards me.

On our way home, the sailor hazarded a few jokes regarding, as he termed the baroness, the crazy old craft he had kept company with that evening; but finding me thoughtful and inattentive to his observations, he became silent; while, for my part, I uttered not a syllable concerning either of the fair ladies whom we had just quitted.

Philosophers cannot deny that there is much seeming inconsistency even in wisdom. For example, the wisest man attends much more readily to the commands of a lovely young woman than to those of a more mature-aged lady, even though the eldest fair one should possess the largest share of wisdom; but perhaps some allowance ought to be made for this apparent inconsistency to the masculine strength of wisdom, which emboldens it to expose itself unnecessarily, purposely that it may shine the more triumphant, and owe its victory solely to its own powers.

I had no sooner breakfasted, the morning after our dinner party, than, in consequence of a *billet-doux* from the duchess, I posted away to her, when I was received by her grace far more affectionately than fastidious dames, who judge of everything from outward appearance, would deem becoming in any lady, save a wedded one, to receive her husband. The less ceremony the more welcome is a hackneyed observation in life, and I had not been long seated on her sofa before the duchess busied herself in the task of bringing anew to my ear the old proofs of her danger and the world's wickedness; but the demon of mischief hovered near, and she had not proceeded far in her story ere, without any announcement of her arrival, Selina suddenly entered the apartment, and on beholding the duchess and me seated together on the same sofa, upraised both her hands, exclaiming, " Good heavens ! what is this I see? Here is a *liaison* which shall no longer be kept a secret."

There is a point of offence at which even modesty grows bold, and, casting aside her imperial robes, steps forward to defy the defier. Highly irritated as she was at this second rude interruption by the widow, none acquainted with human nature can deem it surprising to learn that the lovely duchess's courage had now reached that climax. Rising majestically from the sofa, " Madame," said she, " your intrusions upon me are altogether unpardonable, and must be the result of design."

By her countenance I saw that a storm was now brooding in Selina's bosom, and, wishing to avert it in its progress, I hastily said, " Fair ladies, let mine be the pleasing task to mediate between you. Perfection is not a human attribute; we have all our weaknesses, but it behoves us not to expose the trivial follies of each other. Let charity be the companion of loveliness —division, my charming friends, destroys power—you have hitherto been dear to each other, pr'ythee continue so, and live happily."

" The advice of a philosopher, although he may be of the school of Epicurus, shall not be thrown away upon me," said the satiric widow.

" Madam, I have spoken hastily, and freely do I confess my error," said the now politic duchess; then adding, " Selina, let us both drink from the cup of Lethe, and remain faithful friends."

" My visit of this morning was intended merely as a call *en passant*, to inquire concerning the health of my dear duchess, and this being accomplished, I shall take my departure; however, I must avow that my unexpected meeting with Signor Winpenny here is a lucky event, as I have something of moment to communicate to him, and therefore I must beg of him to accompany me home in my carriage;" then smiling significantly at the duchess, she added, " for opportunity, as your grace knows, is everything with us women."

To play the cards of high life with a fair prospect of success, perhaps deeper cunning and finesse is requisite than what persons in subordinate stations have occasion to resort to in their ordinary transactions; and thereby hoping to soothe the widow's mind, so that she might be deterred from injuring the lovely duchess in the estimation of others, I readily consented to become her equestrian companion; while her grace, though inwardly burning with vexation and vindictive feelings towards the widow, on bidding her guests good morning, said she wished us a delightful ride, and hoped her dear friend Selina would profit by opportunity, since experience had made her so well acquainted with its use.

Selina's carriage had scarcely borne us from the door of the ducal hotel, before the jealous widow reproached me with the crime of entertaining a partiality for a married woman, and upon my requesting her to recal the ungenerous accusation, she not only refused, but strenuously insisted on the justness of her charge, and in support of her assertion provokingly adduced the circumstance of my having paid my first visit of that morning to her rival the duchess.

An angry woman can give free licence to her tongue, and Selina now indulged herself in invidious remarks upon the duchess's character and failings, and likewise on the *penchant* of bachelors for married women; but when these ebullitions of jealous feelings subsided, she with no little tact returned to the subject nearest her heart, and artfully, though by gradual stages, brought the discourse back to the point at which it had met with interruption from the sailor.

"The affectation of ignorance serves admirably well for eliciting treasured secrets from another," observed the widow; then after a sigh or two, added, "and as designing characters usually are both reserved and inquisitive, I presume it is to possessing these qualities that philosophers stand indebted for a portion of their fame; but, to illustrate what I am saying, I must call to your mind the ambiguity of your replies to my candid communications at our last dinner, and remind you that my last question, the same as the memorable one of the prophet to King David, remains unanswered. Now, my dear signor, pr'ythee at once ease my mind; tell me explicitly, and without circumlocution, are you willing to relieve me of the burden of wealth and the cares of celibacy, by taking me for better or worse as your partner in journeying through this vale of happiness, if it be traversed in your company; but otherwise to me—what many of the world pronounce it to be—a vale of misery."

"An honest question demands a candid reply, and the offer you make me of riches and felicity merits my warmest gratitude; circumstances, however, not now to be explained, render it improper that I should benefit by your partiality for one so undeserving of it; therefore, my dear madam, in denying myself the happiness you would bestow, I can only add that I am to be pitied, as being a victim to the stern necessity which imposes so painful a duty on me."

"I see how it is," said the widow, bridling up with rage and disappointment; "I am rejected for the worthless duchess, with whom you have already formed a *liaison*. You, however, ere long, will find cause for repenting of this false step: a crim. con. trial will fix the serpent upon you, and then her love will turn into wormwood, when her deadly sting will either drive you to distraction, or bring you to a premature grave."

"My dear madam, I have formed no *liaison* with your innocent friend, the duchess; you wrong us both by entertaining so uncharitable a supposition."

"If the evidence of the eyes was not conclusive, that of the tongue to corroborate it must be so," rejoined the widow. "Have I not myself seen and heard amply sufficient to justify the duke in bringing his action against you? While now, as if to persist in your folly, you positively reject the proffered hand of the wealthiest woman of this capital."

"Madam, tautology is not to my taste; still must I repeat that I entertain no improper views on the Duchess of Malvedo, and I am again called on to assert that my declining to re-enter the hymeneal state has no relation whatever to my honourable acquaintance with her grace."

"Come, come, signor," said the fair widow, assuming her most bewitching smile, "for once forget the stoic, and condescend to be a plain man. Apollo was less haughty than thou art, and Jupiter would have despised such wisdom as thine. The gods and goddesses, save only the sanguinary Minerva, delighted in the enjoyments afforded by love. Pray, then, my dear signor, be truly wise; let us copy from the immortal powers, and, revelling in the felicity of wedlock, pass happily on through life, until, profiting by the advice of Catullus to his mistress, we continue enraptured with each other, even when age has silvered our locks, and Time whetted his scythe to cut our thread of life."

"I see, madam, you indulge yourself in a poetic vein this morning," replied I; "you are warm as was Sappho, but I trust will meet with a far happier fate than did that famed poetess."

"My fate, like that of Sappho, is meeting with an ungrateful, cold-hearted swain," retorted the now angry widow; "yet I know better than to destroy myself on his account. The wounded scorpion stingeth itself to death, but my sting shall be reserved to sting the first stinger."

"The sting inflicted by a lovely woman is felt further and more severely than what she can be aware of," remarked I, with a smile.

"And that of an unfeeling, worthless man, deeper than it ought to be," was the angry retort.

The carriage had now arrived at the gateway of Selina's mansion, but on our descending from it, I declined the lady's invitation to enter her house, as likewise one that she gave me to dine with her; on which her indignant anger so completely mastered her prudence, that she gave a free licence to her tongue, and in her declamation, among many other things, asserted even within the hearing of her footman, that my love for the Duchess of Malvedo must be of a furious nature, since I was in such a prodigious hurry to hasten back to that treacherous woman; but she vehemently added, she would acquaint the duke with his wife's wanton conduct, and thus be revenged on me, while she brought condign punishment on the duchess for her shameless and infamous depravity.

To reason with an incensed woman would betray simplicity bordering upon madness, and of this truth I was fully sensible; so I contented myself by bowing to the widow, whose features were not a little distorted by the furious passion which agitated her frame; and before she could still her raging tongue, or recover any degree of composure, I faced about, and *sans cérémonie* walked away at a brisk pace, glad to get out of hearing of her unceasing clack.

CHAPTER VIII.

" Unnumber'd maladies his joints invade,
Lay siege to life, and press the dire blockade;
But unextinguish'd av'rice still remains,
And dreaded losses aggravate his pains;
He turns with anxious heart and crippled hands
His bonds of debt and mortgages of lands;
Or views his coffers with suspicious eyes,
Unlocks his gold, and counts it till he dies."

" Short was the conflict; furious, blindly rash,
Th'assailant gave his bosom to the gash:
He bled, and fell."

The most faithful narrator of facts has occasionally to make digressions from his story, and as it relates to a character that has shown conspicuous in these pages, and will long be remembered in Florence, where his misfortune was the general theme of conversation, I must now mention the lamentable catastrophe which befel Counsellor Gotschalk. This hard-hearted miser, who no otherwise regretted the death of his amiable wife than because it deprived him of the friendly services of Prince Swarthyburg, now that he had lost the partner of his bosom, and was become a martyr to the gout, gave up his time and thoughts to usurious projects and telling over his money.

The counsellor's house, as every person in Florence well knows, stood at the corner of a central street, near to the choicest market, and although an old-fashioned mansion, was good and substantial. It was erected a little way further back from the footpath than the neighbouring houses, but what it lost to the street one way was made up for in room by a large wooden first-floor bow window, which projected most ungracefully some distance over the public footpath.

Mischief enters through the gates of security. One day when the miser was engaged at his beloved occupation of counting over his money in the room of which the aforesaid bow-window constituted a part, and which was his *sanctum sanctorum*, containing all that he prized in life, an ammunition waggon broke down in the street fronting his house, and was so seriously damaged, that it became necessary to procure another vehicle; but while this was being got, the ammunition was exposed to rain falling in a heavy shower.

The non-commissioned officer in charge of the party very prudently caused the gunpowder, viz., eight barrels, to be taken out of the broken waggon and placed under the projection of the counsellor's window, to preserve the ammunition dry until his soldiers came with a fresh waggon; but here human vanity might take a profitable lesson, for one was afforded of the uncertainty of life and the instability of worldly possessions, most forcibly showing that man gathers riches together without knowing who shall enjoy them, and in the height of his prosperity is cut off by death with the swiftness of lightning.

The miser, whose attention had been drawn to the accident, heeded not whether the ammunition was wet or dry, but having taken a cursory view of the scene of confusion from his window, returned to his beloved occupation of counting money, without concerning himself to prevent the serjeant having the powder stowed away under his window; but there seems to be a malevolent spirit to blind man to the danger which is to overwhelm and bring him to ruin, and which even causes him to run headlong to the perilous spot he ought to shun. However, this may be wisely ordained, inasmuch as uncertainty strips death of the terrors springing from anticipation of its visit, and enables the surly conqueror of mortality to subdue, without appalling us. Julius Cæsar, perhaps, never uttered a wiser opinion than the one whereby he pronounced the most sudden and the least foreseen death to be the best.

It is impracticable to show whether Monsieur Gotschalk was of Cæsar's way of thinking, but as he was as much a Christian as a miser can well be, most likely he was of the opposite opinion, namely, that pronounced in church prayers against battle, murder, and sudden death. But Cæsar and the stoics advocate sudden death, while the saints of all times and the apostles of yore, backed by the timid of every age, give the preference to a death which is preceded by long lingering misery. Adieu, then, to metaphysical reasoning, which leaves man in the same maze of obscurity in which it finds him.

It remains to be told—yet exactly how the disaster originated has never been discovered—that the aforesaid eight casks of gunpowder exploded, and instantaneously sent the wretched miser, his bow-window, and the sentinel placed over the ammunition, travelling in different directions in the air, blown into innumerable pieces.

The journalists of the day differed much from each other in their newspaper accounts of this lamentable accident; some reported it to have been occasioned by a spark blown from the pipe of a passing waggoner; others, that a flash of lightning had done the mischief; and in more than one ministerial paper it was broadly hinted that the government had got tidings of its having been caused by the radicals, who were then growing in strength, and not unfrequently employed themselves setting fire to corn-stacks and other agricultural property; for somehow it will happen, that men goaded to the extremity of misery by means of corn-laws, to uphold the great stall-fed legislators, lay and clerical, occasionally break out in this way, *malgré* all the diabolical artifices of the law, and whole armies of policemen, to uphold whom in insolent authority over themselves they have to do the threefold work of slaves, and yet (such is the curse entailed by corn-laws) cannot, by the waste of sinew and of flesh, earn sufficient bread to satisfy the ravenous wolf within them.

The superstitious, who rarely see things in the light of reason, got up their edition of the disaster, and on the strength of a dame's testimony, who was addicted to dreaming of numbers in the lottery, which had brought her and many gossips of her acquaintance to ruin, asserted it to have been the ghost of Gotschalk's wife that fired the gunpowder; indeed, the witch took her affidavit that she saw the spirit do the deed with a blue lambent-flamed taper, and that the spectre was habited in a gown of virgin purity. This report being of a marvellous nature, spread far and wide, and a dissenting clergyman or two assisted to promulgate the miracle, which was handled to admiration in well-delivered discourses, of a nature to increase the preacher's reputation and fill his tabernacle. However, to consider this affair dispassionately, and not cast too great a slur on the old woman's testimony, it should be borne in mind that this is not the first instance where a ghost has been charged with incendiarism; for instance, have we not the testimony of a fisherman to the astounding circumstance of its having been Napoleon Buonaparte's ghost which fired the magazine of powder at the great explosion at Ostend, saying, when it did the terrific deed, " With one spark will I shake the reigning dynasty from the throne here?" and truly the Orange family were soon after *châse'd*.

The counsellor's heir-at-law, a small Bulgarian farmer, came hastening to Florence with a joyful heart, but his sanguine expectations were dreadfully baulked when he investigated into his new inheritance.   To explain this, the bulk of the miser's treasure had been deposited in chests, stowed in his *sanctum sanctorum*, but these chests, unfortunately for the farmer, must have stood empty, no doubt for the miser to count his money, at the moment of the explosion, and therefore the Bulgarian touched not a single stiver from this source.

Thousands of gold and silver coins were scattered about the neighbourhood of the destroyed mansion, and people found occupation for many days searching for the precious memorials of the miser's wealth, but not one of the finders of the strewed treasure brought a single piece to the heir-at-law, and yet he caused many advertisements to be inserted in newspapers, informing them what they ought and were expected to do.   These people knew the man had pillaged thousands, and therefore considered it fair game to reap from the crop so unjustly gathered, and so unexpectedly scattered; but what tended to aggravate the heir-at-law's disappointment was, that all persons who had pecuniary transactions open with the counsellor for advances on their landed or other securities, held back from furnishing evidence against themselves; while his bonds, notes of hand, and other documentary papers, having been destroyed by the explosion, there was no written evidence of money due to the estate of the deceased; yet numerous persons knew he had enormous sums lent out at the time of the awful catastrophe.   Consequently the Bulgarian farmer, though he was heir-at-law to one of the wealthiest men in Florence, touched no other property by his death than a few acres of starved land, and a dilapidated, badly furnished country chateau, for the ruins of the town mansion are unworthy of being mentioned.

Having brought the counsellor's tale to a conclusion, I shall mention what accrued to Prince Swarthyburg, as the ill-natured said, owing to the catastrophe which befel the miser.   Public opinion, which can engender movements to change customs and shake monarchs from their thrones, grew outrageously violent against the prince, who, after suffering many indignities from the populace, was glad to make a merit of necessity and remove from Florence, which, being a court favourite, he was enabled to do under the honourable plea of employment on a diplomatic mission to a northern state; for no matter how worthless the character of a court parasite, he has only to keep well with the monarch and his ministry, and the public will be made to uphold him by the imposts they pay.

The catastrophe which befel Gotschalk made so much noise in the higher circle of society on the day it happened, that even the feelings of love, hatred, and revenge seemed stilled by its influence, and I heard nothing of or concerning the fair widow, and the still more charming duchess.   Love and revenge, however, are passions not easily smothered, and on the morning following the accident a *billet-doux* reached me from the fair duchess, wherein she stated that, she had just heard the designing widow had sent for that famous duellist, the Chevalier Bras de Loup, who was an old admirer of hers, and proffered him her hand in marriage, conditionally that before the nuptial ceremony took place, he revenged her wrongs by either slaying or wounding me in fight.   This information given, the fair writer went on to say she was in a state bordering on distraction, for that her character lay at the mercy of the merciless Selina, and my life was on the eve of being exposed to the assaults of the most successful of duellists, who, moreover, had a potent reason for slaying me.   Finally, she entreated I would hasten to her instantly, otherwise she should come to me on the wings of hope, satisfied that I had too much generosity, if not affection for her, to forsake a female at such a critical moment, whom I knew to be entirely devoted to me.

I mused for some seconds on the contents of the duchess's letter, when Monday, who unobserved by me had entered the apartment, interrupted my reverie.   " Your honour," said the sailor, laughing and holding out an open letter for my perusal, " if so be that a man was bound for the harbour of matrimony, d'ye see, there would be no difficulty in his getting into a safe sheltered port, where he might drop his anchor, and lie snug against every wind."

I smiled at the sailor's observations, and taking the proffered letter, perused its contents. "Well, Monday," said I, soon as I had finished reading, "it is not every day that a wealthy dowager baroness proffers her possessions and her person to a penniless seaman, on the easy condition of his becoming her lord and master. Surely, my friend, you can't do better than marry the old lady."

" 'Tis said marriages are made aloft; but d'ye see, your honour, many a black squall lowers from a high quarter; besides, to own the truth, I can't well stomach the idea of making sail against the full current of my inclinations."

" Well, act as you approve; I have no advice to offer on such a delicate subject as that of matrimony," rejoined I.

A servant now entered the room to notify that a gentleman waited in the ante-chamber, desirous of seeing me ; on which I directed he should be shown into our apartment, and a tall personage, wearing prodigious mustachoes, was accordingly admitted, when, having made his bow, he spoke thus:—"I have done myself the honour of waiting upon you, signor, as the bearer of a message from Chevalier Bras de Loup. He calls upon you, signor, to render him satisfaction at the point of the sword for ungentlemanly conduct shown by you to the incomparable Madam Selina Rosa Conova, to whom my friend the chevalier is on the eve of being united in marriage."

" In charity, signor," replied I, " I might wish you a better office than that of carrying messages for, and serving as the second to, a man who knows not what he would quarrel about. Impertinence, however, shall be rebuked; tell, therefore, your principal that I know him not, nor shall I pay any attention to his hostile message; but should he molest me, he may rely upon it that I shall punish him. Now, signor, your business with me is over, and I wish you a good day."

The stranger was so far from profiting by my instructions, that he made use of several taunting expressions, thereby insinuating that my conduct was ungentlemanly; but, without replying to him, I calmly turned to Monday, and requested him to rid the apartment of a man who knew not how to conduct himself. My secretary, on this, desired the mustachoed gentleman to walk down stairs; but he acting obstreperously, and defying the sailor, was rudely seized by him by the shoulders, and pushed outside the door, whence, after a struggle of several minutes, he got helped on his journey down stairs by a kick on the seat of honour.

After the preceding feat of his, I remarked to the sailor, that, since it was not his design to marry the baroness, perhaps taking a journey would not be objected to by him; to which he replied that he never had felt more desirous of quitting a port where he was wind-bound than he now was of making sail from Florence, for that the current of his inclinations set violently against marriage; while on the opposite tack, such, he said, was his desire of doing a good turn and obliging everybody, that his heart misgave him, and he feared if he tarried longer in port, he should fall into the dowager's trap of matrimony, and have to ride at double anchor in all weathers. " Therefore," added he, snapping his fingers, "your honour has but to hoist Blue Peter, and I'll warrant to get under weigh the moment the signal gun is fired."

" Since you have made up your mind not to be a rich Benedict, and are ready to take a journey, you will not be sorry to hear that I purpose quitting Florence for Bologna at sunrise to-morrow."

" Your honour," replied the sailor, " I am accustomed to obey, and not to question orders given by my commodore. Blue Peter and the signal gun are all I look for or expect."

We now sallied forth to execute some business essential to be done previous to our quitting fair Florence, but had not proceeded far before the sailor, happening to look behind him, perceived Chevalier Bras de Loup and his mustachoed second following after us. "Adzooks," said he, " your honour is likely to have another little affair to settle before we make sail from this port."

I walked on without commenting on what Monday said, till a touch on my shoulder, and the stentorian voice of Bras de Loup calling upon me to render satisfaction for ungentlemanly behaviour to Madam Selina Rosa Canova, as also to himself, by gross insults given to his friend, attracted my individual attention.

" As you are resolved to rush on your fate, the sooner you receive it the better," replied I, in a resolute tone. " Your friend and you, I see, are provided with swords, and two weapons are sufficient for our purpose, therefore lead the way to some retired spot where the punishment due for your insolence may be inflicted by means of your own steel."

Indubitably, even the professed duellist would prefer seeing symptoms of backwardness in a man he stands pledged to fight, than witness in him that fiery readiness of manner which awaits not form or delay in proceeding to the deadly work of execution. Bras de Loup and his friend, who both were Austrian officers, had come habited in their regimentals, according to Monday's opinion, that they might cut the more formidable appearance before the enemy; but they looked disconcerted at my extreme readiness for mortal combat; nevertheless Bras de Loup, who was a brave man, showed no tardiness in leading the way to a retired spot, after having briefly declared that deeds, not words, were called for.

The place selected for combat was a retired walled garden near the banks of the Arno, and soon as we arrived there, the sword of my opponent's second was delivered into my possession.

"Signor," now said the fierce chevalier, " I warn you that I am an excellent swordsman, and should you prize life, wise will it be for you to apologize and yield your pretensions to the beautiful Madam Canova;" yet while he spoke, the chevalier calmly took up his ground.

"Take back your advice, and recollect your observation that deeds, not words, are called for," was my answer; then adding, "now stand on your guard, signor."

Bras de Loup's person was that of a full-sized grenadier, and his limbs were muscular as those sculptured for a gladiator. His would have been a picture worth contemplating, had an able artist delineated him in the position he took to stand on his guard against me; yet was Bras de Loup's figure and muscle inferior to mine, for I am astonishingly athletic and more than six feet high.

"He has been victorious in eight duels, and killed three of his opponents," observed the mustachoed second.

"I'll warrant Signor Winpenny will bring him to his dead reckoning," ejaculated my secretary, while we duellists were measuring weapons against each other.

The event proved that Monday was not mistaken in my skill and prowess, though he knew not the school in which I had attained my science, as after we had parried a few passes on either side, poor Bras de Loup, whose violence of manner afforded me advantage over him, was laid extended and insensible on the ground, with a terrific wound almost through his body. "One vessel has struck its colours," now said the sailor, taking up my blood-stained sword, which I had cast upon the earth that I might render assistance to my fallen opponent, " and here I stand ready and willing to engage the other; so, come on, signor, if you wish to obtain revenge for what has passed between us."

Monday's words seemed to imply a want of feeling, when, in reality, he was endowed with an ample share of that most noble attribute; but then the false pride, too oft attendant on martial courage, had whispered him that satisfaction was due to the man he had grossly insulted; and moreover this pride made him think that, as the principals in the quarrel had fought out their affair, it would be acting unworthy of a British sailor to neglect this opportunity of offering to perform the like ceremony with the enemy's second.

The mustachoed gentleman's mind was occupied by far different thoughts than those of engaging in mortal combat, and he heeded not the sailor's bravado, but leaving his enemies to staunch the chevalier's wound how best they could, disappeared like lightning from the garden. However, we were soon relieved from our unpleasant task by his return, accompanied by a grave-looking personage, clothed in black, as also a young man dressed in the same ominous colour. "The wound is mortal, and the poor gentleman's hour of death is near," said the ancient surgeon, soon as he had examined the wound and gone a few paces from the sufferer, who lay groaning upon the earth; then, after an awful silence, the grave practitioner of the healing art resumed thus:—" This duelling is unpardonably sinful; and inasmuch as our laws are extremely severe on occasions where murder has been committed in this barbarous way, my advice to the parties implicated in the sad affair is to fly the country without any delay, for all the world knows that the only possible way of defeating the law is to get beyond its reach."

" Will you undertake the care of this wounded gentleman, and be answerable that every thing proper is done for him?" asked I.

"Give me a reference to the person who is to remunerate me for my professional services and the expenses I shall incur in burying him, and then you may all three of you post away as fast as you can, for life I see is ebbing from my patient," was the doctor's caustic reply. .

The mustachoed gentleman, groaning aloud, handed a card of address to the surgeon, saying he confided in him to do everything proper for his unfortunate friend.

"I will do all that professional skill prompts to preserve the breath of life, and restock the body with new and pure blood ; but if the lungs refuse to do their office, my task shall be to bury your friend where his bones shall lie undisturbed ; for, thank the fates, we live not in a country where graves and charnel houses are robbed for the profit to be derived from a few bones," rejoined the follower of Galen.

"Sir," said the sailor, in a half whisper to me, "I'll warrant, your honour, we shall get aground once more in the billows, unless we bear a hand and make sail from this quicksand."

I was of the sailor's opinion, and no sooner had the chevalier's second satisfied his mind that his friend would be taken proper care of, than turning my face from the ghastly scene of glory, at a brisk pace I quitted the garden with Monday, who looked anxiously about him, following close behind me.

Not a word was spoken for some time ; but the sailor, after we had passed through several streets, broke silence by saying, "Would it please your honour that I should see after your property at the hotel?"

"I will send instructions respecting that by post," was my reply.

We continued our journey at a brisk pace for the distance of five or six miles, when we entered an inn at a small village and ordered refreshments. While the meal was getting ready, I wrote a letter to my *valet de chambre*, in which I enclosed an order on my banker for money to enable him to defray all just charges against me, and notified that I should speedily transmit him instructions where to proceed with my baggage ; which being done, I penned a note to the fair duchess, informing her of what had happened to me, and stating that previous to my last duel I had come to the decision of quitting Florence, for that her honour and reputation demanded this sacrifice on my part, and were dear to me as they ought to be to every friend of hers who felt desirous of hearing of her domestic happiness and general welfare in life, with ardent wishes for a long continuation of which I concluded my epistle.

This letter to the lovely duchess I enclosed in the one to my valet, to whom I transmitted orders to deliver it into her grace's own hand, and the packet I myself put into the village post office ; but when this was done and our meal over, the shades of evening were beginning to overspread the earth, wherefore I resolved to remain all night at the village inn, and commence our journey on foot at an early hour of the morning.

CHAPTER IX.

" Whoe'er perceives with equitable brow
The strange vicissitudes of things below ;
How little labour sometimes wealth secures,
How less of genius fleeting fame ensures ;
How nations, brave and wise, humane and just,
Erect the scaffold, monument, or bust ;
Whoe'er keeps such examples in his view,
Shall give to merit what is merit's due."

" Pride often guides the author's pen,
Books as affected are as men ;
But he who studies nature's laws,
From certain truths his maxims draws."

",This mournful truth is everywhere confess'd,
Slow rises worth by poverty depress'd."

"THE vegetable productions of luxuriant nature look beautiful, and richly scent the atmosphere this morning," said I to my secretary, when, at an early hour, we were journeying on foot, upon a bank of the Arno, after a good night's repose at the village inn.

"Yes," replied the sailor, "the rising sun gives life to the prospect, while the renovating dew makes the flowers and herbs send forth their fragrant and aromatic perfumes."

"I perceive you are an admirer of fair nature," remarked I, smiling ; "say then, my friend, would not this morning's walk, with Lady Sophia Bramble for your companion, be one of the richest of treats to you?"

A more florid colour than ordinary mounted into his cheeks at my observation; but presently, assuming a careless manner, he replied by saying he might whistle all his life for a wind to bring him alongside that little galley, and yet never get one ; but, for his part, he felt satisfied to follow in the wake of the commodore whose flag he sailed under.

"A truce to your waggery," answered I, "I talked of love; but say, is not yon person a-head of us the distressed poet to whom we were introduced?"

"By the cut of his stern, the square build of his patched coat, the lubberly swinging of his arms, and the poet-like manner in which he heels his head over to leeward, I could almost swear to the man; but add to these land-marks his pigeon toes, and I will give up taking observations if it is not that unfortunate slave of all work, as he christened himself," replied the sailor.

Here the poet happening to look behind him discovered us, and immediately came to an halt, that he might join company.

"You are abroad by times, sir, this fine morning," said I, saluting him.

"The traveller who has been out of bed the whole of the night, may well commence his journey at an early hour of the morn," was his reply.

By further discourse we now ascertained that the poet purposed travelling some distance on the same road we were journeying, and after walking a little way, during which the son of Apollo remained so absorbed in gloomy thought, that until a question had been several times put to him, it rarely occurred that his attention could be drawn so as to elicit a correct answer, I jocularly remarked that the solar rays of the morn seemed to have inspired both my companions with the passion of love, evinced by their taciturnity and absence of mind.

The poet, after making a futile attempt to appear gay, declared in reply, that sympathy had made a violent attack on his animal spirits, when, upon Monday's asking him for an explanation of this seeming enigma, he informed him that it was the sympathy between his pocket and animal spirits. However, perceiving the sailor to be puzzled by what he had said, he added that, with permission, he would enter into some explanation of this phenomenon; and on our expressing a desire to hear him, he delivered himself as follows:

"Philosophers and early writers on the sublime and beautiful say that sympathy is a fellow feeling of inclination and affection, a rapid but undefinable communication of one heart with another; in short, that conformity of nature's own qualities, ideas, and tempers, by which two kindred spirits seek each other, grow attached, and in a manner melt into one. If, however, a poor poet may make known his discovery, where will be found the physician or the surgeon, whose business it is to feel for the sympathetic pulse, that can deny its importance, or maintain that a close connexion exists not between the pocket and the animal spirits? Their experiments and their experience must have made them very sensible to this sympathy, for their spirits have risen and fallen in proportion as their purses ebbed and flowed; indeed, this fluctuating fund of life and spirit influences the muscles of the face, the features, and the tongue; while it gladdens the heart, and gives animation to the eye. Kings themselves worship the full purse, for they know all things are attainable by gold, and that it can turn conscience about like a weathercock. In fine, money is a talisman which in my pocket at this time would bestow happiness and a fine flow of animal spirits."

The sailor and I laughed at the poet's description of sympathy, yet a spice of the cunning displayed by Le Sage's hero, in his interpretation of the language of birds, was perceptible in his conduct. However, on our arrival at an inn, I proposed to the bard that he should breakfast with me, when, judging from the pleasantry of his manner in accepting the invitation, I was inclined to think there must have been some sympathy between his animal spirits and the expected meal.

"Love," observed I, after the sailor and the poet had broken the shells of half a dozen eggs at our breakfast, besides devouring abundantly of other food, "love, it is said, weakens the appetite; but I hope, signors, you will now endeavour to disprove the truth of this bold assertion."

"Exercise and the morning air made me ravenous as a shark before I fell in with breakfast here; indeed I could have stowed away in my hold a pound or two of salt junk, and thought it excellent food," observed the sailor.

"A night passed away at hide-and-seek, an appetite ungratified by food since yesterday's dinner, and a two hours' walk this morning, must plead my apology for displaying the greediness of a cormorant at our breakfast," said the poet.

" I cannot," said I, " call to mind that either sharks or cormorants, though they are great lovers of human flesh, are enumerated among Cupid's choice votaries; but, joking apart, a good appetite is a real blessing, and, without giving offence, I think I may venture to say we all three stand upon a par in the enjoyment of such."

The sort of sympathy between the purse and the animal spirits, which the bard had so elaborately defined, seemed likewise to exist between his stomach and spirits, inasmuch as after breakfast he became quite a different man to what he had been.

Our meal being over, we resumed our journey, and had jogged on some considerable way, when Monday, addressing the poet, said, " Messmate, I hope no offence, but thus much must make bold to say, that a night passed at hide-and-seek on shore would to me be more tiresome than taking watch and watch aboard ship for a whole week in a stiff gale, with all hands piped upon deck once or twice every twelve hours."

" He who angles is desirous of catching fish," observed the bard, smiling archly, " but if my adventure of last night, or indeed my whole history, can afford satisfaction to you, signors, I will cheerfully enter into the relation."

Monday and I now signified our desire of hearing the poet's story, and he commenced thus: " It is an old observation, that the life of an author rarely affords matter worthy of record, and though the lives of some few, as that of the immortal Byron, who travelled abroad a little, and lived separated from his wife, which made him the prince of egotists, may form an exception to the correctness of the adage, still it is grounded on too solid a basis to be shaken by a solitary case; but that poverty is the destined lot of some first-rate men of genius, is proved by Cervantes, Otway, and many more authors, who died of want.   To the liberal-minded it will be matter of indifference who were my parents, or what was my pedigree, for such know that the anatomist discovers no difference in quality or colour, between the blood of an archduke and that of a meaner pauper, nor even between that of a despotic sovereign and a blackamoor; neither can the chemist, by any analysing process, find the one to be richer than that of the other.   It follows, then, that hereditary titles are gross frauds on the public, and must ever be so, for they cannot be made to change the nature of a knave, nor brush up the intellects of a fool; nevertheless they serve as grindstones and presses to crush down, and extract wealth from, the great mass of the community.   After receiving a good education, I was cast penniless on the world, when, instead of acting a prudent part by following the business of a husbandman or a cobbler, it was my misfortune to trust for a livelihood to my education and literary talents,—things which have nothing to do with the juggling of authorship.   The navigator whose vessel has ploughed the circumference of the globe; the soldier who has served a few campaigns, and the traveller who has visited pestilential regions of Africa, meets with people ready to sympathize with him for the privations and sufferings he has endured; but, alas! the poor author, whose travels extend only to the purlieus of the town of his residence, and his campaigns to his bookseller's house, may suffer fifty times more misery and privation than these favoured individuals, and yet no person dreams of sympathizing with him. For my part, it is no exaggeration to say that I have run the gauntlet of authorship.   I have been a reviewer of books which I have read, and of others that I never entertained a thought of perusing; yet it is reviewers who decide people whether to patronise or consign new works to oblivion; for in the world how few there are who think for themselves!   I have been the editor of a Sunday paper, which succeeded proportionately to the number of dreadful accidents, police examinations, scandalous reports, and obscene puns with which it was made to abound.   I have had my brains fine-drawn by writing for magazines, and I have taken an active part in spawning forth the insiped matter of a court journal, wherein common sense is outraged by descriptions of court dresses, and statements of the horses with which overpaid princes have travelled; as also by the *on dits*, dinner parties, balls, and other fulsome reports, vamped up to gratify the vitiated taste of fashion.   But, thank Heaven," added the poet, musingly, " I have not very often been guilty of the last-named meanness, though the lesser one of puffery was a fruitful source of gain to me; and of all trades that of the puffer is the most excusable, inasmuch as, more or less, we all practise it.   Puffing, however, is carried to a great length, as an instance of which I shall quote from some of the journals their puffs of a certain doctor's breakfast bacon :—

"A delicious medicated zest, and a valuable remedy."—*Times*.

"An excellent, useful, and effective culinary medicine."—*Herald*.

"Ingeniously simple in its appearance, and unquestionably efficacious in its operation."—*Chronicle*.

"Free from all grossness."—*United Service Gazette*.

"Quite a delicacy."—*East India Magazine*.

"A real luxury, and an efficient medicine."—*Courier*.

"An excellent promoter of the digestive functions."—*Morning News*.

"A delicious morning relish."—*Court Journal*.

"Indispensable at breakfast."—*Dispatch*.

"A nutritious *bonne bouche*."—*Bristol Journal*.

"Nothing can be more effectual and pleasant."—*Old England*.

"It justly merits all that can be said in its praise."—*Plymouth Herald*.

"Paul and Peter wrangled not more violently than the sectarians of the present day, who make scripture clash with scripture, until the apostles seem to be at loggerheads with each other; and in my writings I have been an atheist, a deist, a religious enthusiast, a quaker, a baptist, and an anabaptist; in short, I have supported and attacked every species of religion, from the time of Moses, when he played on the weakness of others, by illuminating the precious stones on the sacerdotal vestments of Aaron and his sons, to prove that the Almighty was present at their meeting, unto that of the glaring impositions of a clergy who sell pardons for crimes revolting to nature. But I have not attained the summit of blasphemy, inasmuch as I have not qualified myself with a proper knowledge of the unknown tongues; and yet, like the trained missionary, I know how far fragments of fiction may illustrate truth, and truth give brilliancy to fiction. To conclude, I have written on almost every head, and brought many an actor and dissenting parson into vogue by my songs paid for with their money, and made to be sung against them. However, though genius may be the genial fount for immortality, yet, when applied to authorship, in nine hundred and ninety-nine cases out of a thousand it passes through life in a state bordering on starvation; and this wretched fate, in spite of my unceasing efforts to avert it, has hitherto been mine."

Here the poet paused; and I, seeing he looked sorrowful, remarked, that a literary gentleman of his acquirements surely might procure some more profitable employ than that of scribbling for journalists and pamphleteers; on which he said he was once of my opinion, but that dear-bought experience had made him wiser; and he gave me the following relation of the employments he had filled.

"The first person I was secretary to was a nobleman, who prided himself on being a poet and prose writer; but the lines he called poetry were unmeaning, and his prose was even worse than his verses; still some malicious relatives of his whispered to him that, after his death, I meant to pilfer from his works, and rob his name of the honours due to him for authorship; wherefore he angrily dismissed me his service. It was now my fortune to enter the service of a noble marquis, whose name stands high as a patron of literary men; but though he was kind and liberal to me, it was impossible I could continue with him, for there was his lawyer, his house steward, his land steward, his butler, his lady, and his valet, to be kept in good humour; and what secretary, at the mercy of such a host, could give satisfaction? Accordingly, I lost my place, and felt too much disheartened to solicit employment again from the aristocracy. The world is wide and abounds in good things, yet an honest man may starve at the door of plenty. I had nearly done so, but at length obtained employment with a great landed commoner. Unfortunately, from his being conversant with two of the dead languages and flattered by sycophants, this gentleman had grown into the shallow-pated monster vulgarly denominated a pedant; yet though his contradictory ways beggar description, I contrived to remain a few months with him, when, out of revenge for my having set the dolt right in a quotation from Catullus, he rudely dismissed me his service. Having thus lost my three places I came to the resolution of never more engaging in domestic servitude, for such I pronounce to be the situation of almost every gentleman's private secretary, though secretaries to public bodies, not unfrequently are the parties who enjoy the largest share of the general pillage. It was now suggested to me by a friendly nobleman, that the office of private tutor to a young relative of his, a ward of chancery, might be procured for me; I, however, begged his lordship not to exert his influence in my behalf, when he inquired what were my objection and I replied, that to an unendowed parson the post would be highly suitable, for it might pave the way to a bishopric; but that I, a citizen of the world, free from local prejudices and bigotry, should be no better than an impostor were I to undertake to instil the dogmas of any church into the mind of my pupil; and moreover, that not being a parson, none of the good things of the church could await me.

"My noble friend, with much candour, pronounced me unfit to be a parson; and," added the poet, smiling, "said I was too honest for the age I lived in. After quitting the pedant, I lived poor and free in my garret, waited upon by no living being, save an occasional dun, and the devils who came to carry away my labours; meanwhile I paid few visits, except to booksellers, who furnished me with employment. Close application to literary business, combined with much confinement to the house, eventually brought on me a fit of sickness, which not only endangered my life, but precipitated unavoidable ruin on me. However, to pass from this scene of misery, it will suffice to say, things daily became worse until I had been five times incarcerated in a debtors' gaol; but, yesterday evening, finding that a bailiff was lying in wait nigh my lodgings, rather than be seized by him to endure a sixth imprisonment, I came to the resolution of taking leg-bail, to recommence my worldly career, and with a mind filled with this resolve, lay hid in an empty house until such time as the city gates were opened this morning, when I sallied forth with the intention of visiting a cousin who resides hard by here, and borrowing a couple of ducats from him, to enable me to reach Bologne, where I hope to get my bread by writing for a magazine edited by an old schoolfellow."

The unfortunate author of all work was thanked for the favour he had done us by relating his tale; after which, the sailor, whose ideas were not altogether clear respecting the pedant, remarked that the learned lubber, who had been the poet's third commodore, appeared to be a skulking swab—a kind of cold-blooded fish, whose character he was unable to fathom.

"There are various sorts of pedants," rejoined the bard; "some are compilers of books, others translators, but the whole are plagiaries. They tell what other writers have told, and no more, nor are they capable of thinking for themselves. Their books lack choice and invention, but have a variety of insignificant matter embodied in them; yet the pedant tries to surprise and bewilder by the extent of his reading, though he possesses no peculiarity nor any originality. In fine, the learning of a pedant is what the rest of the world despise. His is a dry, worthless science, ill adapted for the intercourse among mankind; yet people sometimes mistake him for a profound scholar and a talented man, for, owl-like, his looks are grave and serious, which help to back his quotations; but the well-informed know him to be contemptible —that self-sufficient animal termed a pedant."

"Precious lubbers these," ejaculated the sailor, "they are like hermaphrodite brigs; no matter how crank their spars and bottoms, or how sound and good their rigging and sails, still they are neither one thing nor the other."

Shortly after the preceding remark, we came to a spot on the main road, from which a lane branched off; when, after making the observation that the lane led to the abodes of his relative, the poet said he regretted necessity now called on him to separate from the agreeable companions Dame Fortune, in one of her good humours, had opportunely thrown in his way.

"Take it not ill, my friend, that I offer you this trifle in your necessities," said I, putting six ducats into the poet's hand. "Believe me, signor, I want words to express my gratitude for this unlooked-for bounty," replied the delighted scholar. "What you have given is a little fortune; it will carry me to Bologna, and put me in a way to thrive; but adieu, kind signors; I will haste to pay my visit, in the hope of having the felicity of overtaking you."

"To do that, you must hoist all the sail you can carry," laughingly observed the sailor, as the poet shuffled away at his best pace down the lane.

CHAPTER X.

" The piping swain and bleating flock,
Sound through the woods from rock to rock;
But not a whisper stirs the shade,
Where lurks the insidious ambuscade."

" 'Twill seem this awful rout,
And my mind's dread, distress, and doubt,
Might well have kept me wakeful there;
But hard fatigue sleeps anywhere.
Nature's own medicine! none so sure
For the mind's grief as labour's cure."

AFTER the poor bard had quitted us, Monday commenced philosophizing on the instability of fortune and the uncertainty of merit, especially literary merit, meeting with its just recompense; when I, having acceded to the justness of his observations, he resumed as follows:— " The fair sailor can't make head way in a dead calm, nor against a strong current; but steam is the thing for shooting a-head on all tacks, against all tides, and in all weathers; 'tis fire against water, and, for a time, carries all before it."

" Monday," said I, " what in the name of wonder can steam have to do with poetry? the invention has not yet been so refined upon as to enable it to inspire the poetic brain."— " That's the point I am steering for; steam is comparable to court interest, which is a smooth-going machine, that carries all before it, while poetry, d'ye see, is a plain sailor, unable to make head against the calm of contempt, or the strong current of prejudice. But steam, with all its vast power, will never make a good poem, nor the good poet ever be sure of meeting his just reward. In all things else chance is the predominating deity; but not so in poetry, for here the hero must do everything himself, while in war he is one of the party, a mere dependant on the mercenaries serving beneath him."

" My friend, you will never rise in favour at court if you go on in this manner," now observed I, laughingly.—" I am not cut and fashioned for the people there, nor seasoned for the atmosphere," answered my secretary; then resuming the old subject, he said, " Chance, in defiance of prudence, application, and ability, gives the victory in battle, causes success or failure in business; and chance it is which weathers or brings shipwreck in the storms of life; but did chance ever yet make a good poet? The memory of one great poet is worth more than that of all the butchers of war that ever existed; for what were these last but devastators and murderers, whose sanguinary acts charity would wish should be forgotten? And what was the former but a benefactor, whose instructively pleasing works are bequeathed for the amusement of all ages? Yet, alas! such is the inconsistency of the world, that for the human butchers statues are erected even in his own time, and such is his egotistical vanity, that he intrigues with and sways committee men to erect the granite pillar while he is living; these pillars, however, it is to be hoped, will some day stand, with suitable inscriptions, as memorials of so many philosophers. The great bard's monument is his own sublime work of the imagination, yet statues shall be erected to him when his dust hath long disappeared, and thus will it be with the immortal Byron, the bard who must be highly honoured in future ages, and in ages when Westminster Abbey and its monuments are no more."

A public vehicle now overtook us, and my secretary gladly terminated his lecture to fill a seat in it; when, without any memorable occurrence, we continued journeying in this way until we arrived in safety at the place of our destination, and we soon got housed there in a comfortable hotel. Bologna is a large wealthy city, with a population of a hundred thousand souls, is situated at the foot of the Appenines, surrounded by walls, forts, and ditches, and has a dozen gates. The city has the credit of having given birth to many famous painters, and an innumerable number of cardinals and popes.

It was my intention to have sojourned some weeks, if not months, in this venerable city; but after a stay of a few days, my valet, to whom I had written on my arrival, came posting here with my luggage, and he was the bearer of a tender epistle from the fair duchess of my acquaintance, in which she notified her intention of visiting Bologna, and prepared me to expect her almost immediately, giving me to understand she had relatives in this town, which would serve as a pretence for her taking the journey, but that her real motive was that of placing herself under my protection, for that she found life a burden away from me. " Soho," said I, soliloquizing over the lovely woman's letter, " here is a temptation with a vengeance for a young man ; yet I, who could sli.ht the tender overtures of the banker's rich widow, must act firmly on this occasion, and not embroil myself by resuming intimacy with this charming duchess, otherwise her *penchant* will be her ruin, and fix the fair creature on my hands. I have recommended prudence to the lovely woman as a shield and a buckler, therefore I will arm myself with the god-like quality, and by quitting the site of danger, evade a temptation which I might not be able to resist, and which is greater than any that assailed old St Anthony."

Having formed my resolution, I summoned Monday to my presence, and signified to him my intention of departing that same day on our journey for the eternal city, as Catholic priests have denominated that place of ruins, whence they have long issued their edicts for enslaving the minds and bodies of millions who dared not be known to think for themselves, although endowed by the great bestower of all things with powers of mind equal to those of their spider-like enslavers. My secretary, schooled as he was to obedience, yet was somewhat startled by the avowal of my sudden resolve, but this I attributed to an attachment he had formed to a little Bolognese brunette ; however, after a few hems and a sigh or two, he resolutely declared that sailing orders must be obeyed, and posted away to prepare everything for the journey, which accordingly we commenced, and even proceeded one stage of it that day. The following morning we started betimes, and after passing through several Lombard and Roman cities of great antiquity, yet now of little consequence, arrived at Ancona, which possesses a beautiful and convenient harbour, and is a free port. The population of this city amounts to more than twenty thousand souls, and the wisdom of the governing power is displayed by its allowing every person to worship the Almighty in his own way, without persecution or extra imposition of taxes, which is rarely done by governments where priests hold undue influence.

From Ancona, where we tarried several days, and which is one hundred and eighty miles distant from Rome, we set off in high spirits at the prospect of soon reaching the ancient capital of the Romans ; nor did we waste time anywhere on the journey until we came to Loretta, where we loitered a short space to view the chapel of our lady, which stands in the middle of a church; but neither Monday or I could be coaxed by the clergy, who vend it in small packets ready for the purpose, to purchase any of the dust of the holy house, said to have been brought by four angels from Galilee to Tersato, and four years afterwards to Italy, by the same miraculous conveyance, when all the neighbouring trees, flowers, and shrubs most reverentially bowed their heads, and remained in that lowly posture till they withered and decayed. At Terni, a Roman Catholic priest would fain have persuaded us that our Saviour's heart and a portion of his blood is still preserved in the church there, but this was a lame tale to tell to two experienced seamen.

We had nearly passed the Appenines, and were looking out for a place of rest at Narni, for night was coming on, when our postillion, apparently in a great fright, exclaimed that he saw a troop of banditti approaching from a place of ambuscade behind a clump of trees, and presently a set of ferocious fellows galloped up and surrounded our carriage, one of them pointing a pistol at the driver's head, and calling upon him to stop, which he instantly did.

My party were provided with loaded pistols, and I, jumping out of the carriage, called upon Monday and my valet to back me, and commenced the fight by bringing one of the robbers to the ground with a pistol ball lodged in his body. But these sort of combats, like most others, are a tumultuous scene of confusion ; and all I can remember more is, that I saw my valet cut down by a sabre stroke, when almost at the same instant I myself fell by a similar wound, which rendered me incapable of knowing more of passing events.

When sense was restored to me, the first circumstances I can bring to mind were, that I was lying stripped of all my habiliments, except my linen and trowsers, on some damp and dirty straw spread on the ground at a corner of a dismal dungeon of solid stone, which received no more light than what found its way through two iron bars at the top of the dungeon. My wound, combined with the dampness of the place, caused me to tremble with cold, and well I might, for I had no other covering to comfort me than the few things upon my body and ragged horse-cloth. I lay puzzling myself to know what all this meant ; yet so confused were my senses, that it appeared to me to be a dream, till presently, being tormented by an intolerable headache and the fever of thirst, I felt over my head, which in various places was clotted with blood, and then, on looking about me, discovered a pitcher of water. Now it was that I began to come to a true sense of my condition :—" I have been pillaged by banditti," said I ; " I recollect it all."

My sensations at this moment were frightful ; but though I had been initiated in a life of pleasure, I had also been schooled to bear pain and trouble ; therefore I could in some measure balance the good against the bad, so as to receive visitations of fortune as things of course. I felt feeble as well as thirsty and in pain, but from my water-jug slaked my thirst, which somewhat comforted my frame ; when I extended myself at my length on the damp straw, and covered my frame with the horse-cloth, to try and call to mind what had happened. It was a vain task ;—I could not for the soul of me recollect how I received my wound ; but I was like a man who, when he is recovering from the effects of a concussion of the brain, comes last to a sense of the accident by which it befel him.

" I see that I am in the power of villains," thought I, as I called to mind Captain Quirorga and his mode of providing for prisoners ; and then I said, soliloquising, " would that they had left me to linger on the road instead of bringing me to this dismal dungeon, for the worst would be over, and I should have no more to apprehend from their hostility ; here, however, have I been brought, that they may glut their vengeance on my person, or obtain a weighty sum for my ransom."

After musing for a time, and finding it impossible to come to any satisfactory conclusion, the weakness of my condition occasioned the balmy equalizer of mortality to overwhelm me with its power. How long I remained asleep I know not, but I awoke in consequence of receiving several most uncourteous kicks on my side ; when looking from under the horse-rug, I discovered a ruffianly fellow standing near me. " Ah, signor, so you are alive, are you ?" said the man, grinning ; " I told our captain there was too much metal in you to die of that wound, else doubtless we should have given you a home thrust or two, and left your body near the road, where some good Catholic might have marked the place of your death by a cross of his erection."—" I admire your charity," replied I : " so you spare a man's life in the field, to shut him up in a dungeon, where, unassisted, he may be starved to death or die of his wounds, for what you care !"—" A cool berth and a pitcher of clear water are things befitting such a hot-brained gentleman as you are. But hark'ee, provided you wish to war against nature, we'll send a doctor to plaster up your head."

The fellow, I perceived, was not without humour, and that he possessed a certain portion of good nature, therefore I ventured to question him, but all he chose to say was, that he would go and procure me something to eat. I now waited in suspense for nearly an hour, when my door was unbarred, and my old visitor re-entered my dungeon, and bid me get up and follow him, provided I felt inclined to eat. This I did, though with difficulty, till having entered into a dilapidated chamber, in which was some broken furniture, he told me to sit down awhile, and he would have me looked to and provided with food.

This was a pleasing communication, and I had not been long seated before he returned, accompanied by a club-footed, dwarfish young man, of a pleasing physiognomy, though far from good-looking, and disfigured by a profusion of lank black hair hanging over his shoulders. " Jacobus," said my old gaoler to him, " while I am away at the stable, do you examine and dress this signor's wound, which done, supply him with clothes, and give him some soup with a little bread in it."

The dwarf having signified his acquiescence to the order, my gaoler retired, whistling as he went ; when the little man, without saying one word to me, busied himself in the enjoined task. The first thing he did was to bring from a neighbouring closet the things necessary for washing and examining my wound, a business he then performed with tenderness and care, but not a word was uttered by either of us while he was so engaged. This task being accomplished, he revisited the closet and brought several old coats and waistcoats from out of it, which having thrown down, he drily told me to fit myself. It was no time for ceremony, therefore I effected this task in the best manner I could, and consequently soon sat clothed in an old red coat and a black waistcoat, which were the only articles of clothing I could find large enough to thrust my body into, while, after all, the coat fitted me like a strait waistcoat. The dwarf, who had a strange shyness about him, and rarely looked in the face of one he addressed, but whose manner had hitherto been grave, smiled when he beheld me imprisoned in the scarlet coat, and after passing the back of his hand across his mouth, quaintly remarked that it was a tight fit. Ill and mortified as I felt, still the aptness of the observation touched my fancy, and looking first at myself and then at the little object before me, I replied, " Tight as a laced drum."—" He who has been thirty-six hours without food, must needs be hungry," now said the dwarf; "therefore in mercy I will fetch you a bason of broth before I clothe your legs in leather." The proposition was truly acceptable, for the wolf of hunger gnawed at my stomach, but my caterer promptly returned, bringing with him a bason of soup and a large slice of bread; when saying this would be sufficient for a man in my state, he desired me to eat and comfort my heart, while he went to look out for a pair of boots suitable to the rest of my habiliments. Hunger seasons the coarsest food; I sipped up all my soup and demolished my bread in such quick time, that they had disappeared before the dwarf returned, yet he speedily came, with a huge pair of brown-topped boots in his hand. " I am no son of Crispin," said he, with a sly grin, while he handed me the boots, "yet this I will take on me to say, that if your body is a little straitened for room, you shall have no cause for making such a complaint of your feet. These boots formed part of the stock in trade of a company of players, and were made for an overgrown fellow, who, had we not put his pipe out, was to have performed the part of Goliah before some cardinals at the carnival at Rome." I felt all the better for the dressing of my wound and the food I had partaken of, and without speaking now thrust my legs into the boots, for no pulling was required to get them on, as they were comparable to the boots of a fisherman, much larger than me in the legs.

Again I caught the dwarf grinning at me, when smilingly I said, that he ought to undergo the Jewish rites and set up as a slopseller at a sea-port, where, provided he could bring the sailors into the humour of being rigged out in the way he had rigged me, he would infallibly soon make his fortune.

Prejudice sways the mind of man. My speech outraged the good Catholic's feelings, for though he was one of a band of robbers, to be counselled to become a Jew was intolerable to him, and he stared at me with wildness in his looks, till presently, crossing himself with fervour, he broke into the following ejaculations :—" What! submit to the Jewish rites, and become a Jew ? By Saint Joseph, the husband of the Virgin Mary, and her son Saint Oblia, no true Catholic was ever so insulted before. A Jew, indeed! By the Virgin, where should I then go for confession ? Who would grant me absolution ? A Jew, who believes not in a future state, and whose only dream of hereafter relates to the resurrection and dancing about of a pile or two of human bones."

'Tis bad policy to trifle with a man's religious feelings, especially when you are in his power; therefore, as this dwarf chose to forget that Christ was a Jew, I saw no sufficient reason for impressing this grand truth upon him; but to turn the conversation, smilingly said that he looked too honest for a Jew. Jacobus, who apparently had been tutored in the school of secrecy, was now silent, but I could see that he contemplated with satisfaction his handy-work in clothing me in the fanciful way he had. However, my first gaoler returned soon after the last discourse, when having laughed heartily at my uncouth figure, he threw me a blanket from the closet; then telling me to keep quiet and comfort myself, but as I prized my existence not to attempt getting away from the chamber, he, together with the dwarf, retired, carefully locking and bolting the room-door behind them.

" Well," said I, when left to my reflections, and contemplating my figure, " there is comfort to be found on almost all occasions; for example, it is evident the banditti don't entertain the design of sacrificing me to their vengeance, as, if they did, they would not have troubled themselves to clothe me in the mountebank manner they have. What a figure I cut! Diana Winpenny herself, were she alive to behold him, would not recognise her own son. I suspect, though, that his old commander, Lieutenant Jones, would readily know his apt pupil even in this disguise."

Nobody came to disturb my meditations, so, at length, wearied out by them, I extended myself on a cow-hide which happened to be on the floor, and fell asleep, in which state I remained until the shades of night had darkened my prison room. Why is it that night should have a tendency to shade the mind of man with gloominess, as it veils the world with darkness ?

is a question befitting the learned to decide.   Night makes all man's difficulties and dangers appear more terrible to him.   Night also gives birth to ghosts and hobgoblins ; and when I awoke, which I did before day dawned, my reflections were most gloomy, and kept me awake for hours ; at length, however, wearied by them, I fell asleep once more, and I continued sleeping until the unbarring of my door awoke me from a frightful dream.   " Oh, Jacobus, you are a most welcome visitor," said I, on seeing the dwarf enter with a bason of something smoking.   It was soup, with a profusion of cabbage and a moderate allowance of bread mixed therein ; but never have I enjoyed a breakfast more than I did this.—" I love to see our cookery done justice to, and if it were not for your wound, I would fetch you another bason of soup," said Jacobus.—" My good fellow, run and fetch it," exclaimed I ; " by my soul, it will be doing me a great service."

The obdurate dwarf laughed at me, and replied, that the doctor knew best what was good for his patient, but, for his part, he would not kill me with kindness ; when, without more words, he withdrew, locking and bolting my door.   I had now abundant time left me for moralising, for the whole day elapsed, and night again darkened my chamber, without my being revisited, but happily the fever arising from my wound had subsided, and I was tolerably free from pain.   An hour after nightfall, Jacobus re-entered my room, bearing a lit flambeaux.   The sudden glare dazzled my eyes.   " Come, arise," said he ; " our captain and some of his party have come home, and he has sent me to bring you before them."

I always prefer meeting the worst to a tedious anticipation of it, therefore I promptly arose from my humble couch to follow my conductor, who led me across a yard, and through a stable, when we entered a ruinous old place, like a chapel, lit by several torches, and a blazing fire at the remotest end of the room.   Five ferocious fellows, each armed with pistols and a sword, sat on logs of wood before a table formed of loose planks, laid on two tilted casks ; and on this a large piece of boiled beef and a dish of potatoes were smoking.   " Signor," said the chief robber, addressing me, " I am not sorry to see you in the land of the living ; a nobleman, such as you are, must pay nobly for your ransom, or, by Saint Dominick, we shall have to make an *auto-de-fé* to roast your body."—" You are mistaken ; I am no nobleman ; indeed, so far from being one, I am an adventurer, whose career has been of the daring character of your own."—" He," replied the chief, " who is detected in a lie here, shall be stoned as was Saint Stephen ; therefore, young man, be cautious what you say.   I had tidings given me of your being upon the road, and none save a nobleman, or one with the wealth of such, could lavish away money in the way you are reported to do."

" Captain, excuse me," observed I, " but a man such as you are should not judge of others by appearances.   The world, we know, are the dupes of them."—" Come, no preaching ; you say you are an adventurer, and what are the majority of noblemen but so many adventurers, upheld by plucking that goose called the public ?"   There is nothing like humouring the man who is in power, and when he jokes, the sign is a good one, for few men are of the disposition of Nero, who committed murders, with a joke in his mouth to season them.   Accordingly, to humour the captain, I laughed at what he had said, telling him I had been a buccaneer.

The chief knew not what I meant, but being a *religious* man, who rarely spoke without invoking some saint, he swore by Saint Gregory of Naziente—he, he said, whose wife brought forth another Saint Gregory of Naziente, that I was as comical a fellow in my speech as in my dress ; which, having said, he joined with his comrades in a boisterous laugh at my expense, and then, as if to make amends for the indignity, invited me to make one at his board, adding, that when the meal was over, he would hear my story, and decide on the price of my ransom.

The state of my appetite made this an acceptable invitation, and having thanked the captain, I lost no time in seating myself upon a log of wood, which my friend Jacobus placed for me at a suitable spot.   The party were in good trim for eating, and we soon made the beef a mere shadow of what it was when we commenced upon our meal.   It would, however, be remiss not to mention that Jacobus, who officiated as cook and waiter, more than once took the liberty of reminding me that he was my doctor, and it was his desire that I should refrain from taking much nourishment ; while of the wine, of which a large well-filled jar was provided, he positively insisted I should not be a partaker ; and strange to say, the captain declared he must be obeyed, therefore I drank only from the water jug.

· " By the flying Saint Dandalus," said the chief, when we had thrust our plates from before us, " we have fairly demolished the round of beef; and now, Jacobus, my boy, bring us cigars, that we may puff care away while we listen to this buccaneer signor's story."

The dwarf, at this summons, produced a packet of cigars, and, without ceremony, took his seat on a log with the rest of us, when Captain Manfreda signified his desire that I should commence the relation of my tale, which, accordingly, I did. There is no small art required in a man giving a fit colouring to his history, especially when he has played pranks, and run a career such as mine. In their histories, as in a suit-at-law, experienced persons make truth serve as their beacon, that is, they always keep it in view, to use to their advantage; accordingly, I kept pretty true to my tale, except when I disguised the circumstance of my being wealthy, to make it appear that I was still an adventurer, dependent on his own exertions. The banditti laughed heartily at certain parts of my history, and some of the exploits of my old buccaneering companions afforded them much gratification. " By Saint Simon the fisherman," observed their leader, " those buccaneers the signor tells of were a noble set of fellows. They lived as men ought to do. Their lives furnish a pattern worthy of being followed. I myself should glory in being the commander of a crew of buccaneers, who sail over the boundless ocean, to capture rich merchant-vessels sailing to and fro in all quarters."

The chief questioned me pretty closely touching my finances. " You say," said he, " that you have lost your money. If so, take service with us; you are a brave man, worthy of being in our band."—" I might do so, but that I am not of your country; and my foreign dialect, combined with the broken way in which I speak your language, would bring the chances of war against me, so that when you all escaped your pursuers, I might be detected, and have my neck brought to the halter." " By Saint Antony, there is reason in what you say; we, however, cannot let a man like you free without ransom; you yourself, your friend who escaped us, and your fool of a servant, whom we left to die of his wounds by the roadside, between you all, have wounded four of my party. What, then, am I to do to satisfy these wounded men, let me ask?"—" The fortune of war, noble captain, is various, and not to be averted; one man gets a wooden leg, another a purse of money; but the brave can be generous; therefore let me propose to you to liberate me on my parole, and I will pledge myself to meet you, or who you may appoint, on a given day, say a fortnight hence, to deliver myself up on failure of paying any reasonable sum you may fix upon as my ransom money."—" And how are you to obtain this money?" asked the chief. " How is a man without resources to make himself master of a round sum? You say you have lost your all by our capture of you."—" I shall meet with old acquaintances; there are many such in Rome, who will either lend me money, or else join with me in achieving adventures by means of which it may be obtained; for noble captain, as you know by my story, I am a man who can work his own way."

The captain smiled, and, turning to his comrades, said, " By the Apostle Paul, the man speaks fair; shall we admit him on parole? Shall we let him go at large in home for a week or two, to gather together a thousand ducats for ransom-money, as, d'ye see, comrades, we have taken the poor devil's all?" The four bandits whispered among themselves, after hearing their captain's proposition, and, to own the truth, I augured no good from their manner.

" He it was wounded Jacques," after a time observed the surliest-looking fellow of the party. " He is a very devil in fight," said a second. " Come, comrades," said the captain, on perceiving the indecision of his followers, " you know that I rarely am an advocate for sparing man's life, for, as the saying goes, the dead tell no tales; but, comrades, we should bear in mind that this is a brave fellow, who, though not a bandit, has been of a profession nearly akin to it—he has borne arms as a buccaneer, which, it seems, is what we call a corsair; and he cannot escape, though we let him go free in Rome; therefore, all things considered, by Saint Barnabus, I am for giving him a fair trial; a fortnight's grace on his parole, then to pay us a thousand ducats, or become one of us."

The captain's pleasure was acceded to by his followers, nevertheless I could perceive that their assent to his proposition was not given with much cordiality. It was now resolved that I should be permitted to depart on the following day, after having been sworn to the performance of certain conditions; and the bandits, who it appeared had been abroad for several successive nights on the dangerous business of their trade, and were desirous of rest, spread their cloaks upon bullocks'-hides on the room-floor, and prepared themselves to lie down. Meanwhile Jacobus, by the chief's order, reconducted me to my old chamber, where, preparatory to leaving me, he declared that I was a lucky fellow, and must be one of fortune's prime favourites, for that otherwise I should not be suffered to depart from an imprisonment among banditti, who rarely spared their prisoners, but usually based their conduct towards them upon the maxim that dead men tell no tales.

An easy mind is a great promoter of sleep, and mine, comparatively speaking, was easy to what it had been; some anxiety, however, lurked there, but anxiety and recollection soon sunk together, bound in the chains of sleep.

CHAPTER XI.

> "The Sun had long since, in the lap
> Of Thetis, taken out his nap,
> And, like a lobster boil'd, the moon
> From black to red began to turn,
> When, rubbing first, my drowsy eyes,
> From lowly couch I sought to rise."

IT was broad day when I awoke, but my head ache was not so bad as on the preceding day, nor was my fever near so violent, while the prospect of re-enjoying sweet liberty cheered up my spirits.

I now continued for several hours lying on my lowly bed, tossing and tumbling about, soliloquising and meditating, when Jacobus made his appearance.

"You are in a state of convalescence, and are to be set free," said he, eyeing me with complacency; "had we, however, left you on the road, you would either have perished there, or fallen under the care of a Roman doctor, to be made a living skeleton, ere he trumped forth your marvellous recovery, as evidence of his own incomparable skill."—"My good fellow," replied I, "I know that I am indebted to your services for my quick recovery, but like too many debtors, I shall never be able to pay what I owe."

"Likely enough," answered he, "for mine is a service where I get more hard rubs than coins. I have many masters to please, and none possess a tithe of Job's patience."—"Jacobus, point out what I can do for you after I am free, and depend on it I shall not be tardy in executing your wishes."

"A still tongue shows a wise head," now observed the dwarf, and giving me a few silver coins, he added, "stow these away, and breathe not a word of all this; but when you get to Rome, leave your written address for me with Signor Ambrose, the tavern-keeper in the great market-place, when in good time you may count on hearing from or seeing me."

Here our conversation was interrupted by the whistling of some one, and presently my first gaoler made his appearance. "Well, Jacobus," said he, "you see I've found my way back, and now shall relieve you of further trouble on the score of this prisoner; however, the signor seems wonderfully recovered; he doesn't look like the man I thought to have found dead and stiff in his cage two nights ago."

"Carl," replied the dwarf, "I am glad to see you back in a whole skin, I expected you'd have a brush with the papal troops, but I trust you bring good tidings of the lieutenant's party." "So, so," rejoined Carl, "they are all well except Dominique, who died yesterday of his wound."

Jacobus seemed vexed at this piece of information, and hemmed aloud several times, but said nothing regarding their lost companion; presently, however, assuming his usual composure, he told Carl that he was glad to resign his charge of me, as he had something else to do than be looking after prisoners.

Jacobus now took his departure, apparently unconcerned for my welfare, and soon, on my complaining of hunger, Carl followed him, as he said, to procure me something to eat; but I was kept in a state of hunger and suspense for two hours after his departure without seeing any person. It was verging towards mid-day when Carl paid me a second visit, but it was an agreeable one, for he came provided with my breakfast, and though it was similar to the one I had been furnished with on the preceding day, yet cabbage, soup, and coarse bread, was very acceptable to me.

"Don't fall asleep over your grub," said the gaoler, laughing to see how eagerly I set to at my breakfast, "as recollect, when you've done eating, you are to go along with me to our captain, who is waiting to see you; howsoever, I must say, you are in a precious plight for exhibition by daylight."

Carl was perfectly right. The dirt from my cow-hide couch, on which many a muddy shoe had been rubbed, added to the fantastical dress I wore, made me look a more laughable figure than a merry-Andrew; yet this was of no moment to me, and I hurried over my repast, to accompany my gaoler to the presence of his chief.

On our entrance, Manfreda was sitting, as on the preceding night, with four of his band, and Carl took a seat along with them. "Signor," said the captain, "I have sent for you in accordance with my promise of yesterday. My word is my bond, and by St Crispin, I am too much of a man of honour to swerve from it."—"You are an honourable man, your conduct towards me evinces it," replied I: "the great Quirorga, under whom I served to the day that he perished, and you, noble captain, afford evidence that true honour may be found in every station."

My speech happily touched Manfreda's self-pride, for he loved to hear compliments paid to him on his honourable conduct; but this is a weakness common among thieves in all professions, and therefore it ought not to be marvelled at in this instance. My discrimination does credit to my judgment; yet how infinitely inferior was Manfreda, the bandit, to Quirorga, the staid, the quiet, but the deadly firm pirate. No compliments, no entreaties, no prayers, no promises would have induced that undaunted character to have entrusted a prisoner with his liberty when he thought it his interest to number him with the dead; but Quirorga was a hero at all points, he was always for letting the law take its course, and he was the Draco that made the law. By all the apostles and a host of saints was I now sworn on the captain's sword to fulfil prescribed conditions, and I was made kiss the formidable weapon with infinitely more ceremony than in many law courts the bible is kissed by those who give testimony touching the lives and properties of others. This done, Manfreda threatened me with dreadful threats of vengeance should I betray his confidence, and giving me many cautions regarding my conduct, dismissed me, saying that, as Daniel did from the lion's den, I might now depart peacefully on my journey.

Of the dwarf, who was away at this time, I saw no more; but Carl, by his chieftain's order, conducted me out of the forest in which the ancient building, this haunt of the robbers, was situated; and he also escorted me across some vineyards, till having arrived at the main causeway road, and pointed out the way I was to go, he cautioned me above all things to keep a still tongue in my head, and faithfully perform everything I had engaged to do, when wishing me success in the world, he turned away to bend his steps towards the forest. I was weak from recent loss of blood, and the walk had fatigued me; therefore, when Carl had got out of sight, I sat me down by the road-side to rest and recruit myself. "Well," said I, soliloquising, "all things considered, I have not done so bad. I have so far come the buccaneer over the banditti as to make them believe me a poor wretch, destitute of resources. The fools, the dolts; they ought every man of them to be shot for his stupidity. What an ass they must take me for to think the trivial booty they have had was my whole possession. With half-a-dozen brave fellows, such as were the blacks and mulattoes, my shipmates, I would undertake to break up the entire gang; but avast, I am making sail without carrying ballast; business must be done, and I have something else to do besides castle-building."

While I was engaged soliloquising, several country people passed near where I sat, but my strange habiliments caused them no surprise, which I account for by the well-known fact, that in Italy the priests have long made such rare mountebanks of themselves, and such extreme dupes of the people, that the professed charlatans have no chance of rivalling them.

When my soliloquy was over, I got up and jogged along the road, till after a time I was overtaken by a Jew pedlar, whose conduct afforded proof that adversity banishes flattery, for he thus unceremoniously entered into conversation. "Young man," said he, "may I make bold to ask if you are going to the carnival at Rome, for scaramouches and clowns, to my sure knowledge, will be in great request there."

A man like me, who cared not whether he was mistaken for a king, a scaramouch, or for any other character, but knew that men are much the same in propensities, no matter what their garb, or how varied their titles, would be an idiot to have deemed the Jew's speech uncourteous, and I replied with good humour equal to his own, saying that a man's face might be looked at to see what his features were; or his conversation listened to, to glean from his allusions among whom he lived; but that dress afforded no criterion to go by, as actors and impostors suited their clothes to the part they had to play."

"Exactly so," rejoined the Israelite. "This it is makes me believe you to be no other than a scaramouch."

I could not refrain laughing at the opinion which the Jew had formed of me from my dress. "By Saint Judas," said I, "it is well for you that I am not a proud Spaniard, a hot Welchman, or a quarrelsome Irishman, or I might teach you a way of dancing without music for having presumed to call me a scaramouch."

The Israelite either was, or affected to be, surprised at Judas having got himself canonized, and looking archly at me he inquired if it were Judas Iscariot that I meant; for if so, it must have been the doing of Pope Sixtus, who was elected to the papal chair because he was weak in intellect. "The saints," answered I, "served old companions of mine to swear by, but whether they kept a roster of them, or knew anything of their surnames, are questions I never asked."

"And who are these companions of yours? Were they merry-Andrews and actors?" asked he, with apparent carelessness.

"I am not at confession, signor pork-hater," said I, "therefore what you glean from my allusions is all you shall get from me."

"Pork-hater," muttered my companion, as he walked along, and then, after whistling for a time, he told me as a secret, that a terrible set of banditti frequented the neighbourhood, who once robbed and detained him prisoner for a time, when having given this information, he asked me whether I had ever fallen in with them.

The son of Diana Winpenny was too wary to make a stranger Jew his confidant, therefore he professed ignorance of this banditti, and asked some idle questions concerning them, to which the Hebrew laughingly replied that I need be under no apprehension for my safety, as no robbers would think of molesting a gentleman of my appearance. "But probably," added he, casting a significant glance at my raiment, "the police of the city you are going to may not be quite so complaisant."

After this my Hebrew companion treated me to wine and cakes, and a cabaret on the roadside, and rather perseveringly sifted me for information regarding myself; but I was cautious and said nothing, save what was foreign to the truth; when, after especially recommending me to put up at a certain lodging-house of which he named the landlord, and saying his own name was Suza, and that he should shortly pay me a visit, he bid me adieu at a branch road we came to, and turned away, saying he had business to transact at a neighbouring village.

It was dusk when I entered the eternal city, but though a stranger, with only a small trifle of money in my pocket, I deemed it best not to make use of the Jew's name by going to the lodging-house of his recommending; therefore, being faint and weary, I came to a halt at the first cabaret in my way. Here the widow woman, my landlady, apparently was much of the same opinion regarding my profession as the Jew had expressed himself to be; but although scaramouches might serve to amuse her by their exploits on the stage, she certainly did not approve of such people as inmates of her house; or, at least, until she had ascertained they possessed the means of discharging their reckoning; of which delicate sensibility towards her own interests the lady gave me so many intelligible hints before she thought proper to parade anything in the eating way, that at last, to satisfy her scruple and thereby gratify my appetite, I found it necessary to let her see the pieces of money with which Jacobus had furnished me.

The sight of my coins produced a magical effect on my hostess. She was now troublesomely affable and kind, and cheerfully ransacked her larder to gratify my palate, and this I did extremely to my satisfaction; when, as a suitable accompaniment to a hearty meal, I enjoyed a bottle of the wine of Italy, and then retired to the comforts of a bed, which though a bad one contrasted with my late miserable couch, was to me a bed of down.

After an excellent night's repose, and being further refreshed with a cup of coffee in the morning, I proceeded to the post-office; where fortunately, when at Bologna, I had ordered my banker to send me a letter of credit on his correspondent in Rome, and I had now the satisfaction of finding this letter awaited me. But the step I had taken was a prudent one, inasmuch as great gangs of banditti swarmed throughout the neighbouring parts of Italy, and kept up so good an understanding with couriers and even innkeepers on the roads, that many of the wealthiest travellers got pillaged by them, and not unfrequently an unfortunate gentleman was murdered, especially when resistance was offered against the attack of these formidable outlaws. In addition to the foregoing precaution, I had dispatched my heavy luggage for this capital by the common *roulage* of the country, and the banker now informed me of its having arrived, and also that Monday was in Rome, quite well, but most anxious for my fate. Having obtained my secretary's address, I hastened away to find him, and truly rejoiced was he to see me, whom he feared to be among those only that have been. According to his account, he quitted not the field of warfare until my valet and I were both lying, as he believed, dead; when considering valour unavailing, he jumped upon the fallen bandit's horse, and galloped away from Manfreda's gang, happily to reach Rome in safety.

Betimes next morning I proceeded to find the residence of Signor Ambrose. This tavern-keeper was well known, otherwise, from the vagueness of the direction given me and the many markets here, I might have been puzzled to find his house. Boniface was standing at his street door when I made my appearance, and to him I addressed my inquiries concerning himself. He was a remarkable man to behold; among other peculiarities, having a vast protuberance of body, supported on spindle shanks, and his nose was the very counterpart of that of Falstaff's friend, Bardolph. The landlord looked archly at me for some seconds, when relaxing his features into a submissive smile, he said he had the honour of being the individual I sought after, and my most obedient humble servant to boot. There was an indescribable something in the man's appearance and manner, of a nature to provoke laughter even in the gravest person; I, however, checked my rising inclination to indulge in this passion, while in a half whisper I communicated to Signor Ambrose all that was necessary to be known to him, and gave my card of address. The landlord started on learning who I was, till suddenly recollecting himself he gently pushed me away from a window at which we were standing, while impetuously exclaiming, " Away, signor, away, and hide thyself in thy lodging till thou seest me, for a strange event has happened, and Carl the bandit is now in my house inquiring after thee."

It was evident from the landlord's manner that I was sought after with no benevolent intention; while, on my side, I felt far from desirous of meeting with my old gaoler, Carl; therefore I readily profited by the advice given, and without wasting words in idle speech, turned my steps from Signor Ambrose's house to make the best of my way home; yet, though I hurried along at a quick pace, I kept puzzling my brains to think what could have happened to create this stir after me. " These thieves are a restless, suspicious set of rascals," thought I; " no doubt they want to touch my ransom money before the stipulated time; happily, however, there are two parties of us concerned in this bargain, and by my credit as an old buccaneer, it shall go hard with me ere I suffer myself to become their victim a second time."

I got safe home, and soon after, as I sat at my window, ruminating on what the landlord had said, I spied out, passing along the street, one of the most notorious of the old Genoa gambling fraternity; when, pleased at the opportunity for gaining a partisan, who, for pecuniary advantage, might be depended on in any desperate service, I dispatched a servant after him.

Monsieur le Baron San Lucas, for this was his high-sounding title, expressed considerable joy at our meeting, and after a little conversation, by which I discovered that the jade fortune had of late treated the noble baron most scurvily, I prevailed on him to stay dinner with me; when, at our meal, he made known that the bigamist and several more of our Genoa gaming society were at this time in Rome. After passing a few hours with me and borrowing a few pieces from my purse, the noble baron took his leave for the night, and soon after midnight, when I had retired to my bed, who should enter my chamber but honest Jacobus. I was so much surprised at seeing the dwarf, that I shut and re-opened my eyes to be satisfied of the correctness of my vision; and when the servant who introduced him had withdrawn, and Jacobus closed the door after him, he thus addressed me :—" You seem to be much at your ease here, signor, wallowing away the night in a bed of down, and no doubt you find it more agreeable than a cow-hide couch, such as we accommodated you with in the old castle; but fortune is apt to smile, when she has tried our patience with her frowns."

" My good friend," exclaimed I, interrupting the dwarf, " what in the name of heaven has brought you here? How is it you have contrived to quit the gang of bandits? Have you fled from them, or are you employed here on some service of theirs?"

"Softly," rejoined he, "speak softly, signor, for doors are no security against the passage of aerial spirits and human sounds; while who knows what inquisitive people may be near?"

I felt the force of Jacobus's remark, and in half whisper requested of him to seat himself on my bed, and in a low voice tell me his tale. He seated himself accordingly, and communicated the circumstance of the bandits having captured and imprisoned a noble count and his beautiful daughter, whom, he said, it would be a glorious action to get extricated from their power, as Manfreda had taken a liking to the young lady, who, but for some friendly assistance, never would get spotless from where he held sway.

"Well," said I, "how happens it that you, one of the robbers, should be so deeply interested for this unfortunate fair one?"—"I am their ambassador," rejoined he, smiling; "the count, her father, offers an immense sum as ransom money, if I find brave men to liberate him and his beloved child."

In addition to this, the dwarf gave me to understand that Manfreda had become suspicious of me, and sundry schemes had been laid for trying the sincerity of my promises to the bandits; one of which was that of habiting a man of theirs in the garb of a Jew, and employing him to travel with me, who was to blow out my brains if, on sifting me, he discovered treachery towards them. Happily, however, he remarked, by my courteous discourse I had escaped this great snare, and by not going to the inn which this person recommended, fortunately got housed where my enemies had not as yet succeeded in tracing me out, although Carl was now in Rome for that purpose.

I thanked the good dwarf for the friendly service he had rendered, and assured him it should not be my fault if he ever had cause to repent of trusting to my honour and gratitude; and I inquired whether Ambrose was a man with whom a knowledge of my place and abode was likely to be attended with danger. In reply, the dwarf informed me that Ambrose had married a cousin of his, and was in every respect to be relied upon; nevertheless, on taking leave, he added that benefits raise esteem, and it would be advisable for me to lose no time in making him a present, as, in all likelihood, services of his might be turned to a good account.

Baron San Lucas by appointment came to breakfast with me, when he appeared somewhat dispirited, which I justly attributed to his having gamed away overnight the money which he borrowed from me. But I kept him with me the whole day, the better to discuss matters, and secured a bed at my hotel for him that he might be at hand to proceed to business, should anything arise from Jacobus's next visit to require his immediate services. When the hour of midnight approached, my companion proceeded to his chamber, while in mine I awaited the dwarf's arrival, and he came punctual to his time, but to my surprise, disguised in female attire, which trailed upon the floor, serving to hide his club foot.

"We are environed by enemies, otherwise I should not visit you in this feminine garb," said Jacobus, after having fastened the door; "howsoever," added he, smiling, "where to effect good is the object, surely there can be no great stigma attached to the assumption of a disguise."—"My worthy friend," replied I, "you have assumed the dress of an angel, but what is of infinite importance, you are acting the part of a guardian angel towards me."

Jacobus now smilingly observed that it would be well for mankind if all that wore petticoats partook of the angelic character, as then the world would be a scene of infinite more harmony than it was. We now entered upon the subject nearest Jacobus's heart, and I avowed my readiness to undertake, if feasible means could be devised for accomplishing so desired an object, the liberation of the count and his daughter, even though at great personal peril.

The dwarf signified his approbation of my resolution, telling me he expected no less from a cavalier of my courageous character, and inquired how many associates I could muster, of assured fidelity, resolution, activity, and strength. Having satisfied his inquiries, and afterwards perceiving him somewhat meditative and, as I thought, undecided, the idea struck me that he might deem our means inadequate to the proposed end; wherefore I questioned him to know whether it would be advisable to apply to the public authorities of the city, to obtain their sanction and assistance to destroy Manfreda's band.

The dwarf laughed at the question, and told me I should never have dreamt of the suggestion I had made, if I knew anything of the nature of the magistracy or the police of

Rome, the leading personages amongst whom, he said, were more or less the pensioners of Manfreda, who bribed them in proportion to his booty; and Jacobus gave me to understand, that should I lay a statement of projected plans against the banditti before the magistrates here, the consequences would be their being made acquainted with the same, and my assassination. The dwarf further stated that he had been sent for by his captain, and should leave Rome at an early hour of the morning to rejoin the banditti; while that, as Carl, from the accidental circumstance of my not having engaged a lodging myself, but gone to that of a friend, had not succeeded in discovering me; in all probability he would be recalled in the course of a day or two. Meanwhile he cautioned me to keep myself close hid up and get my partisans ready, armed with good pistols and swords, so that on hearing from him, which I might expect to do in a few days, by the post of the country, which he deemed the safest conveyance, I and my party should be prepared to start on our bold enterprise, in whatever way he might point out in his letter.

I was somewhat surprised at the dwarf's no longer availing himself of the services of his kinsman, to whom, in compliance with his hint, I had transmitted a pecuniary token of my friendship, and I now asked whether he was dubious of the landlord's fidelity. Jacobus, however, thoroughly satisfied my mind on this head, by answering that he had no grounds of suspicion, but prudence whispered him not to place unnecessary confidence in man or woman. The more effectually to guard against any mistake in the execution of our enterprise, I now brought Baron San Lucas into my chamber and introduced him to Jacobus, when an explanation of everything requisite to be done was entered into; and as I, according to the custom of royal personages and notorious sharpers, when on their travels *incognito*, had taken the precaution of assuming another's name on coming here, it was arranged that my letter of guidance should be addressed to me by this my *nom de guerre*. At the same time, for the satisfaction of all parties, it was now agreed on that, in the event of our making a prize of any part or all the bandit's treasure, every person concerned in the enterprise, the dwarf included, should have an equal share of the spoil. Every preliminary measure having been fixed upon, Jacobus, after wishing me an agreeable, though a short imprisonment in the castle of plenty, took his departure, leaving the baron extremely astonished at the oddity of his character and strangeness of his appearance.

<hr />

CHAPTER XII.

" Rome! the city that so long
  Reign'd absolute, the mistress of the world—
Rome! the city where the Gauls
  Entered at sun.rise through her open gates,
  And through her streets silent and desolate
  Marching to stay, thought they saw gods, not men;,
  The city that by temperance, fortitude,
  And love of glory, towered above the clouds,
  Then fell."

As I could not indulge myself in walking about Rome, I occasionally went abroad in a close carriage, when I could not fail being astonished at beholding the filthiness of the eternal city, about one third of which is thinly inhabited, the remainder being used for garden grounds or retired villas. Four or five handsome streets are all this renowned city can boast of, and these, with the solitary exception of the Corso, are never cleansed, save by the wind and rain. The numerous temples, aqueducts, and. countless ruins of magnificent buildings, speak of the might and grandeur of ancient Rome; but, after all, the numerous rich churches and the superabundant number of palaces, contrasted to the poverty of the people, so strongly denote the imbecility of the papal government that I felt no surprise at the population being now diminished to one twenty-fifth of its former number. Indeed, the wonder is, how any considerable population should remain in a city, where the fundamental principle of giving people plenty to eat, that they may increase and multiply, is absolutely violated—where the governing power monopolise and tax the grain, where industry is deemed a crime—and in which the shops are shut three or four times a day for prayers in church, or the shopmen to amuse themselves in theatres.

Diabolical cunning and hypocrisy impose their heavy yoke here, and Rome is the dullest of cities except in the carnival time, when balls, horse-racing, and religious spectacles are tolerated, while to make the indulgence complete, the lottery is drawn, and so drains the pockets of the lower classes that only half the necessary quantity of bread can be procured by them. At this season the indelicacy of Italian dancing disgusts most foreigners, and the eunuchs act the part of females on the theatrical stage; but the priests beat them hollow as actors in their churches. Without an explanation being afforded him, a stranger would vainly puzzle his brains to know what certain ceremonies in established use, and termed religious, can portend. For example, at one place the pope is to be seen scattering ashes upon the heads of cardinals, bishops, and others of the clergy; at another, the decrepid father is busily at work blessing the psalms; and every year this representative of Peter, who is charged with denying Christ once in his life, but whose life of continued pride and ostentation is a constant denial of the Saviour of man, may be seen washing their feet (as touching them is called), and serving twelve priests at table. Priesthood, however, is very accommodating; as a proof of which, a venerable ecclesiastic passes a portion of his time standing at the door of St Anthony's church, where crowds of true believers in the pope's infallibility bring birds and beasts decorated with ribbons to be blessed by this reverend man, who expects no greater reward than a wax candle for preserving a bird or beast from sickness or accident during the ensuing year. Another saintly looking parson invites the passenger into a church dedicated to St Paul, to behold the miraculous crucifix, which priestly tradition tells offered its right foot to a young man to kiss. But of the Roman ceremonies the *festa de morti*, or feast of the dead, which lasts eight days, is said to be the most disgusting; at this the multitude, like an infatuated crowd flocking to see the fooleries of a coronation, got up to blindfold the ignorant, year after year, flock to chapels and charnel houses, to witness and admire the skill of sextons in decorating human bones in the form of hearts, crosses, skulls, and triangles. The Host, too, is often paraded about the streets here in grand review, in consequence of the orders issued by often a superannuated old man, charged according to some sly knaves with representing divinity and personifying infallibility, but more helpless than infancy and weaker than womanhood. On our way from a church ceremony to where my carriage was in waiting, my attention was attracted to a poor aged woman, who sat by the road-side bemoaning her misfortune, and every now and then venting curses against the Franciscan friars; when feeling curious to know what had occasioned her trouble, I presented her with a piece of silver and made the requisite inquiry. "Signor," said the ancient dame, "I thank you for the gift, which is quite a God-send, for, by St Anthony, I was without a zulio. The Franciscan friars have been the ruin of me, and may St Anthony moulder away their bones for it. They promised, if I ascended the top of their church on my bare knees, that I should be lucky in this year's lottery, and fool that I was, I believed them. With great pain and difficulty I knelt my way up the stone steps, the labour of which confined me to my bed for a whole fortnight, but the time for drawing the lottery was near, and I expected to make my fortune; therefore I sold my little property and expended the produce in the lottery; but, alas! not one number of mine has been drawn a prize. Curse the Franciscan friars, I say, and all that belongs to them. May St Anthony smite them to the very bone."

Notwithstanding my situation, I devoted one day to visiting Tivoli, which afforded me much pleasure. It is about eighteen miles from Rome, and tradition says was founded by one Tiburto Argian, nearly five hundred years before the existence of Rome; consequently, so long before Rhea gave her illegitimate twins, Romulus and Remus, to be nursed by the harlot Lupa, whose name enabled the flatterers of power to give those boys a she-wolf for their nurse, as they had previously given the god Mars for their father. Tivoli is deservedly celebrated for the purity of its air, and also for having been the place of residence of Augustus Cæsar, who, after committing more cold-blooded acts of tyranny than perhaps any other man of his years, personally administered justice here from the porticoes of the Temple of Hercules.

Rome, with all its priestly pomp and vestiges of departed grandeur, has little to recommend it to the foreigner as a place of residence, inasmuch as the air about this capital is unhealthy, and the Italians here are dirty and execrable cooks. From the time of Cicero, who boasted of the large snails he could give the friend who visited at his villa as the chief food at their supper, even to the present day, when a hedge hog and a mess of thistles are considered dainties fit for a cardinal, the people of Rome seem to have had vitiated appetites; and he who would satisfy himself that they are still behind some other countries in the art of epicurism, has only to dine at an Italian eating-house, when, should he himself be an epicure of a better school, the coarseness of the viands and the wretchedness of the cookery would most likely drive him hence with an unsatisfied stomach. The attendance at houses of this sort is even worse than the victuals. The half-famished guest may bawl *presto* fifty times, while the indolent waiter to each call answers *adesso*, without increasing his speed. Happily, however, the wines are cheap and good, and the gratification they afford makes the traveller almost forget the bad attendance, the coarseness of the victuals, and the execrable cookery. But though people are epicures in different ways, few are the Englishmen who would be content to dine on snails, hedgehogs, and thistles with an Italian, on frogs with a Frenchman, or on horseflesh with a Tartar.

Through the agency of Baron San Lucas, I busied myself in preparing things for our projected enterprise ; but as a set of needy gamblers, in their pressing difficulties, would, to raise money, pledge to the last portable article, I would not entrust them with swords and pistols, but made the baron's apartment a place of deposit for them ; while, that we might be sure of mustering our party every day, my colleague and I so arranged matters that a luncheon should be provided daily at his lodging, when a small retaining fee, and instructions what to do, should be given to each person. Here the fastidious may exclaim against a distressed fraternity of gamesters as being a despicable set, but truth and justice ought to step forward in their defence, and loudly proclaim that the fees given to barristers, the pay and perquisites of hired warriors, the salaries of statesmen, the tremendous revenues of bishops, and the pluralities of ecclesiastical gentlemen, are neither more nor less than retaining fees, without which these persons, almost to the last man of them, though numerous as large armies, would turn tail and prove false.

On inquiry, I ascertained that my friend the bigamist was in durance vile for a debt incurred in supporting little Rosa Matilda, who had now quitted him to stay with a relative of hers, a resident of the Roman capitol, as, contrary to his usual custom, but happily for her, he had not married this young lady, and she was reported to do like many other beauties, that is, study behaviour rather than virtue. Of course I paid the bigamist's debt, and engaged him in my service ; but seven days elapsed after the dwarf's last visit without my receiving any communication from him ; however, this delay was serviceable, inasmuch as it enabled me to have my associates ready, not one of whom, save the baron, knew more of what he was to be employed upon than that it would be a service of danger, likely to be rewarded with a handsome division of money, and this made the needy set burn with impatience for the moment of action.

The baron, who occasionally called at Ambrose's under the pretence of taking some refreshment, had ascertained that Carl took his departure on the second day after Jacobus's last visit, and, in consequence, he and I began to think the dwarf was rather dilatory in his arrangements, and that the delay boded no good ; indeed the baron's mind grew restless on the subject, and he would sometimes utter language like the following :—" Signor Winpenny, that odd-looking, strange-mannered, hermaphrodite sort of a character of your acquaintance, who has put us to the trouble of preparing for a service of knight-errantry, I fear repents him of the engagement he has made, and, moreover, what is worse, that he may add treason to cowardice, and bring an infinity of trouble upon us."

Fear has many eyes, and the noble baron's apprehensions proved ill-grounded. On the ninth day after his departure, the post brought me an explicit letter from the faithful little fellow. In it he directed me to assemble my party at Terni, a town a few leagues from Rome, and convenient to the robbers' haunts, by a given hour on the ensuing day, and pointed out how we should proceed there singly by public vehicles or other accommodation that might offer, each to be habited in a large cloak over a peasant's dress, and have our weapons carefully hidden from sight. At Terni, to avert suspicion, we were to divide ourselves at four wine-houses, which were named, and, at a given hour after nightfall, proceed, one or two at a time, and warily, to hide ourselves as one party in a vineyard to the rear of a chapel on the road-side, and at this place remain in close ambush until Jacobus made his appearance among us.

The dwarf's letter infused spirits into the baron. It inspired him with confidence, inasmuch as it held out a good prospect of success, and, to use his words, brought the odds on our side. He now busied him procuring the requisite clothing to disguise the party in, and preparing matters so as to insure the attendance of as many of our fraternity as possible; yet, notwithstanding his endeavours to prevent absenteeism, when we assembled next night at Terni, it was found that two out of the number who had pocketed retaining fees were truants, which the baron accounted for in the technical language of a gamester, saying, they had contrived to get into feather, and thus found employment at the gaming-table.

Our party consisted of five, in addition to me, the baron, and Monday; but the associates of my secretary and myself were every man of them needy and disappointed, in the vigour of manhood, and whom poverty had rendered ready for the performance of desperate deeds; in a word, they all bore the ordinary stamp of heroes, their lives having been one tissue of crime. To exemplify this, one gentleman, an Englishman, had been a stock-broker, who, by means of forged warrants of attorney, got possession of considerable wealth, with which, and his wife's niece as his travelling bride, he emigrated, but lost the money at a gaming-table, and the damsel by pandering her to a brother leg. Another, a ci-devant banker's clerk, had once nearly got his neck in the noose of an executioner for putting a customer's name to a money cheque paid to himself. A third was my old friend the bigamist, of whom, at present, I need say no more. Our fourth hero had been a methodist parson, and also a lawyer, but an incurable propensity to the bottle, backed by an itch for throwing the dice, had occasioned him the loss of his business in both professions, and driven him to be an adventurer on the great community. The fifth enlisted in my cause had been a soldier, as, by the bye, were all the others at the lowest ebb of their fortunes, save only the clerk, who served as a sailor. But this fifth gentleman was a Frenchman, named Dashembeau, and a most formidable character. In addition to his martial exploits on the great licensed theatre of war, he had killed several persons in duels, and wounded at least half a score more. As to Baron San Lucas, who completed the number of my partisans, I shall say no more than that he was a man of undaunted courage; but who, like a truly brave character, evinced it not, except on occasions of necessity; while as to honesty, he possessed just sufficient to disguise his want of that unfashionable article.

The dwarf's instructions were so clear and correct that we had no difficulty in finding the proper place for laying in ambush, and the eight of us, enveloped in dark mantles, which we muffled up to our chins, and with broad-brimmed hats slouched over our brows, assembled there in safety; as we believed, without having caused suspicions to arise regarding us either among the people at Terni or elsewhere. We now took the precaution of charging our fire-arms and preparing ourselves for combat, when, after waiting his arrival with anxiety for upwards of an hour, Jacobus made his appearance among us.

"You are punctual to time and place, signor," said he to me in a half whisper, "but tell me, how many of you do you muster altogether?"

"Eight," was my reply.

"Umph," muttered the dwarf, then after pausing a little, he said, "I trusted you would have been two or three more of you, and 'twould be all the better provided you had as many, for ten or a dozen may be the number of our foes. Say, however, can you depend on your friends? are they men capable of screwing their courage up to a fit pitch for the occasion? as otherwise, there is still time to abandon the enterprise."

"Friend," said I, interrupting the speaker, "lead us at once to the scene of action; but never doubt our courage. Were the robbers twice the number they are, we stand prepared for them."

Jacobus now conducted us some distance through woods, vineyards, and over ploughed land, until having arrived near a dilapidated building, the former place of my captivity, he left us hid in a ravine, while he went forward to ascertain how many of the bandits were at home.

The dwarf had been away upwards of a quarter of an hour, which, however, appeared considerably longer to us, who were on the qui vive the whole time, and in great suspense, when, to our extreme annoyance, a dog belonging to the robbers scented us out, and unceasingly kept on barking. We wished this guardian of the night far away, and strove to entice him to us, or frighten him away, but our efforts served only to make the animal more outrageous in his noise; at length, however, Jacobus was heard calling to the faithful beast, and doubtless he took him to some remote place, for we heard no more of his noise.

About an hour after this the dwarf paid us a short visit, when he must have quitted the chateau in an opposite direction to where we lay hid, for he came by a circuitous path, leading to the back of the ravine, or part the most remote from our foe. "The tug of war will soon take place," said he, in a half whisper, "for the banditti may shortly be expected home; but let who will come, and no matter what noises you may hear, mind and stir not a yard any one of you, nor make the smallest noise, but wait patiently until I return here and explain to you how to act."—"We entirely rely on you, Jacobus, and shall attempt nothing without your aid," said I; "only recollect we are not men to be satisfied with slight advantages. We require all the booty the robbers possess, and are willing to use brave efforts to win it."—"Le diable, le diable, lui meme, should not keep us from taking their booty, much less shall a set of thieves," muttered Dashembeau.—"A man can die but once," said the banker's clerk, "and he may as well be killed as hung for trying to secure to himself the needful."—"You have all of you work enough before you," rejoined the dwarf; "the tug of war may be fiercer than you expect. You have brave men to deal with, I can assure you."—"We are prepared for the worst;" but tell me, Jacobus, who are now at home with you, and how many do you expect to arrive?" were my observation and questions.—"Carl and two more are at home, to guard the place and prisoners, while Manfreda and the lieutenant are momentarily looked for, with seven men who went abroad yesternight under their orders."—"And how fares it with the prisoners?"—"Badly, in my mind, as well can be. The count and his man are living on hard fare, expecting to be put to death, and their prison is the place you occupied when first brought here. The young lady and her maid are suffering inconceivable terror from the threats held out to them, and are in the chamber you were last confined in."—"Well, my friend," said I, "provided we are victorious, these poor sufferers will get released from their prison and their fears."—"Good heavens!" exclaimed the bigamist, "I am already in love with the count's daughter: I would go through fire and water for her."—"I can stay no longer," now observed Jacobus, "I have cautioned you enough; do as I have bidden you in all things, and heaven prosper our cause."—"The fellow's off," muttered the impatient Frenchman. "Zounds! does he mean to keep us here cooling our heels the whole night?"—"Silence, Dashembeau; what distant noise is that we hear?" asked the baron. At this observation silence reigned among us. Not a stir; no, not even a breath was heard in the party; but we listened with undivided attention, and soon satisfied ourselves that the noise was occasioned by horsemen approaching. They came at a rapid rate, and speedily passed along the road near the place of our concealment, when, as they drew their horses in, we distinctly heard several of their voices, one of which I knew to be that of their captain. Two men bearing flambeaus came out of the chateau to greet the party's arrival, when they all dismounted, and several proceeded to the stable with the horses, the rest entering the old mansion, their dwelling place. "By my soul," ejaculated the impatient Dashembeau, after the robbers had been some time housed, "I long to be at the fellows. What can keep the lame imp from giving us the signal to commence operations?"—"I have said grace, and am now ready to play my part at feasting or fighting," remarked my partisan, the ci-devant parson. "All my fear is, that their wine will be drunk before the dwarf calls upon us to execute justice on the outlaws."—"Let the fickle dame give me a rich booty on this occasion, and no gaming-table shall strip me of it," observed the run-away stockbroker.—"'Tis a far safer game to kill men for their money, than sign their names to certain papers to get at it," said the old clerk.—"By Saint Benedict, but this may prove a famous adventure, for loveliness and wealth are the prizes we have in view," observed the bigamist.—"I trust we shall make a good cruise of it, and come the buccaneer over the bandits, so as to unship the specie from their castle's hold, and carry it off with us for ballast," said Monday.

"'Tis a philanthropic undertaking, this of ours. If successful, we shall do the world a great piece of service. For the sake of honesty and justice, I wish we were well through the business," observed Baron San Lucas.

It has been said that a man's pursuits and propensities may be known by the observations he makes, and assuredly the foregoing are emblematic of the several characters of my partisans. These gentlemen, however, in the fervour of their anxiety to proceed to the business of gain, whispered many other remarks to each other, which were equally expressive of their sentiments as those I have related, conceiving them sufficient to support the sceptic's assertion that "man does everything by custom;" nor is established custom easily broken, but it needs some great event to shake the system of things, so that life may seem to recommence upon fresh principles.

Our patience was put to the proof. We were kept waiting upwards of two hours in the damp ravine after the captain's arrival at home with his bandits, five in number, during which time our ears were frequently saluted by boisterous shouts of merriment, issuing from the bacchanals regaling themselves. However, at length, when bursts of hilarity no longer reached us, and we had concluded that the carousing party must have retired to the sweets of repose, Jacobus once more made his appearance amongst us. A new day was now beginning to dawn, and I could see the little fellow shook with fear when he approached me, but taking hold of my arm and bidding my friends to follow behind us, he led me along a little distance ; then pointing out to me the main entrance door of the old chapel, he said, " That is the door, within side which most of the banditti are lying down, but unknown to them I have unbolted and unlocked it, therefore approach silently and rush into the chapel with your party, where you will do well to bind with cords all the foes who may survive the dread fight. Meanwhile depend on me to follow, to give you further advice, when this great work of vengeance has been achieved."

" Enough, my cautious friend," replied I, " I feel it would be improvident in you to appear among the thieves until our first brush is over ; but be sure not to be out of the way when I call for you."—" They would slay me," said the dwarf, " I should have no chance for my life, if they found me acting in collusion with you in the fight ; but depend on me, signor, for appearing in fit time."

Having spoken thus, my little conductor instinctively retrograded. Meanwhile I advanced, followed by my armed partisans, and almost instantly commenced on the task of forcing open the chapel door ; but unfortunately, one of the bandits had laid himself down to take his repose against it, and this unexpected impediment not only occasioned us delay in entering the chapel, but also served to alarm some of the banditti. " To arms, to arms ! we are surprised. Where is Captain Manfreda ?" cried out the fellow lying against the door, when he found it on the move, and instantly two or three of his comrades came to his assistance.—" Push, push away, my friends—we must force the door, or we shall get the worst of it," I now exclaimed, straining every nerve of my body to effect this desired object. " Push heartily, my backers ; force the door off its hinges, or, by heavens, the odds will turn against us," vociferated the baron. "Diable, foutre, stand aside of the hinges," bawled the Frenchman, while with a huge stone he broke the door away from its bottom hinge. This feat accomplished, it was scarcely the work of a minute with us to force our way into the chapel, when the bandits near the door made a hasty retreat, and some others who had been laying in differerent places, apparently stupified with liquor, followed their flying comrades' example. However, ere we assailants had well breathed ourselves, Manfreda's gruff voice was heard, cheering his men to the scene of warfare, and almost instantly he and Carl entered the chapel by way of a door at the remotest part from us. " Blood and fury," roared the chief, on beholding the scene before him, " we are betrayed !—By St Paul, the murderer of James and Stephen, I will have revenge. Who is yon big fellow I see ? Hell and the devil, it is the buccaneer. Dastards, cowards, as ye are, why do you stand sculking there ?" Then added he, on seeing several of his party sheltered behind a partition, " But come on, resume your courage, and we will exterminate yon traitor and his party."

" Villain," he now bawled to me in the voice of a Stentor, at the same time advancing at the head of a few men, and brandishing his huge sabre, " stand or fly, it matters not to me, for by St Dominique I'll send your soul unwashed to eternity."—" Take that, you braggart," said I, firing my pistol at his head ; but somehow fate baulked my vindictive intention, for the ball merely grazed his cheek.

" Is it so ?" said he. " Now by St Bartholomew I swear to see your skin stripped from your carcase ; dead or alive you shall be flead ;" and almost at the instant of speaking he dealt so tremendous a blow that, had I not vaulted a little on one side, my head must infallibly have been cleaved in twain. " Surely it must have been the spirit of my mother which saved me," thought I, and before Manfreda could reflourish his tremendous weapon, my sword's point had passed through his huge body. The fall of their leader struck a panic into the rest of his party, and sauve qui peu seemed to be the understood motto of every man of them, for they turned about and fled with the speed of so many Mercurys. Quick, however, as they were, Monsieur Dashembeau contrived to overtake their lieutenant in his flight, when he stopped his further progress by a sabre cut, which, though not a severe one, made him glad to accept of mercy and become a prisoner. Two others of the panic-struck fugitives also failed in accomplishing their wished for object, but these owed their misfortune to pistol bullets, which left them no alternative but to surrender themselves.

CHAPTER XIII.

" In vain her tongue would have expressed
The feelings thronging in her breast:
Her wilder'd judgment—doubt—belief—
Unlook'd for hope ! her words were brief."

" Beshrew my soul,
But I do love the favour and the form
Of this most fair occasion."

THE victory we had gained may be termed a glorious one, inasmuch as we conquered superior numbers; our party consisting of eight, while that of the banditti was nine, for Manfreda it appeared had detached three of his men on other duties, and consequently returned home with only five under him, which, added to three at home, made his number; but we had taken the enemy by surprise, at a time, too, when most of them had indulged freely in the bottle; therefore our conquest is the less to be wondered at.

Five of the bandits had escaped, and the four whom we retained in captivity were all wounded, but none desperately save the captain. However, recollecting the dwarf's advice, we now bound the prisoners with cords, which were laying in the chapel.

Though no one on either side was killed in the fight, yet besides four of the enemy, three of the inmates here suffered from wounds who belonged to my party, and I was one of them, having received a cut from a sabre on my left shoulder and had my cheek grazed by a bullet, which carried away some flesh and a portion of the whiskers. Baron San Lucas was another sufferer from the steel of our foe, and his was an unlucky wound for a gentleman of his profession, inasmuch as the sabre which dealt it to him cut off his thumb and two adjoining fingers. The ci-devant stock broker was the third victim to the horrors of war; and his wounds were three, one of them so severe that I once apprehended we should have to bury him on the site of his glory. Fortune, however, blind as she is said to be, behaved herself with propriety on this occasion, for the banker's clerk, the French soldier, Monday, and the Methodist parson, who all escaped unhurt, are men who had been exposed to great perils in their several callings, and therefore merited some favour at her hands: while her having spared my friend the bigamist, shows she must have been actuated by a spirit of justice, as he, from his lawless engagements, may naturally be supposed to have had his feelings, if not his body, often lacerated.

When we had effected the business of binding the prisoners, I involuntarily stood musing for a time upon the scene before me, but the groans and appeals of the sufferers for assistance soon roused me out of my reverie, when, aided by my unscarred friends, I set to work in affording them what aid I could; this, however, was but trivial, as we possessed nothing fit for dressing wounds, while, to my surprise, Jacobus, who alone could procure what was requisite for this purpose, had not yet made his appearance among us.

"What has become of the dwarf? Why does he keep in the background at a moment like this?" eagerly inquired the impetuous Dashembeau.—"Confound the urchin; I wish he was here to do something to my hand," exclaimed the baron.—"By Heavens! Oh, by Heavens, my account will soon be closed; I have a heavy settling day before me. I shall bleed to death for the want of assistance," vociferated the terrified stockbroker.

These, and many more plaints of a similar nature, reverberated in my ears, till, like the complaining sufferers of my party, I ardently longed for the dwarf to make his appearance; when presently, on hearing a stir at the opposite extremity of the chapel, I turned my head, and was gratified by the sight of Jacobus, cautiously entering with a drawn sword in one hand and a pistol in the other. "My friend," said I, "we have all been anxiously looking for you; your services will now be inestimable, to dress and staunch the bleeding of our wounds; but say, why do you come thus armed? Are we to infer from your appearance that the tug of war is not yet over, but that more foes remain for us to face?"—"Heaven defend us," replied he, "more foes indeed! no, no, signor, you have settled the whole band; still it will not be wise to linger here, as the fugitives may, perhaps, return with bandits of other parties to help them."

" My good friend," rejoined I, " lay aside your weapons of strife, and be as expeditious as possible in performing the duties of a surgeon by dressing our wounds and assuaging our sufferings."

Without uttering another word Jacobus now put away his warlike weapons, and with a key taken from his pocket opened an old chest, that served as a window-seat, from which he took some surgical instruments, together with lint and torn pieces of linen; which done, he commenced dressing the wounds of my party, and at my desire, Baron San Lucas's case was the first attended to; after which the wounds of our *ci-devant* stockbroker were dressed and pronounced of an alarming character; as to mine, they were found to be slight. Having performed the leech's business to the wounded of my party, the dwarf was called on to do the same to the suffering set amongst his old comrades, and this to him was a most onerous office. Captain Manfreda, though desperately wounded, peremptorily refused to have his wound examined, while such were the terrific looks he cast at the dwarf, that Jacobus was scared by them, and dared not approach near him. The little fellow was accustomed to behold his commander with awe, and this was now augmented by some dread imprecations of the dying man, which, coupled as they were by invocations to different saints, whose names Jacobus held most sacred, had the greater effect in filling him with consternation.

But although Manfreda remained undaunted at the prospect of death, and obstinately refused proffered assistance, this was far from being the case with the lieutenant and others who were wounded, for they gladly availed themselves of Jacobus's services, who dressed and bandaged their wounds.

" Jacobus," said I in his ear, soon as he had got through his business of surgeon, " my good friend, much remains for us to accomplish yet; before we proceed to the work of pillage, the more noble service of chivalry shall be performed. Lead me, therefore, at once to the prison rooms of the count and his daughter, of whom you were speaking previous to our attack of the banditti."

The dwarf smiled, and saying, " Safe bind, safe find," was a wholesome motto, called upon the effective members of my party to assist in conveying the bandits to different lock-up cells, bound as they were with cords—a piece of service we did for every man of them, except Manfreda, whose desperate condition, combined with the dwarf's fears of him, induced us to let him remain where he was. This being done, the dwarf re-armed himself with his sword and pistol, and followed by me and Dashembeau, led the way, which I, when a captive here, had traversed, through the stable and court-yard to the ruined chateau. This scene forcibly reminded me of my so recent imprisonment here; and the dwarf having unbolted the door of an inner room, which Manfreda, in his haste to depart hence on hearing the noise of fire-arms of our attack in the chapel, had neglected to lock, I beheld the count's lovely daughter and her maid, who, both in great terror, had retired to the far end of the apartment.

" Signora," said Jacobus, bowing respectfully to the young lady, and pointing to me, " dry up your tears and banish your alarm, for, thanks to the blessed Virgin and this young Englishman, whose powerful arm has brought Manfreda to the verge of death, freedom and happiness again await you."

The news was too great and too unexpected to be comprehended by the terrified maiden. " Where is the dreadful robber?" she exclaimingly asked, with a wildness of manner bordering on distraction. " Is he coming here again? Will no courageous person protect me from the arch villain? is there no champion for a defenceless maid's honour? Where, O where is my father? Does he live? Is my dear parent still living?"

" You are free, young lady—you are safe," rejoined the dwarf; " Captain Manfreda is wounded so severely that I believe he must die, and his band are all scattered or in captivity. To this gallant Englishman and a few of his friends do you owe your honour and your freedom. Your father, too, is on the eve of being freed, and I will conduct you to him."

" Is this a dream, an illusive dream? surely it can be no other," said the doubting, terrified maid. " Are ye not the partisans of the robber chief? Have you not come here to deceive me? What am I to credit? How can I believe your tale, when the wretch himself was so recently with me? when he was here breathing terrible threats against my honour, and prepared to resort to violence to execute his diabolical purpose."

" Mademoiselle," said I, " calm your fears—tranquillize your gentle heart, and let god-like reason be the inmate of your bosom, for we have come here not to deceive you, but as the messengers of good tidings. Manfreda and his band are conquered. Justice has compassionated your sufferings, and extended her arm to punish the robbers in good time for your preservation. Come, young lady, accompany us, that you may be present at the liberation of the count, your father."

The fair damsel looked at me with astonishment, blended with curiosity, but reason was now fast dissipating her terrors, and clasping her hands together in the attitude of prayer, she exclaimed that heaven was just, and had listened to her supplications : then, addressing me, she said, " Signor, you have not the appearance of a bad man and a robber. I believe all that you tell me, and am ready to accompany you to the prison of my poor parent, where, provided you have told me true, my heart will experience the felicity of beholding him restored to the blessing of liberty."

" My present task is a most delectable one, fair lady," replied I, tendering her my arm. " Lead, Jacobus, lead the way to the count's prison, that we may restore him to freedom and the arms of an affectionate daughter."

The young lady's apprehensions regarding me were apparently now set at rest, for unhesitatingly she took my proffered arm, and we followed behind the dwarf to the miserable dungeon which had served as my place of incarceration on the first night of my captivity among the banditti. Our conductor now unbarred the door of this place, which, fortunately, had not been left locked, and on opening it we beheld the count, who was an elderly, silver-headed gentleman, and also his servant, stretched on dirty straw, in one corner of the dismal dungeon, with no other covering over their garments than a torn horse-cloth, which I recognized as that which had protected me from a portion of the dampness of the horrid cell.

The nobleman was startled by the noise we made in opening his door, yet believing us to be a party of the bandit's, and not dreaming of any relief being near, he averted his eyes from us, while exclaiming, " Why do you come here again to torment ? I am ready to suffer death ; but never, never will I purchase life and liberty by consenting to the sacrifice of my child. Give her, indeed, to the embrace of a robber ! no, never ; she has lived virtuous as an angel, and, if Providence so wills it, she must die the death of an innocent martyr, for guilt she shall never stoop to."

" My father, my beloved father !" franticly exclaimed the fair maiden, rushing to her parent and embracing him, as he sat upright on the damp straw of his bed, " give your fears to the wind ; for, heaven be praised, we are free. This brave gentleman and his friends, it appears, have overcome the banditti, and made most of them prisoners. Rise, therefore, rise, and let us fly far away from this detested place."

The noble count was now almost as incredulous as his fair daughter had recently been, yet her presence went far to satisfy him that fortune again smiled upon them. He returned her embrace with warm parental delight, and concisely, but gratefully, expressed his thanks to divine Providence for this unlooked for happy change in their affairs ; after which he rose from his miserable bed, and turning to me, with an expression of complaisance, intermixed with doubt, asked if he might confide in the evidence of his eyes and ears by believing that his and his daughter's captivity and danger were over.

It would be easy, yet it is needless for me to relate how I satisfied the noble count's mind on these points ; but the task of explaining his astonishment on being made acquainted with the events which had taken place within the last two hours, it would be folly in me to undertake. He had heard the firing of pistols, as also had his daughter and their servants ; but this among a set of robbers was no novelty, and they attached no importance to it, but conjectured that they were discharging their fire-arms to reload them.

The delighted parent and his affectionate daughter, together with their servants, accompanied my party back to the chapel, where we found everything much in the same state as we had left it, but the sight of the wounded shocked the gentle lady and her maid. " We must go on with the business we have in hand, lest any mischance should arrive to mar our project now," said the considerate dwarf, in a whisper to me ; and immediately, of his own accord, he led the rescued prisoners to the window near which stood the ancient trunk already spoken of, and putting a couple of logs on the floor at the side of it, requested the noble and his daughter to seat themselves, and have the patience to wait until his friends and he could find leisure to attend on them.   The count and his party readily did as they were told ; however, while this was passing, the dread robber-chief, who had been lying motionless, apparently in a dying way, contrived to raise himself partially from the floor, when, resting his body on one hand, he imploringly besought the count's daughter to approach near, and, as he said, for the Virgin Mary and all the saints' sakes, bestow her pardon upon him before his fluttering soul took its flight to the regions of futurity.   The young lady shuddered at sight of her much dreaded tormentor, and a fit of trembling came over her on hearing his appeal to her compassion ; but while her mind was absorbed with doubts and hesitation at the robber-chief's address, the count, her father, who was a moral man, influenced in all his actions by the precepts of Christianity, addressed her, saying, " Antonia, my dear, this dying man has been a great sinner, and a source of grievous trouble to us both ; but a just Providence has given us the victory over him, and enabled us, almost miraculously, to escape the dread object of his machinations ; therefore, my child, we should remember that our duty as Christians commands us to forgive our enemies ; and let us practise the sweet duty of forgiveness towards this unprincipled wretch, whose soul will have to flee hence heavily burdened with crime ; yet may he not receive some consolation from his hearing the promise of pardon from the lips of one he has cruelly wronged ; yea, and moreover sought to bring to the worst possible state of misery ?"

The dutiful daughter, on hearing her parent speak thus, rose from her seat and walked towards the apparently expiring chief, until, having approached within a few paces of him, his wild, terrific looks, and person deeply stained with blood, struck her with fresh fear, insomuch that she could approach no nigher to him ; but having stopped, the fair maid, in a faltering voice, commenced an address to the hardened brute, promising him her pardon, and her prayers to heaven likewise to pardon him.

The scene attracted every one's attention, and fortunate was it that it did so, for at this critical epoch the remorseless chieftain, seeing the maid would approach no nearer to him, and being actuated by a demoniac spirit, suddenly drew forth a pistol which had been secreted beneath his vest, and uttering a horrid oath denotive of his intention to set their souls journeying together the journey of futurity, fired it at the forgiving dutiful girl ; but most providentially the relentless villain's design was defeated, for Monsieur Dashembeau, who was standing close behind the spot where he was seated, at the instant when he pulled the trigger of his pistol with a blow of his sword lowered his hand to the ground, and consequently the ball passed harmless in a direction remote from the lovely maid.

This new affair created considerable confusion, for the lady fainted, her maid affected to do so, and the count and his lackey were much alarmed on Antonia's account ; meanwhile the ruffian leader of banditti swore dreadful oaths, but Dashembeau and I seized hold of him, and despite his wounds and blasphemy carried him to a dungeon, where we left him, locked and bolted.   On returning from my task, I was extremely amused at witnessing the zeal with which my friend the bigamist bestowed his attentions upon both the females ; in short, such was his assiduity, that to judge by it, even had I not known his character before, I might well have surmised him to be that warm-hearted sort of gallant who unscrupulously would venture to get himself bound in matrimonial trammels with almost any pretty woman he could delude by his artful speech, without troubling himself to reflect upon the number of fair ones he might already be united to.

" Gallantry, signor, as you well know, is an admirable thing for amusing a gentleman at a leisure hour," said the dwarf to me, smiling, and pointing to the officious bigamist; " but," continued he, " at this time it is out of place, as pressing business remains for us to do."

" You are right, Jacobus," replied I, when, ungallant as it was, I disturbed the bigamist in his devoirs to the fair, by telling him the dwarf needed his assistance ; but as we were all much fatigued, and several of the party in a bad state from their wounds, Jacobus wisely suggested that before we attempted more business, we should refresh ourselves by food ; " for mortality," said he, " like a lamp that is kept burning, needs repeated feeding."

This wholesome advice met with general approbation, and while the rest of us seated ourselves in the best way we could, Jacobus and the bigamist visited the larder and wine-cellar, from which they expeditiously produced a good supply of bread, cold meat, and half a dozen bottles of wine, the sight of which cheered the spirits of all persons present.   My friend, the baron, who delighted in presiding at festive parties, was unable to officiate as president on this occasion; but the bigamist, seated with the fair *fille de chambre* at his side, performed the duties of this situation in so admirable and so gallant a manner, that Monsieur Dashembeau and the *ci-devant* preacher signified their thorough approbation of his promptitude in passing the wine, which proved of an excellent quality, while the count jocularly acknowledged that he had never seen a better president in the festive chair; and even Antonia, the charming Antonia, was made to smile at witnessing his gallant attentions to her sex.

CHAPTER XIV.

"The knowing and the bold
Fall in the gen'ral massacre of gold;
Wide-wasting pest! that rages unconfined,
And crowds with crimes the records of mankind;
For gold his sword the hireling ruffian draws,
For gold the hireling judge distorts the laws.
Wealth heap'd on wealth, nor truth nor safety buys;
The dangers gather as the treasures rise."

My partisans, like myself, felt too anxious to put the finishing stroke to our business to permit of our remaining longer at a feast than was absolutely necessary for refreshing ourselves; while the count and his lovely daughter, who had drunk deeply here of the cup of bitters, and whose minds were not to be freed from fearful apprehensions long as they tarried in the detested place, burnt with the fever of impatience to depart from an old castle, the place of resort of a terrific banditti, of whom they conjectured there might be many more than they had encountered.

For the foregoing reasons our breakfast was soon hurried over; but to the disappointment of our noble guests, instead of their then departing, as they expected to have done, they were requested by us to await in the chapel for a time; when, leaving them to their meditations, with the wounded *ci-devant* banker's clerk to bear them company, the remainder of us, agreeably to a summons from Jacobus, proceeded with him to search after that hidden treasure, the prospect of obtaining which had brought us on this daring enterprise.

Hitherto our eyes had not been gratified by the sight of anything of a nature to reward us for the dangers we had encountered, for the horses in their stables, and the warlike weapons upon the robbers' persons, were all the disposable property we had discovered withinside the dreary walls here; while now that my partisans found time for reflection, and consequently contemplated the subject of the bareness of the place, they, some of them, surmised they had been brought here on a Quixotic enterprise, to destroy a powerful horde of robbers at the imminent risk of their own lives, but why or wherefore, except that it might be to serve some sinister end of mine, they could not possibly conjecture. These apprehensions naturally made my fellow-combatants, who had not so much confidence in the dwarf as myself, feel most inquisitive; yet, from prudential motives, no questions of a nature to gratify this passion were asked by them long as we remained seated with the count and his family. Soon, however, as we had quitted them, every individual of us kept pretty close to Jacobus, in the expectation of hearing pleasing intelligence from his lips; but he conducted us to the stable, and with provoking obstinacy fed every one of the horses before he condescended to answer any of his questioners on the subject we had most at heart.

"We are bit, by all that's sacred, I believe we are bit!" exclaimed the *ci-devant* preacher, no longer able to contain his feelings of disappointment on seeing the dwarf employed feeding the horses, evidently in readiness to take a journey with them.—"Bit!" repeated the impatient Dashembeau. "Zounds, by my honour as a gentleman, I'll make a bullet-hole in the man's carcass for his soul to escape by, should the urchin have led us here for nothing more than his own pastime."

"Who the devil, possessing one grain of sense, would have engaged in an enterprise of this sort, unless with the prospect of love or of gain?" muttered the bigamist.

Baron San Lucas, like the rest of my companions, no doubt entertained painful apprehensions of the dwarf's probity and veracity, yet he said nothing of his suspicions, for the baron was an experienced character, nearly arrived at the rubicon of life, whom god-like reason, except in gambling transactions, governed as a good master governs a servant. Notwithstanding that Jacobus must have heard most of the preceding remarks, he, without noticing them, and with imperturbable gravity, perseveringly went on in the task he had imposed on himself, till having fed every steed in the stable, he humorously remarked to the company that substantial loads were necessary to strengthen and comfort the insides of those animals which had to be outwardly burdened by carrying unwieldly loads for the accommodation of mankind; and therefore, now that he had attended to the first essential duty required of him on this occasion, namely, that of providing for its safe carriage, he was prepared to execute the business for which we had collected together and fought so bravely, by putting us in possession of the greatly-coveted treasure. Here one general burst of satisfaction saluted the dwarf's ears, for we all supposed he purposed leading us, without more words, to the treasure. We were, however, egregiously mistaken, for the little fellow had no thoughts of putting us into possession of the robbers' hoards of wealth without previously stipulating certain conditions for himself. It is true he formerly told me that he would entirely depend on my honour and gratitude for his reward; yet now that he saw what a turbulent set of gentlemen I had concerned with me in this enterprise, he very prudently thought it incumbent on him, before we had got possession of any spoils, to ensure the consent of every individual present to his participation in the profits of our enterprise, as also our promises that he should receive an equal share of the booty with the rest of us, and that it should be distributed with the most rigid impartiality. These promises having been called for, were made and sworn to by all about him, when Jacobus conducted us into an adjoining stable, used as a store for keeping horses' forage in; and here he set himself and one or two more of the party to work, in clearing away a quantity of straw which had been deposited next the wall of the inner side of the building; which done, he swept some loose gravel from over a trap-door there, which it had served effectually to hide from view; and then, after procuring a light, drew a key from his pocket, which he said he had taken from his captain's person.

The dwarf unlocked the trap-door, which was very weighty, and I assisted him to lift it up; when he, observing that one of us would be sufficient to descend with him, to hand up the spoils, commenced his descent down a short broken ladder; and I, after telling the baron to remain with his friends where they were, and take care of what I might hand up to them, stepped upon the ladder, and followed the dwarf. The warehouse of the bandits' treasure, which I now entered, bore no other resemblance to the far-celebrated cave of Aladdin's exploits than that it was a receptacle for treasure: this was a gloomy cellar, in which, however, were a number of old chests, mostly in a mouldering condition; but, extremely to my delight, all more or less stored with plate, jewellery, specie, or other valuables. Jacobus, who wisely was bent on making the most of the present time, without wasting words in conversation, set himself seriously to work in unpacking one of the largest chests of valuables, and handing the contents to me fast as he unpacked them; while I, with zeal and good-will equal to his own, passed the same up to the baron, who stood on the tiptoe of impatient expectation at the trap-door to receive the articles thus procured for him. The office we were now engaged in was a most delectable one; but to shorten the story, it remains only to say that chest after chest was despoiled of its contents, until the gloomy cellar had nothing left in it of a nature to further tempt our avarice. We now mounted the ladder to rejoin my partisans, but just previous to our doing so, the similarity of poor Aladdin's state, when the trap-door was closed on him by the wily African, forcibly struck my imagination, and I shuddered at reflecting on what would be my miserable end, should the fraternity of gamesters above take it in their heads, for the sake of more booty for themselves, to provide for my secretary and me in the same way.

We now busied ourselves in dividing the great treasure we had taken into nine portions, as nearly equal in value as we could make them; but while we were employed in this fascinating task, the gamesters and myself were made to laugh most heartily at a sarcastic question put by Jacobus to the *ci-devant* parson, asking whether or not he now considered himself and his friends to be *bit*.

The precious metals glittering before our eyes, and on the eve of being divided between us, had the effect of putting the fraternity of gamesters into such extreme good humour, that Jacobus might have jested with any one of the party without exposing himself to the risk of giving offence, however free his jests might be; but he had other business in hand, and therefore contented himself by making a few remarks, ere, accompanied by Monsieur Dash-embeau and the gallant bigamist, he proceeded to the chapel, to bring from thence our severely wounded companion, that he might be present at the division of the booty we had made, to see justice done. Accordingly, the *ci-devant* banker's clerk was assisted on his way to the stable, which contained our treasure, when the mere sight of it rejoiced his heart with a joy which made him almost forget his wounds. At the suggestion of Baron San Lucas, it was now unanimously agreed upon by my companions, that I should select for myself whichever heap of the treasure I chose; and it was also settled that the baron should be allowed the second choice; while that lots should be cast by the remaining six persons concerned, to decide how they should each be entitled to draw.

Notwithstanding that these preliminaries were agreed to, the preacher, who it was said had never entered a pulpit unaccompanied by these companions, produced a pair of dice from his pocket, when instead of lots being drawn, at his suggestion, these well-known implements of dishonesty were resorted to, to determine each individual's turn for selecting from the piled heaps of treasure. Friendly, however, as they were inclined to be, some bickering took place among the gamesters, from suspicion of the dice being loaded ones; and this was natural, because their owner won the priority of choice; but it passed off in tolerable humour, when, by a cast of the said dice, the last lot of treasure was apportioned to honest Jacobus. Thus, *that* which satisfied me that there must have been some unfairness in the business, served to reconcile the parson's fellow-gamesters to the undue advantage he had taken over them.

Soon as the division of the booty had been made, the dwarf furnished us with a number of strong corn sacks, and every man of us expeditiously stowed away his own portion of the money and jewellery upon his person, and his plate in one of the sacks; when this having been done, we tied the mouths of our sacks tightly up, and each put a private mark on his own, and then we busied ourselves in saddling the horses and packing the bags of treasure in a light cart, which stood near the stable.

Count Anselma and his fair daughter, to whom I now notified our readiness to depart, were highly pleased at the news, and no time was lost in putting the severely wounded gentleman into the cart, as also fair Antonia and her maid, with our bags of treasure; when Jacobus, with a cartwhip in his hand and a smock-frock slipped over his dress, undertook the office of driver to the heavily-laden vehicle, to which he had yoked a couple of horses; and the remainder of us, including the count and his servant, mounted on horseback, prepared to follow behind the cart.

Antonia, the gentle Antonia, was a considerate creature; and though her heart bounded with delight at the prospect before her of quitting this much-dreaded haunt of banditti, where she had been cruelly treated, yet the dictates of compassion moved her now to inquire of us what had become of the wounded robbers; for she hoped, she ardently hoped, she said, they were in a place of safety, where their wounds would be properly dressed, and their other wants attended to.

The evangelical preacher, who chanced to be near the considerate lady when she made these remarks, and whose main avocation in life had been to preach up that charity to others, which, like too many preachers of the gospel, he rarely thought of practising himself, promptly replied to her by saying, the captured robbers were all of them locked up in a place of safety, where in due time the officers of justice would ferret them out, to convey them to prison, where their wants and wounds would be administered to until the day arrived when they must expiate their crimes on a gibbet.

" She hoped not; she hoped they would not be brought to that miserable end;" said the fair girl, with a sigh, for, added she, " though their crimes have been great, their punishment has already been severe; and mercy shown to them might be the forerunner of repentance, by means of which their souls would be saved hereafter, and they themselves might live worthily the residue of their days here."

" By my honour as a soldier," observed the gallant Dashembeau, who had listened with silent attention to the two preceding speeches, and bowing to Antonia while he spoke, " the young lady's sentiments are highly to be admired—their beauty assimilates with that of her fair person; the poor wretches she condescends to compassionate, have been conquered, are more or less wounded, and all of them pent up in a close prison. What are we to do with them? To let them go free would be attended with peril to ourselves; and if we leave them imprisoned here, in all human probability their fate will be to starve,"

"They are all of them outlawed robbers and murderers, irreligious men, the enemies of society at large," murmured the *cidevant* parson."

"I heartily wish they were away at some far distant place, where they might get married and reform," said the bigamist, while looking significantly at Antonia's waiting woman.

"The poor devils! what in the name of charity can we do with them?" observed the baron.

"Jacobus," asked I, "what is your advice on this occasion?"

"What! a set of heroes ask counsel from one like me?" said the dwarf smilingly; "well then, since the fates make me your oracle, I charge you, gentlemen, to give yourselves no kind of trouble concerning the prisoners. We will leave them here safely locked and bolted within their chambers. They have a supply of provision, and may enjoy the advantages to be derived from society: let them, therefore, either wile away the term of their captivity in conversation, or chew the sweet cud of reflection, and moralise on the subject of their past lives. Meanwhile, worthy signors, leave the task to me of finding some person to liberate them, after sufficient time has been afforded us to remove ourselves to such a distance as will ensure us against danger from them."

The dwarf's advice was approved of, and I consequently signified to him that everything regarding the prisoners should be left entirely to his management; upon which, without more words, he cracked his whip, and away went the horses with the cart of treasure; but as it moved off, I observed that fair Antonia's eyes were intently fixed on the dilapidated chateau, and tears of joyful gratitude trickled down her lovely cheeks; while in christian humility her hands remained pressed together in an attitude of prayer, and her lips moved in grateful thanks to the beneficent distributor of all good.

To avoid as much as possible attracting attention, the horsemen followed behind the cart in parties of two or three, and so far off, that in circuitous parts of the road the most advanced of us only kept it in view. In this manner we journeyed some few miles, when our little conductor struck into a wood, where, amongst the thickest of the trees, he brought us all to a halt, and the horsemen dismounted from their steeds.

"All except one of you, signors, must remain here to guard our treasure, while I, escorted by that brave individual, proceed to Terni, to procure the habiliments lying there belonging to the smock-frocked tribe of heroes now environing me," said Jacobus, soon as we had put our feet to the ground.

"You, my good friend, are our guide," replied I, "therefore your will is a law with us. Say, which of the party do you wish should accompany you?"

The dwarf rejoined by observing that we were all brave men, and it signified little which of us became his companion; on hearing which the bigamist tendered his services to him; but this offer all at once changed Jacobus's sentiments, inasmuch as it made him remark that so gallant a Lothario with the ladies might possibly lead them into difficulties at Terni; and therefore he added, provided it was agreeable to that gentleman to do so, he would thank Monsieur Dashembeau, the Gallic hero, to become his comrade. The Frenchman, who was ready and willing to do anything which might be required of him, unhesitatingly acceded to Jacobus's request; yet on doing so, laughingly observed that he supposed his little friend stood in fear of the fugitive thieves; when Jacobus honestly avowed that he would face any other man, or even a ghost, in preference to again falling in with his old comrade, the bandit Carl. Jacobus and the valiant Frenchman, mounted on two excellent horses, now took their departure, to get possession of the clothes of myself and my fellow combatants, which on our quitting Rome, habited in countrymen's dresses, it should be observed we had forwarded to an inn at Terni, to be kept there until applied for. Yet just previous to his departure, the honest dwarf and I so arranged that he was to send post horses and a carriage from Terni to a certain petty inn of his appointing, on the road-side leading to the kingdom of Naples, for Jacobus and I had decided on journeying to the Neapolitan capital in the company of Count Anselma and his daughter, who were going there on their way to Toulon. In spite of the wounds of my party, we were now a merry set; and jokes and laughter made time fleet rapidly away with us, while Jacobus was absent on the business of his mission. The count too, who had almost got rid of his fears for the safety of his beloved child, and that fair maid likewise in a great measure participated in our pleasure; though to have expected them to be as gay as ourselves would have been ridiculous, inasmuch as we, the conquerors of the banditti, had extremely enriched ourselves by the late adventure, while, on the contrary, these noble personages had been despoiled by the banditti of all the wealth with which they travelled. However, my associates fully agreed with me not to accept of any ransom money from them.

The business for which my partisans had engaged themselves in my cause being now happily accomplished, every man of them was free to depart for whatever place he chose, with his share of the booty along with him. Consequently, in a short consultation which we held together out of the count's hearing, it was agreed upon amongst us that all except Jacobus, my secretary, and me, who purposed being the count's companions, as also the bigamist, who, it seems, had taken fire at the charms of Antonia's pretty waiting maid, and therefore would fain become one of my party, should proceed in their own way, and according to their own desire, for the Roman capital. Had such a guarantee been necessary to ensure the return of our messengers with all due expedition, their two sacks of booty, now remaining in our custody, unquestionably would have commanded that effect. I, however, knew that the dwarf had already done too much in the cause in which he had voluntarily embarked, to permit of his acting a shuffling part by my party; and moreover I felt satisfied that should he, contrary to the good opinion I had formed of him, be disposed to act treacherously, and turn informer against us, for any reward he might get promised him by the magistracy, that the presence of his gallant Gallic companion would frustrate his design. Nevertheless, though my mind was easy on this subject, yet I could not avoid feeling apprehensive of evil, which might arise from Carle and his fellow robber, who escaped from us, or from some unforeseen cause. My fears, however, on this head were only trifling, when compared with those of my gamester companions, for these gentlemen, on every occasion, were accustomed to enter into a calculation of the odds and chances for and against them; therefore, as they mostly associated with the most unprincipled part of the community, they could not do otherwise than become extremely suspicious of the dwarf's intentions, and consequently uncommonly desirous of getting themselves removed to a place of safety with their treasure. But this last object could not be accomplished until Jacobus returned to us; for the wounded had to be taken care of, and the party going to Rome required the cart for this purpose. The ci-devant parson and lawyer, whose practices in and knowledge of life made him believe every man to be a rogue, allowed sundry very invidious expressions to escape from his lips; as likewise did our severely wounded gentlemen; but this was by no means surprising, as he no doubt recollected his own old propensities, and therefore could not be supposed to have an implicit belief in the honesty of others. One remark, however, was made during our desultory conversation, which merits being mentioned, because it was of a nature to make the fraternity of us blush, provided blushes could have been extracted from our cheeks, and this was uttered by Count Anselma, who, being ignorant that he was amongst gamesters, and feeling himself called upon, from something previously said, to utter an opinion upon play-men, quoted that of the famous Aristotle, where he ranks gamesters with thieves and plunderers. The count's remark, though it failed in suffusing that gentleman's cheeks with blushes, yet so far nettled his tender feelings of honour as to make the bigamist cease his attentions to the fair fille de chambre, that he might reply to the slanderer of his profession, and this he did by observing that a great proportion of all classes of society, men and women alike, were addicted to the passion of play.

" It matters not," replied Count Anselma, " which may be the sex, or what may be their walk in life; with professed gamesters, plunder is their sole aim. Yet I allow that in gaming, as well as in other vices, there may be different degrees of guilt; as, for example, the youth who commences his career at the gaming table, is a pigeon; but after the infernal crew around him have in good earnest plucked his rich plumage; when they have divided among them his extensive manors, his ancient forests, and his paternal mansions; then, when these leeches have sucked away all his substance, and nothing more remains to gorge their maws, he himself is taught to become a cold calculating sharper; one of a fraternity who denominate themselves honourable men, yet scruple not at defrauding every honest person that places confidence in them. So much for the male gamester, but, alas! with the young female votary to this destructive art, the case is still more lamentable, for high gaming must often be accompanied with great losses; and after all the resources, regular and irregular, honest and fraudulent, are dissipated, game debts must be paid. The winner is no stranger to the necessities of the case, hints at commutations, which dare not be refused, and thus the last valuable jewel of female possession is unavoidably resigned. This indeed is the worst of all evils, but an evil to which every female gamester is inevitably exposed."

Count Anselma's attack upon gamesters was too general and by far too caustic, to be listened to with patience, even by one of the most placid of the gambling fraternity; and the baron, though he was a philosophic character, one who was always on his guard against passion, yet considered it incumbent on him to aid the bigamist in rebutting the violent stigma now cast on their joint profession. To do which, he addressed the count, saying that in his opinion the term "sharper," which the noble count attached to the man who amused himself by play, was unjustifiably severe; for, after all had been said that sophistry could urge on the subject, it must be granted that the successful player, no matter whether with dice, or at games played with cards, stands indebted to chance far more than to skill for his success.

" I respect every gentleman's opinion," rejoined the count." We, however, are all liable to err, and my opinion, baron, as I have stated, is entirely at variance with yours: it is similar to that of Aristotle.

" Gad's blood," exclaimed my secretary, " the count and Aristotle are perfectly right. Gamesters, for all the world, are like land crabs and lawyers, which spare no carcass, nor let go their hold, while there is enough left for another bite."

These last attacks came home to the feelings of the persons to whom they were addressed; but luckily, before any reply could be made, approaching horsemen were heard, when Jacobus and the Frenchman immediately came in sight. Their arrival almost magically banished from every breast the irritable sensations occasioned by the count's and Monday's unceremonious speeches, and in place of them substituted the lively feelings of joy—of a joy which delighted every heart among us. Jacobus had achieved the object of his journey, and the apparel belonging to my party, which he and his companion brought back with them, gave them much the appearance of two enterprising commercial gentlemen, denominated riders, or bagmen, when travelling with bulky commodities, to display before country shopkeepers, who may condescend to permit of these goods being unpacked on their premises. Man is never in better humour than when the cloud of suspicion has just been removed from him; consequently almost every individual present warmly greeted the new comers, and many short questions were put to them. They however, without replying to what was said, cast the packages of clothes upon the earth; when Jacobus, after briefly remarking that diligence was the mother of good luck, told us we should act wisely in habiting ourselves in our proper garments as quickly as possible. We were none of us inclined to act in opposition to the dwarf's good advice, yet with all the haste we could make, it was an affair of many minutes to complete the toilet duty of the party; inasmuch as the badly wounded gentleman required assistance to effect his metarmorphose, while the removal of our specie from the crowded pockets of the peasants' garments we had worn to achieve our bold adventure in, to those of our own proper garments, was a task which we could not be too precise in performing. But notwithstanding all our care; the dropping of money from our over-crammed pockets, and occasionally the picking up of coin by parties to whom it appertained not, as also the oft-repeated examination of the pockets of our discarded clothes, and other ludicrous events which happened on this occasion, gave rise to many jests and much laughter, which more or less served to enliven every person's countenance.

" God helps them that help themselves," said the *ci-devant* preacher, while he was employed pinning up his well lined pockets with pins given him by the *fille de chambre.* " For my part, I verily believe that our two absent friends, who took retaining fees from the baron, and then kept away from this glorious adventure, will hang themselves from vexation when they behold what fine feather we are in."

" Trusting too much to others is the ruin of many. It is well that those truants brought us not all to destruction," seriously observed the dwarf.

" In the affairs of the world men are saved not by faith, but by the want of it; however, a man's own care is profitable, and happily we have catered well for ourselves," said the experienced parson.

"Provided he knows not how to retain what he gets, a man may keep his nose all his life to the grindstone, and die distressed for a shilling at last. For my own part, I ardently wish we were far away and safely housed with our great booty," anxiously remarked the runaway stockbroker.

"We shall have wherewithal to keep the bailiff and the constable away for the remainder of our lives, if we can only take care of it," said the grievously wounded clerk.

"What signifies wishing and hoping?" exclaimed the impatient dwarf. "He that lives upon hope will die fasting. Come, let us be moving, my friends. Signor Winpenny and the party I shall accompany have only a short distance to journey to the inn, where by this time post horses and a carriage must be waiting us; therefore all we need do will be to take our horses, to carry us, our bags of money, and the ladies."

Jacobus's advice was strictly attended to. The bigamist, myself, the count, his man servant, my secretary, and Jacobus, were speedily mounted on our chargers, being the four who possessed bags of treasure, each with his sack stowed in front of him, and the count and his man with the fair ones behind him, for on this occasion even the bigamist's gallantry gave way to his love of the needful, inasmuch as he made no offer of accommodating the fair *fille de chambre* with a seat behind him, though he took especial good care to carry his bag of treasure for a companion. The cart and the horses harnessed thereto were left for the accommodation of my wounded partisan, as well as to carry the booty of those who purposed going to the everlasting city, now mainly upheld by Jews; but at what time, and in what manner, the baron's party contemplated entering the town of ruins, was a subject into which none of my party troubled themselves by inquiring. The dwarf apparently was extremely anxious to hasten our departure, as scarcely had we got seated on horseback, with our treasure packed before us, ere he laconically observed, that "lost time is never found again," and put spurs to steed, without troubling himself to go through the formalities of bidding adieu to our brother adventurers.

"Hollo, my lad," shouted Dachembeau, "why, you are off like a shot fired from one of Gustavus's leather guns. You are afraid of Carlo, I suppose; however, good luck travel with you, for you are an honest little fellow."

Jacobus heeded not what was said, while his sudden departure made it incumbent on the rest of his party to act with promptitude like his own, fearful we might otherwise lose sight of him in the forest; consequently no long adieus were uttered, but we clapped spurs to our steeds and followed after the dwarf; the two females riding behind the count and his man, clinging to them by a firm hold round their waists. Jacobus had told us strictly true. The distance to the road side inn was only trifling, but for propriety's sake the females dismounted before we came to it, and, escorted by the count, terminated their little journey by walking there, where we found a post carriage had arrived and was kept awaiting us. We now stowed our three bags of treasure away in the vehicle, and procured several boys to follow behind with the horses we had made free with belonging to the banditti; when, after Jacobus had commissioned one in whom he could confide to release the bandit prisoners, away we went, light-hearted and merry, on our road to Naples.

CHAPTER XV.

"The bark that quits truth's faithful shore,
To sail on falsehood's treacherous sea,
Feels winds and waves increase the more
It widens from the sheltering lee;
Till seaward, seaward still impelled,
The billows are to mountains swelled."

"I wonder men dare trust themselves with men!
Methinks they should invite them without knives."

"You were in a prodigious hurry to get away from our comrades and well out of the forest: one would have thought you a knight errant, following after a beloved mistress," observed the bigamist laughingly to the dwarf, when the party of us were comfortably seated in our post carriage, journeying away from the inn, with the count's two servants stationed outside of the vehicle.

"The sun shone, and I was for making hay while it did so; for, between ourselves, I conjectured there was a storm gathering near us," was the reply humorously made to the bigamist's observation.

"It was a prudent resolve of yours, and acted on with becoming spirit, which proves you are not a man to put off to another time what ought to be done directly. But tell me, Jacobus, was it the fear of your old comrades who escaped from us that made you clap spurs to your horse, and set off in a gallop, as if you were an agent employed by the good Mercury?" rejoined the bigamist.

"Your ideas all centre in love; but every man to his trade: 'tis the true way to live," said the facetious dwarf.

The bigamist was a good-humoured fellow, or perhaps he might have taken fire at Jacobus's invidious remark, as no person approves of having a direct attack made on the most vulnerable and faulty part of their character. He, however, after a moment's reflection, evidently to turn the subject of conversation from himself, asked what had been the Frenchman's aim when talking of a shot fired from a leathern gun.

The question was a puzzling one, which Jacobus was incapable of answering; while, for my part, I knew no more of the Gustavus alluded to and his leathern guns than of the inhabitants of another planet; but the count, who was a remarkably well informed man, finding no one replied to the question, informed us that Gustavus of Sweden, in the battle he fought at Leipsic, in 1631, against the imperialists under Count Tilly, made use of field-pieces constructed of hardened leather, bound round with iron hoops; in which battle the Scots, for the first time, fired in platoons; and doubtless, he added, Monsieur Dachembeau had alluded to the combat in question. I had seen sufficient of the dwarf's character to judge, from the evasive answers made by him to the bigamist's questions, that there was some mystery attached to our hasty departure from our companions in the forest, which he did not approve of making known to the party of us; yet wishing to satisfy my own curiosity on this head, I took an opportunity, the first time we descended from the carriage, of privately asking him what had been the real occasion of his extreme hurry in getting away from partisans who had acted most faithfully towards us. Jacobus blushed to the very eyes at my question; when, after pausing for a minute or two, he replied by saying, "Signor Winpenny, this is a world abounding in villany, and though I avow that in most cases honesty is the best policy, and the most satisfactory to the feelings, nevertheless, in my opinion, he who retaliates not when the opportunity is afforded him, on the sharper he has been duped by, is a sorry fool for his pains." Here the dwarf paused, and I regarded him with astonishment, for I was altogether at a loss to conjecture what prank he could have been playing; presently, however, he resumed speaking by saying, "He who cheats with the dice merits being kicked and having his head broke;" but for his part, not being a fighting character, he had satisfied himself for the injustice done him by our comrade, the ci-devant preacher, in awarding him the refuse lot of treasure by means of his false dice, in taking advantage of an exchange which somebody had made of the marks placed on their two bags, and thereby left for his more designing friend the treasure we had allotted for him, Jacobus, instead of that lot he had made choice of for himself."

"He must rise betimes in the morning who would get the better of you in a bargain," said I, laughing heartily at what the dwarf had told me. "Your generalship, my friend, would not disgrace a Ulysses. I see how it is; you took advantage of the opportunity afforded you by being our charioteer to exchange the marks which had been placed on the two sacks of treasure, and then you hastened us away from the forest, that your trick might not be discovered before our departure." The dwarf re-echoed my laughter, but neither denied nor acknowledged that he was the individual who exchanged the marks in question; consequently, though his not speaking to the point afforded a proof of his prudence, yet his silence was likewise confirmatory of his cunning.

"You have done well, Jacobus," now said I, "in getting to windward of the parson, who unquestionably is the greatest knave of all my partisans. But, my friend something whispers me that he will follow after us to Naples, there to call you to a severe account for the masterly trick you have put upon him."

" Let him follow if he pleases; the road lies before him," replied the dwarf, looking archly while he spoke; " I ask only to get there a day in advance, and then, should he find and know me, to call me to the reckoning you speak of, mine will be the fault, and I, simpleton as I should be, must be exposed to the preacher's tender mercy."

" You are too deep for me, Jacobus; I cannot delve into your meaning. A remarkable figure, such as yours is, must be known again by whoever once sees it."

" You are an experienced character; one who has come the buccaneer over and brought to ruin Manfreda and his band; time, however, that solver of mysteries, will show whether even Signor Winpenny may not for once in his life be mistaken."

Here our private conversation was put an end to by the count's lovely daughter, who, in her eagerness to journey on, reminded us that the rest of the company were waiting for us; and she knew, she smilingly added, we were both of us much too gallant to wilfully occasion any delay to the party which might bring nightfall upon them before they got housed, and consequently terror to the female portion of it, who, after what they had recently undergone, were ill prepared to brave new dangers. This summons was imperious upon us, and we instantly handed the fair damsel into the carriage and resumed our journey.

An extensive knowledge of the world gives a man many advantages in society; but to shine in it beyond others, an excellent education must be combined with great practical experience. The count, far as book knowledge and oratorical education went, was vastly my superior; but in practical knowledge, youthful as I was, yet I entirely outstripped him. His conversation was highly instructive, while, fortunately for me, I was not exposed to the necessity of showing ignorance before his lovely daughter and him, for though I knew nothing of the dead languages, and like many other persons thought them of almost as little real use as the dead themselves are, yet, as I was of a cheerful character, and had constantly, in proportion to my advance in worldly prosperity, endeavoured to make my personal acquirements keep pace with my upward progress in society, and, among other accomplishments, applied myself sedulously to the study of several modern languages, I was certainly an entertaining companion for any mixed society, though unqualified to be the associate of persons of vast erudition, when they made learning the subject of their discourse.

For these reasons, and, moreover, as the bigamist was a good-humoured gentleman, Monday and Jacobus always facetiously pleasant, and the fair Antonia fascinating to an extreme, while we all had sufficient cause for gratification, our journey, during which we constantly strove to be agreeable to each other, was one uninterrupted scene of pleasure; but to specify particulars, or dwell on the places we stopped at, is unnecessary, for adventures we met with none, and our stay on the road was short as possible, our main object being to get beyond the dominions of the church, and this we happily effected. The first and only town we made any material stay at was Sezzo, in the kingdom of Naples, and here we halted until our saddle-horses came up with us, which, after the first stage of our journey, had been left at a post-house, to be rode to this place, by regular stages, by post-boys of the country.

It happened to be the time of the horse fair when our nags arrived here, and, for sundry good reasons, we deemed it expedient to dispose of them, which job we effected most expeditiously, and at tolerably fair prices; but then we were indebted for this service to an auctioneer, who was assisted in selling the horses by certain puffers; without which last, no man in his senses, whether in the kingdom of Naples or elsewhere, would think of sending valuable property of any kind to be got rid of by auction. While we were detained at Sezzo on the foregoing business, we all went to see a play acted. Moses was the hero of the piece, and the conjuring tricks he was made to perform far outdid those of all the famed jugglers I ever saw or heard talked of; but this was not extraordinary, for when religious affairs are made a mockery of on theatric boards, absurdity is carried to its extreme bounds. Moses, on this occasion, was represented as an unprincipled sinner, guilty of all crimes; but then the actors so completely murdered their several parts, that the veriest Jew would have felt ashamed at acknowledging his law-giver and prophet, or any of the rabbis and other Israelites about him.

It was gratifying to witness the happy lives Count Anselma and his daughter now led together. The avowed wish of one served as a law with the other, while the chief thought of each apparently was to anticipate the other's desires. Antonia, however, was frequently deprived of the services of her waiting-maid, for the gallant bigamist with love discourse beguiled the maid's ear, and kept her away from her mistress whenever he could; yet so great was his partiality towards the fair sex, that at those hours when Angelina was engaged with her lady, he was usually away, gallanting with some other fair one. The dwarf often jested with this gay Lothario on his foibles, for, be it observed, he had two leading ones— namely, he was much addicted to over-feasting the body, as well as to courting the fair; and we were all made to laugh at our dinner, after the sale of the horses, by Jacobus humorously observing to this sensual gentleman, who was feasting at a prodigious rate, that he himself was not experienced in these things, but he had heard it said that " over-indulgence in love and feasting causes the body to waste away like a snow-ball in summer, and brings on dejective melancholy, which leads to mineral waters, medicine, and repentance."

Eloquence, in men of bright parts, has great power, insomuch as to induce people to believe things which have neither actual nor possible existence. This grand truth we have too frequently seen verified by the conduct of certain treacherous senators; but when talented men, possessing the gift of eloquence, use it to uphold truth and virtue, it is as profitable to hear their discourse as the discourse sounds beautiful to the ear. This was strictly the case with Count Anselma; he was highly talented and most eloquent, while his eloquence was resorted to for no other end than to promote virtue, and uphold it in its beauty. I shall not in a hurry forget his remark to me when at Sezzo, on an occasion where, perhaps, he was led to think me not so moral as I ought to be, or as some primitive christians are represented to have been. " My friend," said the worthy count, " let no man have it in his power to say with truth of you, that you are not a man of simplicity, candour, and goodness, for no man can hinder you from being good and pure at heart."

With the produce of the sale of our horses in mine and my partisans' well-lined pockets, the party of us proceeded to the Neapolitan capital the day following that of our having disposed of the animals.

Count Anselma, who was well known in this delightfully situated city, immediately on our arrival procured a supply of money, and insisted upon repaying me his portion of our travelling expenses, which I would fain have left him my debtor for; but his feelings of independence permitted not of his owing an unnecessary pecuniary obligation to any person whatever. The Marquis of Meralvo, one of the brothers of the count's deceased lady, was a resident here, and they were on terms of brotherly affection together; therefore the count, with his family, went to reside at the marquis's mansion, while I and my three associates took up our quarters at a celebrated tavern, and immediately set ourselves to work selling our abundant store of plate and jewellery, which, however, that dangerous suspicions might not arise in the minds of the purchasers, we prudently took the precaution of doing in small lots, and among many different jewellers.

It was now the carnival time, and royalty, which knavery has pronounced can do no wrong, was busily employed at the work of tomfoolery.

There was a corso in the street of Toledo. It consisted of two cars full of masks: the first, drawn by eight superb horses, representing a Russian sledge, in which were the king and twelve nobles of the court, all apparelled as Cossacks; the second, also drawn by eight horses, belonged to a prince, who, with his suite, were dressed as English jockies. The principal sport of these distinguished personages was to frighten the horses of the equipages as they passed along by flinging at their heads balls made of flour and plaster, and to break the panes of the windows of the first and second floors of all the houses which happened to be closed. These princely diversions of an anointed ruler and his august family, however, were attended with serious accidents. A lady was thrown out of her carriage and run over; a gentleman was likewise thrown by his horse, trodden under foot, and killed; but then royalty was amused, and the Neapolitan soldiers, the cavalry in particular, in maintaining order, afforded a glorious opportunity of distinguishing themselves, which they did with their accustomed bravery and urbanity, striking to the right and left with their sabres the foot passengers who crowded to see the masquerade, and, in imitation of their betters, magnanimously leaving the maimed and wretched of the poor to repine unpitied in the streets and on the highways.

CHAPTER XVI.

"'Tis calm, clear night, the streets no more
    Are throng'd; the grand procession's o'er.
    But hie thee forth the city wall,
    And see what will thy sight appal:—
    The maimed and wretched."

"Ye men, who pour your blood for kings as water,
    What have they given your children in return?
    A heritage of servitude and woes,
    A blindfold bondage, where your hire is blows."

"And now being femininely array'd,
    With some small aid from scissars, paint, and tweezers,
    He looked in almost all respects a maid."

THE morning following our arrival at Naples I heard and saw sufficient of the miserable consequences of the corso; but, to pass from the revolting theme, not a little to my surprise, for I anticipated nothing of his intentions, the dwarf, after our breakfast, told me he must beg leave to remove his quarters, for that he had a friend in the neighbourhood of the town who insisted on his becoming his guest. I liked the little fellow too much to willingly allow of his separating from me in so cavalier a manner, and would have persuaded him to delay his departure, at least for a day or two; he, however, humorously replied, that "one to-day is worth two to-morrows," and, in defiance of my entreaties to the contrary, called for a carriage, when, after telling me he should speedily have the felicity of seeing me again, moved away in it with the whole of his treasure.

Jacobus had so thoroughly taken me by surprise in this instance, that I forgot to talk over some other business with him, which I had deputed Baron San Lucas to transact for me in Rome; for somehow the little fellow's sagacity and trustworthiness had so worked upon me, that I not only made him my confidant, but also took his advice on many occasions. However, as he had promised to see me again very soon, I easily consoled myself for the fault of my memory, and passed the day away most agreeably in the society of the bigamist, who, like myself, had never seen the lions of Naples, and therefore we now visited many of them, and went to the opera at night.

"Fly pleasures, and they'll follow you," is a celebrated old adage; but the bigamist must either have disbelieved or despised it. He was perpetually following after pleasure, and at the opera this night made so many gallant overtures to fair ladies, that his great attentions evidently caused several Neapolitan beauties to believe their charms had fired his heart. This conduct of his in almost any country, but most especially the peninsula of Italy, where assassins are ever ready at hand to bathe their daggers in blood for an adequate reward, was of a nature to expose him to considerable danger; but there are females who think so much of the pleasures attached to an affair of gallantry, that they have no thoughts to spare regarding the personal safety of the gallant who affords them these pleasures; or perhaps, like certain sanguinary commanders in war, they deem their triumph glorious in proportion to the number of heroes who are made to bleed. Be this, however, as it may, the bigamist's attentions to them occasioned us to be invited by two ladies of beauty and fashion to a card-party held at one of their houses that night; and, gallant fellows as we were, we unhesitatingly accepted the invitation.

We accompanied the fair Neapolitans to the villa at which the fête was given, and were honoured by riding with them in their carriage. It was a tastefully fitted up residence, just outside of the town, on the Salerno side. The youngest of the ladies, the object of the bigamist's attentions, was a beautiful brunette, about twenty years of age, named Signora Silva; while her companion, Signora Franceschetti, was much older, she being on the verge of five-and-thirty, but volatile enough for any miss in the last year of her teens. The rest of the company invited to this entertainment, like ourselves, had been at the opera, and on seeing us depart from it, followed after us; therefore we were soon assembled and seated at card-tables, but my fortune it was to be placed at a different table to that of my gallant friend.

Cheating, more or less, is universal among gamesters. Though the bigamist and myself were tolerable proficients in the arts and mysteries of play, yet, having another object in view, we permitted ourselves to be tricked out of ten or a dozen gold pieces at this visit; and more-over, by assuming the manners of mere novices at cards, made ourselves great favourites with the sharping train present at this party; for, however severe the term *sharper* may seem when applied to noblemen, chevaliers, and other persons in high life, justice and truth demand it should be used towards all individuals, from the monarch to a scavenger, who take undue advantages of those they play with, which assuredly is done by an infinity of people of fashion in Naples, and was remarkably conspicuous this night in the conduct of our opponents at play at the villa of Signora Silva; but none are blinder than those who don't choose to see, and we wilfully shut our eyes to the impositions practised at our expense.

Signora Silva, whose history we previously had known nothing of, a young chevalier, pre-sent on this occasion, intimated to us was the *chere amie* of a certain duke, who, for the extent of his possessions and unbounded influence at the court, was second to no private individual in the kingdom of Naples. He, however, according to this gentleman's report, although much attached to her, had of late become extremely jealous of the lady, for which she had herself only to blame, as the duke's jealousy had arisen from her frequently giving large parties at her house, and acting with much levity in her general conduct.

This information was of an encouraging nature for my friend the bigamist, who was by far too much a man of the world to live burdened with an over-scrupulous conscience, and he consequently determined to profit by it to the very utmost of his ability. However, what has now been said will be sufficient for my purpose, therefore I shall state no further particulars of what passed at this fair lady's party, but content myself by saying that my friend made great progress in his new amour; and we, after passing an agreeable night, returned home together, highly satisfied with the acquaintances we had made, and bent on pushing our good fortune to the utmost.

"My friend," said I, before we retired to our pillows, "the fairest roses are envi-roned with thorns, and trouble of some kind is sure to accompany or else follow on the heels of every amour. You, for example, have repeatedly drunk from the hymeneal cup, but no doubt the penalty you have paid for the sweet draughts imbibed by you has been more than commensurate to the pleasure you have enjoyed from them. Marriage, however, cannot now be your object, therefore you have no fresh risks to run on the score of bigamy; but, let me ask, is not the duke's anger, deputed, as it will be, to the hands of a bravo, a danger still more to be dreaded?"

"I forget dangers when I embark in affairs of gallantry," replied the gay Lothario; "while, as to wedlock, it is always my dernier resource; yet when the garrison would not capitulate without that formality, or that a fortune was to be gained by it, I hitherto have scrupled not at entering into the desperate tie. For the future, however, when I resort to matrimony, the knot shall be loosely tied; it shall either be done by a mock priest, like our friend the methodist, or else there shall be some flaw in the ceremony, such as the insertion of a false name. In the present instance, with Madam Silva all is plain sailing; I shall carry the fortress and laugh at his grace into the bargain."

"'Tis well, my friend," rejoined I, laughingly, for reason used against passion is like human breath blown against the wind. "Madam Silva, I hope, will prove an angel to you; that's all I've to add; so, good night; pleasant dreams to you."

Desire and doubt admit of little rest. The bigamist sallied forth in the morning to visit his new charmer; but I, who had not yet disposed of all my plate, remained at home to meet several jewellers whom I had appointed to wait on me; and just as I had terminated my business with these gentlemen, somewhat to my surprise a *billet-doux* was put into my hands, in which I was requested to accompany its bearer to meet a lady who had some particular business of a private nature to transact with me.

"Ho, ho," said I to myself as I followed behind the messenger, "I see how it is; Signora

Franceschetti is one of those amorous ladies who think there should be no time lost in affairs of love, and consider it admirable policy to strike while the metal is hot."

Impressed with the idea that an affair of gallantry awaited me, I arrived at a small house, pleasantly situated in a vineyard a short distance from the town, and here was ushered into a parlour, in which a slender little young woman, who was remarkable for a profusion of carroty hair, which hung in ringlets about her face, was sitting with her needle-work before her, but on my entrance the damsel arose from her seat, and received me with a low curtsey.

Red hair is very unusual among the people of this country, and altogether the young lady's appearance surprised me. I could not call to mind having seen her before, and felt disappointed, inasmuch as it was Madam Franceschetti whom I expected to have met here: however I said nothing, but returned the lady's salute with a bow; after which we continued silent for a time, for she seemed in no hurry to break to me the purport of her assignation; while, on my part, I wished to come to the knowledge of this secret before I committed myself by speaking.

" I understand, signor, that you have recently come from Rome," said she, at length breaking silence, and speaking in a peculiar squeaking voice.

" Yes, signora, you are rightly informed; but pray, may I ask how it happens you know anything of me and my movements?"

" Fame trumps forth the movements of extraordinary personages,—especially when they travel encumbered with large sacks of plate," rejoined she jeeringly.

" The devil's in the woman," thought I; " what can all this bode?"

" It isn't every one can carry quantities of plate and jewellery through the territories of the church with impunity," said she, resuming the discourse.

" Well," thought I, " I suppose this is some trap laid for me.'

" Naples, continued the lady, " is a gay city, and a dangerous one for a gallant young stranger to take up his abode in. There are beautiful women here who might make him forget those of Parma, as also certain fair ladies at Rome."

" Confound the girl, she is a downright sorceress," muttered I aside.

" Antonia, the daughter of Count Anselma, is as amiable and virtuous as she will be wealthy and is beautiful. You will act wisely, signor, to privately arrange your other love affairs, and sedulously pay your devoirs to this fair one, who, provided woman can make man completely happy, is the maiden above all others to be coveted."

For a young female, in a private assignation with a man, to recommend another of her sex as worthy of his notice, struck me as so extraordinary, that it made me forget every other circumstance attending this strange interview, and I unconsciously stared at the face and golden locks of the speaker till I completely disconcerted her and brought blushes into her cheeks.

" The most judicious person may sometimes err, and the wisest be mistaken," now observed my companion, laughing and gently lifting from its place the carroty wig which disguised her.

" Good Heavens," exclaimed I, " 'tis Jacobus! How have I been deceived, not to have recognized my little friend, who forsook me only yesterday? But how is it that he has got rid of his club-foot?"

" My club-foot and male attire were both put on for the purpose of disguise. I am a woman, signor, who has nothing artificial about her save these curls; but in confiding this secret to you, I implicitly rely on your honour never to hint at or promulgate anything concerning me, for I would not for the world have any one of your late associates trace me out. I told you that time, the resolver of mysteries, would show whether or not I could deceive you in my personal appearance, and having been successful in imposing upon the shrewdest of the party, I shall feel no fears of being discovered by any other individual belonging to it. My share of the robbers' treasure has enriched me beyond my hopes, and the object I have in view is to live on the interest of my money, enjoying life in a rational manner, and divested of those fears I should be in, was the mock parson or any fugitive of the robbers to trace me out."

I could not fail admiring the sagacity and good sense shown by this able personifier of characters; but, after a pause, I addressed her, saying,—" How am I to know that this is not another fictitious part you are performing, for is not it the second time you have appeared before me in female attire? Provided, therefore, you are in your proper character, say, signora, by what name am I to call you? And, moreover, let me ask to be favoured with a few words of your history, that I may know what is your walk in life."

"Your wishes shall be gratified, signor; but as long stories make weary listeners, my tale shall be embodied in a few words. My father was a merchant at Venice, but unfortunately for himself and his family, he kept too luxurious a table for his income to uphold; and by this conduct ultimately verified the proverb which says, 'Who dainties love, shall beggars prove.' Yet he scarcely lived long enough to be sensible of the truth of that adage, 'Fools make feasts, and wise men eat them,' as he was drowned by the swamping of a gondola before the credit of his house was entirely blasted. The good man had no wife living, but he left behind him a son and daughter, neither of whom knew how to gain a livelihood; while as to friends, all the world knows that poverty has none. My brother was a gallant, brave man, but naturally very idle; therefore we lived how we could upon the remnant of our father's property. However, as I've heard say, 'A small leak will sink a large ship,' and our expenses soon brought us to a state of complete ruin. To ward off the gripe of poverty, the sufferer should pretend to be a stranger to her, and she will then treat him with ceremony; but this it was vain for us to attempt doing, for the desperate state of our affairs was well known throughout the neighbourhood of our residence; and moreover, to be known to absolutely need a favour when you ask one, ensures a refusal of the boon, as permanent relief may be obtained from vanity, from self-interest, or from avarice, but never from genuine compassion. To be poor and seem poor is a certain method never to rise. No person could be found to advance us a trifle of money; and at length my poor brother, being driven almost to desperation, became one of the fraternity of gamblers; when, fortune proving inimical to his views, he descended, or perhaps the term may be more appropriate (for I know not exactly these gradations in society) to say he *ascended*, to the walk in life of a bandit. Plenty, pleasure, and danger now attended upon the brave youth. It suffices, however, to say that he remitted me an ample sufficiency of money, while he himself associated with banditti after banditti, until his exploits had been so many and so daring, that they rendered it necessary for him to remove still further from his old neighbourhood, and thus eventually he became one of Manfreda's famous band. From this time the remittances my brother made me were few and at periods remote from each other, till at length he ceased sending them altogether, and I heard nothing more of him; when, growing uneasy on his account, and being much distressed for money, I came to the resolution of taking French leave of my creditors, and going in search of the brave young man; and that I might effectually disguise my person, I now provided myself with male attire, and the artificial lump which constitutes my club-foot. A long story might be made out regarding the way in which I fell in with the banditti, and got employment among them; but all I need say is, that my poor brother had met with his death from a pistol-bullet, on one of the bandit's predatory excursions, shortly before the period of my joining them; and that by a mere accident I discovered the hiding place for Manfreda's treasure, which, while I remained with the banditti, I was perpetually devising expedients for participating in, and fully hoped that one time or other, through the agency of Ambrose, the tavern-keeper, who, as I have already said, is married to a cousin of mine, I should successfully achieve this object. Diligence is the parent of good luck. I never lost sight of the object I had in view, till deeming the wrongs you had suffered at their hands were sufficient to make a man of your determined character act the part I wished done by Capt. Manfreda and his desperate band, I voluntarily assisted you in carrying the project into execution, by which the whole of the banditti have been destroyed or dispersed, and their wealth got possession of, to be divided by you and your partisans."

I thanked the fair narrator for the story she had told me of herself, but intimated that she had passed over an essential thing, which was that of not having communicated her name; when, after smilingly observing that certainly a half confidence was unworthy of us both, she told me that her names were Julia Ruberto.

CHAPTER XVII.

"Nature is weak, and passion wrong,
And easy 'tis to widen strong."

"The world is nat'rally averse
To all the truth it sees or hears,
But swallows nonsense and a lie
With greediness and gluttony."

"Can this mean peace, the calmness of the good?
Or guilt grown old in desperate hardihood?
Alas! too like in confidence are each,
For man to trust to mortal look or speech;
From deeds, and deeds alone, may he discern
Truths which it wrings the unpractised heart to learn."

I HAD not been many days in Naples ere I received a letter from Baron San Lucas, who informed me how he and his friends had arrived in safety in the eternal city, and then went on to state that he had executed certain commissions I had entrusted him with to the best of his ability; but in concluding his letter, the baron extremely diverted me by the humorous account he gave of the preacher's rage and mortification at discovering the trick which had been played upon him. He had sworn, he said, more than any drunken fish-woman, or blackguard of a trooper, was ever heard to swear; and sometimes he prated about seeking redress in a court of law, while at others he threatened to follow after the person who had so egregiously imposed on him, and insist on having pecuniary satisfaction from him for the great loss he had sustained; or, in default of obtaining this, that he would employ an assassin to avenge his wrongs. But the most amusing part of the story was, that our ci-devant parson fully believed the bigamist to be the individual who had played him the trick of exchanging their bags of treasure, and never for a moment attached the credit of this exploit to the proper person. "Well, fair Julia, alias my good friend, the dwarf Jacobus," said I to Julia Ruberto the first time of my seeing her after receiving the baron's letter, "I have had a communication from my correspondent in Rome, who informs me that the ci-devant parson and lawyer is on the eve of coming here, breathing furious revenge against the individual who made free with his sack of treasure, and determined to have him stilettoed, if he dosen't hand over sufficient money to him to make good the difference between the two treasures." This piece of information startled my little friend, who trembled at the idea of coming in contact with the unprincipled fellow alluded to; she, however, on calling to mind her thorough metamorphosis of character, soon recovered her ordinary composure, and laughingly said "that unless the ci-devant preacher was as accomplished a wizard as he was a cheat with the dice, she would defy him to know her again when he saw her."—"I admire your courage, fair Julia," said I; "you laugh at dangers which you believe to be distant; but when you behold the parson at your elbow, as you soon may, I expect your tone will be changed. If I recollect right, you were not very bold at the time you retrograded, leaving my party to force their chapel door and make a deadly assault on the banditti."

"The better part of valour is discretion, even famed warriors have pronounced; besides," added the cunning jade, "I am a woman, and the policy of women, as everybody knows, is to set men at variance with each other, whenever they themselves can benefit by their brawls."—"'Tis too true, Julia," rejoined I with a smile, "and if doubted, may be proved by history, ancient and modern."

I was now a frequent guest at the Marquis of Meralvo's superb mansion, where, notwithstanding that this nobleman was excessively proud, in compliment to his brother-in-law, he made me extremely welcome. The marquis was a great favourite at the luxurious, depraved court of Naples, and would often have carried Count Anselmo there with him, but that the count, from being a philosopher, set small value on the oft deceitful smiles of royalty. However, example goes far in tainting the best principles, and sometimes the marquis succeeded in persuading his noble brother-in-law to accompany him to the king's levee, while occasionally fair Antonia made one among the ladies of the family in attending the queen's drawing room.

I, too, was introduced at court, the circumstance having been dispensed with, out of compliment to the marquis, of my never having been at a king's levee in my own country; and on this occasion I had the honour, as that degradation to manhood is termed, of kissing the king's hand.

Amongst the buccaneers, gamblers, banditti, and other notoriously unprincipled characters with whom stern necessity, chance, or interested motives had occasioned me to associate, I had, short as was my career, witnessed villany in abundance, both masqued and unmasqued; but all the villanous depravity which had fallen under my observation fell infinitely short of that practised at this corrupt court. Indeed, so great and glaring was it, that even Count Anselmo, notwithstanding the aristocratic honours he enjoyed, and the consequent bias they inspired him with for his fellow peers and the kingly makers of them, more than once has honestly confessed to me, that, in his opinion, no other form of government could be devised of so exceptionable a nature as one which upholds a host of sycophants by places and sinecures, all of them overpaid, and a great proportion unnecessary to the state. " In England," he would say to me, " provided truth emanates from the press, you must be a happy people; for all your ministerial papers, as also your whigs and tories, assert that you have no people to pay or places to support, except what are absolutely requisite; therefore, if a childish paraphernalia is exhibited at court, you have the consolation of knowing that it is not at the people's expense; but here, what between the knavish equeries, aids-de-camp, grooms of the stole and bed-chamber, lords in waiting, an all-grinding priesthood, and an infinity of other leech-like characters, who grin like so many monkeys before the face of royalty, though they laugh at and impose upon royal personages, and who have nothing material to do more than show an excess of servility to their superiors in power,—which meanness usually revenges itself by the display of insolent vulgarity to those beneath them,—the country is drained of its treasure, while those who contribute to the taxation are exposed to insults from those wretches in place, many of whom are so ignorant of common gentility, that they scorn to answer the letters on business of their fellow-men, though nobler than themselves, because not such arrant paupers. I am involuntarily made to laugh," the count would say, in concluding this subject, " almost on every occasion when I see either of their *Neapolitan* Majesties taking their accustomed equestrian exercise, for then these gallant grooms and others (who some of them affect bluntness of manners, and others great condescension, as their hidden daggers to stab with when away from the royal presence) are on their good behaviour, showing their smiles and curvetting their horses in the most attractive manner; yet, after all has been adduced, undeniably these are the very worst of the vermin of a court."

I, who knew nothing concerning what description of persons usually attend the British court, felt a degree of national pride rise within me on learning from so well-informed a personage as Count Anselmo that they are most of them independent characters; and it was also gratifying to me to learn that in England, according to the assertions of certain of her leading journals, there are no unnecessary pensions paid or places supported by the state. Nevertheless, though this news afforded me pleasure, doubts of its truth forced themselves upon my imagination, and I even thought it possible that editors of the stamped press might be bought over to help to deceive the people; for when a corrupt administration can squander away millions of a slaving multitude's money, and get tyrannic senates to approve of their conduct, as we read in history has sometimes been done, why should it be marvelled at if such personages act invidiously to the interest of their daily customers, in return for adequate ministerial *douceurs*? These, my doubts, however, I think, were attributable to the sentiments which my poor mother Diana had often expressed in my hearing, of the excessive venality of persons in power in my native land. She would say that an absolute monarchy would be infinitely less expensive than our government, for that then there would exist but one chief, while that now, what with the requisite ministerial majority of lords and commons, it was saying too little to assert that Great Britain was under the government of a thousand absolute men, no matter by what name they were called,—all of whom, and their kindred and friends, must be fattened on the great community. Believing, therefore, there was some truth in what my mother had said, how could I conjecture that such a thorough change as Count Anselmo had represented, could have taken place for the better? how could I credit that so wonderful a reform could have happened in so short a time, and this without a terrible revolution?

Here, again, is a proof that education moulds and fashions the human mind. Unquestionably, had the prince, her paramour, united himself in wedlock to Diana Winpenny, or even had I, in her time, received a tithe of the honours and pensions bestowed on many of the spurious offspring of royalty, my mother would have preached a very different doctrine in my hearing to that which now made an infidel of me regarding the assertions of ministerial papers, or the opinion of my friend, the count, on the subject in question.

Power naturally follows property. Although I had no title to make a flourish with before my name, I was made much of by all the courtiers with whom my noble friend and I associated; while, as I lived in the city of Naples in lordly style, keeping hired horses, servants, and a carriage, the houses of those personages were readily opened to me, and I was a welcome guest wherever I went: one whose avowed wishes were respectfully attended to by all the persons, noble and simple, who called themselves my friends.

"O Fortune! thou art an admirable attendant," I would frequently say to myself, when I was receiving courtly attentions from first-rate personages, which no virtues, no talents, nor the most exalted nor brightest genius on his side, could have obtained from them for the poor man, "thou art all that is excellent and lovely in the eyes of mankind, and so well art thou known, that heroes and other robbers make rivers of blood to flow; chastity casts off her robe of purity with contempt; and priests glory in roasting and damning their brother men, to get thee yoked to their chariot-wheels. Have I not, therefore,—has not the son of Diana Winpenny done well in braving all kinds of dangers to win thee? And now that thou art his attendant, should he not make the utmost he can of thee?" Thus would I often apostrophize, hugging myself with feelings of infinite delight as I reflected on the great ability I had shown in playing the cards of life. But is it not so with the majority of persons whose careers have been fortunate? Do they not attribute everything good that has befallen them to their own prudence, valour, or sagacity?—quite forgetting in these paroxysms of their vanity, that life is no more than a game of cards, wherein chance gives the honours and decides the game. And, after all, the most favoured condition of life has nothing to be proud of;—a hair, a fly, or an insect is able to destroy this mighty being, whose life is of such importance. Great and wealthy personages, &c., many of those called the wisest of men, have committed determined suicide to rid themselves of it; others have plunged headlong into the yawning gulf of futurity in preference to submitting longer to live in the universal sameness of life, which is but to eat, drink, and sleep, and must earlier or later cease to be. In this manner did I frequently apostrophize, invoke fortune, and reason with myself; yet I exerted my best endeavours to enjoy that life which innumerable persons of both sexes and of every country have found to be a burden, and have gladly rid themselves of,—that life which Hume, the philosopher of modern times, and Seneca, of ancient days, boldly maintain that man is not prohibited from depriving himself of, there being, as the former says, no text in Scripture which forbids it; while the latter observes, that many of the sufferings endured in life are worse than death, which is not feared by infants, boys, nor lunatics, and therefore should be viewed with indifference by wise men.

I have just made the observation that I now did my best to cull the sweetest flowers of life; and with the lovely and bewitching Antonia, and her learned, liberal, and philosophic father, for my companions,—which, more or less, they were every day of the week,—how is it possible that I could fail in making my time glide pleasantly away? Besides, could more than this have been required to render me happy? was I not on the true classical ground of Italy—the land of antiquities, of mighty recollections, and of the fine arts—yea, and in the near neighbourhood of the awfully majestic Vesuvius, the great wonder of all ages of the world? To this country belong the romantic scenes described by poets and travellers; the beautiful moonlight nights, the glowing azure of the sky, the dark-blue sea, the purple-tinged mountains, the forests of orange, lemon, and olive trees; and here is found a full portion of female beauty, and men lawless and impassioned. In Naples, however, the fair are

"Soft as her clime, and sunny as her skies."

The count, his lovely daughter, and myself, frequently made excursions together into the neighbouring country, one of which I can never forget. We were away on this delightful jaunt for several days, and most highly were we gratified by the beautifully-diversified scenes that we saw; among which may be enumerated delightful valleys, stupendous crags, scanty rivulets bubbling over the pebbles of their rocky beds, plains strewed with ruins of former greatness, and dilapidated ancient castles and towers, perched on lofty peaks, among beautiful forests of chesnut-trees and wild solitary glens. On our entering Naples from this excursion, fair Antonia, in the warmth of a grateful heart, made the remark that the present were the happiest days of her life, and she felt thankful to Providence for blessing her with so many of them; when I, being animated by sentiments of a very similar kind to those of the lovely maiden, expressed myself in unqualified terms of satisfaction on the continued happiness I now enjoyed. Count Anselma, however, who had overheard our observations, smilingly remarked, that although youth was the peculiar season for enjoyment, still, with the feelings we possessed, we ought to consider ourselves among the most fortunate persons in life; while to show that happiness is not the companion of grandeur, he instanced to us how Abdalrahman the renowned, who reigned for fifty years caliph of Cordova, and was almost constantly victorious in battle and prosperous in his affairs, kept a journal, specifying therein all the *happy days* which he had spent during his long and brilliant career; and on summing them up just previous to his death, the monarch found they amounted only to *fourteen.*

To return to the bigamist. Though this gallant friend of mine was a gay deceiver, so given to intrigue, that, like the women of Egypt, he would unscrupulously have carried on his gallantry in the public cemeteries, yet it was impracticable for him to give general satisfaction to the many fair ones of his acquaintance, and Antonia's waiting-maid happened to be one of those who felt mortified by his neglect of her. His attentions to this damsel, until very recently, had been most marked, but now Signora Silva and several other ladies of fashion engrossed all his time. For some days the maid fretted much at the gay gentleman's neglect of her, till having ascertained in what manner he employed himself, she became angry with him, naturally looking upon his conduct as a gross insult to her charms.

It is said that "women repay flattery with favour, and reserve vengeance for insult;" and, as will shortly be seen, the truth of this observation was abundantly proved by the conduct of both the fair females in question; but whether the much coveted favours granted to my friend by Signora Silva, or the vengeance taken on him by Antonia's maid servant, are things which shall decide if woman's love or her hatred it is that in the sequel proves most beneficial or most injurious, I must leave to the opinion of others, for I dare not hazard giving my own on so dubious an occasion.

Assuredly had our bigamist changed his religion for that of Mahomet, or of any other creedmaker who has shown himself tolerant on this head, and taken up his abode in a country where no punishment attends having a plurality of wives, saving what those wives themselves may occasion the husband, he would have stood on a proud pinnacle; but there is no gaining a permanent hold of happiness.

Besides the dangers brewing from Angelina's vengeance at the signora's fondness, an unforeseen peril threatened the bigamist in the midst of his triumphant career. The methodist, as Baron San Lucas had foretold he intended doing, at this epoch came raging and fuming to Naples, determined to bring this mutual friend of ours to a severe reckoning for the injury he falsely conceived he had done him.

The first thing the *ci-devant* parson did on his arrival was to call upon me to make known his grievances, when I told him he laboured under a mistake, for that I felt satisfied the bigamist had not exchanged booties with him.

This piece of information at first somewhat startled the preacher, but on my persisting in the opinion I had given, he eventually seemed to come into my way of thinking. However, the conduct subsequently pursued by this gentleman shows that what I had said failed in satisfying his mind regarding his friend's probity towards him; but, if the comparison may be made, as usually happens in a love affair carried on with a wedded lady, the guilty party is the very last suspected, so was it in this instance with Jacobus, alias fair Julia, whom the injured individual, shrewd as he was, yet never even hinted at as being suspected by him.

To hear advice and follow one's own, is the general way with the world. The preacher's conduct formed no exception to the rule, for he soon procured an interview with the bigamist, who, to be near his favourite signora, had removed from my hotel, and taxed him, in pretty plain terms, with having taken the unwarrantable liberty of exchanging treasures with him:

however, on perceiving that the bigamist was waxing wroth at this charge on his honour, he, no doubt, from being actuated by a conviction of the truth of that saying, "when Greek meets Greek, then comes the tug of war," subdued his arrogant tone, insomuch as to intimate his opinion that his friend probably had done it by way of a joke, and would be found ready, when called upon, to account with him for the difference in his favour between the two heaps of treasure.

The bigamist, who felt gratified at thus unexpectedly seeing his fellow-gamester, was exceedingly astonished at hearing the charge that was made by him; yet, as the other concluded his speech by saying the business complained of might have been intended for a joke, he, after a little reflection, considered that the complaint itself was meant as nothing more than a joke; and therefore smilingly observed, that an exchange could be no robbery, let them be who they might that made it; but, for his own part, he knew nothing whatever of the story in question, nor had he a pecuniary difference to account for with any man breathing.

Trifling differences lead to great feuds. The bigamist's speech inflamed the parson with fury; luckily, however, for both parties, his anger raged too violently to admit of his speaking, and before he could properly articulate what he had to say, a ray of returning reason had cleared the ominous cloud on his brain. So far was he now from answering in an angry tone, that he entered into an explanation of the trick which had been played upon him, and told how he discovered it not until he was absolutely bargaining with a jeweller in the Roman capital for the sale of his articles of plate.

The bigamist, now seeing that a scurvy trick had been practised on his old colleague, assured him of his total ignorance, until that moment, of any such exchange of properties as he told of having been made; and on a little reflection, said that it could have been executed by no other individual than the dwarf, as Mr Winpenny, under no circumstances, could be suspected; for that, in addition to his known respectability of character, he was very wealthy, and had been allotted the primary choice in the division of booty.

A word to the wise is sometimes enough, and the bigamist's speech instantaneously opened the parson's eyes. He now expressed astonishment at his own stupidity in not having attributed the trick played him to the real perpetrator of it, for that Jacobus was the guilty party he declared his conviction; and after giving vent to several violent exclamations denotive of his feelings at the liberty which had been taken with him, he requested information as to where the dwarf was to be found, saying at the same time, that he himself had disposed of the plate which had been substituted for his to the best advantage he could, and had brought with him a certified statement of the money it had sold for, that he might come to an immediate settlement with the unauthorized exchanger of their respective booties.

The preceding inquiry led to a further explanation, in making which the bigamist, whose gallantry had hitherto left him no leisure for reflection on the subject, had to express his astonishment at having neither seen nor heard anything of Jacobus since the day of their arrival in Naples; but if he felt surprised, it may well be imagined how much greater was that of his friend, whose consternation at the news absolutely struck him mute for a time. However, as nothing better could be devised at this consultation, the aggrieved man posted away from it to pay me another visit, this appearing to the two friends to afford the best, if not the only chance, of procuring information by which the dwarf might be found; and it so happened that Julia Ruberto, who had called upon me on business relative to the banditti, one of whom, Carl, she had the day previous seen lurking about in Naples, was with me at the time this visitor was announced.

Julia would fain have beat an honourable retreat on this occasion, but there was no time allowed her for doing so, and she was therefore compelled to face the man she had injured. He came almost breathless into the apartment, yet seeing a lady seated near the window, where she had promptly taken up her station, to be at a respectful distance from the unwelcome visitor, he paused and bowed to her before he made inquiries of me, in a low tone of voice, respecting Jacobus, and where he was to be found.

Self-interest has a fascinating power, and contracts the mind. It now had the effect of putting Julia extremely upon her guard, while it made the ci-devant preacher become very earnest in the business he had in view; but all the information he elicited from me was, that

Jacobus had quitted Naples, and I could not inform him where the little gentleman had retired to.

"The villain! would that I could come athwart him, and my sword should find its way to his heart," muttered this *ci devant* pastor of a christian flock, when he found he could gleam no useful tidings from me.

"I recollect, friend," said I (for I felt a strong inclination to play a little with both the gentleman and the lady's feelings), "that you expressed some suspicion of the dwarf's probity at the time he kept us dancing attendance upon him in the robber's stable. How then, in the name of charity, let me ask, did it happen that you neglected to inspect the marks on your bag of plate previous to your allowing the old guardian of it to part company with you, and this, too, although you had once declared yourself apprehensive that the whole party of us had been bit by him?"

"The double-faced villain, his organ of acquisitiveness must be very large; he would take in the very apostles if he had to deal with them. Believe me, sir, I was not fool enough to neglect examining the marks on my sack, but the wily knave overreached me, for he had taken care to exchange them with those on his own bag of the spoils."

"I recollect," said I, "your saying the banditti we overcame were all of them robbers and murderers—irreligious men, and the enemies of society at large; while the dwarf in question, it appears, was one of them."

"He it was," replied he, "that caused us to spare our prisoners' necks from the halter; and who can say he had not some sinister object in doing so? He may yet betray and bring the whole of us to destruction."

"Never fear," answered I; "we have divided the booty among us, and every man must take care of himself."

"Those who can't take care of the wealth they obtain, can hardly be trusted to take care of themselves," muttered the dissatisfied parson.

"If I remember correctly," observed I, "you once remarked to me, that in the affairs of this world men are saved, not by faith, but by the want of it."

"'Tis as true as any gospel that ever was preached," rejoined he with a groan.

"To use our friend the stockbroker's language," said I, after a protracted pause, and speaking in a sarcastic manner, "some of us may be doomed to keep our noses to the grind-stone the whole of our lives, and die poor and distressed after all."

"'Tis the fate of every gamester to live in the miseries of Tantalus, and that of most of them to die in the poverty of Lazarus," whispered he in my ear. "For my part, I have had a cursed run of bad luck, which has eased me of a great portion of my spoils."

By the preceding speech, I found the subject was too cutting to the complainant's feelings to allow of my jesting more upon it; and after declaring his determination to ferret Jacobus out, and either extract a supply of the needful from him, or bring him to his last mortal reckoning, he made his obeisance to the carroty-haired young lady, entreated of me to assist his views in finding the absentee, and took his departure.

"Well, Julia," said I, soon as our visitor was gone, "you have maintained your part to admiration, and imposed on us all; but tell me, signora, does not compassion move your heart towards this poor man, who, to use the gamester's language, has got himself nearly *cleaned out?* and notwithstanding your bump of acquisitiveness, you, no doubt, purpose coming down with a round sum to help him on in the world."

"If I do, may the sun of good fortune smile on me no more," said the hard-hearted fair one. "What! part with my precious money to uphold a gambler,—a man whose thoughts are upon odd and even till his last coin is gone? Aristotle and Count Anselma are much of my way of thinking—gamesters are no better than common thieves and plunderers."

"Then you really feel no compassion for the man you have tricked out of a part of his treasure; but you denominate him a thief and a plunderer, quite forgetting your own handy-work," said I, laughingly.

"Fair play is a jewel, and one good turn deserves another," rejoined little Julia; "he cheated me by means of false dice, and I retaliated on him by exchanging our marks. We are now quits, and my object shall be to steer clear of his notice."

" You will act with your accustomed prudence, I make no question," said I; "but, Julia, you tell me Carl is in the town, therefore you have two open foes to guard against."

" Yes, 'tis true Carl is here; yet never fear for me, as I shall take good care to steer clear of them both. You, however, signor, I must counsel to go armed, and be constantly on your guard, for depend on it, whoever Carl may discover belonging to our party will not be let walk the streets of Naples in safety. Now adieu for a time, and may good fortune attend you; but expect not to see me again at your hotel until Carl and the preacher find other employment than that of searching after me."

Julia now took her departure, but whether she had any plan in view for getting so dangerous a neighbour as Carl out of the way, she did not explain to me; though, judging from her known sagacity, I make no question that she meditated something not over-beneficial towards him.

I went to a magnificent dinner this day at the Marquis of Meralvo's mansion, after which the company stood up to dance, and with me, at least, the night was passed away most delightfully. However, fate so decrees, that while some are rejoicing others shall be sorrowing; and on my return home I found a messenger awaiting me from the bigamist, who wished me to visit him immediately. From what this man told me, it appeared that the bigamist and his friend had been set upon that night in the public streets, either by thieves or assassins, and both of them got wounded.

I lost no time in proceeding to my friend's lodging, where, in a double-bedded chamber, I found the two unfortunate gentlemen extended on mattresses, with a brace of nurses in attendance on them. Their wounds had been dressed, and the sons of Galen into whose clutches they had fallen, had taken their departure from the house; therefore, notwithstanding the injunctions which these gentlemen had left, that no person should be permitted to speak to their patients, I hazarded holding an interview with him.

The bigamist, whose wound was in the thigh, and, as it turned out, of trivial importance, had received from his medical attendants numerous cautions about his wound; he, however, not being a man to be terrified by squibs, and knowing something of the nature of wounds, was not alarmed on the occasion. He told me that his friend had returned to him after visiting me on the preceding day, and that they had dined together at a certain restaurateur's, celebrated for the excellent cookery of fish; when, as they were on the way home after dinner, flushed with wine, they had been set upon by two ferocious fellows, who had given them their wounds, and would undoubtedly have slain them outright, as they had nothing more than their sticks to defend themselves with, had not some persons opportunely arrived to their assistance, at whose appearance the thieves and assassins fled.

I asked him whether he or his friend had sufficiently noticed the villains to know them again by sight; on which he gave me to understand that their persons had been wrapped in large cloaks, and their faces hid in masks, which had rendered it impossible to make any particular observation of them.

The poor parson, who, in our combat with the Roman banditti, may be said to have come off with flying colours, for he escaped nearly unhurt, was now lying a pitiable object, suffering from a dagger wound in his side; but though he often groaned under his torments, his danger subdued not his rancorous spirit, for he not only swore bitter hostility against the villains who had occasioned him this evil, but also frequently indulged himself by uttering exclamations of anger against Jacobus, to whose cunning in surreptitiously exchanging treasures with him he attributed even this last misfortune.

I promised the discomforted gentlemen that I would use my best endeavours to get the villains who had maltreated them apprehended and brought to justice, and requested them to command my services in every respect; after which I took my departure from the hotel, to court the sweets of sleep

CHAPTER XVIII.

" That young and old may in thy praise combine,
The virtues of humanity be thine:
Trust all to heav'n; but thou, thy cares engage
To calm the passions and subdue thy rage:
From gentle manners let thy glory grow,
And shun contention, the sure source of woe."

" Her breast was peaceable—
A quiet conscience makes one so serene!
Christians have burnt each other, quite persuaded
That all the apostles would have done as they did."

BETIMES in the morning I revisited my wounded friends, whom I found doing well, but extremely mortified at being kept confined to their beds at a time when they were desirous of being employed abroad, one of them to fulfil an assignation with Signora Silva, and the other to search after the truant Jacobus. However, I shall pass over their complaints, and content myself by stating that I left the unfortunate gentlemen in the hands of their surgeons, and proceeded to consult the noble marquis and my friend the count, on what could be done to discover the perpetrators of the gross outrage which had been committed on the persons of my two friends.

I found both the noblemen at home, and one of the Neapolitan ministers of state was with them at the time of my visit, who most obligingly took an interest in the business, and sent for that servile character, the chief commissioner of the police, when he, having heard what I had to say, and written down the description I gave of Carl, took his departure, to set his myrmidons at work in all quarters to ferret out the daring culprits.

Not to dwell unnecessarily long on this part of the story, the result of this proceeding was that, extremely to fair Julia's contentment, a day or two afterwards, Carl and the other robber, already mentioned as having escaped from us, were captured by the police when in bed together at a lodging-house, which was well known as a place of rendezvous for notorious characters of the lower kind; and although the evidence against them at their trial, which took place almost immediately, was not very conclusive, yet partly through the good offices of my powerful friends, and partly owing to the bad characters of the men themselves, they were condemned to a year's service each in the galleys, and sent there accordingly. Their sentence undoubtedly would have been more severe, had it not been for the charitable interference of Count Anselma, who notwithstanding he had been instrumental in bringing them to justice, yet on finding the gentlemen they had wounded were doing well, compassionated their sufferings. He knew they had been stript of their hard-earned treasure, and he recollected that the man Carl had treated him and his daughter more kindly, when confined in their dungeons, than had the captain of banditti, or any other person of his party; therefore, through the medium of counsel, he contrived to soften matters on the trial, so as to prevent a more severe sentence being passed.

I must avow that I was rather surprised at the lenity shown by the worthy nobleman; and by the parson's desire I inquired of him into his motives for acting as he had done, when his answer spoke so strongly the innate benevolence of his heart, that I should act remissly were I not to insert it in these memoirs.

" Tell your friend," said he, " that I have acted from motives of charity and humanity ;— of that charity which the christian religion strongly inculcates, and it has been a main part of his business to preach. I could not help compassionating the fate of the poor wretches, and in the hope of their reform, I have done them this little service. It is true, every one could not have accomplished the object which I have done; but certainly, whenever we can so manage it, our good services should go hand in hand with our feelings of compassion, inasmuch as charity, which is to think well of, and do well to, every other human being, is the most amiable and most exalted of virtues,—a virtue which happily the most beneficent author of human nature has placed within the reach of every individual."

When I communicated the nobleman's speech to him, the parson expressed no kind of admiration at his noble sentiments; yet no sooner was his health sufficiently re-established to enable him to return to Rome than he availed himself of the benefit to be derived to him from the count's compassionate way of thinking, by putting his goodness of heart to the proof, in soliciting a pecuniary present for himself, to enable him to get back to the eternal city.

The appeal was not made in vain. Count Anselma recollected that his liberators had taken no ransom, and he subscribed a handsome sum, as did I likewise. The bigamist also assisted his friend, and Julia, feeling glad to get rid of him, notwithstanding her former declaration, now opened her purse, and generously, but under an assumed name, administered to his wants. Thus amongst us a good round sum was collected, with which the broken-down gamester (a designation justly befitting him, as he confessed that a run of ill luck had eased him of all his wealth) returned to Rome to invoke the smiles of fortune, for more than the thousandth time, at the gaming-table. Previous to his going, however, the bigamist gave his old friend a dinner, at which I was present. On this occasion the unfortunate clergyman, doubtless from being stung by a sense of his own avaricious folly, as greediness after wealth it is leads people to the gaming-table, as likewise to embark in other desperate hazards, and consequently is the forerunner of pauperism, and not unfrequently of suicide, preached us a very eloquent discourse, pointing out that propriety, necessity, and wisdom imperiously demand that parents should make a staple provision for their children, the principal money of which cannot be touched by them, to secure their offsprings through life against the miseries of poverty, a condition to which innumerable evils may bring even the wisest and the best of us in old age.

Whatever may have been the parson's own failings, and I know they were great, inasmuch as he was a drunkard, a gambler, and a man of an unforgiving, rancorous disposition, yet this discourse of his does him infinite honour, and for the sake of mankind at large I sincerely hope he may put the sentiments and matter it contains into print, which, indeed, he declared his intention of doing. This one act would make ample atonement for all the peccadillos of his life, and his most ungenerous foes, when they read his work, so far from bawling out with the ignorant, "O, that mine enemy had written a book," would be ready to go and hang themselves for vexation at thus being made sensible of the benefit this gentleman had conferred on the world.

I myself would attempt the task of declaring some of the sentiments I heard from his lips, were it not that I should mar a good subject by doing so; therefore I shall pass to other matters, after briefly but ardently expressing my hopes that the fortunes, life annuities, and other schemes proposed by him in the speech I heard may soon be established by all governments, for the protection of the children of affluent persons from the miseries of want in their old age. When this has been done through his recommendation and advice, our *ci-devant* preacher's name will stand on a prouder pinnacle than do any of those of the countless bishops and swarms of church pluralists for long generations, who have, like the locusts which bred famine in Egypt, thanklessly devoured the best produce of the land.

Julia Ruperta was highly delighted at the priest's departure; she had now got rid of the three persons she lived in terror of, and therefore could enjoy her wealth in peace of mind, and go abroad with pleasure and comfort to herself.

"Well, my little maid," said I to her, the first time we met each other after the parson's departure, "I presume I may congratulate you on the liberality you have shown, since it was contrary to your declared sentiments?"—"A branch may be lopped off to give vigour to the tree, and I could have no rest while the sectarian preacher was watching to destroy me," was her reply.

"The dark clouds of mystery, like those of the weather, not unfrequently obscure our view; and, fair Julia, certainly there was a something unaccountably strange in the circumstance of Carl and his associate falling foul as they did of my two colleagues."—"I have heard it whispered," said she, with a significant smile, "that one of them received an anonymous letter informing him that the parson was in Naples, and probably they expected to get possession of some of the banditti's lost treasure by attacking him."

"The secret is out," said I, "the mystery is cleared up. A blind person may see which way the wind blows. I reverence your cunning, fair Julia, and beg to repeat once more that

those persons need rise betimes, and be wide awake, who would get to windward of you."—
"The parson is an unprincipled fellow in every respect," returned the red-haired damsel; "he
has no more real religion in him than a fish, or a bird, or a four-legged beast. Will you
believe it, signor, he told me, when we were busy packing our bags of treasure in the cart,
preparatory to starting from the old chateau, that religion is a trade, in which the greatest
impostors thrive the best. In proof of which daring assertion he mentioned that in olden
days the priests of Egypt were wont to make choice of a bull for their god; those of the
Chaldeans, of the fish oannes; the Scandinavian nation, of Odin, styled the Father of
Slaughter; and that the Celts, the descendants of the Scythians, chose the misletoe as theirs;
while that the Christian built his fabric of theology upon a miraculous conception, disbelieved
to this day by the nation, now a widely scattered people, whom, nineteen centuries ago, it
was destined to bring to salvation."

"His doctrine must be revolting to your Catholic feelings, fair Julia," said I.

"Name it not; it is altogether so," was her reply. Then presently she added,—"Will
you believe it, signor, he said that the religion of the present Romans is entirely derived
from that of their heathen ancestors, which, he asserts, is seen by the use they make of incense,
holy water, tapers, and lamps in their worship, as likewise in the practice of pomps and
processions, pretended miracles and pious frauds,—in the making of votive offerings and gifts,
and the erecting of rural shrines; also in the orders of the priesthood, nuns, monks, begging
friars, &c.; in the use of boys clothed in sacred habits to attend the officiating priest; all
which, according to his declaration, were practised by the Pagans, and are practised by the
Popes in imitation of them. It should be observed, too, that the Mahometan and all other
religions fall equally under his censure with that of the Christian. The parson told me the
Alcoran was not written until thirty years after Mahomet's death, and that therefore it must
abound with lies; for at that time the Mahometan empire had been founded, and it was com-
piled as a state religion, to give it support."

"It is well for him," I observed, "that the Inquisition reigns not in its pristine power;
for if it did, he might probably find himself tied to a stake some ill-starred day, ready to be
burnt with Jews and other unfortunate persons, as so many peace-offerings of an inveterate
clergy to God, of whom they arrogate to themselves many of the attributes."

"Yes; and the scoffers at our divine religion ought to be brought to condign punishment,"
said the rancorous little bigot, crossing herself while she spoke. "One thing, however, I
must say," added she, in a subdued tone, as if struck with a sense of shame at her illiberality
"and this is, that our religion aside, his general remarks were excellent. One of them, in
speaking of Mahomet, I well recollect.—'Those,' said he, 'who make great changes in the
universe, do it not by gaining over the chiefs of parties, but by winning the crowd to their
wishes.'"

"This," said I, "is the secret reason why he is an enemy to the hierarchy established in
his country. He would have every preacher of the gospel left to his exertions to gather
together as many of the crowd and as much of their money as he is able. 'Those who object
to support a national church, because they differ from its tenets,' I have heard him say, 'have
truth, reason, and justice on their side; inasmuch as truth says, to compel men to support any
religion is wrong. Reason says, to compel them to support the religion of a different sect is
tyranny; and justice exclaims, it shall continue no longer.'"

Like the brilliant set in gold, so is good sense in appropriate phrase. During the time
the events recorded in these pages were passing at Naples, I had almost every day the gratification of being edified by the liberal and enlightened conversation of my noble friend, Count
Anselma; and what was of still greater moment to a young man in my situation, as it tended to
afford me the highest possible terrestrial happiness, was the being blest every day by the society
of the highly accomplished and beautiful Antonia. I should have been a deplorable dunce in
matters of worldly wisdom had I neglected to profit by the flattering advantages. I made the
most of them I could, and so effectually wormed myself into the good graces of both the father
and daughter, that nothing more now remained wanting on my side to ensure to me possession of the lovely Antonia and the large fortune she was heiress to, but that to which assuredly
my birth had given me no pretensions namely, an ancient and noble pedigree. My income
—thanks to my own management, aided by not a few of the smiles of fortune—was at this

time princely, and what is more, all derived from interest money on my own unencumbered capital,—not from places, sinecures, or unjust leases of landed property, under any capricious government under the sun.

Perfection is not the lot of humanity; consequently the wisest and best of men have their peculiar weaknesses, and my friend the count was not free from such; but his failings were in a manner contradictory to each other, as, for example, he entertained a strong bias towards the ancient aristocracy, whom he looked to for everything virtuous; while, with an erroneous judgment, comparable on this head to that of the great Bacon, he considered them as the emblems of time; and, more justly, the new-fangled nobility as the mere creatures of power, whose nobility is bestowed for qualities which favour the personal views of their chief ruler.

His other peculiar weakness was that of showing too much condescension, which, though 'tis amiable, is a most dangerous thing; for few deserve our confidence, and those most eager to gain it are ever the first to betray it. This last named weakness, however, I made subservient to my purpose, inasmuch as it enabled me to obtain minute information of the count's family secrets, amongst which the particulars of his large revenue were the most interesting to me.

Had I derived my descent from an ancient and a distinguished family, unquestionably I might now have carried the lovely and wealthy prize of beauty in glorious triumph; but the low, vulgar, stupid name of Winpenny stood an impediment in my path to success; indeed, it was so sorrily thought of, that I knew not how to get it grafted on a good genealogical tree. The count was partial to me, insomuch that, could my origin be shown to be noble, he would have preferred me to any other man for a son-in-law, which he candidly avowed to me. But then Winpenny was so intolerably low a name, that there was no possibility of his stomaching it. He could not, he said, have one of the *canaille* as his son-in-law and heir, even though he might have inherited the wealth of the wealthiest Jew contractor.

As to Antonia, I knew that she loved me, but she was a most dutiful daughter, who would have suffered her charms to wither away to old age in celibacy, rather than act in opposition to her father's avowed wishes; therefore, with both the parent and child, the confounded name of Winpenny stood an obstacle in my way to good fortune; it was like a dangerous rock right a-head of a ship in full sail, which she can pass neither to windward or leeward of.

I was put to my wit's end to get over this difficulty, and eventually stood indebted to the bigamist, who knew many of the shuffling tricks practised in furthering matrimonial alliances, for suggesting the practicability of getting myself perched upon some ancient genealogical tree, under a different name from that of Winpenny.

This hint infused new spirits into me, and to profit by it I lost no time in seeking out the most skilful genealogists in all Naples. To him I explained my case, and intimated that he might fix his own terms, provided he carried me triumphantly through the difficulties attached to my name and the want of a proud ancestry, when he gave me to understand that my case was by no means an uncommon one; and having taken a large fee, as earnest money of my intentions, promised he would lose no time in examining certain old records, from which he would endeavour to make a pedigree for me, and further said I should hear something satisfactory from him in a few days.

The genealogist's promise was soothing to my hopes, and I met Count Anselma and his lovely daughter in exuberant spirits at their dinner the day I received it. However, to shorten the tale, the pedigree-maker sent for me within the term of his promise, when, not a little to my pleasurable astonishment, he found an ancestor for me in the Neapolitan Count de deux Sous, a most renowned commander, who flourished before the time of the French Emperor Charlemagne.

Having reflected on the nature of this communication, the pleasure it occasioned me began to give way to apprehensions that it was too good to be realised; not that I cared a sou concerning the vaunted fame of Count de deux Sous, nor the honour of being a descendant of such a hero, but because on the management of this affair hinged my prospect of becoming the husband of the beautiful heiress Antonia; and in my anxiety on the subject, I bluntly inquired of the genealogist how this Neapolitan Count de deux Sous, who lived a thousand years ago, could be shown to be an ancestor of Andrew Winpenny, an obscure English-man?

The genealogist could not forbear smiling at my ignorance, but he apologised for his rudeness, and said, that with the wealth I had at my disposal, backed by my powerful friend's influence at the Neapolitan court, the pedigree he chalked out for me could be made to pass valid with the world easier than a child is taught its alphabet. "Indeed," added he, rubbing his hands together with joy, "circumstances seem to conspire in your favour, as do but observe, signor, how closely the name Winpenny approximates to deux Sous. Few are the titles recovered from olden times, or the pedigrees which have to travel far back, that are half so clearly established as I hope to make out your claim to the countship of this once famous commander. Winpenny! the name speaks for itself; it must have been derived from deux Sous *gagner*, and this celebrated count, I shall be able to show, from his oft-repeated success in battle, was called the Victorious, and sometimes *le gagnant*."

"But, my good sir, I must once more ask how it can be practicable to make a pedigree for me, as the descendant of this Italian warrior?"

"A man's pedigree," replied he, "in many instances, has nothing to do with his ancestry; it is a thing fabricated for him by some able genealogist, who grafts his name upon a branch of a leafless tree, and thereby brings the old wood to a state of foliage. The fraud of the transaction confers a benefit on monarchy and the aristocracy, inasmuch as it gives another of time's old pillars for the pride and support of both; and, what is more, is made to serve the interested purposes of harpies about the court, who vend the old title at a higher rate than they could a new one, while it enables the lawyers to spin their musty yarn to great advantage, and the monarch to metamorphose a favourite into a very ancient peer of his realm, which is a feat not easy to be accomplished, although a monarch can make new peers thick as drones, and comparable to them, as living in idleness on the labouring community."

"I bow submissively to the august mysteries of your learned profession," said I; "nevertheless, as the pedigree you intend to honour me with requires being made out in England, I cannot see how you can effect the desired object."

"Distress not your mind by doubts on the subject," rejoined he; "your genealogical tree, far as it can be done here, will be completed to-morrow, and by it will be shown that one Moses deux Sous, the direct and only descendant of the famed count, served under the banner of William the Norman, bastard, who made a conquest of England, and in the fourth generation this man's descendants changed their name to Silverpenny, and a century after to Winpenny, which they have borne ever since."

"All this," said I, "may look very well on the genealogical tree of your planting; but what documents can be forthcoming from England to crown your labours with the desired success?"

"Pardon me, signor, for saying so, but you know nothing of these things," answered the pedigree-maker. "The strength of your claim will be bottomed upon your foreign extraction, while your pedigree itself will be the less scrutinised into from its coming from a foreign land. I need only to add, that my correspondent is one of the leading genealogists in England, where his influence is predominant at the heraldic college, and he will fill up your pedigree from the time of the first Moses deux Sous to that of your birth; when, on the transmission of this document to Naples, your court friends here will readily succeed in purchasing the restoration of the deux Sous title to the rightful heir of the family, which is yourself; though, in all probability, to guard against jealousy among the peers, your title o count will be dated only from the grant."

"Then be it so," said I, with a smile. "I suppose I must stomach this little indignity; but, my friend, are you really of opinion I shall get ennobled in this easy way?"

"There can be no doubt of it," replied he. "Everything tells in your favour—you have powerful friends, and are ready to pay a high price for your title. Besides, you are a foreigner and extremely rich, therefore there can be no fears entertained by the government of your soon becoming one of those pauper peers who bring disgrace upon the aristocracy, and who need place and pension to uphold their lawful families; and assuredly as that the land must sometimes lie fallow, sooner or later every peerage and branch of it has to be supported from the public purse, to the injury of the people, wherefore each new title is a curse on the great community."

There was sound reason embodied in what the genealogist had said; consequently, after furnishing him with the names of my parents, together with those of my grandparents on the paternal side, and stating the parishes in which these unassuming people were born, married, and died, I departed, leaving a check on my banker for a handsome sum, that the genealogist might do what was needful with his London correspondent, as also satisfy himself that in his transactions with me he had to deal with a liberal character.

CHAPTER XIX.

"Heavens! what is this?
Lord have mercy upon us!"

"What black magician conjures up this fiend?
What! do ye tremble? Are ye all afraid?
Alas! I blame ye not, for ye are mortal,
And mortal eyes cannot endure the devil—
Avaunt, thou dreadful minister of hell!"

My friend, the bigamist, during the time many of the preceding events were passing, was revelling away his hours in all the felicity that Signora Silva's cheerful acquiescence in his amatory views could occasion him, and such was his success, too, with other females, that I recollect saying to him, "My friend, you are over-fortunate. I am alarmed at your constant prosperity; and therefore shall give you the advice of Amasis to Polycrates, to procure some mortification or suffering to yourself."

My caution, given in jest, the superstitious, judging by what followed, might have mistaken for inspiration. Peril, however, is an attendant on our most blissful enjoyments, and surely an evil spirit must have been at work, not only to terminate my friend and the signora's reciprocal delights, but also to make this, by him, beloved fair one, the means of inflicting a supernatural punishment on the poor bigamist.

I have said that the signora was the mistress of a certain wealthy and potent duke, who, in consequence of the levity of her conduct, and her entertaining much company, had become jealous of the lady; and I must now add, that about this time, as was reported, from his having received private information, but conclusive as to his culpability, and which it was believed came from Antonia's serving-maid, the vindictive Angelina, his grace's revenge was particularly directed against my gallant friend, whose attentions to the signora fired his breast with such fell feelings, that he came to the resolution of having him assassinated.

The duke's black intention got bruited abroad, and the report came to my ears, when I lost no time in consulting with my friend, the bigamist, on what should be done to guard against the impending danger. The result was his coming to a determination to fly from Naples, to hide himself somewhere in the neighbourhood of Salerno, until an opportunity might offer of his embarking at that port for Toulon, where he knew it to be my intention to proceed soon as my business and that of Count Anselma at Naples should be terminated, and where he himself purposed residing for a time, to keep up an intimacy with me and the count's family.

To serve my friend, who felt rather dispirited at the necessity there was for his flight, and purposing to remain a day or two his guest there, I accompanied him to a village, which must be a few leagues beyond Salerno. The day following our arrival, as we sat discussing some prime wine after a late dinner, the bigamist, exceedingly to my consternation, suddenly started from his seat, and with horror depicted in his countenance retreated, stepping backwards to the far end of the apartment, his eyes constantly fixed towards a vacant spot near the door, and he deeply absorbed in attention, as if listening to the speech of some one, though, be it observed, I heard nothing; and in this manner he remained stationary during some minutes, trembling violently from top to toe, when suddenly he shrieked aloud with terror; then, presently assuming a little courage, exclaimed, "Heaven be praised, she is gone."

I now got my friend to resume his seat, and questioned him as to what was the matter; when he said, "What! is it possible? and did you not see the spectre of Signora Silva? She came, habited in the ordinary dress of the signora, but with bosom bare, and a bleeding wound in her right breast, while her hand grasped a bloody dagger."

" My friend," replied I, " surely you are jesting; you cannot be in earnest."

" Jesting," rejoined he, " who dares jest with immortality? Heard you not the angry ghost speak to me?—yes, you must have heard her; ' Ungrateful wretch,' said she, looking sternly, ' why did you forsake me?' "

" Friend," said I, putting on the appearance of greater courage than I felt, " your imagination must be deranged. You are like Brutus, when he fancied he beheld the gigantic spectre in his tent; but the dead can do us no harm, therefore let us not be appalled by deceptions of the imagination, of which this is one."

" The malignant—the wicked spirit," exclaimed the poor fellow, convulsively shuddering as he spoke; " it was the real ghost of the departed signora. She is dead, and I shall speedily follow after her. Mark the time, Winpenny; mark to a minute what the time is."

I affected to make light of what was said, yet I looked at my chronometer, which was in good order, and an excellent one, and the time was exactly eight o'clock. Moreover, I lost no time in dispatching a messenger to Naples with a letter for Count Anselma, privately soliciting to be informed if anything extraordinary had happened to Signora Silva, and he returned next day with the news of that famed courtezan's death, which had happened exactly at the time the bigamist stated that he had seen her spectre, and in the very way it had given him to understand the signora perished.

This affair of the ghost exceedingly bewildered my imagination, for although, during my diversified career of life, I had been embroiled with many terrible characters, and beheld many terrific sights; yet it was with mankind only that I had got embroiled, and men it was who enacted the desperate deeds I had witnessed. However, not to add to the bigamist's alarm, which had already become too frightful for his peace of mind, I avoided as much as possible all conversation with him regarding the apparition; and, as soon as with decency I could, left him in his village retreat, awaiting his passage to Toulon, that I might return back to Naples.

I made Count Anselma my confidant in every particular regarding the bigamist's intimacy with the late Signora Silva, and the apparition he had seen of her, for things which appear incredible should be communicated to none save the wise. He was extremely interested, but not much surprised, at the tale, which last circumstance somewhat startled me, because having myself given no credit to ghost stories, but always considered them the fables of weak or designing persons, I expected from him a similar opinion of supernatural appearances of this sort.

" Your poor friend's fate is fixed," said he, soon as I had finished my tale. " He will shortly be numbered with the dead, for apparitions, such as he has seen, come not to deceive."

" Count," replied I, " until now I believed not in the apparition of disembodied spirits to mortal eyes, but what my friend has seen in my presence cannot be forgotten by me."

" He," rejoined he, " has beheld what few are permitted to see : departed spirits, however, or rather guardian and bad spirits, for the scripture tells us there are both, are sometimes permitted to manifest themselves, and preternatural impressions are occasionally communicated to us."

" I am almost satisfied these are truths," observed I.

" We," resumed the count, " have the authority of scripture to prove that departed unembodied souls sometimes revisit mankind. In the first book of Samuel, the witch of Endor calls up a bad spirit to personify that old personage's ghost, which says to Saul, ' Why hast thou disquieted me, to bring me up?' Then we have testimony here of the reality of apparitions, as it respects the souls of departed persons, in the appearance of Moses and Elieas with Christ in the mount at his transfiguration."

" Is it, count," asked I, " your opinion that it was the spirit of Signora Silva which my friend beheld?"

" No," replied he, " I am decidedly of opinion it was not her spirit. I apprehend there are few speculative delusions more universally received than this, that those things we call spectres, ghosts, and apparitions, are really the departed souls of those persons whom they are said to represent. We see, or believe we see our dead friends and relations actually clothed with their old bodies, though we know those bodies to be rotting in the grave. We see them dressed up in the very clothes which we have cut to pieces and given away amongst different persons. We hear them speaking with the same voice, though the organ which formed their former speech, we are sure, is gone and perished. These similitudes of things fix it upon our thoughts that it must be the same—that the souls of our late friends are actually come to revisit us, which to me is most incongruous and unlikely; for, in the first place, they must have a mean opinion of the future state and the exalted condition of the blessed, that can imagine they are to be interrupted in their joy, and even disquieted, by the power of a despicable witch, as Samuel is represented to have been, when speaking the words quoted; and, secondly, they must have mean thoughts of the state of the wicked hereafter, who can think that the spirits in prison can get loose to come and attend upon the trifles of life."

"Then," asked I, "since it was not the spirit of the late signora, pray what was it that did appear?"

"It was one of the world of spirits which inhabit this globe, and which are termed invisible, yet occasionally are permitted to become manifest to our sight. If apparitions of the departed could appear at pleasure, there would be no place for mankind. Unembodied souls would then be perpetually coming back here to harass their executors for injuring their orphans; and in this case, how could Henry the Eighth of England have reigned in peace to the day of his death, after having seized upon the revenues, rents, lands, monies, and estates bequeathed by unnumbered charitable persons to found and maintain hospitals, colleges, churches, and religious houses? Resentment all dies with the breath of life; and whatever the apparitions which we call souls have pretended, or we have pretended for them, the souls of the departed are perfectly unconcerned at it all."

"Then, Count Anselma, if I understand you right, you think that neither the souls of the blessed or the cursed, the happy or the miserable, are concerned at these appearances; who then, let me ask, are the inhabitants of the invisible world?"

"There must," answered the count, "be a world of spirits, or of spirit, from whence we receive the frequent notices in private, which are so perceptible to us, and which we are so uneasy about. These may, without any absurdity, be supposed capable of assuming shape, conversing with mankind, either in the ordinary way, either by voice and sound, though in appearances and borrowed shapes, or by private notices of things, impulses, forebodings, misgivings, and other imperceptible communications to the minds of men, as God, their great employer, may ordain; and when all's said, 'tis but soul conversing with soul, spirit communicating to spirit, one intellectual being to another, and by secret conveyances, such as souls converse by. Neither is the apparition of these spirits any absurdity: these may be intimate with us, appear to us, be concerned about us, without anything intelligible to mortal. Thus they are guardian angels to the very letter, without being obliged to attend at every man's ear or elbow. Mankind are thus truly said to be in the hands of God always; and Providence, which constantly works by means and instruments, has the government of the world actually in his administration, not only by infinite power, but by immediate deputation."

"Count," observed I, "you have said that this terrestrial globe is frequented by bad spirits as well as guardian angels, and surely that which has appeared to my friend must be one of the infernal kind."

"Assuredly so; it was a diabolical spirit, that came to harass and affright your friend, perhaps expecting it should bring him into a fit of desperation, so as to destroy himself, as the woman it appeared in the shape of had done before. He too, poor man, was the more affected at the sight, inasmuch as he was conscious of crime, for he had not only acted dishonestly with her, but it seems had been dishonest to her, which had led her to be her own executioner. Many are the authenticated histories of apparitions of this description—of the apparitions of persons whose souls have just previously—yea, at the very instant—escaped from their prisons of clay, some of which have appeared to friends of the deceased at exceeding great distances—even thousands of miles from where the spark of life was ejected from the mortal frame; and moreover, people renowned for their wisdom, of all countries and in all ages, have believed in the reality of these spirits. By their own angelic and spirituous penetration, I believe the good spirits know everything of us needful to be known, and are capable of being affected in our behalf, so as to concern themselves for our good on many accounts; and also that the demon of evil, from the beginning of the world to the present day—from when he made a murderer of Cain and tormented Job almost to death—has sometimes been permitted to haunt people for their crimes—to worry, terrify, and perplex them ; yea, and by evil counsel, to endeavour to bring them to destruction ; but he can do no more, and good advice he never gives."

" Alas !" I involuntarily exclaimed, " my poor friend's fate, I see, is irrevocably fixed."

" Yes," said the count ; " from time to time he will be tormented by this fiend, and eventually perish in the way that has been foretold." Then, having mused for a time, he added, " There are many well-authenticated tales of apparitions, which bear me out in my reasoning, but it is unnecessary to go into them.   One, however, that of a ghost that assumed the appearance of a deceased lady who had been the mistress of a Lord Littleton, and came to terrify and warn him of his death, which took place at the predicted minute, may be glanced at, as being applicable to our case ; as also may that of the ghost which tormented Cassio Burroughs, until, according to its prediction, he was slain in a duel, for these must have been fiendish spirits, like unto the one which your friend has seen.   Another—that of an apparition which personified Sir George Villiers, the father of the first Duke of Buckingham, and appeared several times to Mr Gowes, an officer of the king's wardrobe in Windsor Castle, telling him certain secrets known only to the duke, and directing him to go to his grace, and warn him that, unless he did something to conciliate the public favour, he would, a quarter of a year from that time, be slain by a dagger, which he accordingly was—must, on the other hand, have been a guardian spirit, for it came for a good purpose ; but that it was Sir George Villiers' spirit cannot be maintained, as Sir George had been dead many years ; and how could his soul have been disturbed for this world's affairs, or he have known of his son's conduct after his own death?   The famous Lord Clarendon, in his ' History of England,' relates all the particulars of this apparition ; and referring you to it for further information, I shall, after commenting upon a remarkable dream of more recent occurrence, turn to a gayer subject. The dream was that of Mr Williams, of Scorrior House, near Redruth, in Cornwall, and happened in the night of the 11th May, 1812, when he *three* several times dreamed he was in the lobby of the House of Commons, and saw a man shoot with a pistol a gentleman, said by one of the crowd seen in his dream to be the Chancellor. Mr Williams told his dream everywhere, and minutely described the appearance and dress of the man that he saw in his dream fire the pistol ; and it so happened that, on the evening of the 11th May, a man named Bellingham had shot Mr Percival, the Chancellor of the Exchequer.   Six weeks after, Mr Williams having business in town, went with a friend to the House of Commons, where he had never been before, and instantly, on coming to the steps at the lobby, he said, " This place is as distinctly within my recollection, in my dream, as any room in my house ;" and he made the same observation when he entered the lobby, and pointed out the exact spot where Bellingham had stood when he fired, and which Mr Percival had reached when he was struck by the ball, where he fell.   The dress, too, of Percival and Bellingham agreed with the description given by Mr Williams, even to the most minute particulars.   Now, my young friend, judging from this dream, and some other remarkable ones on record, as also from the clearness with which we behold things, persons, and places in our sleep, which are far distant from us, and moreover, reflecting on the infinitely superior brightness of our ideas and reasoning, when dreaming, to what we are capable of while awake, I am inclined to believe that the embodied soul quits its earthly case or prison, when the body is asleep, to wander free and far, enjoying itself in spirituality with aerial companions from the world of spirits."

" This last idea of yours is a noble one, my lord," said I, " and it will often fill my imagination. Tell me, however, since you say there are good and bad spirits, which last can do us no bodily harm, whether it is advisable to speak to an apparition ?"

" Yes," answered he, " in my opinion we ought ; and I am borne out in it by that of many worthies who have written on the subject. It would be well of us to ask it, ' In the name of God, what business hast thou here?' These worthies are mostly agreed that the evil spirits very rarely appear, and that almost all apparitions are of friendly and assisting spirits, which come of a kind and beneficent errand to us ; therefore, that we need not be terrified at them as we are. When an evil spirit does appear, it is limited by a superior power, and can do us no harm without *special licence*, and this, methinks, should take off the terror from our minds, and cause us to arm ourselves with resolution to meet the satanic fiend, whatever shape he thinks fit to assume. Moreover, he that is not able to face the devil in any form or shape, is not really qualified to live in this world—no, not in the quality of a common inhabitant!"

"Moreover," added the count, after some little contemplation, "do not many persons maintain that the charmed magical mirror furnishes unquestionable testimony of the secret communication which exists between the imprisoned spirit or soul of man and the free unembodied world of spirits; which last, some imagine, at man's invocation, often curiously shows things and people to him in the magical mirror, in the order and way whereby they have or shall affect his worldly interests."

More conversation on the foregoing gloomy subject was entirely out of the question, for at this moment the charming Antonia made her appearance in the apartment, and we entered into conversation with her; therefore the count's recommendation was attended to, for we certainly turned to a gayer subject than any spectre could have been in our eyes; or that the charmed magical mirror could have furnished matter for as a topic of converse between us.

CHAPTER XX.

" He who has but impudence
To all things else may make pretence,
And put among his wants but shame,
To all the world may make his claim."

" 'Tis not her skin surpassing fair,
Contrasted with her dark-brown hair;
'Tis not her dark blue eyes' mild flash,
Nor pencill'd brow, nor silken lash;
'Tis not her lips of ruby bright,
Parting on teeth of purest white;
Form, stately as the mountain pine,
And graceful as the clustering vine.
'Tis that expression undefined,
At once recalling to my mind
Those fancied traits, which e'er did seem
To be the idol of my dream ;
When all my thoughts, in one bright move,
Have pictured out a thing to love."

MY friend the bigamist repeatedly wrote to me during the time he was detained at his place of retreat in the country, waiting his passage to Toulon; but when the vessel he purposed departing in was on the eve of sailing, I quitted Naples, with the intention of staying away for two or three days, to make what I much feared would be a farewell visit to him.

He was even more than usually delighted at seeing me, but I soon discovered that *toujours gai* could no longer be a suitable motto for his character. Indeed, care marked his countenance; yet she was a visitor I had never seen there previous to the appearance before him of the accursed apparition, which so uncourteously disturbed this friend and me at table, and occasioned the remarks to be written on good and bad spirits which appear in the preceding chapter of these memoirs.

He told me that the malignant spirit had paid him a second visit, and that she came at midnight, when he was lying in bed, wide awake, with a candle burning on his table. The door of the chamber, he said, was fastened, and he saw not how the ghost first appeared in the room, but her threats and reproaches were the same as before; and moreover, on this last occasion, the terrific scene was still aggravated by her repeatedly flourishing the gory dagger in her hand.

With pain it was that I heard my friend describe this unearthly object's second visit, for I deplored his misfortune from my very heart; what, however, could I say of a nature to cheer up his spirits, when the subject of his complaint was beyond the power of mortal to redress? The sturdiest buccaneer that ever inhaled the breath of life, the most undaunted bandit that ever shed his fellow-man's blood, yea, even the stipended leader of armies, whose gods are his king and himself, would certainly, in my poor friend's situation, have felt their courage sink within them, on beholding the dread apparition which had now twice appeared to disturb his rest.

Friendship and compassion demanded of me to do everything in my power to raise the poor sufferer's spirits, and by the aid of wine, facetious tales, and diversions of various kinds, I strove to effect this purpose, but to bring them to their ordinary standard was impracticable. However, it is consolatory to me to know that I performed my duty, and on taking leave of my friend on board the vessel, just as she was getting under weigh, I strongly impressed on his mind the wisdom of confiding in Providence, to give him the victory over his tormentor, and, as the count had advised, recommended him, should this evil genius of his again appear, to call upon it in the name of his creator, to tell what business it had to disturb him.

I hastened back to Naples with the speed of a Mercury, soon as I had seen the vessel, with my friend on board, borne several leagues away from Salerno with a favouring breeze; but, to conclude his tale, it remains only to be told, that about two weeks from the time of the vessel's sailing, I received a letter from her captain, in which he stated that my friend had unfortunately perished in the sea, wherein he had been precipitated by the sheet of their ship's main-sail, which, when the sail was flapping in the sea, had accidentally caught hold of him round his leg; when, though the boat was lowered down, and every means resorted to to save him, it was impossible to do so, he never having risen to the water's surface after falling overboard.

The captain, in his letter, further stated, that a will had been found among the gentleman's papers, whereby he bequeathed the bulk of his property to a lady therein mentioned by her maiden name, although by a memorandum appended to the testament, it appeared she was his wife, as also the fourth spouse he had taken to himself.

This enigma, he observed, I might, perhaps, be able to clear up, and that it was to be hoped I could do so, more particularly as the gentleman had named me his sole executor, and left me a legacy of two hundred pounds conditionally that I undertook the trust. The property the unfortunate gentleman had on board his vessel, he concluded by saying, had been sealed up after an inventory had been taken of it; and on his arrival at Toulon, for his letter, it should be observed, was written at sea, he intended to deposit the will, as well as the property of the drowned gentleman, with a celebrated banker whom he named, to await there either my arrival, or until I transmitted a power of attorney, enabling some person to act in my behalf.

The news of the poor bigamist's untimely ate diffused a damp on the spirits of his old associates; but Count Anselma and myself, though we deplored his loss, had felt so thoroughly satisfied that his days would be few in the land of the living; and also that since the apparition's visitation life itself was more painful than pleasurable to him, that we soon consoled ourselves at his death. Angelina, however, that jealous and mischievous *fille de chambre*, by the ungovernable grief she showed on hearing of the catastrophe by which the bigamist came to his death, gave us cogent reasons for believing her to have been the authoress of the anonymous communications which have already been alluded to as having been conveyed to the duke, and consequently the primary cause of the lamentable deaths of Signora Silva and my poor friend. But, as the count observed to me, ill-requited love and scornful treatment often drive the female mind to a state of frenzy; while suspicion not affording justifiable cause for conviction, we deemed it the best policy to let the maid's only punishment be her feelings, and provided she was guilty of the mischief which led to my friend's death, heaven knows her affliction would be amply severe.

In concluding this melancholy story, which is true in every particular, and could be vouched for by many of my acquaintances, I take the opportunity of explaining what are my motives for never having mentioned by their proper names either the bigamist, the methodist parson, or several other persons who appear in these memoirs. The plain fact is, they are all real characters, and I have felt actuated by delicacy towards their friends and relatives, which has made me forbear giving their names, and yet I feel confident that doing so would vastly increase and promote the circulation of my memoirs; for many people love to obtain information which enables them to talk of their neighbours, and this they might then do of many, owing to their connexion with the enterprising gentlemen of whom I am treating. However, even modesty should be confined within limits; therefore, notwithstanding that I keep their names secret, to prove to the world that two at least of my heroes are not imaginary characters, I shall go so far as to mention that the bigamist was own brother to a certain well-known knight belonging to one of the corporate companies of the city of London; and that the methodist parson, who had been a pettifogging lawyer before the spirit moved him to become a minister of the gospel, was thought highly of as a preacher in the neighbourhood of the British metropolis, until such time as his propensity for the bottle, and his notoriety as a gambler, had rendered it impracticable for him to uphold the evangelical character any longer; he having violated decorum so greatly, as on more than one occasion to go intoxicated into his pulpit, and been proved to have pledged property belonging to the chapel he officiated at, to raise fresh stakes for the hazard-table of a petty gaming-house near Saint James's palace.

The bigamist's untimely fate, cut off as he was, too, in the flower of his age, gave rise to much serious conversation in the domestic circle of which I had the happiness of making one; and Count Anselma's remarks on the event were listened to by every person with greedy ears. "Human life," he would say, when discoursing on the subject, "resembles a lamp, which may be extinguished by a sudden blast, or by the gradual exhaustion of that which supports it. Since therefore, my friends, life is at the mercy of every breeze—since a pestilential blast, or any one of thousands of other things which might be enumerated, can instantly extinguish it, one of the great duties of man is to divest himself of pride and study humility—humility, which may be thus defined:—We are truly humble when we permit others to discover faults in us which we ourselves are not willing to own, and when we receive their rebukes and corrections with patience, and a sincere desire to profit by them. Self-love conceals from our view many of our frailties; and while we indulge this passion we cannot but be surprised that they should be discovered in us by our fellow-creatures; but true humility will make us distrust and think lowly of ourselves, turn to God for his grace to conquer our evil dispositions, and bear with patience the corrections of our fellow-creatures."

The language of good sense and virtue, flowing as it did from the lips of a benevolent philosopher, carried with it irresistible conviction, and each day that I listened to Count Anselma's discourse left me a better man than it had found me. The sweet converse of Antonia also wrought a blessed change in my mind; consequently, how could my improvement be other than rapid, when the siren though innocent strains of the daughter, and the wise discourse of her parent, were two powerful causes at work to produce the same effect on me?

Impatience has been defined as arising from a want of fortitude to suffer pain; but this definition must be an erroneous one, for I, who now lived in a continued round of pleasure, yet grew impatient, when sufficient time had elapsed for the purpose, and still my much coveted pedigree arrived not from England, and more than once I called upon my friend the genealogist to consult him on the subject of its non-arrival. He was a humorous fellow, and on these occasions would say to me,—" Signor Winpenny, for so I must call you a little while longer, time is necessary for producing all the good fruits of the earth, and if the poet is to be credited, those of heaven likewise,—

"For Time, which kills, sets all things right and even;
Time is man's dread,—Time brings the bliss of heaven.' "

The poet and the genealogist both told true. After a little more delay my pedigree came, and an admirable one it was. The English-pedigree maker, however, to enhance the price of this article of his manufacturing, arrogated to himself a wonderful degree of credit for the masterly manner in which he had filled up the genealogical tree with Winpenny, from the time of one David Winpenny, whom he made it appear was the descendant in the fourth generation of that Moses Deux Sous who followed the fortunes of William the Norman, who conquered England, and was the individual that changed the family name from Deux Sous to Silver-penny, unto that of the present representative of the family,—the claimant of the Deux Sous countship.

By the parish registers he had searched, this gentleman said, it certainly appeared that the Winpenny family were of some antiquity; though, from information derived from other sources, he found they had never been known, even by tradition, save as a poor family, many of the members of which had been burdensome on their parishes. This last circumstance, however, my genealogist remarked, might be deemed favourable to the claimant of a title, inasmuch as needy persons cannot thwart the views which their wealthier relatives may entertain this way; while, on the contrary, rich and powerful relations are perpetually jealous of each other's rise, and ready to impede their progress to grandeur above their own, directly and indirectly, in every way. But this is a subject scarce worthy of being discussed, though one thing I must not forget to mention, as it tends to show the real value of pedigree and pride of ancestry · namely, that Andrew Winpenny, my *reputed* father, was still living, yet on my genealogical tree he was marked down as one of the departed members of the Winpenny family, and of course a certificate of his death and burial accompanied the pedigree.

The arrival of this valuable document afforded great pleasure to my friends and me; and as all preliminary arrangements had previously been made for ennobling me, while the money, to be given as an equivalent for the proud honour attached to my being made a count, was ready at my banker's, I had little remaining to do more than sign cheques for the sums that certain harpies in office had to receive for their services, and for fees and perquisites to some other agents in the business. Very little delay took place in getting my title made out, but precisely as my Neapolitan genealogist had prophesied, my Deux Sous countship was dated only from the time of the royal grant to me, whereas had it been ante-dated, in conformity to the petition that was made out in my behalf, grounded on the antiquity of my family pedigree, I should not only have been the most ancient count of the kingdom of Naples, but have possessed the oldest title, by half a dozen centuries, that all Europe could boast of, as existing at the present day. However, all things considered, I verily believe that Count Anselma and the Marquis of Meralvo were correct in telling me that it was best as it was; for otherwise the jealousy among the nobility would have been unbearable, and no trouble or expense would have been spared by them in sifting into my pedigree, to discover a flaw which might invalidate my title; whereas now no peer would care a solitary sous about it.

"Well," said I to myself, the first time my breast was dedizened with the star of my order, and my person clothed in a suitable way to attend at a royal levee, to kiss the hand of my cousin, the monarch who had ennobled me, "well," said I, "here do I stand, the creature of power—the counterpart of a crafty lawyer, who has procured himself to be ennobled as a recompence for the service he has rendered mankind by the strength of his lungs, his unconquerable insolence, and the pliability of his principles. This, however, is honour," added I, patting my star; "this is one of the baubles by means of which the great blindfold and prey upon the multitude: but I forget myself, I am a count, and must be upon my good behaviour. I ought to take a leaf from the book of worldly wisdom—the book of silk-aproned bishops and lawyer knaves, who mainly assist in upholding the aristocratic fabric, and with sanctified faces gravely pronounce every institution and law excellent, which brings grist to the great, and presses heavily on the poor."

It is a rule at courts to shower down honours where they are not wanted. The only difficulty a man has is to procure one lofty title, and a string of inferior ones follows as a matter of course. For my part, after I had been well received at court, I was indirectly offered several inferior titles, which were represented to me as necessary appendages to garnish my grand dish of honours; but, contrary to general custom, I felt satisfied with the possession of a single title, and thought meanly of my fellow nobles, who coveted knighthood, ribbons, or servitude to royalty in any shape; besides, I prized my money above subordinate distinctions, and therefore, though in delicate terms, declined profiting by these overtures, thus balking the expectations which certain courtiers had formed on my purse. I was also solicited to accept of military rank, or take office under the crown; but I rejected the temptation with a smile of pity, for I knew better than to relinquish the enjoyment of happiness for the pursuit of power.

My title of count being thus happily attained, Count Anselma felt proud of acknowledging me to the world as his intended son-in-law, an honour which hitherto his aristocratic dignity had forbid of his doing me; and such of his relatives as he deemed worthy of this attention were made acquainted with his intentions regarding me, and several invited to the wedding. Meantime suitable preparations were made for this ceremony, and the lovely Antonia received me in the character of her intended husband, while with candour worthy of her other virtues, she avowed the partiality she felt for me. May I not therefore, as her pure mind inhabits a pure body, confidently look for happiness from my alliance with the mild, amiable, innocent, and benevolent girl?

The noble count's gratitude to me, like that of his daughter, was great in return for my having rendered them the service I happily did in extricating them from their captivity among the banditti; but neither this service, nor the wealth I was master of, would ever have gained the count's consent to my union with his daughter, had I not contrived to impose myself upon the world as being the representative of a very ancient family; for Count Anselma, as has been already stated, though in other respects a philosopher, was an aristocrat in the strictest, yet probably in the most favourable sense of the word. But if he was proud of the noble blood that flowed in his veins, he did not forget that nobility of mind and conduct must be combined to command the esteem and respect of mankind; yet was he blind to the truth, that to confer any hereditary privilege is to do an injustice to posterity, as also that it is improper to permit degenerate children to enjoy privileges which parents received as rewards of talent or virtue. In fine, he was the counterpart of the polished courtier of the old regime, whose virtues and foibles, not vices, are alike combined in his person.

Integrity stoops not to flattery. The count, who, from the commencement of our acquaintance, had been observant of my habits and disposition, now that I was on the eve of becoming his son-in-law, gave me some salutary advice for the guidance of my conduct; when, among other things, he earnestly cautioned me against the vice of gaming, saying, the more effectually to impress upon me his abhorrence of this destructive habit, that it would be well if the edict of Richard the First of England was enforced everywhere, by which persons winning or losing more than twenty shillings within twenty-four hours, were to be publicly and nakedly whipped for three successive days. Moreover, he truly observed, that as we are none of us equally judicious and wise at all times, which is remarkably exemplified in the conduct of men of genius, who readily become dupes to the low and ignorant, his advice to me was to take council in everything, and endeavour to distinguish the best, so as to pursue it.

Count Anselma's discourse gradually made an altered man of me. It instilled into me a new education, teaching me far different customs from those which I had hitherto followed; but as the desperate cards of life had been played by me, and I had gained all that I required, little credit is due to me for listening to the goddess of prudence, who whispered that it was wiser to seat myself peaceably in the lap of affluence than re-engage in hazardous adventures.

My affairs were now all happily settled, my agent at St Thomas's having remitted me bills for twenty thousand dollars, eight of which had been recovered for me at Porto Rico, and twelve thousand for my claims at Jamaica; and, thanks to the kind offices of Signor Albini, my baggage, so unceremoniously seized upon and detained at Parma, was now once more safe in my own custody, while from his correspondence I have reason to hope I shall, ere long, be gratified by again seeing this great and learned gentleman.

The virtuous sentiments now infused into my mind, could not fail of making it a matter of great satisfaction to me to see some of my old friends and associates well provided for, as they now were. My secretary, for example, has fitted out a ship, and become a merchant at Naples, where, with such capitalists as Count Anselma and myself for his backers, he needs only to continue diligent and prudent to be very successful; but the fair orphan, Lady Caroline Bramble, is still the star of attraction to him, and judging from some sly, lover-like communications which have passed between them, I verily believe that the Honourable Mrs O'Shufflewell will see her ward the wife of a merchant, although she designed her to be the lady of a peer. My friend Baron San Lucas has been taught wisdom by the tricks the jade fortune has played him, and is now in the receipt of a comfortable life annuity, purchased with his share of the spoils taken from the banditti. But of all the parties of whom I have to make mention, perhaps the fate of my fair Parma flame gives me the greatest satisfaction; for Rosa Matilda, I rejoice to say, is restored to a life of virtue and of happiness. She is now the wife of a wealthy English country squire, who, being on his travels at Rome, was introduced to her on the Corso, fell desperately in love with, and got wed to her, after a brief courtship. As to Julia Ruberto, I would gladly have taken her as an inmate of my family; but home, her sweet native home, pleaded too forcibly with her to admit of any arguments of mine altering her decision, which was to return to Venice, and accordingly she did so, after humorously telling me that the robber's wealth had now made a lady of her; yet, notwithstanding the artful gipsy's professions, I am of opinion that an old Venetian lover was loadstone which directed this movement of hers.

The case of my poor mother's husband, and those of the three children she bore to after my birth, I took into consideration, and consequently have made arrangements by w the former will receive a stipendiary allowance of money, and the latter be placed o learn useful employments, when, provided they are industrious, they might pass honestly comfortably through life.

To conclude: The law papers having been duly prepared, and every other prelimi measure taken necessary to our marriage, the happy day for this long and much-des ceremony has at length arrived, and this blessed morning has given me for a bride one of loveliest and wealthiest maidens in all Italy. Our intention, and that of Count Anselm in a few days to embark for Toulon, in the neighbourhood of which he possesses a very and castle and a large domain; and at Toulon I shall execute, to the best of my ability, the t reposed in me by the poor bigamist. Meanwhile, during my absence from this country, Co Anselma's man of business will do what is necessary with regard to my property at Ge and elsewhere.

Thanks to Providence, my cup of bliss is unusually well filled; and though the burde riches is heaped upon me and I am a Benedict, wedded to a second wife, with the *Deux S* countship to uphold, yet surely none, save a philosopher of the Martinian school, resolu determined to be dissatisfied with everything, would deny that I have now a most promi prospect before me of passing through life in felicity; and that I may deserve happiness, study shall be, as Pontanus advises from his sepulchral marble—*to know myself.*

THE END.